Mansfield Tracy Walworth

Delaplaine: or, The Sacrifice of Irene

A Novel

Mansfield Tracy Walworth

Delaplaine: or, The Sacrifice of Irene
A Novel

ISBN/EAN: 9783337001322

Printed in Europe, USA, Canada, Australia, Japan

Cover: Foto ©Andreas Hilbeck / pixelio.de

More available books at **www.hansebooks.com**

DELAPLAINE:

OR,

THE SACRIFICE OF IRENE.

𝕬 𝕹𝖔𝖛𝖊𝖑.

BY

MANSFIELD TRACY WALWORTH,

AUTHOR OF

WARWICK. — HOTSPUR. — STORMCLIFF. — LULU. — ETC.

NEW YORK:
G. W. Carleton & Co., Publishers.
LONDON: J. C. HOTTEN.
M.DCCC.LXXI.

This Book

IS DEDICATED TO MY FRIEND,

JOHN McB. DAVIDSON,

[The Safe Manufacturer of Broadway, N.Y.]

A MERCHANT PRINCE,

IN EVERY SENSE OF THE TERM.

———

THAT I RECOGNIZE THUS PUBLICLY

THE NOBLE, GENEROUS CHARACTER OF THE MAN,

THE FRIEND OF EVERY ONE

WHO IS TRUTHFUL, EARNEST, AND STRUGGLING,

WILL MEET THE APPROBATION

OF THE MANY MEN WHOM HE HAS ASSISTED, ENCOURAGED,

AND BUILT UP IN LIFE.

To Their Hearts

I ENTRUST THE EMOTIONS AND THE MOTIVES

WHICH HAVE PROMPTED

THIS TESTIMONIAL

FROM

THE AUTHOR.

IRENE.

CHAPTER I.

THE sky was overcast, and the wind moaned over the solemnly gliding river. Upon the banks of the broad stream the scattered trees stood leafless, and a dread sense of approaching winter and storm and desolation seemed to pervade all things. Even the town on the river bank was wonderfully quiet. Few of the inhabitants cared to be abroad in the chill air; and even half a dozen empty row-boats on the shore looked as if they were drawn up from the water, and huddled together to keep each other warm.

Near to the town and close to the water's edge loomed up heavy and extensive buildings of gray stone. Firmly and durably constructed, the vast pile of masonry reared its towers and turrets solemnly against the leaden hue of the sky. There was mystery and awe in the appearance of the massive architecture. At the first glance the long outlines and angles of this durable structure appeared to be deserted. The eye roamed wearily in search of human life, but found at last an indication of the presence of man at the summit of a lofty wall, and exactly at the angle it made with another wall. Here, perched high above the earth, was a sentry box, from which a man with a musket emerged and contemplated the huge enclosure beneath him.

A painful interruption in the dread silence of the scene was approaching the massive building from the front. A boy of perhaps fifteen summers was being led, or rather dragged, between two men towards the entrance of the structure. At the very door he dropped upon his knees and begged piteously for mercy.

"Oh! for God's sake don't put me in there. I'm innocent."

The officers jerked him to his feet again, and then dragged him in through the great iron door which was opened for them. He cast one upward despairing look at the leaden sky. It was his last sight of free air. The door was closed behind him and he was a prisoner of the State. He was condemned to six years imprisonment at hard labor. *And he was innocent.* The poor wretch would not yield even within the enclosure of the walls, but fought desperately with the officers; seizing the hand of one with his teeth and biting to the bone. The man uttered a curse and exclamation of pain, and then dealt the offender a blow which felled him to the floor. Dizzy and half blinded, the boy rose to his feet, and realizing that the officers had released him, gazed about him in wonder and terror. No sound escaped him, though the blow had been severe. For an instant his body reeled, and then he caught at the neighboring wall to save himself. The two officers looked at him indignantly, and the warden, who was the only other occupant of the guard-room, said sternly, —

"You little *devil.* You make a promising beginning."

"I'm innocent," muttered the boy clinging to the wall and his eyes beginning to realize the hopelessness of his situation. He saw another iron door before him which gave ingress to the prison proper, and beside it a narrow grating four feet up on the wall, which enabled the warden occasionally to cast his eye along the stone corridor, passing by the cells of the prisoners within. Ha! something bright attracted his attention on the opposite wall. It was the gleam of muskets loaded and ready for immediate use in case of insurrection among the convicts. They stood in a rack against the wall, polished to an attractive brightness, and orderly as soldiers. With the bound of an antelope the boy crossed the room, grasped a musket before he could be intercepted, levelled it, and fired. One of the officers fell. Quick as lightning he seized another from the rack, fired, and his second enemy fell. The warden darted across the room after him. The boy summoned all his strength, and by a skillful lunge of his empty musket jammed the muzzle into one of the warden's eyes. The pain of the blow was intense and bewildering for an instant; and the warden, stumbling over one of the fallen officers, nearly landed on his face, in the effort to reach the telegraphic alarm which communicated with the sentry boxes on the summits of the prison. This delay was fatal for the interests of the State. The boy turned the key of the outside door, and was out and off like the wind, the warden following with a loaded musket. A sharp report was heard outside, and a ball whistled beside the fugitive's cheek. The warden's shot had missed, and he returned to his guard-room, afraid to be absent from his post, and confident that the sharpshooters on the walls of the prison would soon bring down this refractory youth. He listened for the challenge of the sentry, heard it, and then a shot; another report followed, and he heard a shout from some laborers working on the rail-road. Looking up the rise of ground to the east, he spied the fugitive, apparently unharmed, running along the upper ledge of a stone quarry, and making for the river bank. Two of the prison guard were in pursuit, but far behind. The boy ran for dear life. They could not overtake him. He never looked back, but ran straight on for the river, gained the bank, and leaped into the water. He disappeared in foam, rose again, raised his hatless head, looked about him, and then struck out boldly for the opposite shore. He swam bravely, and the spectators on the railroad raised a shout of approbation. The pursuers were rapidly nearing the shore, and had taken a shorter route to intercept him by musket balls, when they should come within range. This *détour* proved to be of no service to them, as it brought them directly upon a pool of water, which they were disinclined to wade. They skirted this obstacle, and the swimmer thereby gained on them, steadily cleaving the waters for the opposite shore. It was probable the little fellow would fail to reach his goal, and sink exhausted in mid-stream. They reached the shore at length, and fired upon him, one after another. The shots were fair, and whistled close to his ears; but the little desperado bore a charmed life. They exhausted their ammunition, but could not harm him. Then they searched the river bank for a skiff. Before they could find one, the little swimmer was far off upon the bosom of the broad stream, struggling heroically to gain the opposite shore.

The river was fearfully broad at this place, spreading out into a great lake. There was apparently little chance that the youthful swimmer could gain the distant shore. He must soon go down. But an unexpected succor hove in sight.

A yacht, manned by three sons of Neptune, was sweeping

down the river like a bird, before a fine breeze. The gray-beard who handled the tiller was the captain and owner, an old sea-dog, who had won scars and reputation in the naval warfare just ended. He had witnessed the firing from the shore, and seen the human head bobbing up and down in the water, and conjectured immediately that a prisoner had escaped from the clutches of the State. He intimated to his crew of two men, that if the convict was wounded and needed help, he would pick him up ; otherwise he would let him shift for him-self, as he was determined to lose no time on his passage to the metropolis. He ordered a sailor to be ready to cast the swim-mer a rope if necessary, as the course of the yacht was directly for him. When the little vessel was within hail, the boy raised himself in the water, and cried for help. The brave lad was nearly exhausted. When the captain heard that pitiful and juvenile cry, his heart was moved, and he ordered the coil of rope to be heaved at the swimmer. The order was admirably executed from the starboard bow of the yacht, and the boy clutched the line as its coils fell around his neck, and was dragged in by the sailor in a sinking condition. One minute more would have been too late, as the poor swimmer's strength was swiftly failing him, encumbered as he was by his clothing and boots. The rescuer carried the dripping boy in his arms to the small cabin in the stern of the boat, where the captain's wife and daughter were seated, wrapped up in their cloaks and shawls, and begged them to look after the poor lad's comfort, as he had fainted away from exhaustion and fright, and lay on the floor of the cabin like one dead.

The captain of the yacht in the meantime held on his course as if nothing had occurred, knowing full well that, as the boy had been hauled in from the starboard, his pursuers far away on the larboard side could not have witnessed the rescue, and might be left safely to make their own conjectures as to his fate. When far away down the river on his course he could see the pursuers laying on their oars and looking about them as if uncertain where the fugitive could have gone down to his watery grave. He smiled at the skill and rapidity with which he had carried off the object of their search, and then fell into a meditation as to the probable consequences to himself if by any mischance the State should discover that he had aided a prisoner to escape. There is an unaccountable propensity in the minds of some men to exult at the escape of a criminal from the clutches of the law, when effected in a gallant and heroic manner. The youth of the culprit, moreover, enhanced this exultation of the captain of the yacht, and he was rapidly preparing himself to believe that there must have been some extenuating circumstance in the boy's case. He determined to give the brave swimmer a chance to be heard in his own defence, at least, before he would consent to deliver him up to the authorities. Stern disciplinarian as he had learned to be when in command of a government ship, he had not relinquished his sympathies for youth, and was ever inclined to lend an attentive and sympathetic ear to their complaints.

Filled with these reflections, he descended to the little cabin of his vessel, when he had made such disposition of his sails for the night as he deemed prudent to secure his craft from danger, in the event of sudden gusts from the hills which every navigator of the river is accustomed to anticipate. He found that his wife had lighted a lamp and was sitting beside the rescued boy, whom she had nearly divested of all his dripping garments, substituting for them a pea-jacket belonging to the captain, and then enveloping her charge in a huge boat-cloak which effectually shielded him from the cold wind struggling at every crevice to enter the cabin. The chances were that the poor boy could not escape a severe cold from his exposure in the river so late in the fall. His teeth were fairly chattering with the chills which crept over him.

The boy was now sitting upon a lounge with the huge boat-cloak wrapped snugly about him, his large dark eyes roving about the narrow apartment. Opposite to him, and curiously regarding his every movement, was the captain's daughter, her sweet face partly shaded by a straw flat and her juvenile figure carefully enveloped in a black-and-white plaid travelling shawl. There was a peculiar air of independence about the girl, and a precocious ease and self-possession rare in a little lady who had not yet entered her twelfth year. . She was delicate and fairy-like in figure, but by no means of short stature, and her large brown eyes looked intensely brilliant in the lamplight, shaded though they were by her flat. There was surely a mysterious fascination for the child in the wild roving eyes of the escaped convict, for she seldom withdrew her gaze from his face, save when his eagle glances met her own. Then her eyes drooped their lashes, so piercing was the boy's gaze.

" Well, my lad," exclaimed the captain upon entering, in his bluff, hearty style, " I see you are provided for ; now give an account of yourself. What is your name, what were you put in that prison for, how did you escape, and what have you to say for yourself generally? Out with it like a man. If there are any extenuating facts in your case, I am the friend of boys, and will do all in my power to help you. But, by Jupiter! if I see you don't come square and boldly up and toe the mark, I'll put you back in the power of the State. Speak out; make a clean breast, if you want my help."

To the amazement of all, the boy sprang to his feet, muffled as he was in the cloak, his eyes kindling with terrible emotion, and regarding the captain with a bold, free glance, as if there was no discrepancy in their ages or positions. He looked as fearless as an untamed eagle of the crags. "I am innocent, sir, God knows. They were dragging me to prison. I killed two of them; I'd kill *fifty* before I'd let them take away my liberty. God made me, and gave me fresh air and sunlight; nobody shall shut me up and make me work for them. They can kill me, but they nor no other man can make me work for them. I am innocent, sir; I never stole no money. I was a messenger boy, sir, for Deems, Barnes & Co. They missed a roll of bank notes and some of the money was found in my hat a-lyin' in the window of their office, right before their eyes, and they thought I was fool enough to steal their money and then put it right under their nose, where I put my hat every day; yes, sir, right in their window, — that's where I put my hat every day, — right there. Why, any fool wouldn't do that. You know that, sir. You wouldn't steal money, sir, and then lay it right in your hat that was lying in the window with the other hats where everybody couldn't help seein' it. Somebody did it to ruin me, sir; and then they swore away my character, — that is all a poor boy's got, and the judge said as how I'd got to work six years at hard labor in the State's prison. And that's how I come to kill 'em, and I'll kill all the men on the earth before they put me in there. They've no right to shut me up; I'm innocent."

The amazement caused by this brief speech, delivered with all the fire and rapidity of youth, was overpowering, and for a moment no one replied to the little orator as he stood there so resolute, wrapped in his cloak. Then the captain exclaimed:

"Why, youngster! do you know what you've done? They'll hang you sure."

"That would be mercy, sir," replied the boy advancing straight up to the captain, and looking in his eye. "It is better to die than be a convict six years, and then come out in disgrace ; it would be a mercy, sir, to kill me ; but it's worse than death to be innocent and have the light taken away, and the air taken away, and my liberty too, when God gave them to me and I ain't done nothing to forfeit them. Would you stand, it, sir, if you was in my place ? Ain't it agin the law of God to shut up an innocent boy and break his mother's heart ? Would you let 'em put you in there, sir ? "

" That's a difficult question you propound," replied the captain ; " I believe I could fight pretty hard for my liberty, if I was innocent. But you talk bravely, my little orator. You look like an honest boy, and I shall screen you sure, if you satisfy me you are."

" Will you read the evidence, sir ? " said the boy eagerly. " Do read it — read it carefully, sir. You will find it all in the newspaper ; you will say I am innocent, — I *know* you will."

" Yes, father, read it," interrupted the captain's daughter, coming up to him and laying her hand on his arm. " I feel quite sure he is innocent. See how earnest he is ! That face is not the face of a thief. *I* believe him — every word."

The boy's face lighted with rapture as he turned to this unexpected advocate. " Oh ! miss," he exclaimed, " the good God will bless you for that word. I don't know what I wouldn't do for you ; you are the first voice that has declared me innocent. Everybody was banded agin me, and now your voice sounds just like music."

The wife of the captain had remained silent ; now she added her calm voice to that of the girlish advocate.

" Madeleine is right, Henry. This youth bears an honest face, and we must shelter him until something can be ascertained regarding him. But I fear he has compromised himself dreadfully by killing the keepers."

" Self-preservation is nature's first law," said the captain bluntly ; then he added, " but I will take the responsibility of hiding him in the city until we know further of this matter. You and Mady keep your mouths shut, and I will see that those fellows outside do not talk to our detriment." Then turning again to the boy, he said, " What is your name ? You didn't answer me that."

" Alfonso, sir ; Alfonso Debaena."

" Have you a father ? "

" No, sir. He died when I was a baby."

" A mother ? "

" Yes, sir ; she lives in New York."

"Is she poor?"

"She is a washerwoman, sir."

"And what have you been doing to earn your bread?"

"I was a messenger boy, sir, for Deems, Barnes & Co."

"Yes, yes, you told me *that.* But what was your occupation before?"

"I was a target boy, sir, at a rifle gallery. I kept the targets clean, and picked up the balls and moulded them over again, and sometimes I loaded the rifles."

"Are you a marksman yourself?" inquired the captain.

"They said at the gallery, sir, I was a capital shot. I often rung the bell a dozen times hand running."

"That's very fine shooting, my lad."

"Well, sir, I can *do* it."

"And how did you kill the men that were dragging you to prison, Alfonso?"

"I shot 'em, sir. The muskets were standing in the room where they dragged me to, and I snatched 'em up and fired the first time they took their hands off me."

"Your practice at the gallery made you a dead shot, it appears."

The boy made no response. His eyes were studying the face of the captain's daughter. Then his teeth commenced to chatter again, and he shivered repeatedly.

"Come to the lounge again," said the captain's wife; "you will be sick, Alfonso. Lie down there, lie down."

The boy obeyed at once, and sank down upon the cushions, trembling with cold. They covered him with every available blanket and shawl, and after a time he ceased to shiver, and fell asleep, with the two females watching beside him. The captain of the yacht left for the deck, muttering, "So youthful, and yet with such an infernal will. That boy will make his mark in the world if they give him half a chance."

The elder watcher who remained beside the sleeper indulged in a milder remark:

"Madeleine, the eyes of this boy haunt me. They resemble eyes very familiar to me, but I cannot locate them. Somewhere I have seen a pair of dark eyes like them. Yes, the very same large, dark, lustrous Spanish eyes."

"To me," was the response of the young girl, "they recall Lord Byron's corsair. Do you remember the lines, mother?"

> "There breathe but few whose aspect might defy
> The full encounter of his searching eye."

The mother smiled at this appropriate quotation, and then, arranging herself comfortably for the night against the luxurious cushions of the cabin, covered her face with a shawl, and was soon asleep. But Madeleine sat long in a reverie beside the sleeping convict, looking out through the little cabin window upon the waters sparkling and dancing in the moonbeams, and perplexing her youthful brain with the arguments regarding the several instances of justifiable homicide.

CHAPTER II.

ALONE and in agony!

The luxurious couch with its golden satin and lace canopy, the soft, warm temperature of the room, the tapestry carpet muffling every footfall, and the attentive nurse within easy call, seemed mere mockery to the invalid. To each and every physical comfort about him he had ever been a stranger; from infancy he had lived and toiled among the poor. His bed had been the plain straw pallet, and in sickness the hard, coarse hand of the toiling washerwoman, his mother, had alone soothed the pain from his brow. Suddenly, as by a magician's wand, the scene had changed. He had been rescued from a watery grave and transported to a luxurious sick chamber, where wealth and kindness were ministering to him.

He was indeed alone. His mother, overpowered by the anguish of his conviction and sentence, had succumbed to the disease which had long afflicted her. Her boy had been torn from her, and made the companion of convicts; before the tidings of his escape could reach her she was a corpse. The sad news had been broken to him at last; he was recovered sufficiently to bear it. He had inquired for her so often, that his kind-hearted rescuers had not power longer to withhold the secret of his loss. What a world of anguish and apprehension beset that emaciated sufferer, as he lay there in the midst of luxury recovering from the fever! His mother, his heart's all, was no more. His reputation for honesty was gone; who would give him employment now? He was that detested thing, an escaped convict. The cruel taunts and curses of men would follow him; he was an outlaw; every citizen of the busy world

would avoid him as a pestilence. Aye! more than this, a reward had been offered for his apprehension, and he knew it ;
he had seen it in the city paper. What did the vindictive public want of him further? *His life.* They had offered a large
reward for the murderer of the officers. He knew that the gallows awaited him ; he shuddered at the grim death which confronted him.

Would the kind friends who had arisen so unexpectedly on
his path be able to conceal him effectually from the government detectives? They had assured him that they were now
convinced of his innocence ; they had repudiated the evidence
adduced on his trial as insufficient. They had promised to ship
him secretly to some foreign port, where he might start the
race of life anew. It was evident to him, that they sympa-
thized with him in his desperate struggle to regain that which
had been wrongfully wrested from him — his liberty. His frank,
bold, independent ways had a strange fascination for them. He
had developed day by day attractive qualities of head and
heart ; it seemed a shame to suffer that manly boy to be crushed
by a felon's doom. He had been desperate in choosing his
manner of escape, but then the foundation of his cause was
innocence. The eagle-eyed boy had followed the instinct of
liberty. Youth, innocence, truth, had wrestled with injustice,
wrong, falsehood, and had come off victors. No doubt, questions had arisen in this case for casuists ; but what had the
young eagle to do with casuistry. He knew that liberty was
his *right ;* he knew that the officers were perpetrating a great
wrong. Right triumphed over wrong; hence the bluff old
sailor concealed the boy and sheltered him.

But the boy was suffering bodily and mental anguish. The
ravages of the fever were evident upon him ; the greater suffering was in the mind. No mother, no kinsman left, the gallows
imminent, and he but a boy.

A light step sounded upon the carpet, the rustle of a silk
dress was heard, and Alfonso was no longer alone.

" Poor Alfonso," she said, as she took her seat beside his
couch. " The doctor says you are daily growing better, and yet
every day your eyes are growing more sorrowful. Why does
your cheerfulness not return with your health ?"

He looked up eagerly to those lustrous eyes ; he noted the
wonderful luxuriance of her golden hair, which covered her
girlish shoulders with the *abandon* of the Grecian Aphrodite.
Then he said with an effort at cheerfulness, —

"You always bring the sunshine with you, and if I could always be with you I should never be sad."

" Do you miss me so much, then, when I go to my lessons ?"

"Yes, and I shall miss you more when they send me across the sea."

" I don't know about that," she said; "there are so many wonderful sights beyond the sea. You will become engrossed in them, I've no doubt. And then, you know, you have promised me to make wonderful efforts to become great in your profession ; I shall expect to see you captain of a ship some day."

" Whatever I do I shall miss you ; I shall miss your reading to me. Do you know that what you have read to me has fired my heart to become great like those men ?"

"Why shouldn't you become great ? If I were a man I would cut *my* way to fortune and fame, I assure you. And I know it's in *you* to do it ; father says so, too."

"If I had any one to care for me, or any one who was my relation, I could succeed. But this being all alone chills me and breaks my spirit."

"Hush ! Alfonso, *I* care for you, and I told you that long ago. I shall watch for every word about you, and if you succeed I shall clap my hands for joy."

The dark eyes flashed with enthusiasm at this reply, but before he could respond the nurse entered the apartment with a message for Madeleine.

"The new washerwoman, miss, is below, and wants to see you."

" Tell her to come to the head of the stairs ; I will meet her there."

This order was obeyed, and Madeleine left the room to meet her. To her amazement the washerwoman had pushed her way through the upper hall, and into the sick chamber unbidden. She had already passed the threshold.

"This is presumption," she said indignantly to' the woman. " This is a private bed-chamber. Were you not told to await me at the head of the stairs ? "

"Yes, miss."

" Well, go back there, as you were directed."

The woman retired in confusion, but not until she had seen distinctly the face of the invalid, which was turned towards her. Great care had been exercised by the family in keeping inquisitive persons at a distance from the sick chamber. The police were on the alert, and this discovery on the part of the new washerwoman, who had been recently recommended to the family, was suggestive of possible trouble. Madeleine followed the woman out, transacted her business with her, and then sent her away. Upon returning, she found Alfonso seriously alarmed. The nurse, who was a trusted inmate of the house since the infancy of Madeleine, was endeavoring vainly to dispel his apprehensions.

"I am lost! I am lost!" exclaimed the poor boy.

"Nonsense," replied the captain's daughter. "That old woman may never hear of your case."

"Ah! but I know *who* she is. I will never forget those eyes. Oh! save me! hide me."

"Who is she? Speak, Alfonso!"

He pronounced a name that made the listeners shudder.

"*Gordon!*"

"Impossible! Alfonso."

"Yes, that old woman is Captain Gordon — the same man that arrested me. I saw his eyes. Oh! hide me, quick!"

For an instant the girl seemed paralyzed. The name of the great detective, with whose exploits the whole metropolis was ringing, bore with it a sense of mystery, of terror, of hopelessness. Rumor had it that *Gordon* on the trail of crime was as unerring as destiny. He followed up the slightest clue to the whereabouts of a rogue with the tenacity and the scent of a bloodhound. Disguises, artifices, impenetrability, were his servants. The most crafty of outlaws trembled at his name. He was commonly believed to employ secret agents in every haunt and den of the city. He could worm secrets out of a man with the unconcerned air of a Fouché. Concentrated, determined, and indefatigable as Le Tellier, he bent his entire energies to the service of the State. There appeared to be little hope for Alfonso if this terrible detective was upon his trail.

The paralysis of terror was but momentary. The girl darted from the room and summoned her father. A hasty consultation ensued. There was evidently but one safe course— Alfonso must be shipped for foreign parts. A friend of the captain, the master of a sailing vessel, would sail for China on the following day. Feeble as the boy was, he must be hurried in a carriage to the vessel, and they would trust to Providence to give him strength for the voyage. The secret agent of the State had penetrated their sanctuary, and there was no time to be lost. There was but one word for all in that house—*haste!*

.   .   .   .

The shades of evening were creeping on. The darkness of
the night would be the signal for flight. Unquestionably the
vigilant Gordon had placed a guard upon the house. Certain
of his victim, he could patiently wait for his recovery and
thereby save expense to the State. No one believed he would
make the arrest at once. It was arranged that the father of
Madeleine should bear the invalid boy in his arms along the
roof of the long lines of galleries which were built in the rear
of the block of buildings, until he reached the second story
window of a dwelling occupied by Madeleine's aunt. Then,
with that lady's connivance, he was to pass through that window,
and to make his way with his burden to a carriage on the street.
There were hazards of exposure from the occupants of windows
which the two must pass. But at the late hour of the night
selected for the enterprise it was expected the rear curtains of
the dwellings would be dropped, so that they might escape
observation.

Alfonso and Madeleine were alone together. If their ruse
proved successful, in a few hours they would be parted and the
ship would bear one to a distant land. The convict boy and
the golden-haired girl were silent in the gathering twilight.
For days and weeks she had been the teacher and he the
scholar. Every book that had wrought its charm over her
young life she had made known to him. She had read to him,
talked to him, instructed him in her little world of knowledge,
and witnessed the development of his youthful intellect and his
enthusiasm in a field before utterly unknown to him. In his
humble and obscure life he had known only the hard struggle
for bread. She, the child of affluence and of culture, opened to
the convict boy the portals of a higher life. She read to him
of heroes, of poets, of scholars, and at times the intense brilliancy of his dark eyes assured her that the seed had fallen
upon good ground. The dormant, uncultivated intellect of
the boy was aroused, his enthusiasm was awakened ; ambition
sprang to sudden life. He forgot at times that he was a
convict. He yearned for the triumphs of the future, and he
looked upon the lovely face of the girl as that of his angel.
She had instructed him in the love of the angels. She had
pointed out to him the splendors of the Christian faith. Her
youthful intellect had copiously poured out before him the
treasures it had amassed, and as her acquirements were those
of a precocious brain, the boy could have enjoyed no better

school.   The consciousness which had dawned upon Madeleine that the escaped convict possessed intellect as well as courage and will, deepened her interest in his fate.   And now that they were about to part she found that he had become the object of very tender interest to her.   She felt vaguely that the boy was destined to wield a trenchant sword in the battle of life, and that her influence was going forth with him for good.

She was sitting beside his bed, unconscious apparently of her surpassing loveliness, with her unrestrained mass of misty, golden hair sweeping back upon her shoulders, and her fair, rose-tinted cheek resting upon her clinched hand.   Her dark eyes and darker lashes contrasted strangely with her blonde beauty; and it was no wonder that the boy thought her the most beautiful girl that could be imagined outside of the celestial land.

"You remember," he said at length in tremulous tones, "that you were the first voice that called me innocent.   I shall never forget that, and if I return from that far-off land I will lay at your feet beautiful things, rich things, that will make your eyes sparkle.   Remember that promise.   Remember that."

"Yes, I will remember all you have said to me, and I want you to remember this.   Every night I will pray to the good God for you.   When you see the evening star just rising, then think that Madeleine is kneeling down and praying for you, that you may be everything that is noble, grand, and good."

"I will," he answered solemnly.

Deeper and darker lowered the night, and the winter winds began to raise their mournful voices upon the silence. , Then the evening star lifted suddenly above the clouds and like an angel messenger moved on its way.   The eyes of these silent children were instantly fixed upon it, and in their souls that solitary sentinel of the early night was established as an eternal memory of the pure and the beautiful.

"I will call it *our star*," she said softly.

"And I will call it," he said, "*Madeleine's star.*"

CHAPTER III.

" Push him into the river, and he will rise with a fish in his mouth."
Arabian Proverb.

MAN stood upon a mountain crag impending over the Strait of Ormuz. The night was coming on. The wild gale howling over the sea lashed the waves into foam beneath his feet. Checked in their headlong fury by the lofty wall of bare gray rock, the mad waves hurled their malediction upward to the impeding cliff in hissing spray, which was at intervals caught up by the wild wind and scattered. The gale gathered intensity with the fall of the night and the man was unsteady upon his feet, tottering in the violent force of the wind sweeping inland. The sombre sky grew darker, the agitated sea blacker, the booming of the waves against the cliff more appalling. The twilight slowly faded away into blackness, and the demons of the night held undisputed sway. The silent man was lost in the gloom. Ha! the keen, bright signal of human agony blazed in the offing; the solemn boom of the gun followed the flash, and was hushed again by the sweeping gale. Another and still another gun moaned from the sea, and there was none to help.

A gallant ship was beleaguered by the treacherous waves. Behind her stretched the dangerous shoals and reefs of Oman. Before her lay the rocky mountain walls of Mooristan. She was heading apparently when the night fell for the Persian Gulf, which she could only reach by entering the strait of Ormuz at a point something like a cannon shot distant from the cliff where the solitary man stood watching her movements. An hour before sunset this purpose seemed feasible. But the stiff breeze had freshened and gathered power until it blew at last a terrific gale. She had advanced far enough by nightfall to render her position hazardous in the extreme. To run for the open sea again in the teeth of such a violent gale was impossible. To lay off during the night and avoid a lee shore, or to run boldly for the Strait, were the alternatives presented to her commander. She was evidently at dusk, by the quantity of canvas she spread, destined for the latter alternative. The man on the cliff, before he was obscured by the night, had deprecated this manifest intention by words; so earnest was he in his sympathy for the strange vessel and her crew.   But the wild winds only hurled his words over his shoulder.

Treacherous submarine foes awaited the approach of the ship, and over their fangs the white froth of rage was curling. Air and water were allied to the hidden enemy. Fire alone remained true to man. A bright gleam trembled upon the summit of the cliff, waxed larger, brighter, and then shot up into the blackness of the night with sudden brilliancy. Tongues of fire darted from the swelling, luminous mass, and spoke to the mariners, shrouded in gloom, of their proximity to the coast. Beside this new and friendly demon appeared the figure of the man who had evoked it. He was clad from head to foot in robes of *white*, belted at the waist. Like a ghost, solitary and startling he stood beside the signal fire with his strange and loosely fitting garments fluttering away from him in the violence of the gale, which also caused the flames at intervals to lick the rock before the prostrating power of its fury. The sea thundered away beneath the fire, and its ghostly guardian, the wind, howled savagely on its path of ruin, and a blackness horrible as Tartarus enveloped space. And still at intervals came the sudden flash and the sullen booming of the gun from the doomed ship.

The man listened eagerly for each successive report, to ascertain if the vessel was nearing his standpoint. For a time he fancied the signals of distress boomed closer to him ; but finally the gun ceased firing. He listened patiently for another report. None came. The gun had performed its last duty. It was never fired again. Had the vessel gone down ? He stood in the attitude of expectation, his eyes peering out into the horrible darkness which overhung the sea. The roar of the waters, the howl of the gale, and the *slashing* of the surf as it madly essayed to climb the cliff, met his ear. No sound that indicated the existence of man came to him. He approached the edge of the rock and gazed down into the waves. His fire served to illumine a narrow space about him. It revealed a short belt of glistening black water breaking into foam. The face of the rock was perpendicular. A bullet dropped from his hand would fall into the surf. He watched the fearful blows dealt upon the adamantine wall by the Titans of the deep. Higher and higher they seemed to mount at every new effort, and then receding left a gloomy abyss behind, into which the ensuing waves rolled heavily, and sweeping upward made a fresh assault upon the rocky barrier.

The solitary watcher grew weary at length with his long vigil. His eyes were no longer bent seaward. He turned from the cliff's edge, and replenished his fire. The supply of fuel he had gathered was meagre, and after heaping the remaining fragments of the wood upon the blazing pile, he sat down upon the rock, and contemplated the play of the flames as they mounted upward for an instant, and then swept backward from the cliff's edge in the fierce pressure of the gale. His thoughts were with the unfortunate inmates of the vessel, tossing upon the mad waves, or already engulfed in their triumphant embrace.

Seconds, minutes, hours rolled away, and still the motionless figure of the white-robed watcher sat by the sea in reverie. At length, when his fire had burnt itself out and the winds had begun to scatter the remaining ashes and sparks from the dying coals over the surface of the rock, he arose, and walking inland over the table rock, was about to descend a natural stairway to a cavern which was his solitary abode, when a crash as of breaking timbers startled his ear. He paused in amazement. Then his very soul was pierced with a cry of mortal agony. Another crash ensued, filling him with terrible apprehensions. Piercing yells of terror arose upon the darkness. The ill-fated ship had been forced upon the very cliff lighted up for her salvation. Borne along by the fury of the gale, she had become unmanageable, and head on had struck the rock when lifted up on the crest of an enormous wave. At the first shock the jibboom was broken and thrown over the bow into the vessel. The second shock carried away her bowsprit, head and cutwater, lodging the timbers across the bows. Turning away from her enemy and swinging clear, she was dashed again upon the rock, receiving on her larboard quarter the last awful shock which opened her hull to the waves. The cries of the drowning men were soon hushed in the roar of the sea vaulting over her, and the shrieks of the gale waxed louder, and the surf rushed more frantically up the face of the rock. Grim death claimed the throne where the beacon fire died.

So unexpected was the catastrophe at that point, and so sudden the crash, that the listener's blood went violently back upon his heart, and he stood for a brief time paralyzed in the darkness. The ship had miraculously passed unharmed through the breakers from which his beacon fire was intended to warn the mariners, only to be dashed in pieces at his very feet. He recovered from the first effect of the great horror, and groped his way down the rocky stairs, seeking for a light. He came

at length to the mouth of his cave, and passing in, found a
torch in a cleft of rock. Grasping the light, he retraced his
steps to the summit of the cliff, and advancing to the edge of
the rock held aloft his torch, and gazed down into the agitated
deep. He detected, after his eyes had grown accustomed to
the wild scene, fragments of the ship's timbers and some of her
spars floating upon the waves. But no human wrecks were
visible, no ghastly images of men swayed back and forth or
rolled and fell with the capricious waters. The sea was hiding
its victims, and the ghostly torch-bearer was appalled at the
completeness of her triumph over men.

Strange tableau ! Midnight, an aged man in white, a fluttering torch-light, a storm-wrapt cliff, an angry sea. Mysterious life looking for mysterious death. . He found none. Of all
the gallant crew, not one had come to land. Gladly would the
watcher have welcomed one human face upturned to him in
entreaty. Gladly would he have tendered the hospitality of his
cavern to the shipwrecked. Alas ! the remorseless sea spared
none. He turned away at length from the frantic waves. He
walked slowly to his rocky retreat. He gained the entrance,
passed in, and replaced his torch in the cleft of the rock.
Then he sank into his chair, a seat which none but a hermit
would have planned. It was formed entirely of great branches
of red coral. In the markets of the world that graceful *fau-
teuil* would have commanded a fabulous price. How had the
aged hermit wrested it from the grasp of the Oceanides?

In his torch-lighted cavern, and seated in his coral chair, the
man in white pondered long and deeply the mysteries of that
fearful night. Keenly alive to all human sympathies, and
grieved to the heart that his arm had been powerless to help,
there was, nevertheless, one source of disappointment connected with that eventful night which seemed to bewilder this
solitary being more than all else. *The stars had deceived him
for the first time in all his life.* They had been false to their
most ardent votary. He was an astrologer. The occult lore
of the Orient regarding those luminous inhabitants of the sky
was his birthright. His father was an astrologer before him.
In his upturned eager face the mysterious planets had sifted
their holy light, and in their service he had grown gray. Had
the world known how thoroughly that venerable hermit had
studied the stars, that same gay, thoughtless world would have
trembled when his name was pronounced.

Zenayi was a mystery to his race. No man claimed kindred with him. Whoever disputed his knowledge was eventually proved to be a fool. The *savans* of the East mentioned his name with profound reverence. Knowledge of the tree, the plant, or the flower; knowledge of the tides, the winds, or the temperatures; knowledge of the maladies of men, knowledge of the properties of minerals or metals, knowledge of the flora or fauna of all lands, knowledge in every department of human research — was, by universal consent, admitted to have been mastered by Zenayi. It was beyond human comprehension, however, that he should have so thoroughly mastered learning in sixty years of mortal life. That he was only sixty, was his own statement. And yet no one would dispute this figure. For Zenayi's word was unimpeachable. *Learned* as Zenayi, *truthful* as Zenayi, had become Oriental proverbs.

The stars had deceived him for the first time. The mysterious science of reading destiny by the position of the planets had proved false. On the night preceding the wreck, his astrological calculations had informed him positively of the arrival in distress of a stranger who should become a great benefactor to Persia. The designated night was far spent, and still no stranger had come. Were the stars no longer friendly to their great servant?

The chagrin at his loss of power kept him from sleep. He sat in his coral chair, thoughtful and silent through the lonely hours, listening to the roar of the sea and the whistling of the wind which came to his ears even within the shelter of his cave. The sounds were subdued in the distance, but he knew the wild work was still going on. And thus moody and silent he sat until morning. His torch had long ago flickered out, and the first light that replaced it was the dawn, showing faintly at the mouth of his cavern. He moved not from his seat until the sunlight burst upon the earth. Then he knew that the storm was ended, and he walked forth again to view the sea and the strait. He mounted to the cliff in the full blaze of the Persian sunrise, and watched the waves slowly subside with the advent of the day.

"Ha!" he exclaimed; "the stars never *will* deceive me."

His eye had discovered the promised stranger. Seated upon a rock, a hundred yards from the face of the cliff, and entirely surrounded by the waters, was a lone sailor boy. That rock was never covered by the sea during the most violent storms. To this safe haven had destiny swept the boy when the ship foundered. Zenayi shouted to him in the English tongue to be of good cheer, for succor was at hand.   He knew by the build and canvas of the lost ship that she hailed from Anglo-Saxon lands.   The poor boy rose to his feet, and answered back :

"For God's sake send off a boat."

Zenayi called again, "Will you trust to the boat I send?"

"Ay! ay! sir," came back the manly response.

"Wait, then, till the sea goes down, and I will send you a safe boat, such as you never saw before."

"All right!" was shouted back from the rock, and the young sailor seated himself again to wait for the tranquillity of the sea.   The astrologer immediately sought the rocky stairway and disappeared.   The boy sat quietly upon his rock, eagerly watching the mainland.   An hour passed, and no one appeared to succor him.   Still another hour, and no boat came to his relief.   The waves had gone down and the sea was tranquil.   He spied at last the astrologer mounting to the summit of the cliff.   This white-robed being approached the sea and hailed the young sailor again.

"Trust to the boat I send you without fear.   Don't attempt to swim, for there are quicksands on the shore more deadly than the sea."

The boy promised obedience to this behest, and instantly the astrologer raised to his lips a silver call and sounded upon it a shrill summons, which travelled far away upon the air. Again and again the shrill notes were repeated, and then he paused.   From a point far inland the answer came, but it was not the response of a human being.   The strange cry came nearer, now appearing to descend into the valleys between the barren rock mountains which lined the shore, and again waxing louder, as if uttered from some summit nearer to the sea. Nearer and nearer came the mysterious sound, uttered only at intervals.   At last the mystery was revealed to the young sailor. He caught a glimpse of some white object winding among the rocks.   It came nearer, and then descended once more into a valley; then it rose rapidly to the summit of the cliff where the astrologer stood, and burst at once into full view.   It was a magnificent, spotless young Arabian stallion, snow-white, proud, and spirited as Bucephalus.

Dashing up to the astrologer, the horse rubbed his nose against his arm for a caress.   He received it, then wheeled away, and with a circular sweep around the summit of the cliff, returned again to his master's side and stood there motionless.

"This is my boat," shouted the man in white to the young sailor, who wondered at this unexpected *dénoûment.*" The horse is familiar with this shore; I will make him come to you; trust him with your life, and cling tight to him."

Without waiting for a reply, the astrologer commenced to descend laterally the cliff, and the steed walked after him. He made his way down to the shore at a point far away from the rock where the young sailor was now standing in eager curiosity. This youthful son of Neptune had never mounted a horse in his life, and this wild creature of the deserts was to be his boat to bear him to safety. Gaining a low beach far away, the astrologer pronounced some words to the Arabian, in the ancient Achæmenian Persian dialect. The steed seemed to comprehend his master perfectly, for with a toss of his head and mane as a preliminary to his adventure, he stepped daintily into the surf now reduced to a low white frill along the beach, gave a dozen convulsive plunges into deeper water, and then swam steadily for the isolated rock. It was doubtless no new destination for his imperial highness. With his superb white head proudly lifted above the green waves, he held directly on towards the young sailor's place of refuge. The boy clambered down from his rocky perch to the water's edge to meet the Arabian. A broad, flat rock, from which the waves had receded after the storm, was just visible above the water line, and upon this level platform he sprang with easy effort, and awaited the upshot of this extraordinary message.

The faithful and intelligent beast gained at length the table-rock, but experienced some difficulty in raising himself from the sea on to it. He assayed two or three points before he accomplished this difficult feat, but at last he mastered the difficulty, and stood triumphantly beside the sailor on the rock. The boy, deeming a little rest necessary for the steed, stood patting his neck, which the Arabian took kindly, occasionally stretching out his neck to take a look after his distant master. He appeared to be perfectly docile, and as well trained as a dog; but when the boy assayed to mount him, there were some decided manifestations of impatience on the part of the horse, who soon discovered that the sailor was a tyro in this art. At the sailor's first awkward attempt to clamber up his dripping side, the steed shied away from him, and he sprawled out upon the rock; this ridiculous failure was followed by another and more successful effort. Twisting a lock of the Arabian's mane round his forefinger to secure a hold, he sprang quickly up to his back, and then threw his right leg clear over the horse. The steed plunged for a moment, but the sailor clung tenaciously, and maintained his seat. The horse needed little urging to induce him to take to the water a second time, and with a tremendous splash he sank into the waves, rose again, and struck out for the shore, bearing his young rider in triumph.

Steadily the beautiful beast breasted the waves, heading for the low beach and the astrologer. The latter stood anxiously watching the inexperienced horseman. "The man of destiny," he muttered, "is tenacious — a good quality! I will teach that young rascal how to mount and ride a horse before I'm done with him. See him! see him *cling!* That's a sailor's art, after all. He'll learn — he'll learn."

The Arabian was now rapidly nearing his goal; he had evidently often before borne riders through the yielding element. He manifested no uncertainty of purpose, but swam right for the astrologer, reached at length the beach, and rose proudly from the surf with his dripping rider. His master caught him by the head as he landed, and gave the sailor an opportunity to dismount, knowing full well that otherwise the chances were in favor of his being flung over the Arabian's head. The boy slid from the back of the steed and stood upon *terra firma.* The astrologer released the horse, and gazed curiously at the sailor boy, the mysterious stranger who was to become so thoroughly identified with the welfare of Persia. What had the eternal stars sent to him? A youth of seventeen, muscular and beautiful as Cleobulus; a figure full of grace, a countenance sharply chiselled but of princely beauty, and an eye piercingly black, large, almond-shaped and *chatoyant.* The silky black waving hair was singularly luxuriant in growth, and clustered upon his white temples in unkempt masses. He was fair, but with eyelashes and eyebrows dark as jet. His breadth of forehead was of the poetic type; his mouth large, but exquisitely cut; and at times the thin lips clenched together as if they would never part again. His chin was long and singularly pointed, curving outward. The whole effect of the features was to induce the belief that rare manly beauty and indomitable will had blended in one face. But the eye, the terrible eye, ever roving, ever varying in expression, attracted instant attention by its well-like depth and clearness, its luminous blackness, its power of command. It seemed to penetrate into the hidden arcana of men's thoughts, and to order those thoughts to be abandoned, or to be employed at once in vigorous action. It is essential to a proper comprehension of certain scenes to be portrayed in the ensuing pages that the reader should form a vivid idea of the large, black, commanding eyes of the young shipwrecked sailor — eyes which admitted of no parley, and recognized the existence of no will but their own. There were moments of softness and kindness for those dark eyes, and the depth of that tenderness was unfathomable. But the habitual, predominant expression of those dazzling lamps of thought was this: "We are born to command, and our will *shall* be accomplished, or we perish in forcing it over obstacles."

Watching the powerful and wonderful play of these dictatorial eyes, Zenayi, the astrologer, stood for a moment abashed, bewildered, awed. Recovering himself, however, and ashamed to have been so influenced and dazzled by a boy, he extended his hand to the young sailor, and kindly welcomed him to the hospitality of his cavern in the cliff.

CHAPTER IV.

EEKS and months flew by, and still the young sailor remained an inmate of Zenayi's cave. Without a relative in the world, it mattered little to him where he tarried or whither he sailed. The cave, moreover, had been tendered to him as a permanent home so long as he chose to regard it as such. He was informed that for a portion of each year Zenayi would be absent. Indeed, a summons from the Shah of Persia might at any moment recall him to the capital of the empire. But so long as the sailor was content to remain, so long was the shelter of the cave guaranteed to him. The humble repast of the *quasi* hermit was also free to him as long as he remained. This consisted of bread, grapes in their season, the delicious dates of Dalaki, and clear water from a mountain spring. These came to the cave twice in every week from the governor of the province of Kerman, by direction of his royal master. But the privileges of the spacious cavern included something more precious than food and shelter. *There* was the opportunity and *there* were the facilities for mental culture. Zenayi was teaching his young guest. The cave was his own sanctum for study, and surrounded by valuable books, he willingly encouraged the youthful sailor in his aspirations after knowledge. He held out to the eager boy hopes of advance- ment in life if only he would implicitly follow the directions of his instructor. He intimated that his own influence at the Per·sian court was great, and that industry and application would prepare his pupil for a favorable presentation to the Shah. He fostered in the youth the ambition which he soon ascertained was far from being dormant.

Zenayi was a scholar of marvellous intellectual gifts, and his adscititious endowments were almost incredible. Under the magic influence of his stupendous learning and his scholarly enthusiasm, the youthful student was thoroughly aroused. "*Labor ipse voluptas,*" he said to the student ; and by his judicious arrangement and division of the duties of each day, he made labor a pleasure indeed. "Toil vigorously in your studies," he said, "if you would gain power over men. Your intellect will rule your fellows, if you add to its development the study of men. The clastic muscularity of the gladiator results only from systematic culture. If you would equal Tamerlane, that marvel of Asia, emulate his systematic and persistent application of means to ends."

When these words of wisdom fell upon the student's ear, there was to be seen an expanding of the pupils of those marvellous dark eyes which thrilled Zenayi. A great intellect was slumbering in those luminous depths. How anxiously the sage watched its development, for had not the eternal stars foretold the great influence of the stranger on the future of his beloved Persia ?

But when the boy looked in Zenayi's dark eyes, he was filled with an undefined awe. Something far away and deep in those mysterious eyes gave the impression of superhuman intelligence, the idea that the sage reached his conclusions regarding the motives and characters of men by a process unknown to mortals. It was impossible to shake off this awe when a full, fair look was had into those strange depths. From that dark abyss an illimitable memory seemed to beckon, an omnipresent consciousness, a fathomless intelligence. Not that the sage was aught but gentleness, kindness, tenderness personified. But to this student boy, and to all men, there looked out from those eyes a depth of mystery, *a far-off soul*, that made one gaze again, and gaze in awe. Like objects viewed through an inverted telescope, there appeared to be far-off realities, but no presences. And yet the genial smile would ripple upon the man's lips, the merriment would bubble up from his generous heart, and one's very soul would warm towards him, until his eyes *contemplated* you. Then, you would fall a-dreaming of the earliest consciousness you ever had, and wonder why his look suggested so much and told so little. He was the living, moving, breathing sphinx of Persia. He knew too much; his intellectual grasp was too extensive; his memory too vast. The Oriental *savans* shook their heads. What wonder, then, that the sailor marvelled, standing as he did, expectant, only at the threshold of science. His brief experience on the sea had given him a fair knowledge of seamanship; but this mysterious, white-robed scholar, with his lambskin cap, and white, sweeping beard, and penetrating black eyes, had told him in a few months more of the practical handling of a ship, than he believed the drowned captain and the mates had ever learned on the deep. Zenayi, in the hours of relaxation from study, had named to him every rope, spar, and sheet in the various styles of shipping. He had designated their uses, and their proper handling in various emergencies on Neptune's realm. The sailor would not have hesitated to sail under such a captain, as a practical seaman.

And when, in addition to this thorough knowledge of the tides, winds, waves, and manœuvring of vessels upon the surface of the sea, Zenayi commenced to instruct him in the lore of submarine plants and shells, his amazement knew no bounds. In this subtle reaching of the young sailor's heart, through his profession, had the sage undermined the boy's prejudices against landsmen. It was evident enough that his instructor was a *sailor* — a genuine blue-jacket. He would trust and follow such a man to death. It was an easy step after this to take an interest in the varied learning which was spread so seductively before him. He studied then, and he studied zealously, every book that was opened to him. He acquired the Persian language, assumed the habits of the people whom Zenayi presented to him in their occasional visits to Kerman, the capital of the province, and he rapidly became expert in the use of their arms.

He soon realized that his mysterious instructor contemplated great destinies for him. In that consciousness his soul awoke. He devoured every book of history that he was allowed to open. The exploits of great men thrilled him. But he was seldom permitted to indulge in such intellectual diet. Zenayi held him down to drier studies. He was being educated in practical manhood, in military science, and in oratory. His hours for physical exercise were devoted almost exclusively to horsemanship. From the day Zenayi discovered his awkwardness upon the back of the Arabian steed, he was flung upon the horse again and again, and made to fly over the rocky hills and valleys, without saddle or bridle. He had many a fall and many a bruise from the caprices of the white beauty that gave him the mountain air, but he was allowed no respite until he had mastered the Arabian. Then his instructor sent away the stallion from that barren neighborhood, and had him replaced by a fiery devil of the Kochlani breed, which traces its pedigree to King Solomon's matchless coursers.

"You stand upon the soil immortalized by the triumphs of Alexander. Through Kerman itself that conqueror marched, while his Admiral Nearchus led the fleet through the strait at the foot of this cliff. You shall learn to ride like Alexander. By Ormuzd! I swear it."

This was Alphonso's first introduction to those fleet and fiery steeds whose ardent temperaments aptly entitle them to the appellation, "horses of the sun."

The impetuous beast was led up to the mouth of the cave, saddled and bridled, by a mounted rover belonging to the tribe or clan of the fierce Bakhtiaris, whose turbulence and plundering propensities so frequently oblige the Persian monarch to employ his regular troops in their chastisement. The head of this high-caste Arabian steed was more beautifully formed, and more intelligent, than that of an English thorough-bred. His forehead, too, was broader, his muzzle finer, his eye more prominent. The eye lighted up occasionally with great brilliancy. No doubt that brilliancy would deepen and grow permanent when he was at full speed. His ear was beautifully pricked, and of exquisite shape and sensitiveness. The nostril was singularly thick and closed, but it would expand ere long in the excitement of motion, and when the lungs were in full play. Then, too, the membrane would show scarlet, and as if on fire. The point where his head was put on the neck was delicate. His neck was strong, light, and muscular, a little short when compared with the English stallion, and thick. The neck ran into the shoulders gradually, and came down rather perpendicularly into them. His shoulders were flat and thin. Between the knees, and behind the saddle, where the English thorough-bred falls off, he was barrel-ribbed. This gave him wonderful endurance, and his great constitutional points. This, too, gave him power to endure severe training and long marches on scanty food. His chest was amply broad and deep for strength and bottom. The elbow point, that essential bone, was prominent, fine, and played clear of the body. The fore-arm was strong and muscular, and rather long, and the knee square. Below the knee was manifested wonderful power in the ligaments and flexor tendons. The shank bone was small, dense, and solid like ivory. The feet were dainty; his hind quarters beautifully made, his tail came out high, his hind leg straight-dropped, his thighs and hock good. His stride in going was like a bound. He manifestly could not exceed fourteen and a half hands high, and came, no doubt, from the province of Khorassan.

This silken-coated, chestnut-colored prince of flight possessed a nervous organization sensitive and delicate, a nature susceptible to the alternatives of love or hate. Whichever was uppermost or developed was carried to the extreme. The rover of the clan of the Bakhtiaris had maltreated this imperial courser. There had been trouble already — more was brewing.

Zenayi took the reins from the hand of the rover and held the fiery steed by the head, while Alfonso took his position (preparatory to mounting) opposite the near fore-foot of the horse. The sage thus addressed his pupil :

"You are now to demonstrate whether you are qualified to command a troop of Persian horse. The horsemen of my country are the most daring in the world. They will dash up great and fearful acclivities — they will tear ahead at break-neck speed amid crags and broken masses of rock where the cavalry of other lands would pick their way daintily. They are not madmen, though they often ride like them. Skill in the management of their steeds is the whole secret. This friendly rover of the tribe of the Bakhtiaris will lead on his horse: follow him if you can. Upon your success depends your future in the cavalry of the Shah. I have taught you the history of the battles where our cavalry and those of the Circassians were posted on crags and mountain tops. Boy, you have the eye of a commander; you have wound yourself around my heart. I trust the good Ormuzd will permit me to see you return safe. But you will, before you have followed this rover far, discover that the flight of a Persian horse is no trifling matter. He is of pure, noble blood, from both sire and dam. The Arabs would class him, for this reason, under that most aristocratic head, *El Horr*. I warn you in advance that he is angered. He has been tantalized, worried, and maltreated until his blood is on fire for revenge. I know it by his eye and other indubitable signs. Cling to him like death, and follow your leader. Yonder mountain top is your limit; gain that without being unseated, and you are then ready for the first campaign against the Shah's revolted subjects, the fierce Bakhtiaris."

He pointed away to a far-off peak of the naked rock mountains which line the Strait of Ormuz. Valleys and ragged mountain crags intervened. It was a fearful field for cavalry practice. Then he looked in the face of the young recruit. No sign of shrinking from the dangerous duty was manifest. Alfonso had from his experience on the white Arabian, acquired a firm seat in the saddle and a ready hand and eye. He deemed one who had taken his first lessons on the bare back of an Arabian stallion equal to the management of any horse. He therefore signified his readiness for the adventure, took the reins, mounted and was off, the rover leading.

The sage stood looking after them until they disappeared in their headlong career going down into a valley. "Great Ormuzd, spare him, spare him!" he ejaculated, looking up reverently to heaven. Then a smile crossed his venerable face, and he exclaimed, "How dare I doubt the stars? They have announced that youth as the benefactor of Persia."

While the sage meditated, the fiery steeds had crossed the ravine, ascended the adjacent cliff, dashed rapidly through the rocky path beyond it, and were flying like the wind along the brink of a chasm bearing the ominous title, *Melek al mowt dereh* (Valley of the Angel of Death). No tree or shrub or blade of grass was near. Desolation and broken rocks were everywhere, while the black chasm beside the madly rushing horsemen seemed a long, narrow pit of fathomless gloom. Closer and closer still to the brink sped the leader and his steed, until the eye could look into the blackness below, where Eos, goddess of the dawn, will never swing her torch. Close at the heels of the rover bounded Alfonso, leaping rocks, sliding down declivities where the steed lost his foothold, for the instant, only to plunge to his feet again and bound wildly on. The leader was traversing familiar ground, and never tightened rein. The rattling hoofs of the horses passed so close at times to the edge of the abyss that the loose stones were struck by them and hurled sidelong into the gloomy pit.

No answering sound came back to tell of their having reached
the bottom. Suddenly the leader disappeared from sight, descending straight downward into the abyss, a large mass of
rock appearing to break off and fall beneath him. The steed
of Alfonso reared on the very brink of this fatal fracture, and
plunged to one side, thus saving his rider from death. The
leader and his steed had fallen through empty space, more
than *two hundred* feet, on to the rock bottom of the abyss, and
lay there, a crushed, lifeless mass. The frightened horse that
bore Alfonso reared and plunged again and again to unseat
his rider. Failing in this, he took revenge by running away
like an exasperated demon. All control over him was lost instantly. He cleared huge rocks in single bounds, and soon
turned again, circling round once more towards the very chasm
of the Angel of Death. With his horror-stricken rider clinging
to him, he cleared the chasm at a single leap, and dashing
through the rocky gorge beyond, followed the bed of the pebbly
stream which wandered through it, until he reached a cliff overhanging a ravine. Down this he plunged, and failing thus to
unseat his rider, held on his pathless way amid boulders and
fallen rocks, until he came to a long level valley. Ungovernable still, he flew like a frantic tiger in a long, terrific sweep,
onward and still onward, the wind whistling past him, until he
came to a rude, rocky mountain path. Up this he commenced
to bound, Alfonso now lashing him with his whip, and urging
him to greater speed, knowing full well that now had the time
arrived to reduce him to eternal control. He lashed the
frantic brute to his work, with every energy of power that was
left in his sinewy arm, driving the stinging spurs into him at
the same time, until they dripped and dripped again with
blood. Upward, and still upward, he goaded the proud, beautiful, ungovernable demon, whose frantic limbs still cleared
rocks, leaped ravines, crushed through mountain passes, and
scraped their marks of blood upon the sloping terraces of rock
down which they slid. Blood and dust were now fast mingling
with the foam that streaked the sides of the proud rebel of
Khorassan. He was learning the indomitable will and fearlessness of the youth who clung to him like an edict of destiny.
His strength was failing him, his fire of rage was dying out, and
still upon his sensitive sides beat and beat again the cruel
spurs, and the lash of the whip fell incessantly upon his back.
A level and open space appeared before his inflamed eyes, and
for it he broke away with his lingering remnant of impetuous

rage ; but the spurs galled him to more violent speed. He cleared the plateau, bounded through a short pass in the rocks, and then sank upon his knees in helpless submission to the indomitable master who rode him. The triumphant Alfonso on the instant leaped to the ground, raised the horse to his feet again, and stood beside him in eternal mastery.

On the summit of the mountain selected by Zenayi as the goal to determine his military merit as an officer of cavalry, he was at that instant standing. He had followed his leader *to death*. Then his path to the mountain top lay over obstacles, horrors, and dangers such as no sane Persian horseman would ever attempt while the world revolves. He was *there* at last, and *alone*.

CHAPTER V.

" She appeared like a sunbeam among women, and her hair was like the wing of the raven." — Ossian.

THE clans of the Bakhtiaris were gathering for battle. These turbulent wandering bands of mounted plunderers, enraged at the detention of several of their chiefs for misconduct at Teheran, the capital of the Empire, had vowed vengeance. Their fierce but skillful horsemen were ravaging the provinces of Fars, Kerman, and Khorassan. They had even been seen as far to the north-west as Koom, between Teheran and Ispahan. A large portion of the Persian army had been concentrated near the capital for its defence. Another portion had been dispatched to the assistance of Ispahan, the governor of which city had become alarmed, closed the gates, and was taking vigorous measures for defence. When or where the blow would fall, was problematical. Ispahan, however, was generally deemed to be most in jeopardy. The villages at the foot of the Taurus range of mountains were almost entirely deserted by their inhabitants, who had fled to the walled cities for safety. Houses, gardens, crops, fruit, everything but humanity, had been abandoned to the exasperated marauders. The *sarkardah* or colonel of horse at every post on the line of the rebels' expected advance received orders to risk no battle with superior numbers, but to fall back before them, and concentrate at designated points.nearer to the centre of the Empire. Vigilant and sleepless espionage was enjoined upon all post-commanders until the Persian army was in a condition to take the offensive. No remarkable novelty attached to the insurrection of these fierce desert riders. Such outbursts of violence had been of frequent occurrence, and had been always suppressed by the superior activity and discipline of the army. The present *emeute* derived its importance from the rumors that other nomadic tribes of the Empire were in sympathy with it.

Pending the solution of this military problem, the leading personage of this narrative, riper in years and more mature in mental accomplishments than when he tamed the spirit of the fierce Kochlani courser, rises into prominence amid the fiery Asiatics. . . . .

On the road from Koom to Kashan, with the lofty peaks of the Taurus mountains close on the west, and a gentle rill-furrowed slope of emerald grass leading down to picturesque villages on the east, stood the caravansary of Shoor-Aub. Partly hidden in the gorge of a narrow rocky valley leading into the heart of the mountains, it commanded an extensive view of the broad emerald slope in front, the foliage-girdled villages on either hand, and the vast desert of Khorassan beyond. Close to its eastern front rippled a stream of crystal water through the grass, and parallel with the stream was the road from Koom to Kashan. A traveller to or from either town would not dream of finding a caravansary until it burst upon his view upon looking up the narrow gorge.

On one of those clear, luminous nights when an Oriental moon makes every landscape a *paradise*, this caravansary and gorge were full of Persian cavalry. Their spear-heads twinkled like stars — a sea of stars, so densely were they crowded in the defile. Thousands of burnished points reflected the moon. Mars and Selene blended to glorify the night. The dark-visaged Bakhtiaris might at any moment dash by. Then the paradise would become an Aceldama. The gorge was once defended by a strongly-towered castle, whose dark ruins rose in heavy but majestic masses overhead. The reign of the silent silver queen was undisturbed by the sounds of human tumult. Her luminous light glorified all things. Even the gray lizards, struggling among the loose stones of the gorge, were glancing silver under the moonlight. Occasionally, some mounted soldier would turn in his saddle, till his whole body appeared to shiver in silver glory. It was only his burnished coat-of-mail, whose steel rings undulated upon him like a vesture of soft silk. The high range of mountains were crowoed with peculiar magnificence, their varied heads shooting up into the cloudless and luminous blue of the vaulted sky, and reflecting the moon's rays on their summits with all the pearly hue and lustre only to be seen in Oriental climes, while the deepened shadows at their base gave a profounder majesty to their heaven-tinted brows. Countless little streams pouring from. the mountains adown the grassy slopes toward the embowered and distant villages carried their molten silver treasures to enrich the soil.

The mountains were bare rocks, but the valleys and plains were wildernesses of fragrant shrubs, flowers, lofty *chinár* trees, thickly set rows of cypresses, and wide branching cedars mingling with pomegranate and mulberry trees, and all sleeping peacefully under the spell of the Oriental Selene.

Lights were glancing from the windows opening into the courtyards of the flat-roofed and foliage-girt dwellings far away at the foot of the grassy slope. An officer, superbly mounted, rode out through the gate of the caravansary, and with easy pace crossed the bridge over the little stream, descended the gentle slope, and entered the streets of the village. His saddle cloth was scarlet, with a silver crescent flashing in each of the lower corners. He was clad in glittering mail from head to foot, and his sabre rattled at his side as he rode. A black lambskin cap with scarlet crown surmounted his head. His bridle was covered with silver bands, and scarlet tassels of silk depended at each side of the horse's bit. He was an officer of the royal cavalry, his rank *yuzbashi* or centurion, commanding one hundred horse He had risen from the ranks step by step. Sharp fighting at Ferozabad, Jarun, and Forg, with the revolted subjects of the Shah, had indicated his merit. He had repeatedly routed four times his number of men, by the skill and impetuosity of his charges. The fierce Bakhtiaris had fled before him like a flock of galinazos before the king vulture of the Andes. He had been transferred from the *goolams* (an immense corps of irregular cavalry deemed competent at any day to compete with the Cossacks) to a body of twenty-five hundred cavalry which constitute the Shah's body-guard, the *élite* of the army. The officers for this fine corps are usually selected from the sons of Khans or persons of other distinction in the Empire. The rule had been violated in favor of this young "lord of the scimitar," through the influence of the Prince Royal of

Persia, to whose ear a certain mysterious character named Zenayi had unaccountable access. That a priest of the persecuted sect of the Ghebres should be allowed to offend the sight of pious Mohammedans on the soil of Persia, was mysterious enough to Moullah and to devotee. But when this white-robed representative of the ancient faith was welcomed at court, and even consulted as the royal astrologer, orthodoxy was astounded. But Abbas Mirza, the heir-apparent to the crown, was too thorough a statesman, too able a soldier, and too thoroughly a master of *la science du monde*, to be a bigot or to be influenced by one. Hence he turned a friendly ear to the learned and loyal Ghebre, and his gallant young *protégé* was retained in the honorary corps.

As the young *yuzbashi* walked his horse along the streets of the town, he was struck by the remarkable stillness of the place. Not a human voice was heard. No sound came to his ear, save the occasional yell of a solitary jackal that was prowling near the village. There were many lights burning, as he could see when he passed the arched entrance into the court-yards. Presently his horse's hoof struck something metallic. He bent low from his saddle to examine it. The light from a court-yard whose entrance-way he was at that moment passing, revealed the flash of silver. It was a goblet of the precious metal, which had fallen in the street. As the adjacent house apparently belonged to a Persian of the upper class, he dismounted, secured the prize, and then led his horse up to the archway, and loudly clapped with his hands for a servant. None answered his summons. He repeated the call. No response. Harpocrates had assumed dominion over the town. There was a delicious aroma of roses on every side, and the moonbeams sifted noiselessly through the luxuriant foliage. The tinkling of water in the fountains dipped out its monotonous melody, and a blaze of waxlights poured out through the archway. But human sounds there were mysteriously hushed. Some enchantment as potent as Viviane wrought about Merlin with her wimple, held these luxurious rose-gardens and wax-lighted avenues silent as death.

After a moment of further reflection, he secured his horse, and passed into the court-yard through the arch. The marble fountains were flinging diamond-like drops up into the moonlight, and the odoriferous shrubs that bordered the canals of glistening water filled the air with voluptuous fragrance. But no one was to be seen. The place was apparently deserted.

He passed on to an apartment, whence issued a pure, brilliant
light.   To his amazement, it was a banquet-hall, illuminated
for a sumptuous entertainment, with every luxury spread upon
silver trays on the floor, which was covered with a superb carpet from Khorassan.   The great variety of beautiful porcelain
bowls and dishes upon the trays were filled with the most
savory meats, conserves, sweet cakes, delicious fruits, both
dried and fresh ; sherbet of orange, and pomegranate, and willow water cooled with ice.   Where were the guests, and where
the master of the feast ?   The lower parts of the walls of this
spacious banquetting hall were formed of fine white marble
slabs, painted and gilded in patterns of birds and flowers ;
while the ceiling and walls above were fashioned in delicate
Arabesque figures, with occasional diamond-shaped and oval
pieces of looking-glass inserted to add to the brilliant effect.
Twisted columns of Melos marble, snowy white, with golden
spots, raised their slender shafts to the arches overhead.   Exquisite shawls of the fine hair of the goats of Kerman had been
spread for seats for the Oriental banqueters.   Through the
open casements, the rose-trees nodded their flowers in the faint
breeze, and the soft play of the fountains was heard.   What
Eastern Hortensius had spread the feast ?   What hospitable
Lentulus awaited his Flamen Martialis?   No guest arrived.
No master of the feast appeared ; and the soft, dreamy atmosphere of the Oriental night seemed to hush itself in expectancy
of the coming revellers.   Were the guests shod in wool, that
thus their coming footsteps might harmonize with the dream-
like stillness of the hour ?   Was it not all a dream of the young
soldier, standing in amazement within the banquet-hall, still
grasping his silver goblet?   Were these peaceful scenes not all
false dreams sent to him through Virgil's *ivory gate?*

Surprised at the quiet of the luxurious abode, he entered an
adjoining apartment, where the lights and the silence appeared
to invite him.   This, too, was deserted.   Luxurious divans
were against the frescoed walls, and in the centre of the white
marble floor a fountain was playing.   Here were evidences,
however, of hasty departure.   Female apparel was scattered
about upon the divans and floor.   He passed to other rooms,
and found additional evidences of flight.   Everything was in
confusion, scattered, out of place.   Disorder reigned in what
was evidently the home of some illustrious Khan of the Empire.
He explored the whole house.   Every soul had fled.   He
realized then what had been told him in the army.   The

Bakhtiaris had depopulated towns in advance of their march. This village must have been panic-stricken within the hour, by the same rumors of the enemy's advance that had halted the royal cavalry that night in the mountain gorge. He soon regained the street, and mounted his steed. He traversed the village, looking in at the various entrances to the paved courts, and found that his conjecture was correct. Fear of the lawless marauders had driven off the inhabitants in haste. As he stood at the entrance of one of the better class of dwellings where his horse was fastened, irresolute whether to ride further on and execute the orders of his superior officer in making the desired *reconnoissance*, or apprize him of the army supplies which might at once be secured in the deserted village, he was startled by a hand laid suddenly on his arm. He turned, and beheld a vision of loveliness which thrilled him. A Persian girl, *unveiled*, elegantly arrayed in garments indicating her connection with some family of wealth and distinction, had stolen noiselessly up to him, and now stood in her helpless loveliness, beseeching his protection. She had entered the village, so her story ran, that very night with her mother, and other ladies belonging to the *anderoon* of a Khan whose name was well known in the Empire. They were escorted by a powerful guard, and had sought the village for shelter until morning, when they intended to resume their march towards Ispahan. In the confusion attending the night alarm at the sudden approach of the main body of the Bakhtiaris, she had been separated from her party and escort, who had dashed off toward the headquarters of the main body of the Persian army, leaving her entangled in the mazes of a strange garden, from which she could not extricate herself until it was too late. Fearing then to join the terrified groups of strange men who were flying away to a place of safety, she had concealed herself again in the garden until the villagers had all departed. Hearing the tramp of a solitary horseman in the streets, she had peeped out through the shrubbery, and recognized with joy the uniform of the Shah's body-guard. "Would the officer conduct her to the headquarters of his commander, where her father's name would be recognized, and means afforded her to regain his protection?"

'This appeal was addressed to a soldier, beautiful as Hylas, and she knew it, looking up into his dark eyes with undisguised admiration, and that implicit confidence which the features of a noble-souled man inspires. The young officer

was bewildered by her beauty, and confused by her appeal.
Her felicity of expression indicated culture of the highest order.
Her knowledge of the positions and probable movements of
the different corps of the army manifested in her detail of the
routes by which she expected finally to regain her friends, could
only have been acquired in the family of some officer of high
military rank.   Such an elevated position did the Khan occupy,
whom she designated as her father.   In her ludicrous account
of the night alarm and its consequences, she had evinced her
possession of a gift the most dazzling, and the most evanescent
of all intellectual gifts.   Entirely ignorant as he was of female
coquetry, and an enthusiastic admirer of female beauty, the
loveliness of this young and high-born Persian girl produced a
marked impression upon his susceptible nature.   He saw
before him a face beaming with expression, and a figure fashioned in the most perfect symmetry to delight a sculptor.
Tall and graceful, with a complexion of most exquisite beauty,
in which the dash of Circassian blood from her mother was
plainly visible, she stood contemplating him with admiration
sparkling in her large dark eyes.   The transition from an
existence of constraint, study, and seclusion to the excitements
of a border warfare had been sufficiently stimulating to his
ardent temperament to arouse all the enthusiasm of his nature.
But now in the hush preceding another martial conflict, and
with the seductive influences of the moonlight, the peaceful
gardens, and the soft dreamy atmosphere of the Orient lulling
his professional activity to sleep, he was assailed by a temptation and an excitement before which the illusion of military
glory faded out, and was forgotten.   His vanity was flattered
by so marked evidences of his power over the feelings of a
young and beautiful daughter of one of the most elegant and
illustrious nobles of the Persian court.   This sentiment was
heightened by the consciousness, almost electric, that she was
superior intellectually to the mass of unrivalled beauties who
hide their loveliness in the *anderoons* of the wealthier Khans.
The recollection of Zenayi's words of warning flashed upon him
on the instant :

" Beware the matchless loveliness of the high-born women of
my country !   Yield not to their influence until you have
carved a high name for yourself with your sword.   Shun them
as impediments to your exalted purpose !   Aye ! avoid them
as the Arab sailor avoids the demon-haunted isle of Poelsetton.
The black scorpion of Cashan will harm you less ! "

The words of this salutary counsellor seemed enigmatical as the officer contemplated this marvel of loveliness, whose eyelashes drooped before the earnestness of his gaze. His senses were entranced. The urgency of his military duty, the brief time he had to perform it, and the possibility that delay might isolate him altogether from his command, all fell into oblivion. He heard nothing, saw nothing but the immaculate loveliness that had so abruptly and so wonderfully chained his imagination and his senses. He wandered away with her through the gardens, unconscious where his steps led him, strolling on and still on, and watching the stars which from time to time peeped through the foliage as it swayed gently beneath the voluptuous breeze of the dreamy night, and listening to the musical murmur beside him, which was narrating her girl's life, hopes, and ideas. They were mutually enthralled in each other's perfections. The novelty of unrestrained intercourse in that land of female isolation was rising upon them like the charming hallucinations of a dream. The accident of war had emancipated the high-born maid from the supervision of watchful eunuchs. Such an opportunity for unbounded freedom might not occur again in a lifetime. To look upon a handsome, manly face was no novelty to the inmate of a harem. To peep through lattices, to study the busy scenes of human life and traffic, to frequent the bazaars and streets, are privileges of every-day occurrence to the Oriental maid. But converse with strange men, the casting off the eternal veil, the triumph of being *contemplated* as well as of contemplating, are novelties as rare as comets. This exquisite daughter of Eve had flung aside her veil at the first realization that she was indeed free, and had wandered through the marble-paved courts and luxuriant rose-gardens with a sense of exultation which her knowledge of her danger could not wholly quell. And now she was listening to a voice all harmony, which had not been forced upon her girlish life by paternal authority. She was realizing the poetic tales of Ferdusi, Hafiz, and Sadi, that there were companionships voluntary, congenialities arising from one's own perceptions of the beautiful and the noble, which filled the heart and the understanding with infinite enjoyment, far beyond those established by the dictates of parents and kings. And the mail-clad soldier who walked beside her in a dream, knew that his life might at any moment pay the forfeit of his temerity in conversing with an unveiled daughter of a proud Khan of the Empire.

But the sweet witchery of the night, the adventure, and the *presence* was upon each; and for an hour they ceased to remember duty, fear, the world, and might for another hour, have wandered on and on, had not a fearful interruption dispelled the dream and resuscitated thought. The dazzling flash of fire-arms, discharged in rapid succession, notified the soldier that the enemy had come. Then the clear, ringing notes of a bugle sounded the charge. The Bakhtiaris had been surprised as they reached the mountain gorge. A column of disciplined cavalry had severed their dense mass of desert riders and the work of death was going on. The young and thoughtless *yuzbashi* was cut off from his command.

Hurriedly secreting the Khan's daughter in the dense foliage of the garden, and promising to return, he sought his steed, mounted, and was off. Riding like the wind up the slope towards the mountains, he was soon engaged in the thickest of the fight.

CHAPTER VI.

NE of the brilliant *"Princes de la pensée"* sat by the couch of pain. The great, the mysterious, the tender Zenayi watched like a mother the form of his prostrate idol. The turbulent storm of sedition had subsided, but had left that wreck of the Ghebre's hopes. The lance wounds of the Bakhtiaris were many and deep. The desert riders had hurled to the earth a soldier gifted with a happy genius for command. Entangled in their routed and flying squadrons, he had maintained a gallant fight with superior numbers, until, borne to the earth, he was found by his own soldiers, severely wounded, and insensible. That he had neglected his duty as a scout, was known to one only besides himself. There was little danger that she would reveal his delay in the deserted village. Her own fate was still a mystery. But for her, for himself, for the army, he had thus far had no opportunity for thought. His insensibility had resulted in delirium. His situation had long been deemed devoid of hope by the army surgeon. One alone pronounced in favor of his recovery. That almost celestial intelligence, which never seemed to err, was on the side of hope. Zenayi, whose medical discrimination was proverbial, who comprehended surgery as thoroughly as he comprehended every science, declared that the young officer would be on his feet again. His only apprehension was that he might for a long period remain weak and sickly after his wounds were healed. The army surgeon was awed at the Ghebre's comprehension of the case. Did that mysterious being possess the power of penetrating the veil of the flesh and reading the secrets which were hid from human vision? He questioned the Ghebre upon the anatomy of man, and the proper remedies to be applied and operations to be performed in difficult cases of gun-shot wounds, and lance thrusts, and sabre cuts. The responses were clear and satisfactory. The man knew *everything*. The surgeon had heard this extraordinary rumor of his knowledge before. Now he *knew*, at least, that Zenayi was a surgeon.

But hopeful as the astrologer was of Alfonso's ultimate recovery, he could not conceal the yearning tenderness of his heart for the helpless young officer before him. He knelt beside him, and with his arm about his neck, murmured to the delirious soldier in touching accents:

"My beautiful and noble hero: my heart goes forth to you in your suffering. The heart of the old man mourns for you as if you were my own child. Kindred I have none. Hopes I have none, save of you and Persia. The two are my life. The two must never be severed from each other or from me. In my old age, boy, my heart clings to you. When shall those beautiful eyes shine clear to me again? They have softened again and again in love and kindness for the old man, and his very soul looks out for those love-tokens again. Speak to me once more, boy, as you spoke when the fierce courser was delivered at my cave, tamed and submissive. Let me look once more upon the eyes which blaze for glory and for Persia. Ha! the delirium is gone."

The young officer opened his eyes upon his benefactor, and like one arousing from a dream, said faintly:

"Tell me, Zenayi, why am I here? What have I done? Where am I? What means this dizziness, this pain?"

"You ask many questions, Alfonso. This is my answer: you are in your hospital wounded sore. The Bakhtiaris are routed, and you are covered with glory."

"Will I recover?"

"Yes, by long-continued patience and repose."

"But I came late into the battle," he said, the memory of his dereliction of duty pressing painfully upon him.

"That," responded the Ghebre, "is the very cause of your distinction. They informed your commander that the enemy advanced in a direction totally unexpected, whereby you were misled, and rode on far towards the desert of Khorassan. Returning from your futile expedition, you encountered the enemy in full retreat, and exposing yourself with the reckless impetuosity of the Athenian Chabrias to overwhelming numbers, you, single-handed, slew four of the enemy, and among them, fortunately, the chief of the Bakhtiaris. You can claim the reward offered for his head, and your promotion is beyond question."

A flush of pride mounted to the cheek of the invalid; his eye lighted up with the old fire. The Parcæ had woven, from the threads of his neglect and absorption in the village, a fortunate web for his fame. His arrival upon the battle-field so late had afforded him the opportunity of encountering hand to hand the rebel chief. The latter had fallen. This good fortune needed confirmation, and he anxiously inquired:

"Do you *know* this, Zenayi?"

"I *do* know it, Alfonso. I have your new commission in my own keeping. It is signed by the Prince Royal."

"What is my grade?" he asked faintly.

"You are *sarkardah*, and draw one thousand *tumáns* a year for your pay."

A thrill of delight warmed the blood of the poor invalid.

"O Zenayi!" he exclaimed, "*you* have done this. My benefactor, my friend, my only father!"

"You were never so much mistaken in your life," replied the Ghebre. "The intelligence of your splendid conduct and your destruction of the rebel chief was carried to the Shah himself by your commander. Abbas Mirza notified me that you had been promoted by command of his royal father."

How wildly throbbed the heart of the emaciated sufferer. *A full colonel of horse in the royal army!* The dreams of the boy, the aspirations of the young man, might now be realized. He was prominent now before the army. Aye! more, he had attracted the notice of the mighty and absolute potentate who held the sceptre of Persia. It was not his friend, the Ghebre, this time, but his fortune and impetuous daring, that had singled him out for honor. He contemplated the dark, mysterious eyes that watched his emotion. He saw that they were full of joy at his good fortune.

"My father; my father! I owe all to you. Education, horsemanship, and my first promotions were your gifts; they were the foundation. To you, therefore, my heart ascribes all that has been, all that shall be erected thereon."

The eyes of the Ghebre beamed with tenderness for the young soldier who had so tightly wound himself about his aged heart. Then he uttered an exclamation of distress. The young *sarkardah* had fainted away.

. . . .

Upon the shoulders of Zenayi the mantle of Melampus had surely fallen. Every prediction regarding the recovery of the young officer proved true. His apprehension that when Alfonso should be able to walk, great and prolonged debility would return to him at intervals, was also verified. When dread Azrael spread his dusky wings and fled from the sick couch, the astrologer raised his eyes in gratitude to Ormuzd, the god of the Ghebre. Then bending his entire energies to the work of restoration, he watched patiently beside his wounded friend, applying every remedy which experience and profound study had familiarized him with in the medical art. What self-sacrifice and assiduity could the patriot priest withhold from the gallant soldier who had sacrified all for Persia. With the unhesitating heroism of the Theban Menœkeus, had the young officer presented himself singly to death. In recompense of this abnegation of self, that marvellous intellectual sphinx, who blended in himself the medical genius of Paracelsus, Hippocrates, and Galen, devoted all the fertile resources of his cultured brain to the revival of the exhausted and lingering humanity before him. Familiar with the *habitat* and properties of every healing plant, he administered decoctions of desert herbs, which amazed the attendant surgeon of the corps. This admirable healer gently but gradually supplanted the surgeon, and assumed into his own hands the treatment of the convalescent. "Are you Allah or *deev*," exclaimed the official, "that you comprehend all science and the essences of matter!"

"Study, profound study, honest Malek, and a vigilant observation of nature, compress great and varied knowledge into the space of a human life. I am old, and I have studied much."

So modestly and gently came this response from the Ghebre, that the charmed surgeon was emboldened to continue, —

"But the memory of man, Zenayi, shirks the greater portion of its burden. Else might we all attain to heights of knowledge near to Allah's realm. We cannot all claim a memory like yours."

"'Tis true, Malek," responded the Ghebre, "'tis true. Memory is the golden key to kn•wledge." Then looking full in the eyes of the surgeon, he added solemnly : "Pray to the incomprehensible Ruler of all things, that you may never remember *as Zenayi remembers.*"

The deep, sonorous termination of his sentence boomed like a distant bell in a far-off cavern. It seemed as if the ever-receding and dying echoes of that cadence would never cease. The surgeon started at the sound, and in the mysterious eyes of the *savant* saw a far-off light, a mysterious something that awed him with a sense of immensity, a profound, *ever-receding* grandeur. And then he fell a-dreaming of his own earliest consciousness, and forgot all present objects in his reverie. *Such was the power of Zenayi's look.*

As the physical strength and natural elasticity of spirits gradually returned to Alfonso, he began to realize the material paradise in which he was sheltered. Slowly upon his awakening senses came the odor of flowers, the rippling of waters, the distant murmurs of music ; occasionally he caught the merriment of laughter, the inspiration of song, and the exquisitely modulated voice of women in badinage. To each and every question he propounded to the sable eunuch who watched beside him after Zenayi had departed for his cave, he received the single response, "*Negauristan.*" The impenetrable mystery of the slave regarding the locality and the ownership of the summer palace which was his hospital gave out to his curiosity this single key. That it was a palace or the abode of a powerful Khan of the Empire, the officer surmised from the elegance of the "mother-of-pearl" ceiling above him, the frescoed walls about him, and the silken draperies of his couch. With his returning strength and appetite, came also presents from some unknown hand of every luxury that the climate afforded. No sooner had one delicate meat or fruit become familiar to his taste, than it was replaced by some new and equally palatable luxury. He pondered long and frequently upon that mystic appellation, "*Negauristan.*" It was an occult and novel region of the Empire to him. He could not make it out.

One day his attendant bathed the invalid carefully, clothed him in soft, delicate textures of white, threw about him a robe of golden-hued silk trimmed with white Siberian fur, ar-d placing yellow morocco slippers upon his feet, carried him in his arms to another apartment. Here he was seated upon a divan of pearl-colored silk, between enormous pillows of the same delicate hue, and directed to look through the open gold-cased window upon the scene below. He believed for an instant that he revelled in an Oriental dream.

Far away before him, in successive terraces, stretched downward voluptuous and varied gardens of oriental plants and flowers, pavilions, fountains, and lakes; rose-trees, shade-trees, glistening canals, and water-falls. The Pisa gardens of Cosmo de Medici, the botanic paradises of Alfonso d'Este, and the sumptuous terraces of Breslau, sank into insignificance before the voluptuous Eden here presented at a single *coup d'œil.* The great Semiramis herself was eclipsed upon her own soil. Her Bagistan was but a single terrace beside this luxurious dream. The atmosphere was laden with the perfume of countless roses and lilacs, which gently undulated above the cuts of clear and sparkling water. The trees were full grown and luxuriant in foliage, their lofty stems nearly covered by a rich underwood of roses and aromatic shrubs. A Kooleh Frangy or temple appeared at intervals between the spacious arcades of trees, and from an artificial cliff a sheet of white roses was trained to fall downward like a cascade, fragrant and white as the celestial waters of *al Cawthar,* the river of Paradise. Springs were gushing bright from their native rock, and sparkling in the ardent glances of the sun, and over the delicious vistas and flower-enamelled lawns a soft glamour seemed to hover, born of the golden light and the rich coloring of the flowers. From the emerald clusters of luxuriant plants the sheen of sculptured marbles peeped. The Persian Shireen timidly looked forth from her pedestal.

> " She lives in stone, and fills
> The air with beauty."

The precepts of the Koran were forgotten in this sensuous retreat, and the images of " the infidel " had found a lodgment here. Beside the grand avenue stood the Venus of Melos, with her ideal beauty, and her conquering arms outstretched to Mars. Here, too, was Ferhaud, the sculptor, for whom in the olden time the lovely Shireen drooped her head, and died. The Persian Sapor here led captive the Emperor Valerian ; and near them, in a mass of roses, was the reclining Cleopatra in the repose of death, a statue immortalized by Castiglione.

The view beyond the vast garden was intercepted by the chain of the Elbrooz mountains, whose dim outline was marked in tints of chalky purple ; and beyond them loomed in solitary grandeur the loftier peak of Demewand, clad in eternal snows. Near to the summer pavilion where the invalid was seated, and girt with shrubs of white-blossomed rosaceæ, crown imperials, tulips and red-flowering amygdaleæ, stood a white marble imitation of the graceful and exquisite Choragic monument of Lysicrates.   On the same luxuriant terrace, in happy unison with this terrestrial paradise, stood the " golden-haired " Rhadamanthus, " sovereign judge on the Elysian plain."   Here the graceful Tyro, enamoured of her river, gazed into a flower-girt stream ; and under an arched trellis of roses knelt the doctor "*en gaye science,*" to receive the violet of gold from the marble hand of Clementina Isaure, Countess of Toulouse.

Entranced by the exquisite vision of this varied and far-reaching loveliness, rivalling the gardens of the Fairy Morgana beneath the Italian lake, the invalid soldier inhaled the delicate perfumes, and in the vivifying light of the sun felt a dreamy languor stealing over his senses.   His ear was enchanted by the wild and beautiful notes of countless nightingales in close proximity to their beloved roses, and in the lull of the summer noon he sat in sensuous absorption amid the arborescent plants, exhaling their sweetness upon the dreaming air.   Familiar only with the stretch of grassy vales, or sunburned desert wilds where his courser spurned the sands too often glistening like myriad daggers in the ardent sun, this soothing vision of Elysium and peace came to him like a new creation.   To his insatiable longing after power and glory was being added rapidly a new ambition, *Wealth.*   Why might not he attain such heights of sensuous bliss as the master of this paradise ?   Who was its master ? Who had the means, the taste, the far-reaching liberality of sentiment and wisdom, to cull the masterpieces of foreign lands, and in violation of the precepts of his religious faith make them part of the treasures of luxurious Persia ?   The capacious intellect and the unbounded liberality which planned this voluptuous seclusion, where the masterpieces of art might be enshrined, could belong to no common Khan of the Empire.   The fabulous wealth employed must rival that of Karun.   The proprietor was a consummate master of effect, whoever he might be. Symmetry, fitness, harmony, reigned supreme in all the voluptuous appointments of this spacious, dream-like *charbagh.*

For an instant he surmised that Zenayi himself was master of the place.   He had learned from his years of study and tuition under this extraordinary scholar, that the owner of the hermit's cave was a power in Persia. Might not his influence at the court have conduced to his pecuniary success? This conjecture was at once abandoned. The astrologer had informed his pupil again and again that he owned not one foot of land on the surface of Persia. The Shah had confirmed his claim to the cavern, which had belonged to his father, the astrologer, before him. Who, then, was the gifted master of this lovely realm of taste and beauty? He turned for the first time to study the apartment in which he was seated. Curtains of rose-colored silk, with under curtains of lace, adorned the windows. These flung upon his pale face a delicate shade of light, and softened the effect of his manly beauty. He was closely shaven, only his black military moustache being suffered to grow. His dark eyes roved now over the apartment, in examination of its furniture and appointments. The softest velvet carpet of blue and pearl covered the floor. The divans, with their pillows, were all of the same delicate shade of silk as the one upon which he sat. His attendant, while he had been engrossed with the landscape without, had noiselessly covered the entire carpet with fresh pink rosebuds, until its patterns were nearly obscured. The apartment was octagonal, and on each wall was painted a medallion portrait. Here again was the Koran ignored. The ceiling, the walls, and the window-casings were of white Elbrooz marble, upon which birds and flowers had been inlaid in gold. Opposite to where he sat a Saracenic arch opened a view to the "court of the bath," a luxurious circular saloon open to the skies above, with a snow-white marble basin in the centre of the floor, full sixty feet in diameter, and full of crystal water, sparkling in the sun. Rose-trees and fragrant flower-bearing shrubs, nodded around its brink, their shadows quivering at times over the bright water, which was freshened every instant by a flowing spring.

At the sight of the medallion portraits, executed with the force and delicacy of Isabey, the young *sarkardah* started from his luxurious attitude. They were family likenesses, a race of sovereigns. He knew several of the faces well, so frequently had he seen common copies of them in possession of Mohammedan shopkeepers, who for lucre bartered away the principles of their prophet. He was filled with awe at his situation,— the terrible realization which burst upon him instantly. He was in a *royal palace*, and before his astonished eyes was the image of its master. There was the likeness of the dread potentate Futteh Ali Shah, the man whose word was law, whose will gave life or death to the subject.   He was the guest of the sovereign, who could make or unmake his military fortune by a word.   Wonder, awe, hope, darted in succession through the brain of the young officer of cavalry.   He scanned every lineament of that pale face for an idea of his character.   He noted the habitual expression of languor given him by the artist ; the perfectly formed, dark, beaming eyes, and the jet-black ample beard which tapered to a point below the hilt of his jewelled dagger in his waist-belt. His robe was of fine gold brocade, with a deep cape of dark sables falling on his shoulders.   Eminently kingly was the mien of the sovereign of Persia.   The *sarkardah* had attained his present rank in the royal army by the direct interposition of his sovereign.   Doubtless the Shah had acted in the matter solely upon the recommendation of Alfonso's superior.   But the ambitious young officer could not divest himself of the idea, that once having been forced upon the attention of the Shah as a soldier deserving of promotion, he might, by securing a personal interview with his sovereign, so impress him that his subsequent promotions would be of easy accomplishment.   This anticipation was not without reasonable foundation, inasmuch as he actually belonged to Futtch Ali Shah's honorary bodyguard, and might at any moment be detailed for service about his immediate person.   Thus far the exigencies of war had withdrawn a portion of the body-guard from the neighborhood of the capital, and Alfonso had never yet looked upon the countenance of his sovereign.   He could not look forward, therefore, to his entrance into the camp at Teheran without an eager hope of attracting the Shah's notice by his superior military conduct.   Thanks to the incessant schooling and admonitions of Zenayi, he had become a thorough disciplinarian. His command of one hundred men was, by the testimony of the astrologer, the best-drilled body in the army, with the exception of the artillery, which was under the supervision of British officers detailed for this service by their government. What, then, might not be expected from the Shah's favor by an ambitious officer, who was now in a position to introduce that same superior discipline into an entire regiment.   His own unmilitary conduct had been overlooked, and his neglect of duty had strangely enough resulted to his advantage.   And now what might not be expected from a sovereign who had gone to the amazing length of making a wounded officer the inmate of his royal palace ?

In the midst of such startling good fortune, and the wild

dreams it suggested, the young *sarkardah* was amazed to see a white ball fly through the window and alight directly in his lap.

CHAPTER VII.

MAZED at the precision and suddenness with which the white projectile had been flung into his lap, the *sarkardah* looked up through his window at a long stretch of lattice work, which covered the entire side of a wing of the palace. A short slide in the lattice was open, revealing a face beautiful as Ægle, mother of the Graces. Instantly the face vanished and the slide closed. The audacity of this exposure was only equalled by the skill with which the missile had been projected. The attendant eunuch was busy about his apartment, and failed to detect this female manœuvre. The officer unwound the white ball and found it to be a delicate handkerchief, redolent of rich perfumes. It was loaded with a large Budukshân ruby to aid its flight. A note was enclosed, traced in the delicate characters of the Persian language, and in the most graceful female chirography. He read with amazement, not unmixed with pleasure, these lines :

"Ha ! ha ! my young Abou Hassan, caliph for a day. How grand you are in your new state ! And so luxurious, too ! Who would have dreamed this of the soldier who was bent on glory alone ? Your senses were to be iron-clad, you said, until you had gained eminence in war. 'Abstemious at the banquet, headlong in the battle ; ' these were your words. Ha ! ha ! you look like it now. The rose curtains become your complexion well.

> 'Beds of hyacinths and roses
> Where young Adonis oft reposes,
> Waxing well of his deep wound
> In slumber soft.'

Listen to me, gallant soldier. Your flight upward has been swift as the arrow of Acestes. Beware lest you share its fate and be consumed in going. You are in danger now. Ahrimanes circles you with subtle darts. Beware the temptations of these gardens. Hold your passions calm and unruffled as the

Lake of Wulur.   Thus will you climb still higher in your sovereign's heart.   Alas!   I am a prisoner once more.   Would you see me again?   There is danger.   But the soldier fears nothing. I can whisper words in your year that will aid you.   *There is a power behind the throne that elevates swifter than feats of arms.*   If your memory of me has not passed like the summer cloud, wear a white rose when you see a red rose on the lattice. Then follow my messenger and I will teach you the *arcana imperii.*   Princes rule their slaves, but their own passions rule princes.   Condescend to listen to a woman, and you will soon attain your meridian splendor.

"IRENE."

He crushed the delicate missive nervously in his hand, while his face flushed.   "How came she here?   Is she one of the Shah's wives?" he asked himself, while his bewilderment increased.   There was nothing extraordinary in his last question. The beautiful being he had encountered in the deserted village might indeed be the daughter of a Khan and a wife of the sovereign.   What should he do with her extraordinary proposal? To meet clandestinely the wife of the Shah or one of the ladies of his extensive *anderoon*, was at present a physical impossibility.   He was too weak to walk or to follow her messenger. The proposal was sheer madness in any event.   Death would be the immediate penalty of such folly if discovered.   That he had obtained access to the palace was a profound mystery in itself.   His highest ambition was to please his sovereign.   To listen to her proposal would so exasperate the Shah that both their lives would pay the forfeit.   This exquisite being had fascinated him.   She had evidently studied to become proficient in all the graces and intellectual acquirements that would elevate her character.   She was evidently a woman of that upper class of Persians who pride themselves upon their intellectual culture.   She was, moreover, surpassingly beautiful.   Such combined attractions, both of person and mind, could not fail of their effect upon so susceptible a nature as that of Alfonso. But now he started back with a shudder from the abyss on whose brink he had been so unconsciously treading. The Shah's wife! The words were a horror.   The malignant jealousy of a Persian monarch was proverbial.

But as he re-read the dainty missive, and realized the power he had gained over this lovely woman, two temptations assailed him violently.   His vanity led him to look with complaisancy

upon an adventure from which his better sense would have dis-
suaded him.   His thirst for advancement suggested the possibility of her power to perform what she promised in making
him acquainted with the secret springs that influenced the
actions of the Shah.   Temptations are very sweet that are
backed by beautiful eyes, high rank, and a subtle pen.   The
longer they are suffered to engross the attention, the weaker becomes the power of resisting them.   The first encounter of the
young officer with this lovely woman had in its consequences
nearly shivered to pieces his military hopes.   She had caused
him to neglect his duty.   Supposing Irene to have been a maid,
he was not disposed to criticise his own conduct too severely.
But now serious doubts were tormenting him regarding her
actual position.   If she proved to be a wife, his path of duty
was distinctly marked before him.   In any event, it was folly
to meet her in such a locality as his sovereign's palace.   .   .

Days and weeks glided past, and the wounded officer found
his strength sufficiently restored to enable him to walk from
room to room.   Finally he was able to leave the palace and
rove through the delicious gardens.   The attendant eunuch
never was out of sight, but was all courtesy, kindness, and sympathy.   Every luxury was provided for the officer.   He saw
eunuchs occupied in beautifying the gardens, but never for an
instant was permitted to look upon a female face.   He imagined
the ladies of the royal *anderoon* frequented the garden at hours
when he was excluded from it and restricted to certain apartments in the palace.   But of one fact he was convinced :   the
expected red rose had never made its appearance upon the lattice.   He had seen no opportunity of yielding to or resisting
the fair Irene's temptation.   His eyes had daily sought her
lattice, but no signal rose appeared.   Had her own courage
deserted the fair tempter ?   The anxiety which finally took possession of the mind of this gallant officer regarding the ' non-
appearance of the signal was extreme.   A stern conflict had
been going on between his sense of duty and his aspirations for
distinction.   Of high spirit and reckless bravery, great personal
beauty and noble aspirations, he had dwelt long upon the thought
of gaining the ear of the Shah.   He was growing impatient of
inactivity.   He was speculating daily upon the probabilities of
being released from this luxurious hospital and restored to his
regiment.   He had no one to converse with but ignorant slaves.
It became evident at length that "Negauristan" was occupied
only by the ladies of the Shah and the eunuchs.   He finally

allowed his discretion and firmness to yield under the *ennui* of his monotonous existence. He hailed with joy everything that looked like a change in his daily routine. He determined to take advantage of any opportunity that might offer to have an interview with the mysterious and gifted Irene. Perhaps she possessed genuine power to aid his projects. He believed or hoped that he might secure her services without compromising either her interests or his own. He was willing at last to incur some hazard to gain his ends. He would sacrifice to the furtherance of his ambition something of the tranquility of mind that attaches to a perfectly safe career. He would risk the interview with the fair Irene. He was not prepared as yet to analyze his regard for this lovely stranger. She interested him, and he would know more concerning her. His ambition alone had stifled his scruples, and he finally awaited the appearance of the red rose with eager interest. He was unconscious of the firm root her adroit flattery had taken. She had appealed to his ambition, and suggested for it a brilliant culmination. His belief in his exalted destiny was his predominant thought, and this lovely woman had fostered it. He could not fail to admire one possessed of so great discrimination.

At length, after the lapse of many weeks, the singular absence of the Shah from his summer palace still continuing to perplex Alfonso, he was relieved by discovering a red rose clinging to the mysterious lattice. It must have been thrust out through the white wood-work during his last half-hour's stroll through the garden. Concealing his delight from his attendant eunuch he sought an opportunity to pluck a white rose from its branch, and soon attached it carelessly to his robe. He cast no looks towards the lattice as he walked past, and finally seated himself in a bower, whence he could examine the locality as on ordinary occasions. A glance sufficed to inform him that the red rose had been withdrawn. No doubt the watchful beauty was satisfied with his assent, and had removed all traces of the dangerous intrigue. How anxiously throbbed his heart for her next manifestation of herself. The day wore tediously away, the night came, the moon sailed upward to the zenith. The anxious officer sat by his window in expectancy, occasionally elevating his eyes from the loveliness of the *charbagh* to the hidden loveliness behind the lattice of the *anderoon*. Presently his attendant was relieved, as was customary, by another sable eunuch. The new-comer placed before the *sarkardah* a porcelain bowl heaped full of the luscious grapes of Astrachan, and then drawing from his waist shawl a tiny note, handed it cautiously to the officer. "Follow this eunuch fearlessly, and keep silent," was traced in the delicate chirography of Irene. The anxiety of the officer was not fated to be of long duration. The silent guide conducted him across the "court of the bath," opened a door beyond by means of a ponderous key, and disclosed to his view a private garden of exceeding loveliness, cooled by fountains and illumined by the moon. Placing his finger upon his lip in token of the silent caution to be observed in the place, he pointed to a rose-covered bower, and immediately withdrew. The officer entered the fragant retreat, and was confronted by the fair companion of his former moonlight adventure on the road from Koom to Kashan.

Seated upon a divan of marble elegantly cushioned, she motioned him to a seat beside her. She was agitated naturally enough at the hazardous interview and for a moment was silent.

Then, as she resumed her self-control, she raised her lovely eyes as on the night of their first interview, and said with the faintest tremor in her voice, —

"I have summoned you in this extraordinary manner to my presence at the request of your friend. I have taken great interest in your career on your own account. I now have additional reason to aid you on the Ghebre's account. He has requested my services in your behalf, and his word is law."

"Zenayi!" exclaimed the officer in surprise.

"Hush! you will be overheard. Those apartments are full of ladies." She pointed to a row of windows behind her, open, and flooded with the moonbeams.

"Yes, Zenayi," she resumed. "He has desired me to point out to you the road to success."

"And you know him?"

"Yes, far better than you. You have been his pupil for a few years only, but he has taught me nearly my whole life."

"You amaze me. He never mentioned your name to me, and he has conversed familiarly with me for years."

"Zenayi keeps his own counsel," she answered.

"And may I ask why you are in the Shah's palace?"

"And I keep mine," she replied, as if finishing her sentence.

Slightly annoyed at this rebuff, he said, "I would not be inquisitive, lady; but some things I have a right to know. Before I consent to proceed further in an interview attended by so

3*

much danger, I must know if you are a wife, or if any one has claim upon you as a member of any *anderoon* in Persia."

She looked up in surprise at this, and fathomed at once the depths of his thought.

"Oh ! no," she said gayly. "I am only a girl. You need have no fear of me."

The charming *naïveté* of this response dissolved his long-entertained apprehensions. He experienced an instantaneous sense of relief, and his previous embarrassment of manner vanished.

"Then as you are untrammelled," he said, "save by the absurd custom, of Persia, which make you all prisoners, I will listen to you cheerfully and gratefully, particularly since the Ghebre commissions you. Had you notified me before that he was acting through you, a great load of apprehension and doubt would have been removed from my mind."

"I do not act exclusively," she replied, "because the Ghebre desires it. I have my own wishes regarding your advancement."

"That is generous and kind, lady, for I am almost a stranger."

"No soldier is a stranger who hazards his life for my country."

These words were uttered with the pathos and the majesty of an empress. The listener was deeply moved. "I could know from those words alone," he said, "that you had been a pupil of the Ghebre."

"Yes," she replied, "Zenayi is a sublime patriot, and had our great Khans one tenth of his zeal and wisdom and energy, those Muscovite bears would not dare issue their mandates that our boundaries should be thus circumscribed."

"I have consecrated my life to Persia," he said, thrilled by her tones, so full of power and sweetness.

"Yes, brave soldier, I know it. Zenayi has told me all. It is for this that you meet me here. We both seek your advancement because we realize that energy and will like yours are vital to the defence and aggrandizement of Persia. There is but one regret for both of us, and that is, that you will not early and promptly adopt that line of policy which will place you at the summit."

"What can you mean?" exclaimed the officer.

"The Ghebre has informed me that you have declared to him your system of policy in the army."

"And what is that ?" inquired the amazed *sarkardah*.

"That you will never be the temporizing slave of expediency."

"Nor will I," he replied. "He has given you my very words."

"Then you are a pious and fanciful enthusiast."

This avowal of laxity of moral principle startled the high-minded officer.

"The standard of morality is elevated or depressed according to the tone of morals which prevails around us. I pardon you, therefore, lady, in consideration of the laxity of principle which popular rumor ascribes to the *anderoons* of the Shah."

She laughed a scornful laugh. Then composing herself she replied :

"Such frankness impresses one with a conviction of the sincerity of your acceptance of the rumor. But the world knows little of the secrets of the royal *anderoon*, except what it derives from its own experience. The *anderoon* is but the world in miniature. The same passions and prejudices, hopes, and jealousies are known in the house of the subject as in that of the Prince."

After a brief silence she resumed : "Your ambitious hopes will be frustrated unless you abandon your position and resort to diplomacy. You must take the world as you find it. Artifice, tact, compromises, and suppression of the truth make and unmake states. The mother cannot even rear and protect her child without resort to them. The friend cannot gain advantages for the loved one without employing them."

Fascinated and thralled by the strength and subtlety of her intellect and her radiant beauty, he contemplated her with admiration. Then he said :

"I cannot stoop to measures detrimental to my honor. Dissimulation is foreign to my nature. I prefer an open, fair, fearless career."

"You have not attained your present eminence, gallant soldier, by an open, fair, *fearless* career."

He started, and his face flushed with anger. "I have cut my way to rank by my good sword."

"Aye !" she responded. "You have been bold in the field, even reckless. But you know, as well as I do, that you would never have been transferred to a command in the honorary body-guard if you had not practised deceit. I call your concealment of the truth, diplomacy — the justifiable diplomacy of life. Soldier, a woman knows your secret. *You are a Chris-tian.*"

He was utterly confounded, and looked at her in blank amaze-ment. She continued, —

"You could not hold your rank an hour if you did not fre-quent the mosque. You know that the followers of the Prophet alone, are allowed to hold position in the honorary corps. Ha! ha! Is this an open, fair, fearless career. Soldier, you have been acting sense and talking nonsense."

. The *sarkardah* was utterly routed by this truth boldly spoken. From the first instant of his discovery, that advancement under the Persian Shah would be greatly facilitated by embracing the religion of Mecca, he had followed the Ghebre's advice, and become a professed believer. In his heart he did not assent to a single dogma of that faith, and Zenayi knew it. In certain departments of the army, the denial of a foreign religion was not essential to command. But in the body-guard of the Shah no "infidel" could hold rank or place. And yet that was the real corps for an ambitious soldier to enter. He remained si-lent. Irene, conscious of her triumph, resumed :

"The artifices and deceits of the mother are only the coun-terparts of the dissimulations of states. A great good in both instances justifies the deceits. They alone are false who are false to what they are bound to love, protect, and advance. When you are false to your friend, the Ghebre, false to the mother who reared you, false to Persia, which you have sworn to defend, then you become my enemy. The fealty you owe to your God is in your heart. No man has the right to criticise its outward manifestation. Hence I do not charge you with blame in frequenting the mosque. But I do argue, that since you have chosen to become a defender of my country, you should seize every opportunity to advance her interest by strat-agem, by diplomacy, and by skill. Zenayi unites with me in the hope that you will prove the benefactor of Persia. Hence we join to advise you to seek promotion at an Oriental court by the tact, flattery, courtesy, address, and craft by which princes are influenced."

Divested of her natural timidity, and radiant with the inspira-tion of her theme, her eyes sparkled as they regarded him, and she awaited eagerly the soldier's reply. Conscious that he was detected in his religious artifice to retain his position in the honorary corps, and easily led by his indomitable ambition to adopt any line of policy that would secure his further advancement, he made little opposition to her political schemes. Her diplomatic subtlety and flattering interest in his fortunes gradually weakened his power of resisting her arguments. Already were the beauty and magnificence of the Persian Court inflaming his imagination, and his military promotions had only aroused his ambition for still loftier heights. If the sophistry of the fair tempter had failed to convince her auditor that expediency was lawful in the moral and religious sense, it had nevertheless shattered his power of resistance. He said, after a long and painful silence :

"I cannot oppose the united verdict of two friends like you and Zenayi. You have pronounced in favor of strategy. I deem it the highest honor to afford the slightest gratification to those who have befriended me. Your love for Persia cannot be questioned. I place myself, therefore, under your guidance, as the ally of the Ghebre."

The eyes of the brilliant beauty fairly blazed in her triumph. The mortal whom her ardent nature had invested with all the perfections of a hero and a man, had consented to become her pupil in the artifices of the court. She was no less ambitious than he for his future glory. To the natural products of his military genius and valor, she believed her knowledge of the court would enable him to add laurels that he little dreamed of She was one of the most beautiful, patriotic, least scrupulous and most intriguing women of the age. Her originality of. thought and power of brilliant expression had attracted the notice of the Ghebre, and he saw in her an able coadjutor in his schemes for advancing the glory of his beloved Persia. She had been the medium of his secret correspondence with Abbas Mirza, the heir apparent to the throne, and the ablest modern statesman and soldier of that sunny land. His influence over Abbas Mirza was even greater than rumor admitted. To evade the jealous eyes of moullahs and princes near the throne, the correspondence of these two noble patriots was entrusted often to the hands of the intrepid, brilliant, and youthful beauty, Irene, who, from her relationship to Futteh Ali Shah, had the *entrée* of the royal *anderoons*.

Under such favorable auspices had the *sarkardah* been established near the Court of Teheran. His extraordinary dsiinction, in being selected as a guest of the Shah during his illness, was due to the fact that during the battle with the Bakhtiaris he had recklessly dashed into a squad of the marauders, and at the imminent peril of his life rescued a prisoner they were bearing off towards the desert of Khorassan. That prisoner was the youngest son of the Shah.

CHAPTER VIII.

"My tongue took an oath, but my mind is unsworn."
Euripides.

ICTATOR and amanuensis. Both were beautiful, and seated on a divan with their feet tucked under them.

Dictator. "Hush! If you laugh so, we will never get through."

Amanuensis. "I can't help it. This thing is too ridiculous."

Dictator. "You must help it, or your head will be in a basket."

With a determined effort at self-control, the last speaker composed her features and proceeded to dictate the love-letter. The amanuensis smoothed down his countenance also, and proceeded to write. The astounding epistle, which was finally completed after the risibilities of both had been taxed to the utmost, read as follows:

"Light of my life. I have followed you from Ispahan, as the Chaldean followed the star. I have never gazed upon the loveliness of your face; but I have stood near you, and watched your graceful form, and listened to the music of your voice until my reason is well nigh shattered. I know that the countenance which lies hid beneath that veil is the face of an angel. Grace is the first attribute of Israfil. But you have stolen that precious gift from the celestial. Music is the matchless power of Israfil. But in the sweetness of your voice, that resurrection angel has veiled his face and wept for joy. Once I had deemed it joy and bliss unspeakable to enter Paradise and listen to the voice of Israfil singing before great Allah's throne. Alas! there is no more Paradise for me, save where your footsteps linger and your voice breathes melody. I saw a young mother bending over her first-born, and the cooing of the child ravished her heart; but when you laughed in passing, the mother abandoned her child, and followed you. I saw the lover when the maid's voice whispered 'Yes,' but he turned from her when your words made the garden flowers bend their fair heads to listen. Ah! sweet voice, ravishing voice, you combine the melodies of angels and of men. All turn to follow you. All other sounds are discord when you speak. Can you wonder, then, dear woman, that my heart and ear were thrilled when that voice beneath the veil first met my ear? Can you wonder that your graceful form and step at Ispahan gained for you the title 'Lily of Iran'? And yet upon your face I have never looked. And I have followed you timidly from hill to vale, from town to city, but no glimpse of that veiled beauty rewards me. I love you, and yet my eyes feed only on the air. In Sanscrit the *mirage* is called ' the thirst of the gazelle.' This is my thirst. You are my *mirage*. I see not your face, and yet I follow. Ah! will you never become reality to me. Will you not, for the burning heart that follows you, remove that veil, that I may see, blended with your grace and music, your beauty too? My heart is young, my life is young, and all their freshness and unsullied power reach forth to you in worship. Hear me, see me, call to me, that I may come and pour my heart's treasures at your feet, and I will kneel to you in such pure and humble mien for one sweet smile that all the angels will approve! I have followed you, my star, until you pause at the sweet bowers of roses circling Negauristan. I have dared the sabre, I have faced death, to see you. Reward my love with one sweet smile, and I will die content.

" ALFONSO."

Her eyes, large, beautiful, and full of light, contemplated the amanuensis while he re-read the entire epistle, that the full effect of a continuous reading might be ascertained.

" What do *you* think of it ? " she inquired, when he had finished.

" Superb ! nothing could be better. The lady, doubtless, will consider me a lunatic."

" No ; she will be in raptures. You will be the gainer, if you follow up the plan with vigor. Trust me to read the vanities of women."

" Well, lead on ; my word is pledged."

The dictator arose, and left the room ; the amanuensis remained seated on the divan. After the lapse of an hour, the eunuch of the dictator appeared at the door, and with the single word " follow," led the way down the steps of the palace, to the main avenue of the garden. The heat was intense ; and the shade of the shrubbery was particularly agreeable. The guide passed on through the lanes of roses, slowly conducting the officer to a far-off grotto, or temple, which, from its construction, materials, and encircling fountains, was delightfully cool and secluded. At the door of the temple, the slave bowed and turned immediately away, leaving the officer to pass in alone. The latter, upon entering, discovered a lady, magnificently attired, seated upon a divan. She was veiled, but immediately extended her hand, which was wondrously fair. The officer pressed it to his lips, dropped it again, and remained standing. Two piercing eyes were contemplating him through the opening in the veil; they gave no clue to the age of their owner. Glancing out through the rows of luxuriant poplars, willows, and fruit-trees, he saw that they were free from danger of intrusion, and commenced at once to pay court to the veiled lady before him. She appeared to be perfectly self-possessed, and desired him to be seated beside her. Her voice was very feminine and gentle. He began at last to realize that his extravagant praise in the love-letter was not, after all, so great a departure from the truth. His interest deepened in the veiled beauty who was to be the victim of the court intrigue.

"Have I not offended you, lady, by my presumption in avowing my love?"

Two penetrating eyes were regarding him with interest, but being the only features of her face that were visible, they afforded no clue to her emotions. The opening for the eyes barely afforded the wearer of the veil the opportunity to look out.

"Your admittance to this garden should convince you of my true feeling. We are not prone to take offence at those we admit to our presence at the peril of our lives."

"Then you pity me, lovely stranger," he inquired, his interest waxing greater at each glance he cast into her eyes.

"I respect you," she said gently ; "but still I cannot conceive of love which is not based on acquaintance."

"Did not my letter convince you, fair lady?"

"Yes, I believe you ; you have the countenance of truth. And so you have followed me all the weary road from Ispahan?"

"Yes; and the road to me was not weary. I could follow you forever, if only you would deign to smile upon me sometimes by the way."

"Ah! then your constancy would only continue on the pledge of sometimes looking on my face."

"You mistake the ardor of my love, dear lady With such a voice and form you can hold me your slave if that cruel veil is *never* raised."

"Suppose I try you," she said.

"My love for you will endure any test, however cruel. Try me by any test, and see how passionately I will follow you, if only you will say that you will love me after the trial is over."

"I will love you upon such terms," she said, coquettishly. "Mark my words now. I accept you as my lover, provided that you will never ask me to unveil myself. When the trial is satisfactory to me, when I have tested your constancy long enough, then will I reveal myself to you. Then will I be to you all that you can desire."

"Ah! light of my life," he exclaimed, passionately seizing her exquisite hand, "you have conceded everything."

She did not withdraw her hand, but it lay there folded in his, soft, warm, and loving. This contact seemed to thrill them both, and they sat in silence in the fragrant atmosphere of the garden. He had come there to intrigue for power; he remained to love. Without one glance into her face, he loved. The eyes, the white neck, the partially revealed and snowy bosom, and the grace of form, joined to that low, sweet voice of tenderness, had thralled him utterly, and the two strangers were from that instant lovers. His letter had won her; her presence had enchained him. With but the single barrier of the veil between them, they were accepted of each other. She trusted him. She knew the veil would remain intact, and he, with all his eagerness and fire, would have died before the sanctity of his promise was violated. He drew her at length to him, and she faintly resisted him; then her head fell upon his shoulder, and he passionately kissed her eyes. They were all of her features that were left to him from his pledge. If the concealed lips of the woman were ravishing as those of Aphrodite, he could not reach them because of the veil.

And there, in the soft, voluptuous hush of the summer time, and with the air laden with perfumes, the strange beauty clung to the ardent lover whose words and mien had enthralled her. And he, bewildered by the loveliness which trembled in his arms, whispered on and on, in accents of tenderness, which were born of nature and of the hour. The intended victim of the state intrigue had become his ruler; and for the first time in his eventful life he loved, and loved desperately.' Whoever or whatever she was, he loved her, and the consciousness of the absorbing nature of that love grew upon him the longer she remained clasped in his arms. She was young, ardent, and glowing with womanly charms and graces. By some singular combination of events that he could not fathom, his letter had fallen into unexpected hands — the hands of the veiled woman beside him. It was intended for the hands of an old and influential wife of the Shah, ugly in feature and form, and of harsh accents, but of wonderful power in the state. Her excessive vanity was to have been played upon by the schemers, in order to secure her influence at court.

Irene had incited him to this diplomacy, and had portrayed to him the advantages that would attend upon his becoming the professed lover of this old crone. The female schemer had in some unaccountable manner been thwarted in the delivery of the love-letter, and it had fallen into the possession of some one young and lovely. This, at least, was the solution to the young *sarkardah* in the first moments of his astonishment. So entranced was he by the appearance of this exquisite being upon the scene (who evidently believed the letter was intended for her), that he dared not divulge the secret of the real destination of the missive. That would destroy the charm of her hallucination that she had been secretly loved by a stranger. Encouraging her delusion, he led himself on to love, and before he was conscious of it, was bound with fetters stronger than steel.

"Who are you, darling angel?" he said at length, holding her head tight to his breast, and looking down into the luminous depths of those eyes, that regarded him with boundless tenderness. "I have followed you and dreamed of you until I have been almost crazed. Tell me, are you a spirit of the celestial realm sent down to tantalize me with your loveliness?"

She hesitated for an instant; then, as if her purpose was suddenly taken, she murmured, "I would not attach any harder terms to such a noble lover, than the inviolable mystery of the veil. But this question I cannot answer now; when the veil is removed you shall know who I am. If you love me, do not press this question."

"Mystery upon mystery," he murmured, pressing her closer to him. "Now will you realize the boundless nature of my worship for you. I will not seek to solve your secret. Only give me that heaven of my heart, the knowledge of your love,

and I will wait your revelation of yourself to me at your own
time."

"I do love you, then," she whispered, hiding her face in his
bosom. A storm of passion swept over his heart at those sweet
words, and he folded her again and again to himself. He had
won a priceless and a passionate heart, a love that was eternal.
Some instinct told him this, and in the fierce joy of such a possession the world and its ambitions faded out and were gone.
He ceased to remember and to hope, for all joy seemed bound
up in the fruition of this summer hour.

How long he lingered in those white, peerless arms, he never
knew. He only bent his gaze tenderly upon those eyes that
held his life, and wondered if those hidden lips were rosy red
and moist for his chained kiss. For each and every feature of
the veiled face, his countenance was eager and his heart beat.
But in the honor of his soul those lips were sacred, and their
warm, eager kiss remained untouched, untasted, and concealed.

The return to life and reason originated with the maid, if
maid she were. Withdrawing herself gently from his arms, she
sat erect once more, adjusted the rose wreath that his ardor
had displaced, and then placing her hand quietly in his, said in
her clear, sweet voice:

"Tell me, Alfonso, what are your great aims in life. Tell
me, that I may help you."

"First, yourself; second, a name," he replied, rousing himself to his accustomed activity of mind.

"What honor would you have next? What power do you
crave in the State or in the army?"

Her manner had changed on the instant, and her stronger
character was coming out. He was amazed.

"I would prize above all other honors," he said at length,
"a separate command. I am a *sarkardah* in the royal horse.
I would be the sole commander of an expedition, untrammelled
by orders other than the orders of the Shah or Abbas Mirza."

"Define your wishes, Alfonso; I can aid you."

"Impossible!" he exclaimed. "Who are you?"

She laughed a merry laugh before she reminded him of the
inviolability of her secrets.

"I will tell you, then," he said, "to what particular command I aspire."

"Very well. Say on."

"Do you know," he said, looking curiously at her, as if

some suspicion was aroused, "that the Turcomans were band-ed with the Bakhtiaris in the late rebellion?"

"I do," she replied.

"Then hear me. Those wild plunderers beyond our borders will never respect the domain of Persia, until they are chastised on their own soil, amid their wives and their herds. If I had power over five thousand horse to lead them across the border, I would deal such havoc among those wild riders that they would behave themselves in future. This is the command I crave. If I return unsuccessful, the Shah is welcome to my head." He spoke vehemently.

"You shall have that command, Alfonso."

"You speak confidently, dear lady," he said; "are you the wife of the Shah?"

"Would you hold me in your arms if I were his wife?" The tone was reproachful. He remained silent.

"Speak, Alfonso."

The position was a perilous one. But the reproachful tone had given him his clue, and he hazarded a bold response.

"No, dea rlady, I would sink into my grave by my own dagger before I would fold to my heart the wife of another."

The reply was a happy one; for she instantly exclaimed, "I knew it! I knew it! You are still uncorrupted by the Persian court. Now you shall have the command against the Turcomans without fail."

"How can you secure me that?" he inquired eagerly. "It is my wildest dream to gain that opportunity for distinction."

"Wait patiently," she said, "and the order shall be sent to you after you rejoin the army. Perhaps sooner."

"I can believe in your love, dear lady, but not in your power."

"True love is ever powerful, Alfonso, and cuts its way where friendship falters. You will find that I speak truth. The expedition shall be placed under your command."

"Why, dear lady," he exclaimed, "it has not even been projected."

"It shall be projected," she answered firmly.

"I am too young and obscure to secure the honor and responsibility of such an expedition."

"You *shall* command it — mark my words."

"Who gave you my letter?" he inquired.

"I cannot tell you that, Alfonso. I have no right to tell you."

"You will not gratify my curiosity in any way, dear lady?"

"No. When you wrote that letter you had not a single thought or wish in life but to gain my love. You have secured that; you have stolen my heart. I have given you a woman's highest gift, and on sacred terms. Let that suffice. You have loved an unknown. You must still continue to love an unknown until she chooses to raise the veil. You intended that letter for me, did you not?"

This interrogatory was startling, but there was only one bold answer that could be given. It was promptly given.

"Yes, for you."

"And you have no suspicions as to who I am?"

"No, angel of grace and music. Nor do I care. If you are a queen or a peasant, it matters not to me. I love you."

"And you can love a veiled face?"

"Yes! with my whole being and with all the ardor of my heart."

"Will you ever love another?"

"Never!"

"Swear it, then, holding your face towards Mecca."

"I swear it."

"Now I believe you," she said; "and when the time of your probation is over, you can withdraw this veil and see to whom you have pledged your faith."

"Ah! happy hour will that be, dear lady, when I may withdraw the veil and see the beauty which belongs to the ravishing voice and the graceful form. But how shall I know that the dear hour has come?"

She meditated for an instant; then placing her white fingers beneath her silk shawl girdle, she drew out a folded paper, opened it, and revealed its contents. It was a flame-colored ribbon, to which was attached the badge of the Order of the Sun Lion, an honorary decoration given by the Shah to distinguished commanders of the army. The *sarkardah* eagerly examined it, for it was a distinction which he hoped some day to wear. Feth Ali Shah founded the order. The badge of honor was a golden, white-enamelled, six-pointed, rounded star with golden balls, which rested upon a green-enamelled wreath of palm-leaves. The central field displayed the rising sun, and on the reverse was a couchant lion.

"You will notice," she said, when he had satisfied his curiosity in the examination of the badge, "that one of the star-points is broken off. Mark this particular badge, that you may know it again wherever you chance to see it. When you see in the future this decoration of 'the Order of the Sun Lion attached to my veil, withdraw the veil from my face, and claim me if you wish."

She replaced the badge under her girdle, and the officer studied curiously her person for some clue to her future identification. Who could she be? Doubtless a person of some consequence about the court. The confident tone in which she predicted his future advancement convinced him that she was in some way related to the Persian monarch. He dared not question her concerning Irene, satisfied as he was that that crafty girl had in some way been foiled in her plan. This assuredly was not the ugly old crone who had occasioned them so much merriment in the composition of the love-letter. This lovely woman before him was, moreover, evidently determined to baffle his curiosity in every particular. There was but one course, therefore, for him to pursue in the matter of her identification. He must be patient, and carefully note every occurrence at Negauristan, and in the meantime cautiously draw out from Irene the secrets of the palace.

While the lovers were still engrossed in the sweet intercourse of a new and ardent passion, their conference was abruptly terminated by the appearance of the eunuch. The startling intelligence was communicated by the watchful slave of the unexpected arrival of the Shah. There was manifest trepidation on every side at the advent of the dread sovereign to his summer palace. The lovers were parted instantly, the eunuch conducting the officer hastily back to his apartments adjoining the "court of the bath." The veiled beauty fled precipitately away through an avenue of willows, and was seen no more. Negauristan was instantly restored to its rigorous discipline. Intrigue of every kind assumed a double veil.

CHAPTER IX.

HE excitements of the unexpected love scene in the garden had proved detrimental to the nervous system of the convalescent officer. Subject as he was to sudden and protracted attacks of nervous prostration, in accordance with the predictions of the Ghebre, the intense strain upon his brain and heart occasioned by his instantaneous precipitation into a mad, bewildering passion, had caused a tremor to pass over him, even while he sat with the strange beauty clasped in his arms. The startling advent of the Shah, and the apprehensions it excited, gave the *coup de grâce* to his failing strength. Upon reaching his quarters at the palace, he swooned in the arms of the eunuch, and lay for hours like one dead. When he revived it was night, and the moonbeams were flooding his room and couch. Through the open windows the ever present odors of the gardens were stealing, and the faint breeze was at intervals waving the rose silk draperies of the room to and fro. He had been laid by his faithful attendant on a divan in the octagonal apartment adjoining the "court of the bath." This tall, athletic African, with his red turban, yellow trousers and vest, and red shawl girdle, stood near the Saracenic arch in silent watch, with his steel sabre glistening in the moonlight. The officer recognized him as the eunuch who had admitted him to the first interview with Irene.

At the instant of opening his eyes upon the motionless slave, Alfonso was conscious of something pressing lightly upon his forehead. He put up his hand, and found it to be a rose, which had been placed there during his unconsciousness. At the same time he discovered a female kneeling beside his divan, and steadily regarding him with her large, lovely eyes. It was the intriguer who had sent him on the garden expedition to the aged wife of the Shah. The moment the officer revived she waved her hand to the eunuch, and he withdrew into the "court of the bath." The beautiful girl who had taken such marked interest in the fate of the Ghebre's *protégé*, was regarding him with tender interest. When she realized, however, that he was fully restored to consciousness, she arose from the carpet upon which she was kneeling, and brought to him his accustomed beverage, recommended by the Ghebre for his use after every relapse into the fainting fit. He gratefully ac cepted her services, and she supported his head while he drank. After a time his inclination and strength to converse returned to him, and his first thought was for her safety.

"You have incurred double risk this time, fair Irene, in ministering to my comfort. You must be in great peril here. Where is the Shah?"

"Gone to the Ark, hours ago; there is no longer danger from that source."

"And where is the Ark?" he inquired.

"Inside the walls of Teheran. It is sometimes called the *citadel*. It is the Shah's residence a part of the year, when he resides in his capital for the transaction of official business."

"How far is it from Negauristan?" he inquired again.

"Only half a mile," she said. "He often walks out here to look after one of his numerous *anderoons*."

"His *numerous anderoons!*" exclaimed the officer. "How many wives has the Shah?"

"Two or three hundred, at least," she replied. "You know, of course, that the Koran only allows four *wives*, properly speaking. You remember the words: "Take in marriage of such other women as please you, two or three or four, and not more.""

"The Shah, then, gives a free rendering to '*the verse sent down from heaven,*'" he said.

"Yes, the Shah multiplies the *four* by a hundred. Generous natures are always liberal." She uttered these words bitterly; then abruptly turning the conversation, she added, "I am anxious to know your experience in the garden with Ayesha, the Shah's wife, when you are strong enough to converse."

"I was very successful," he said.

"Did she unveil?"

"No! indeed," he replied, determined to disclose no more than was the legitimate intelligence for the two conspirators.

"I knew she would not, Alfonso. You remember I told you so. She is too anxious to keep you under the illusion that she is beautiful."

"She would not give me even a glimpse of her face."

Irene laughed. Then she asked, —

"Did she listen to your vows of eternal constancy?"

"Certainly she did; and promised, too, that some day I should look in her face, if only I proved constant."

"Ha! ha!" laughed Irene; "she will not lose you as her lover in a hurry by exposing her features; though some day her vanity may be wild enough even to test your judgment on the subject of beauty, her voice and grace have gone so far with you."

" Her hand is beautiful," said the officer.

" Yes, that is her only remaining attraction ; it is soft and white as a girl's. But what did she say about the letter ? "

" She declined to tell me who gave her my letter."

" Ayesha is true to the honor of the *anderoon*," replied Irene. " I knew she would be that. No woman here who is not utterly vile would mention the name of the one who brings tidings to her of her lover. The messenger as surely suffers death here as the principals. Should you chance by accident to reveal the name of the letter-carrier to one of the Shah's spies, my head would be off. Hence Ayesha's reserve with even the writer of the letter. Had you been a spy counterfeiting the letter writer, you might thus have gained from her knowledge that would have cost me my head. When outside love steals into the inclosure of the *anderoon*, a woman sacredly refrains from whispering to any mortal the name of the messenger."

" But *you* would not hesitate to tell me who gave Ayesha my letter, would you ? " inquired the officer.

" Not when I gave her the letter myself, as I certainly did. I, the messenger, may risk my own life by naming myself, if I choose."

" You gave my letter, then, into the hands of the Shah's wife ? "

" I did," replied Irene. " The celestial dog, Al Rakim, guards letters no more faithfully than I."

The mystery of his interview in the garden deepened at this response. Who had been counterfeiting Ayesha ? How had the mistress of his heart gained possession of his letter ? Why had she appropriated its terms of endearment to herself?

" How old do you think Ayesha is ? " he inquired.

" Half-a century at least. But why do you ask ? Do you meditate the possibility of loving that old woman ? Ha ! ha ! that would be a strange termination of our intrigue."

" I will never love mortal woman," he said, wondering at the eagerness with which Irene watched for his reply.

" I am glad of that," she said. " Make Persia your mistress. Love her eagerly, madly. She is worthy of all your love. Make the great heart of this lovely empire your own. Thrill my people with your splendor. Love them, fight for them. Make your name among them the synonym of all that is pure, heroic, noble, self-sacrificing ; and your fate will be happier than any woman can make it. Be a second Cyrus. He started in a secluded mountain region like you, and by his good sword cut his way to power, and founded an empire which has made its indelible stamp upon the ages. Ah! I have stood beside his marble tomb at Mourg-Aub. Go visit it, still surviving the wanton hand of ages, and see if you are not inspired to be something great, noble, heroic. Be not like these Khans of Persia, finished voluptuaries, unmindful of the glory of their native land where heroes have worn the diadem ; but strong and self-denying, assert the loftiest manhood, and carve an honorable name high on fame's arch. Yes, you are right. Love no mistress but my Persia."

Her intellectual expression, her striking beauty, and her eloquent tongue, fired with all the ardor of her clime and country, aroused wonderful sympathy in his heroic heart. He attempted to rise, but she forbade him.

"Forgive me," she said, "for my thoughtless enthusiasm on that subject, old, yet ever new — my native land and its heroes. You are too weak. Forgive me. Now tell me what promise you extorted from Ayesha. That isthe point of all this intrigue. What is she going to do for you in the army?"

"I told her I had conceived the project of entering the country of the Turcomans, and striking terror among the marauders."

"Well, what then?"

"Ayesha assured me of her power to aid me in securing the command of the expedition."

"That she had influence enough to further your advancement, I told you."

"She promised me, moreover, that I should be appointed soon to that command. She spoke confidently."

"Then it will be done, rest assured. May Allah give you strength speedily to take the field!"

"Then you feel confident of Ayesha's power to influence the Shah?"

"I *know* it, Alfonso. He refuses her nothing. She has secured some of the most lucrative offices in the government for her relatives."

"If I am advanced in the army, I shall owe it to your superior wit, and knowledge of character."

"That is the very reason," she replied, "why the Ghebre put you under my tuition ; that you might learn to divest yourself of all sentiments except those that conduce to your advancement and the interest of Persia. The Ghebre and myself will look after your promotions from time to time, and give you suggestions as to the secret of court influence. *Your* especial part will be to satisfy the people, by your fighting qualities and by your successes, that your promotions are merited. Do you know who left that rose upon your forehead ? "

" I fancied it was your gift," he said.

" No ; I had nothing to do with it. It was the Shah himself. The slave says he bent over you in your unconsciousness, kissed your forehead, and then left the rose upon it."

" The Shah ! " exclaimed the amazed *sarkardah.*

" Yes, the Shah. You need not look so astonished. The Shah is a man and a father. You saved his youngest son from a terrible captivity. Had you not scattered his captors they would have tied a rope around his neck, tied the other end to the tail of a horse, and made him run over weary miles of trackless sand to keep up with the cruel pace of the horse on his way to the borders. In this way he would have been dragged across the entire width of the desert of Khorassan, with clouds of dust beating into his eyes and nose. The prisoners of the Turcomans often die on the way, for thus are they all treated."

" And the Shah has gone ? "

" Yes, and it is rumored that he leaves the Ark to morrow night for the camp at Sultania. It is said that Abbas Mirza will leave Tabreez, his own capital, and come down to Sultania to meet his father."

" Have you ever seen the Prince Royal ? " inquired the officer.

" Seen Abbas Mirza ! " exclaimed the girl in surprise. " Yes, I have seen him as often as I have seen the sun, and he is fully as glorious. My heart feels a throb of exultation when only his name is mentioned. That superb being is the pride and the hope of Persia. When he comes to the throne, there will be wild work on the borders of the Muscovites. He hates them as I hate them and as the Ghebre hates them."

The girl was thoroughly aroused by the theme. The listener had never seen her manifest such enthusiasm.

" That image haunts me," she continued. " I can never despair of the glory of Iran while Abbas Mirza lives. Oh ! he is so great, so noble, so possessed of every virtue and trait that becomes a prince. He is the greatest thinker in the realm, except Zenayi."

"Describe him to me, Irene," said the officer, whose imagination had been often excited by the comments of the people
upon their great favorite.

"Describe him!" she said, fervently.   "I might as well attempt to describe the morning sun.   He comes like a great,
proud demi-god of fearlessness and goodness upon every town
in this land.   The people go wild over him wherever he rides.
The women hold up their boys to him, and cry from under their
veils, 'Here are your future soldiers for the Muscovites.'   Every
child knows how he hates those northern bears, and how he
loves the Persian people.   When he comes to the throne, the
sleepers will wake up."

"But tell me how he looks, how he rides," said the *sarkardah*, raising himself upon his elbow, and steadily regarding her.

"He has barely passed the age of thirty.   His countenance is
noble ; his complexion fair as the Georgian blood in his veins
can make it.   His eyes are dark, and beaming with intelligence ; his nose aquiline ; his pointed beard heavy and long,
and like his finely formed eyebrows, of a jet-black hue.   He is
a hardy soldier, a superb horseman, and equal to any fatigue that
a common soldier can endure.   He is a thoughtful statesman,
and his garb on horseback, though rich and tasteful, is far from
equalling in magnificence that of his illustrious Khans, some of
whom are indeed worthy of his regard.   Do you see him from
my poor picture of him ?   I cannot describe him ; you must see
him."

"Is he affable ?" inquired the officer.

"Yes," she said, "to all *worthy* men.   At his court, the
mendicant and the prince are alike welcome."

"Has he a fine command of language — lucid and powerful expression ?"

"Remarkably so.   He is eloquent when aroused. But reared
in the school of absolute and uncompromising obedience, he
has habituated himself to wonderful self-control."

"Zenayi tells me," said the officer, "that he has displayed
the most consummate ability in debate in the councils of the
Shah."

"So it is reported," she replied ; "but they say there was
nothing oracular, magisterial, or dictatorial about him."

"What is the best avenue of approach to him ?" inquired
Alfonso.   "How shall I proceed to gain his favor ?"

"Convince him of your superior soldierly qualities.   Let
him know that you detect and lament the apathy of the Persian

nobility regarding the honor of their country; that you depre-
cate this decay in the national spirit of Persia, and this extinc-
tion of her military courage. He will listen to you. You will
be in communication with him some day — you are in the line
of advancement now. Be bold, maintain rigid discipline in
your regiment, and fight like a *deev* when you have the opportunity. Every step in advance now is a longer and bolder
stride than the preceding one. But your achievements must
in every instance be proportionate to your rank. You must
not only dazzle the multitude; you must also win the admiration and good-will of the military commanders, who are
keen-eyed to detect real merit, and who will admit its existence,
and use it for their own glory. Be cautious not to exhibit to
them too great anxiety to be advanced. But appear to be
zealous, and devoted to their personal interests. Thus they
will allow you driblets of glory, and before they know it, you
will have slipped quickly into a position where you will not need
their influence. But maintain courtesy ever, with high and low;
for men are more easily caught with honey than with vinegar.
You have seen already, in the case of Ayesha, how it is with
women."

"I have not seen her influence yet," he quietly remarked.
"I would trust sooner to your eloquent tongue and marvellous
intellectual powers to move princes."

The adroit are rarely invulnerable to their own weapons when
employed skilfully against themselves. The lovely eyes of the
girl brightened with pleasure. She valued a compliment from
one whose eyes fairly blazed intellect.

"Zenayi told me you would respect me."

"Respect you! I admired you from the first instant of our
intercourse. And when I fell wounded from my horse, and my
consciousness was ebbing away, my last thought was of you,
and your helpless condition in the village. Great Allah! how
bitter was my reflection, when I thought the angel of death had
me fast, and I could not rescue you from those fierce devils
who were falling back upon the village."

"And you thought of me *then?*" she asked, with a scarcely
perceptible tremor in her voice.

"I thought of nothing else," he said firmly.

"And I only a girl, and a stranger?"

"Say rather a *woman* in the realm of lovely faces and empty
heads — an eagle among butterflies."

The *sarkardah* pronounced these words too vehemently to

leave the slightest doubt of his sincerity.   He indeed gave her
the generous allowance which brain yields to brain.   He appreciated her.

   Their conference was interrupted by the entrance of the
eunuch.   The slave had been entrusted with a package to deliver to the officer when he should recover from the fainting
fit.   Deeming the moment favorable for the presentation of the
paper, he advanced, and gave it into the hand of Alfonso.
Immediately upon the slave's withdrawal the officer desired the
girl to examine its contents, as his strength was again giving
out.   Irene opened the paper, and uttered an exclamation.
   "What is it?" he inquired. ."Who sent it?"
   "The Shah."   ·
   "You cannot mean it, Irene — the Shah?"
   "Yes.   Futteh Ali Shah.   This is his own handwriting," she
said, as she glanced down the page.   "It is all right.   This is
more rapid work than usual.   Ayesha has been prompt, and
here you are designated as commander of the Turcoman expedition."
   "Already! I must be dreaming," exclaimed the *sarkardah*,
pressing his hands to his throbbing temples.
   "This is no dream," continued the girl, still determined to
finish the perusal of the royal document before she laid it down.
"Here you are empowered by the Shah to select from the
goolams five thousand horsemen, and to remove them to a
separate camp, to be chosen by yourself, in any part of the
province of Fars.   The officers are to be designated by you,
and the commissaries, and quartermasters of the army are
instructed to furnish you with every needed supply for the encampment.   And here you are ordered to introduce in the
camp the most rigid system of discipline, and to familiarize the
troops with every desirable evolution in the science of cavalry
warfare."
   The prostrate soldier was all eagerness.
   "And what limit is prescribed to the duration of the encampment?" he inquired.   .
   "None at all.   Your discretion is to be the guide."
   "And what then?" he said.
   "Then you are to observe the utmost secrecy as to your
designs and line of march, which must have for their ultimate
object the devastation of the Turcoman country and the chastisement of the insolence of their plundering bands in the late
alliance with the Bakhtiaris.   You are to fall upon their terri-

tory with the suddenness of the thunderbolt, and bring away with you whatever you can lay your hands on."

"And you believe that Ayesha's influence with the Shah has effected all this?" inquired the officer.

"Most assuredly I do. I gave her your letter, and she promised you in the garden to secure it for you. The Shah was closeted with her during the two brief hours of his visit to the *anderoon*, and then she solicited the command for you, without doubt. Every one here knows that you saved the Shah's son, and Ayesha, doubtless, urged some extraordinary honor for you in consequence."

"Well," responded the *sarkardah*, "you are an admirable schemer. I shall follow your suggestions hereafter, make love to innumerable old women, make vows of eternal constancy to every man or woman you select, and resign myself to every conceivable intrigue that may be propitious to my fortunes. If Eblis makes a claim upon my soul, I shall expect you to satisfy it."

"If you do nothing worse," she said, "than say a few silly things to an old woman who ought to be preparing her soul for the journey over *Al Sirât*, I will undertake to adjust with Eblis his claims upon you."

The eunuch again made his appearance, and intimated that it was time for Irene to withdraw into the women's quarter of the palace. The hour had arrived for closing the gates between the private garden and the *anderoon*, and she must at once retire, or suspicions would be aroused. Bidding the officer farewell, she obeyed the summons, and disappeared across the "court of the bath."

After Alfonso had retired, with the slave's assistance, to his sleeping apartment, he remained awake for a long time, looking out upon the gardens, revelling in the moonlight, and dreaming of the lovely stranger who had, a few hours before, clung to him with apparently a girl's fondness and ardor, developed by his utterance of eternal vows. Who was his veiled companion of the grotto? Who had secured him the military command? He knew no woman of fifty had won his love. Ayesha and his charming mistress were not identical. How were they connected?

CHAPTER X.

TWO men were stretched at ease upon the grass beneath the shade of a group of lofty *chinár* trees. The white dress of one indicated that he was a priest of the ancient religion of Zoroaster The other was an officer of cavalry, beautiful as Alexis, but apparently indifferent as to his personal appearance, having little to distinguish him from the common soldier but a richly jewelled sabre. The smoke from his *caleeoon* curled lazily away upon the mild atmosphere of Southern Persia, and his whole bearing was in keeping with the luxurious repose of the tropical day. The intolerable mid-day heat was still hours ahead, and the two companions, though so apparently at their ease, were nevertheless carefully inspecting the military evolutions going on below them, and exchanging remarks upon the spirited scene. A large body of horse were in full view, executing their graceful movements upon an unobstructed field of two miles in extent.

The whole scene, as witnessed from the commanding position at the group of *chinár* trees, was strikingly grand and beautiful. The eye ranged over an amphitheatre of many miles, hemmed in by distant mountains of bare, verdureless gray rocks. An immense sweep of dark-green grass, occasionally broken by groups of cypresses and flowering shrubs, led the eye on to the distant and naked mountains, and through the wide-reaching verdure a small river held its tortuous way and glistened in the sun. Far away to the right, on gently undulating ground the tents of the cavalry stood like tiny marble pyramids in the grass, and above the larger pavilion of the commander floated the blue banner on which was blazoned the lion and the sun. Behind the officer and his companion ragged and verdureless cliffs of dark rocks rose to an amazing altitude, and upon one of them stood the ruins of an ancient castle. This range of cliffs extended far to the north and south on either hand. In advance of this mountain range, and on the left, arose abruptly from the plain another range of barren cliffs, holding its way northward and parallel to the first range, and formed with it a lovely valley rich in foliage, contrasting strangely with its lofty, adamantine, naked barriers. The eye ranging down this valley detected, less than half a mile away, white-marble ruins scattered here and there amid the grass, as of ancient temples or palaces. Groups of hewn blocks, isolated pillars, and lofty terraces of marble rising to a level with some of the lower gray-stone cliffs, attracted instant notice. Civilization of a higher order had in the long-gone ages made its mark in this luxuriant wilderness. What people had reared halls and temples of chaste marble, then passed away and been forgotten?

But from the front the views of nature and of moving art were multiform. Squadrons of fiery steeds crossed and re-crossed the plain, now sweeping round in long ,and graceful curves, now forming into line and again closing into solid column, till the spear-heads of the dark-eyed riders glistened in the sunlight like one single sheet of steel above them. Then, again, they broke into regiments, and charged at full speed across the grass, the sun flashing upon the silver and gold trappings of the horses dashing on in all the fiery impetuosity of their Asiatic blood. After watching the various evolutions for a time, the young officer saw a regiment of lancers halt, and one-half the men dismount and place their lances in the left stirrup boots of the men who remained mounted. This man-œuvre, seldom necessary, and then executed for the purpose of holding or carrying some post, was performed with manifest confusion. The officer arose from his comfortable position, laid aside his *caleeoon*, and called to a mounted *sarjaukas* who was near at hand, and engaged in holding the commander's war-horse. The fiery courser of Khorassan was brought forward by the corporal, and looked as wildly beautiful and spirited as when he carried his young master across the fear-ful chasm "*Melek al mowt dereh.*" The officer mounted the chestnut-colored beauty, and promising the Ghebre to return after the drill was over, dashed down the slope to the plain to instruct his lancers in their duty.

The white-robed follower of the "*Bactrian sage*" watched his *protégé* as he dashed along the line of his bright-robed and sunburnt Asiatics, and then halting before the inexpert regiment of lancers, promptly and skilfully taught them precision in their novel movement of transferring their lançes. He saw them again and again repeat the evolution until skill and rap-idity had taken the place of awkward confusion. Then, with kindling eye the white-bearded sage heard his trumpet-voiced pupil issue his clear and forcible orders, wheeling regiments into line and line into column, and then leading them in a terrific charge over the country, seeking out the rugged and broken ground that intervened between the river and the level plain of their daily parade. To the natural ease and grace of horsemen trained to the saddle from infancy, they now added the skill and power for complicated movements that fitted them for every emergency of changeful battle. Their commander had neglected nothing calculated to bring them to the highest degree of efficiency in the field. Gifted by nature with a robust frame, indefatigable in exertion, and of unconquerable resolution, he had been occupied on horseback night and day in looking after their wants, perfecting their equipments, and familiarizing them with sudden and unexpected calls to arms and to the saddle. He had succeeded in infusing his own energetic and vigilant spirit into his officers, until they had come to regard him as one who was preparing them for some great and secret service, where each of them was sure of making his military fortune. Indeed, he had hinted to them that they were on the verge of great events, and that the Shah himself had expressed remarkable interest in each one of them. By nature an orator of decided power, he had impressed them with a sense of their own dignity and their exalted destiny. The rank and file, too, were under the magnetic influence of his vitality and zeal, and were ready to follow him with eagerness on the mysterious expedition, the rumor of which had passed through the camps. They realized at last that his discipline was inevitable, and his care for their individual comfort when off duty incessant. Their enthusiasm was aroused for the skilful leader, who dashed off at the head of their column at such a headlong pace, that they named his charger Al Borak, after the famous celestial steed of their Prophet. With ready tact he adopted the suggestion, and his impetuous steed ever after bore that appellation.

Farther and farther away over the plain sped the wild riders until they reached the distant river, into which they plunged, and fording it with ease, rose to the opposite bank, and then dashed on again towards the Eastern mountains. Soon their onward sweep was known only by the far-off glitter of their spear-heads, and then they seemed to sink into and blend with the plain. When they had vanished in distance, the Ghebre said aloud, —

"Ormuzd be praised ! my hope is realized. The stars have sent me a great commander."

This mysterious being sat then for a long time buried in reverie. Some subject of reflection occasioned him great uneasiness, for. at times he muttered and shook his head in doubt.

"He is young," he said, "and the knowledge might ruin him. It might destroy a great incentive to exertion. Ambition might be paralyzed."

Whatever conclusion the sage might have reached regarding the propriety of clothing his *protégé* with the mysterious knowledge, his doubts were forgotten in the excitement, of an unexpected arrival. A band of some thirty wild-looking but admirable horsemen dashed rapidly up from the south, and without a moment's hesitation invaded the defenceless camp, and commenced an indiscriminate plunder of everything they could lay their hands upon. They were a party of wandering Eelauts — a tribe of people similar in habits to the nomadic tribes of Arabia and Tartary, and who nominally owe allegiance to the Persian monarch, but are really the scourge of the defenceless travellers and villagers of the Empire. At sight of this startling episode the Ghebre manifested the natural ire of honesty at the unchecked depredations of cowardly theft. But the first ebullition of his wrath having subsided, he was attacked by a fit of inordinate laughter at the absurdity of the scene.

"I will laugh my young commander into a fury," he said, "when he returns."

But his merriment and depreciation of the military prudence of the young general were short-lived. For a party of cavalry under command of a *naib*, who had been concealed in a gorge of the mountain for precisely such contingencies, were spurring on like *deevs* for the marauders. Before the Eelauts could disengage themselves from the camps, the cavalry were upon them, and after a brief skirmish shot or sabred every man of them. Their bodies were flung into a hole and covered with earth ; and their horses swelled the complement of asses that were allowed by the army regulations to each company of cavalry for the carriage of the men's kit. After witnessing this speedy act of vengeance, the Ghebre said to himself, —

"Always on the alert, and reticent regarding his plans ! I have misjudged him again. He will surely succeed !"

Again the watcher fell into a reverie, and during its continuance the morning wore away. As the noontime approached, when the Oriental of every condition in life resigns himself to repose and sleep, on account of the overpowering heat, the great body of horse again made their appearance. They had made a grand *détour* to the northward of several miles, and were now returning through the valley by squadrons. Arriving on the plain before the Ghebre, they were formed in the order of review, the officers received their instructions, and the regiments were dismissed to their encampments. The commander rode up to the group of *chinár* trees, dismounted from his panting steed, and surrendered him to the attendant *sarjaukas*, who rode off with him towards the encampment. The commander flung himself upon the grass beside the Ghebre, and commenced to devour the provisions which had been placed under the trees for their comfort by the *sarjaukas* during the absence of the troops. Water from a limpid spring issuing from the rocks behind them was their only beverage.

"You came near losing your dinner, Alfonso," said the Ghebre.

"How so?" inquired the officer.

"The Eelauts have been visiting your camp. While your thoughts were occupied with glory, they were attending to more sublunary affairs."

The officer looked away towards the mountain gorge, where he had stationed his *naib*. Nothing of life was visible in that direction.

"I can tell the result of their temerity," he said, "within a couple of men."

"Well, try your power of telling the unknown!" said the Ghebre.

"My *naib* routed them with the loss of a man or two, and of the Eelauts two may have escaped by the superior merit of their horses' heels."

"No; you have not surmised the truth," replied the priest. "Your *naib* is a better officer than that. With excellent judgment, he allowed them to get fairly at their work, and then was upon them like a tiger. With twenty men he slew thirty; and one alone of his command was wounded. Not one of the Eelauts escaped. Their horses are now the property of the Shah, and the riders are under the ground."

"Did you witness the fight?" inquired the officer.

"I did; and the *sarjaukas* brought me the details."

"To-morrow, then," said the commander, "I will make that *naib* a *sultán* of fifty horse."

"You will do wisely," said the Ghebre, as he nibbled away at a handful of Dalaki dates. After the noonday repast was concluded, a proposition was made to the officer which obtained his immediate assent. It was, that when the sun had dipped sufficiently low behind the rocky range to their left, so that a shadow would be flung across the entire valley, the two should make a personal inspection of the marble ruins, which so mysteriously testified to the decadence of an ancient people. The Ghebre assured his companion that the marble fragments were, without question, the sole surviving ruins of the ancient temples and palaces of Pasargadæ. The site for the present encampment had been selected by the officer of cavalry at the suggestion of Zenayi, who informed him that it was the classic ground of Persia. Here was the white marble tomb of the great Cyrus on an eminence, and known to the ignorant natives of the province as "*Mesched Madrè-i-Sulieman.*" When the common people do not assign to the devils the construction of an ancient architectural marvel, they are in the habit of ascribing the work to the great King Solomon, whose supernatural fame extends over the Orient. To the white marble terrace or wall in sight of the cavalry encampment, rising perpendicularly against the cliff to a height of thirty-eight feet, the Ghebre informed the officer that the common people attached the name "Tackt-i-Sulieman," or the throne of Solomon. In this valley, known by the modern name of Mourg-Aub, the astrologer assured his pupil once stood the sacred city of Pasargadæ, founded by the illustrious Cyrus, as a memorial of his national achievements. Here were the colleges of the Magi, and here the altars of their religion, where the illustrious conqueror was wont to celebrate with pomp the rites of that venerable faith. In this sacred valley, his tomb had wonderfully outlived the ages ; only the inside ornaments of gold and the purple hangings having been removed by the hands of the military spoilers.

How artfully had the court-astrologer, the confidential friend of Abbas Mirza, and the correspondent of the brilliant Irene, worked upon the ambition and the imagination of the young officer, to rouse him to the energy and activity requisite for lofty achievements. This was to be the crowning point of his intellectual skill. The selection of this encampment on the very spot rendered memorable by the tramp of the great conqueror's horses, and by the munificence of his royal soul, was to be the key of the arch of inspiration the astrologer would rear in the young soldier's brain. Here, on this consecrated ground, would he wring from that intrepid son of Mars a thrilling oath that he would be true to Persia — true to her

honor, true to her military glory. How keenly, in the heart
of the patriotic Ghebre, must have burnt the hate of the Muscovite ! How earnestly and devotedly must his aged heart have
loved his native land, to have kept alive in his own bosom so
long this eager hope and yearning towards the day of vengeance. How carefully, wisely, and patiently was the patriot
training up all his forces, princes, women, and soldiers, for the
great day of reckoning with the encroaching, the brutal, and
the infamous Russia, the Christian fiend, whose tramp has ever
been upon the prostrate faces of heroic patriots.

On the ground hallowed by the former presence, and the
monumental remains of the noble Cyrus, the Ghebre hoped
and believed the young officer would breathe in inspiration.
He designed to introduce to the commander in detail the
ruined wonders of architecture, and to decipher for him the
venerable cuneiform inscriptions which are carved in the marble.
He had often remarked that kindling of his pupil's eyes when
the deeds of mighty conquerors were related. The successes
of the cavalry officer had already awakened in his ardent mind
those lofty visions of ambition, which he hoped he was soon
destined to realize. The theatre of glorious achievement was
now apparently opening before him, and his former instructor
proposed to aid his entrance to the arena of enlarged command, by a revelation of a marvellous secret which would tend
to quell the grosser motives of his ambition and fire him for
the loftier objects of a soldier's pursuit. In furtherance of
this purpose he thus addressed the friend he loved so well,
beneath the shade of the *chinár* trees :

"Alfonso, I believe that the attachment you formed for me
in the cave by the Strait of Ormuz was the friendship of a noble
and true heart. Every act, every word of yours since those
happy days of study has been only a confirmation of your
tender regard for me. You have consulted my wishes, and
paid that deference to my age and experience, which ennobles
your own heart at the same time that it warms mine. It is
because I know you to be deserving of confidence, that I propose this day to open to you a mystery that will startle you.
But as it is calculated to advance your ambition for military
distinction, and to facilitate your attainment of your high purposes, I am desirous that you shall bind yourself to me by a
solemn oath, to bury in your bosom the secret which I shall
reveal. Swear to me, then, that what I disclose to you this

day shall never be employed against my country or its interests. Swear that the secret shall be shared with no mortal but
Zenayi, and swear that you will be the faithful soldier of Persia
when she needs your sword. Give me the assurance of this
oath, and I will ere long convince you how dear you are to my
heart, and how zealous I am for your advancement."

The officer looked long and thoughtfully at his mysterious
friend, before he replied. It was impossible at times to divest
himself of the awe which the Ghebre occasioned. The marvellous learning of the astrologer, the vague rumors he had
heard in the army concerning him, the suspicion among all
classes that there was something supernatural about the scholar,
— all these reflections and remembrances crowded upon the
officer's mind when Zenayi sought to bind him with an oath.
Would it be binding himself in any sense to supernatural influences? He pondered the proposition for a time, and then as
by sudden impulse he answered, —

"Zenayi, many men of intelligence fear you as one under
the influence of Eblis. But I trust you as my father, my benefactor, my dearest friend. I will believe in your integrity and
trust you with my fate if every mortal on this globe deserts
you. Here on this instant I swear allegiance to you, your secrets, and your country. When I sleep in a soldier's grave carve
upon the headstone, 'He loved Zenayi.'"

The old man was deeply moved. He attempted a response,
but his quivering lips would not utter a word. He calmed his
emotion after a time and said, —

"Now nothing but death can part us. Alfonso, I am the
owner of three secrets. The first you will soon share, the second is more profound, and it may be your lot in after-times to
share that too. But the *third* is of ineffable loveliness, something that your imagination will never conjure up, and were the
Shah of Persia to offer you his realm in exchange for it you
would laugh him to scorn. It may be that fortune has this
third mystery in reserve for you. But inasmuch as the possession of this secret involves a degree of purity of life to which few
men attain, and a self-sacrifice to which few are equal, you must
look forward to the disclosure of it from my lips with as little
hope as you do to the day when you shall fly through space with
wings. The first mystery will be yours before another sun shall
rise. Sleep now, and take your rest during the heat of the day.
When yonder mountain flings her shadow over the vale of

Mourg-Aub we must spring to our feet, for we have many weary
steps before us."

In a few moments the two were sleeping quietly under the
shade of the *chinár* trees.   .

CHAPTER XI.

F the reader will bear in mind the following accurate
sketch of the ruins at Mourg-Aub, in Persia, he will
better appreciate the influence of locality which the
Ghebre brought to bear upon the ardent soul of the
young commander.   He will also realize more perfectly the
astounding mystery which Zenayi revealed to the bewildered
gaze of the soldier, and which that astrologer had designated as
the *first* of his *three great secrets.* The valley and ruins of
Mourg-Aub are thus described by a famous English traveller :

"On mounting my horse this morning for my excursion, I
took a direction down the valley for about four miles ; when
quitting the road and turning to the right my attention was
arrested by a view of the first grand object amongst these ruins.
It is not far from the road.   The natives have given it the name
of 'Tackt-i-Sulieman,' or the throne of Sulieman.   It appears
to have been the platform of a building, and consists of a mass
of hewn stones raised nearly to a level with the summit of a
rocky hill to whose side it adheres.   The materials are of *white
marble*, put together with a labor and nicety scarcely to be supposed.   Every stone is carefully clamped to its neighbor on
their upper horizontal surface, and at a small distance from the
perpendicular face.   The great front looks to the north-west,
and measures in length about 300 feet ; its sides from the front
to where they touch the hill 298 feet.   At the distance of 72
feet is a retiring right angle of 54 feet, which, after running
again in a direct line of 168 feet, forms a corresponding face to
the opposite angle of 72 feet ; leaving 48 feet to complete the
whole of the northern and southern faces.   *The height of the
great front* is 38 feet 6 inches, formed of fourteen blocks of
marble, all of the same thickness, namely, 2 feet 9 inches.
Their lengths vary from 7, 14, 13, to 19 inches.   They are

beautifully chiselled, and have a rough surface over each about an inch from their edges. Their breadth also is variable — from 3, 4, to 5 feet. This imperishable casing-structure has been filled up to form a level at the top with different-sized pieces of the native rock, a dark limestone. The marble must have been brought from some considerable distance ; the nearest I could hear of is that of the mountains of Yezd. I remarked on every block a peculiar figure, probably to guide their situations on the spot of erection ; a proof the stones were adapted for their places at the quarry. Great depredations have been made on this and all the other ancient buildings of the plain by the rapacity of the natives of some former period tearing away the masonry to obtain the iron by which it was bound. The top of the platform is now strewed over with fragments of the hill, and very much sunk in the centre. I found no trace of columns, and not even the smallest bit of broken marble. What may have stood there, whether palace, temple, or fortress, it might be difficult to conjecture.

"The hill unquestionably commands the entrance to the valley or rather plain of Mourg-Aub, now received to be that of Pasargadæ ; but the strong natural barriers which the mountains present to the south and to the north render additional walls unnecessary. Nevertheless Pliny calls this spot 'the Castle of Pasargadæ, occupied by the Magi, and wherein is the tomb of Cyrus.' The city of Pasargadæ may, therefore, rather be considered a holy city, consecrated to the colleges of the Magi and the officers of religion, than as a stationary royal residence. And nothing can be more probable, since it was built by Cyrus to commemorate the great victories which made him king, than that he should consecrate it to the gods. Cyrus, according to Xenophon, made seven visits into Persia proper, his original kingdom, after his accession to the vast empire to which he gave its name ; and although that historian does not specify the particular place in his paternal land whither he went to perform his accustomed religious duties, yet as he was the founder of Pasargadæ avowedly as a memorial of his achievements, what can we more naturally suppose than that Pasargadæ would be the scene of such rites? The idea seems to be corroborated by the fact that it was long the custom with his successors, on their accession to the throne, not only to receive here the usual insignia of government, but attended by their nobles and priests, to make the most solemn sacrifices on the summit of the mountain. Why, therefore, may we not consider this *immense* platform (evidently raised to enlarge that of the hill) the spot on which the altar, priests, and royal party stood during the awful ceremonies of their religious convocation?

" I now descended into the lower ground, and at the distance of a quarter of a mile from what I would denominate the *sacred platform* I came to a square, tower-like building, which Mr. Morier calls ' The Fire Temple.'　It is formed of the same lasting materials with the former structure, the blocks of marble not being much less in size ; but the extent of the edifice does not seem in proportion to the magnitude of its component parts, its square not measuring more than nine feet along each face, and its height not appearing to exceed *forty-nine feet.* . . .

" A quarter of a mile due south, I came to a square pillar of only two stones one over the other, the lower one 12 feet high, the other 7 or 8, the whole terminated above with some broken work like a ledge.　Three of the faces are beautifully smooth, and on that to the north is a short inscription of four lines in the *arrow-headed character*, perfectly uninjured, and so clear and sharp that it seemed scarcely possible to mistake a wedge. . . . In proceeding south-east for rather more than a quarter of a mile, no vestige of ruins appeared till I reached a low mound which bore evident marks of having formerly been ascended by steps.　To this the inhabitants of the plain give the name of the ' Court of the Deevs ' or Devils.　From the centre of it rises a perfectly round column, smooth as the finest polish, but the base of which is totally buried in surrounding rubbish. The length of the shaft cannot be less than from *forty* to *fifty* feet, and is composed of four pieces of marble.　The lower division comprises almost half the whole height, and in circumference measures *ten* feet.　I should imagine that the column has been higher than at present, there being no fragment of a capital discernible at its top.　A spacious marble platform supports this immense fragment of a column, the square shape of its area being marked by four pillars of similar style and demensions to the one I had recently passed.　The four are distant from each other *one hundred and eight feet.*　Those that denote the north-west face of the building are not much dilapidated ; but the ruinous state of the place alone showed where the opposite ones had been by baring their foundations. The most northern of the pair, which are in the best preservation, is composed of three stones surmounted by a sort of cornice, the whole being 15 feet in height.　On one side is an inscription near the top corresponding exactly with the one I had transcribed from the preceding pillar. A third mass of marble in a yet more mutilated state stands thirty feet in front of these, dividing exactly the middle of the face of the square. There is an inscription on the north-western side of this mass. I conjecture the place to have been completely open to the air, as I found now all. In viewing the plain from the elevation of this building it appears one rich velvet of vegetation, without the interruption of the smallest unproductive spot rendered barren by fallen rubbish. I mention this as an extraordinary peculiarity, that amongst so many fine ruins there should be no trace of minor ones between.

" Perceiving to the south-east another columnar appearance, I rode in that direction for half a mile, and on arriving found an immense single elevation of the kind belonging to a former edifice, now entirely swept away ; and which, but for the fragment which attracted my attention, could only be marked by the bases on which stood its ancient columns. Its shape is a parallelogram, one hundred and fifty feet by eighty-one. Two rows of pedestals divide it, each composed of four stones, the whole (with the exception of one of white marble, which stands the third on the north-east range, and is six feet square) being of the dark rock of the country. . . . .

" If this tract is allowed to be the site of the city established by Cyrus, this very edifice may be that which Plutarch mentions (Vitæ Artax. X.) as the place where the Persian kings, his successors, received consecration ; and which, he observes, *was dedicated to a goddess in whose guidance was the affairs of war.* By the general plan, there appear to have been two entrances, one from the north-east, the other in the opposite quarter. They are both twelve feet wide, showing something like a step advancing beyond the outer line of the floor. At about six feet distant from the north-east side of the building, and standing out in a parallel point to its centre, rises *the square pillar* which had drawn me hither. It appears perfectly distinct from all others, no trace of a second being found. *One single block of marble* forms it, and as far as I could judge, it is *full fifteen feet* high. On examining it *I was delightedly surprised at discovering a sculpture in bas-relief,* occupying nearly the whole length of the north-west side of the pillar, surmounted by a compartment containing a repetition of the usual inscription. I lost no time in measuring and drawing this invaluable piece of antiquity.

" It consists of a profile figure of a man clothed in a garment shaped something like a woman's shift, fitting rather close to the body, and reaching from the neck to the ankles. His right arm is put forward, half raised from the elbow ; and a s far as I could judge from the mutilated state of its extremity, the hand is open and elevated. His head is covered with a cap close to the skull, sitting low behind, almost to the neck, and showing a small portion of hair beneath it. A circle, of what I could not make out, is just over the ear, and three lines marked down the back of the head seem to indicate braidings. His beard is short, bushy, and curled with the neatest regularity ; the face is so much broken, only the contour can be traced. From the bend of the arm to the bottom of the garment runs a border of roses, carved in the most beautiful style, from which flows a waving fringe extending round the skirt of the dress ; the whole being executed with the most delicate precision. From his shoulders issue four large wings : two spreading on each side, reach high above his head ; the others open downwards, and nearly touch his feet. *The chiselling of the feathers is exquisite.* But the most singular part of the sculpture is the projection of two large horns from the crown of his head. They support a row of three balls or circles, within which we see smaller ones described. Three vessels not unlike our European decanters, and regularly fluted, rest upon these balls, being crested again by three smaller circles. On each side of the whole, like supporters to a coat-of-arms, stand two small creatures resembling mummies of the Ibis, but having a bent termination to their swathed form. Over all is the inscription. The figure from head to foot measures *seven feet.* The width of the stone where he stands is five feet. Two feet from that line reaches the present level of the ground. The proportions of the figure are not in the least defective, nor can any fault be found with its taste, being perfectly free from the dry, wooden appearance we generally find in Egyptian works of this kind ; and in fact it reminded me so entirely of the graceful simplicity of design which characterizes the best Grecian friezes, that I considered it a duty to the history of the art to copy the forms before me exactly as I saw ; without allowing my pencil to add or diminish, or to alter a line. I cannot omit stating that on some of the bas-reliefs in the great temple of the Isle of Philæ, in Egypt, several figures are found bearing attributes on their heads very similar to those on the horned mitre just described.

"But with the exception of the mitre, there is nothing I have ever seen or read of which bears so strong a resemblance to the whole of the figure on the pillar, as the ministering or guardian angels described under the name of Seraphim or Cherubim by the different writers in the Bible. And if we are to ascribe these erections to Cyrus, how readily may he have found the model of his genii, either in the spoil of the temple of Jerusalem which he saw among the treasures at Babylon, or from the Jewish descriptions in the very word of prophecy which mentions him by name, and which doubtless would be in the possession of Daniel, and open to the eyes of the monarch to whom it so immediately referred. . . . . .

"At the distance of about a mile southward from these remains, rises the singular structure commonly known as the tomb of the mother of Solomon, and in the language of the country called "Mesched madré-i-Sulieman." This interesting monument, however, is probably the "*Tomb of Cyrus.*" It stands on an eminence not far from the foot of the hills that bound the plain to the south-west. A wide area marked outwardly by the broken shafts of twenty-four circular columns surrounds the building in a square shape. Each column is three feet three inches in diameter. Six complete each face of the square, distant from each other fourteen feet. *Seventeen* columns are still erect, but heaped round with rubbish, and barbarously connected with a wall of mud. Within this area stands the tomb. The great base on which it rests is composed of immense blocks of the most beautiful *white marble* rising in steps. At the bottom of the lowest step, two sides of the base measure forty feet; the other two sides forty-four. It first rises five feet six inches, so forming the lowest step. The second begins two feet interiorly from the extreme edge of the first, rising three feet six inches, and receding one foot ten inches; at which point the third step rises three feet four inches, and recedes one foot ten inches, and so on. Thus a succession of giant steps completes, in a beautiful pyramidal shape, the pedestal of this royal tomb, majestic in its simplicity and vastness. At the base of the lowest step, a projection or sort of skirting stone runs all around the foundation of the building almost even with the ground above, and not striking very deep into it below; probably to what was the ancient level of the earth. The charge of this interesting place is given to females of a neighboring village, and none but that sex are permitted to enter the supposed repository of the remains of the mother of Solomon.

"The door opens into the north-western side of the tomb; the whole width of the side being sixteen feet ten inches, of

which measurement the entrance dividing it occupied two feet
ten inches.   The height of the door was exactly four feet.
Four layers of stones composed the elevation of this super-
structure.   Just over the door are two ledges, which from their
parallel I should suppose held an inscription.   When I entered I
found that the thickness of the walls was one solid single mass of
stone measuring *five feet* from the outside to within.   The extent of the chamber was seven feet wide, ten long, and eight in
height. . . .   The learned world are indebted to Mr. Morier for
the first supposition, that the ruins scattered over the vale of
Mourg-Aub are those of Pasargadæ, for the unanswerable arguments which establish his supposition and for the first accurate
accounts of the two most corroborating proofs, namely, the general cuneiform inscription found on the columns and the details of
the tomb I have just described.   In comparing what has just been
said of this structure with the account given by Arrian of the
Tomb of Cyrus at Pasargadæ, the resemblance between each is
too exact not to bear an instant conviction, that they are portraits of one and the same place.   Arrian writes from the testimony of Aristobulus, who had visited the spot :

" ' The tomb of Cyrus was in the royal paradise of Pasargadæ,
round which a grove of various trees were planted.   It was
supplied with water, and its fields covered with high grass.   The
tomb below was of a quadrangular shape, built of marble.
Above was a house of stone with a roof.   The door that leads
into it is so very narrow, that a man not very tall with difficulty
can get in.   Within is the golden coffin of Cyrus, near which
is a seat with feet of gold.   The whole is hung round with cov-
erings of purple and carpets of Babylon.'   He adds, ' In the
vicinity was built a small house for the *Magi*, to whose care
the tomb had originally been entrusted, and so continued since
the time of Cambyses from fathers to sons.'

" The above description arose from the visit which Aristobulus
made to the tomb by order of Alexander.   Plutarch tells us
that Polymachus, one of Alexander's officers, rifled the tomb
of Cyrus.   Alexander commanded his immediate death for the
act.   Aristobulus describes the tomb as being situated " within the royal paradise at Pasargadæ."   The paradises of the
ancient kings of Persia were like those of the more modern
Shahs at Ispahan — spacious gardens adjoining their palaces, and
often so extensive as to contain ground which we would call a
park for the preservation of animals for the chase.   Aristobulus dwells with minuteness upon the details within.   He speaks

of 'robes and under-garments of Babylonian and Median man-
ufactory, richly dyed in violet, purple, and other colors. There
were likewise chains, scimitars, and ear-rings of gold, the whole
beautifully set with precious stones.'

"I shall now speak of the inscription written in the cuneiform or arrow-headed character which is so generally met with
on all the pillars, etc., of this place, and without the de-
viation of a single curve. Professor Grottefund gives it the
following translation :

"'Dominus, Cyrus rex orbis rector.'
"'Cyrus, lord, king, ruler of the world.'

"From his epitaph as given by Strabo, we find in its simplicity the same greatness even in death :

"'O man ! I am Cyrus, son of Cambyses, founder of the
Persian empire and sovereign of Asia ; therefore grudge me
not this sepulchre.'"

Trembling with emotion, the mysterious Zenayi stood before the tomb of the mighty conqueror, holding the hand of
the young commander of cavalry. A priest of the Magi, a
descendant of that illustrious line of hierarchs who marked
their learning and their piety in letters of fire upon the heroic
ages of Persia, was overpowered by the memories and the as-
sociations connected with that sacred spot and that holy city.
The priests who had ministered in those open temples and
upon those free, airy mountain heights, were his brethren.
Honored in their characters and their sacred functions by the
illustrious Cyrus, they had been a proud, wise, free-hearted
race. Their day of honor had gone by. Their power waned,
and from their height of dignity they had fallen to the position
of a persecuted race. The fanatical sword of the Arabian
Prophet had decimated their followers, and scattered the
ancient priesthood over Asia. They had long been a persecuted and a down-trodden race. They could no longer publicly
look in the faces of the holy stars and worship there the symbols of the one true God. The sacred fire which symbolized
the attributes of Ormuzd burned faintly and secretly in the wilds
of India and Persia. But the persecuted Ghebres were a true
and faithful race. They never deserted their faith, but through
the ages of blood and tears and anguish still revered the
memory of Zoroaster, of Cyrus, and of glorious Persia in her
prime, as mistress of the East.

On this sacred ground had the Magi watched the tomb of

the great Cyrus, and now one of their descendants stood there in the fire and the emotion of his undying love for Persia, to inspire a soldier's heart to emulate the great virtues of a noble conqueror, who had gone where the martial cry sounds never.

"I hoped," he said at length, "that you would here breathe in some of the pure, proud air that nourished my country's hero. I hoped that here you would aspire to lead the life of Cyrus, heroic, noble, forgiving, living for the happiness of his countrymen, and in the chaste pursuit of truth ignoring self. Be from this day like Cyrus in his noble mood, magnanimous. Live to be loved like my Cyrus."

CHAPTER XII.

THE setting sun gilded the summit of the "*sacred platform*" of Mourg-Aub. The marble glistened in the effulgence of the receding orb for a moment, and then the shadow of the western mountain fell upon the sacred structure. Still were the summits of the highest mountains radiant with the touch of the dying day's sceptre, and from a distant crag a tiny object flashed like fire, a star of brilliant fire. It was the polished spear-head of a sentinel watching the approaches to the camp. This tiny fire went out quickly, and the shadows fell deeper across the valley. In the shadow which now lay at the base of the cliff against which the wall of marble was erected, stood the astrologer and the young commander. Their horses were in charge of a soldier on the northern side of the "*sacred platform.*" The two friends were hidden from the curious eyes of any one connected with the camp. Having completed their examination of all the ruins of Pasargadæ in the valley, they had reached at last the broad front of the terrace upon whose summit the great Cyrus had offered sacrifice of the noble horses of the Empire to the King of Heaven. The platform of rock upon which had congregated in the olden time the noble and powerful of the kingdom of Persia on the occasion of the grander ceremonies of state and of religion, was silent, deserted, and rapidly growing obscured in the fall of the evening.

The two stood in silence, occasionally casting glances about them to see that they were indeed unobserved. They were about to penetrate by a secret entrance the very heart or centre of the cliff against which the marble terrace stood. The Ghebre assured his companion that within the apparently solid mass of mountain rock which the marble terrace embraced on three sides, was a marvel of antiquity, the knowledge of which would bewilder by its magnificence even the Shah of Persia. To the young soldier of fortune in the very flush and fire of his manhood was to be unveiled the first of the astrologer's three great secrets. He had sworn to preserve this secret in his own bosom. That which he was about to explore in the bowels of the earth was to be his property forever. It was to be his by the gift of the mysterious intellectual giant who had adopted him as his son and heir. Often, in the course of his years of preparation and study, had the Ghebre assured him that he owned not one foot of land *on the surface of Persia.* Now the sage who loved him was about to present him with a property *beneath* the surface of that empire. So much of mystery attached to the astrologer in his every movement and expression, that the young commander had learned to expect something of great weight and importance in every revelation of the future and the unknown. The Ghebre had never deceived him. Everything that he had been taught to look forward to in connection with his individual fortunes as significant or valuable, had always proved to be so. He was confident now that something of unusual magnitude was about to burst upon his vision, something that was to advance him in the path of power. He was to be clothed with property, the existence of which he had bound himself by oath never to speak of to any one besides his instructor. All the enjoyment of this property was to be free to him, provided only that he would guard the secret until his death. The usufruct of this subterranean estate was only limited by the term of his life. At his death the estate was to revert to the astrologer if he survived him. If the Ghebre preceded him to that land, "the bodies of whose inhabitants cast no shadow" then the secret, by his oath, must die with him."

Here was mystery enough to make the commander serious and thoughtful before the ancient monument of the Magian worship. He looked upon the admirable solidity of the marble wall before him. Master workmen had reared that pile of masonry more than two thousand years before the young commander was born. How thoroughly masters of their craft had been the builders of the terrace. Kingdoms, dynasties, races had passed away, or been blended irrevocably with others, and still the *"sacred platform"* of Mourg-Aub survived. And the ghosts of those ancient builders returning to their material bodies might smile triumphantly, pointing to their indestructible handiwork. There was an irresistible fascination in the contemplation of the beautiful fabric, when coupled with the thought of its immense antiquity. As the evening shadows deepened upon the massive work before him and the mysterious hour of darkness drew near, when it would be safe to enter the hidden passage to the mysteries within the cliff, the commander could not refrain from communicating his thoughts to Zenayi.

"I wonder," he said, "why it never enters the heads of the modern rulers of Persia to erect durable fabrics, massive marble palaces, that will outlive the ages. They build beautiful palaces, airy and graceful as the palatial temple of Demogorgon on the Himalayas. But their frail structures crumble in a lifetime, and are gone. The Shah has built a dozen palaces, and not one of them will outlive the reign of Abbas Mirza. Why does he not, with all his exquisite taste in fairy-like buildings and in sculpture, grasp the idea, so natural to an artistic mind, that a durable palace of marble will delight his own eyes, while he watches it gradual erection, and not only augment the grandeur of his own reign, but cause Abbas Mirza's name, and the names of his grandchildren, to be honored on his account ? Were each Shah to invest but a portion of the immense revenues of Persia, in a few reigns this land would be magnificent. Each succeeding monarch would look back with pride, and strive to emulate this princely architecture. Tell me, Zenayi, why, in families of so much taste, the idea of *massiveness* never seems to enter ?   How can a Persian monarch look upon these ruins, and then ride south-west only some twelve farsangs (forty-eight miles), and view the ruins of Persepolis, and not have his pride and artistic taste aroused to erect something *durable* in marble ? Why, Zenayi, these ruins fire me, poor as I am, to emulate the vastness of these ancient works. Poor as I am, I eagerly long for power, for wealth to erect something durable, grand, imposing. I can appreciate the exquisite taste of the Shah's aerial palace. It thrills me when I look upon it. But it puzzles me, that the same intellect which appreciates grace and airy beauty in art, does not feel the kindred fire of massive, durable beauty. Grandeur and grace are no strangers to each other in art. They

burn in my soul with equal intensity. The flight of a body of
Persian light horse over the plain is to my mind graceful and
beautiful as the flight of birds; but I could not fail, if power
were in my hands, to mass the infantry for battle, and rejoice in
the thunder of a hundred heavy cannon pouring in pounds of
iron where my horsemen only showered their hail of tiny bullets.
If the quick evolutions of horse charm me, the heavy roar of
cannon exalts my very soul. Would to God I could command
both. So are my thoughts blended as to grace and majesty in
art."

"Ha! ha! my young commander," exclaimed the delighted
Ghebre. "So my ruins of Pasargadæ are working upon you,
after all. I knew you had a *kingly* soul. For this, I brought
you here. Stupid heads and stony hearts never see anything
but rubbish in massive, ancient ruins. But the *superb* of soul
are never blind. The mean and the penurious of a country
would never raise monuments to their heroes and defenders —
would never honor a great and noble name. But the grand of
soul *aspire* to do what their purses cannot do for their heroes ;
and these are the noble of every kingdom — prince or peasant,
potentate or mendicant. Now, listen to me, for it is not dark
enough yet for our purpose. I have believed in you. You
have given me love and confidence unbounded. You do not
believe that Zenayi is the tool of the evil Ahrimanes, but the
servant and priest of Ormuzd. I am a mystery to you, and to
all men. But you have judged me by my life. In this you have
followed justice. You have loved and trusted the Ghebre. Now
for your reward. But it is a reward which, I hope to convince
you ere long, if you live, is not to be mentioned in the same
sentence with other mysteries which your upright life may in
time induce me to reveal to you. True, you will be amazed
at what I am about to show you. But if you will restrain and
hold in perfect control the impulses and the passions which my
secret will certainly awaken in your heart ; if, instead of following out the selfish suggestions that will arise in your very soul,
at the sight of the subterranean estate I am about to place
under your control, you will listen to my counsel, you may in
reality be preparing yourself for the future revelation to you of
my *third and last secret*. Oh ! the ineffable loveliness and value
of my third secret. If ever you are privileged to know it, you
will ridicule the thought that my first secret has any charms for
a mortal that can compare with it. If ever you learn the third,
the *great* mystery, Zenayi will no longer puzzle you as he now

puzzles his countrymen.　Why he knows so much, will then be clear to you as the daylight.　Now I will test the firmness and the strength of your character by disclosing to you the first secret.　Claim what I exhibit to you, absolutely and without fear.　I give it to you, the whole and entire ownership, subject only to the condition of your oath, that no other man shall ever know it.　Come on, now; you have given Zenayi your heart and your noble trust.　See how the Ghebre appreciates that precious gift, *a heart.*"

He led the way, as he concluded, to a corner of the marble terrace.　The darkness nearly obscured the view of the ancient work.　No curious eyes could now watch their movements. The Ghebre, stooping at the angle of the wall, placed his hands against the lowest block of marble visible above the surface of the ground.　He pushed this stone inward with apparent ease. It seemed to swing in towards the cliff on hinges.　He then applied his hands with like success to the block of marble next above it.　Thus a low door or means of ingress to the interior of the terrace was revealed.　He bade the officer enter before him, and descend a flight of stone steps that his feet would encounter directly.　The amazed Alfonso obeyed his direction, passed in through the opening to impenetrable darkness, and immediately felt firm stone steps beneath his feet.　He descended the flight, and was closely followed by the Ghebre, who had closed the marble doors behind him.　Encouraged by the guiding voice of Zenayi, the officer descended slowly and cautiously what seemed to be an interminable flight of steps. He counted two hundred of these before he reached a level platform of stone.　Here he paused by direction of the Ghebre, who now swept past him with his robe, and appeared to be occupied just ahead of him in striking a light.　A flicker of light now became visible, it burned up brighter, it illumined the face and long beard of the astrologer, it waxed brighter still, until the walls and arch of a subterranean gallery became distinctly visible about them.　This mysterious passage appeared to lead on directly from the foot of the steps down which they had come, into the heart of the rocky hill which above ground had been embraced between the three walls of the marble terrace.　This arched way, however, was not constructed of the dark, native rock, but was covered and formed with blocks of glistening white marble.　They were walking, also, upon blocks of the same pure white material.　This passage way was ample enough for two persons to advance abreast, and the arch was full two feet above their heads as they walked. The guide was already in the highest glee, and laughed and chatted with his companion, as if a burden had been suddenly removed from his spirits.

"Don't fancy, Alfonso," he said, "that I am a Mohammedan Eblis, conducting you down to his realm, Sajin. But believe me, I am leading you to a sight stranger than any ever seen since the Arab Prophet *'split the moon in two,'* when the infidels demanded of him a sign."

He held a lamp in his hand and walked on through the tunnel as he talked, the officer following, and carefully scanning the walls as they advanced. It was a perfect and solid specimen of ancient masonry, and every block of marble was firmly in its place. It looked as if it were the perfect work of the preceding day. But the Ghebre assured him the same race had built it that laid the marble of the "sacred platform."

"But will there be no end to this marble walk?" inquired the officer, after they had proceeded rapidly ahead for several minutes. "We must have come already half a mile; I could swear it is that distance from the terrace."

"Be patient," was the response. "We are going straight on into the heart of the rock mountain, which you will remember overhangs the rear end of the terrace."

"Impossible!" ejaculated the amazed officer. "That mountain is a mass of solid rock."

"That only proves," responded the astrologer, "that the workmen of the days of Cyrus were a persistent set. Not only is that mountain rock, but this tunnel we are travelling is also cut through solid rock. This marble is the facing only of the tunnel."

"What are those brazen balls that occasionally hang so close above our heads?"

"Ancient lamps," replied the guide; "those people needed light to walk, as well as we."

They were indeed lamps, formed by suspending with brazen chains a hollow, half-globe of brass from the arch above. How the wick was arranged above it, was impossible to discover from where the two were walking.

"The estate you promised me," said the officer at length, astonished at the extent of the excavation, "appears to be all alley or tunnel."

"There was very good reason for all this length of tunnel, as you will discover ere long," said the Ghebre as he hurried along under the arch. "They were anxious to reach something ahead, which could only be effected by making this wonderful length of tunnel. This was to be the only avenue of approach to it, secret and permanent. There was a secret hidden in the heart of the rock mountain, which Cyrus alone was acquainted with. It was a marvel, indeed, how he could discover something to which there was no visible means of approach, and which was buried deep in the mountain. But he did find it, and he tunnelled patiently until he reached it. What he did at length excavate his way to, is to be your estate. I give it to you ; wait patiently until I lead you to it."

This was unaccountable to the officer ; to reach the object ahead could only be effected by constructing this tunnel. How, then, could any man have known that there was an object in the heart of the mountain worth tunnelling for ? He was determined not to be put off in this way, so he inquired again, —

"Was Cyrus at the object himself before he cut this approach to it ? Had he ever had any access to it before this work was made ? "

The guide laughed heartily at this interrogatory ; then he answered, "No ! no ! no ! Cyrus knew it was in the heart of the mountain, but he had never been there. He had no means of access to it, and no one knew it was there but Cyrus himself. He cut this secret way to it, and this way was the only means of access to it that he ever had."

"And still he knew positively that it was in the heart of the mountain ? "

"He did know positively that it was there," replied the Ghebre. "But until he cut this avenue through the solid rock there was no means by which he could reach it."

"That passes comprehension," exclaimed the officer.

"It will be plain enough to you when you see the place, and are instructed in its mysteries," replied the astrologer. "There is nothing supernatural about it ; he knew it was in the heart of the mountain, and he was determined to gain access to it, and he did by means of this excavation."

"I am bewildered," exclaimed the officer ; "you never deceived me, and still what you say appears to be absolutely impossible. Did Cyrus ever *see* this object before he cut this avenue to it ? "

"No ! no !" shouted the Ghebre with laughter ; "he never saw it until he cut this avenue through the rock."

"Then he was a madman," retorted the officer, "to cut into

a solid mountain in search of something that had never been seen, and to which there was no access."

"No! he was no madman," replied the Ghebre, "because he *knew* that the object was in the mountain, and that it was what he wanted for his purpose."

" That is an impossibility," replied the officer, " unless some one told him who had been there when it was accessible, and later by some means that accessibility was destroyed for Cyrus:"

" No!" replied the Ghebre ; "it never was accessible until Cyrus made it so."

"Well! lead on, Zenayi ; you talk in riddles. When, in the name of Heaven, will this arched way terminate ?"

" The termination is not far off now," replied the guide.

At length the tunnel did terminate in an ancient door of brass, standing as an impenetrable barrier across the way. It was fast locked, and covered with all manner of military devices cast in the brass. Ancient warriors in full armor, swords, lances, and banners, were portrayed in the brass, and exquisitely fashioned in just symmetry and proportion.

"This door," said the Ghebre, as he held up his lamp that the officer might examine the details of the casting, "is the cotemporary of Cyrus. That great monarch has stood where we stand now, looking at those martial scenes."

When the young commander of cavalry had expressed himself satisfied with the examination of this marvel of ancient art, the astrologer informed him that now he should look upon the estate which from that hour was to be his own. The door alone divided him from the gift of Zenayi. A panel of marble was then pushed back into the wall of the tunnel, swinging into the wall on hinges. The Ghebre applied his hands to two small carved heads upon the block of marble, and thus was the door swung inward, revealing a large brazen key hanging within the masonry. He took it from the iron plug on which it hung, and placing it in the hand of the officer, said, —

" Take the key of the estate. I have given it to you in return for the gift of your heart. Love Zenayi unto the end, follow his counsel, and he will exhibit to you some day a mystery that will appall you with its splendor, as this estate beyond the door never can. Now unlock the door, and you will live in the great Past."

Overpowered with some undefined awe, which the vicinity of the underground tunnel and the martial door occasioned, the soldier with trembling hand fitted the massive key to the key-hole. He was so agitated that he could not at the first effort unlock the door. He applied stronger efforts to the key. The bolt of the lock yielded to the pressure and slid back. He pulled upon the key ; the massive brazen door of the subterranean mystery slowly swung in upon him. Wider and still wider swung back the door. He flung it back against the side wall of the tunnel with an exclamation ; then with every vein of his body running fire, his eye dilated, his face pale with excitement, he stood gazing upon the wonders of the estate the mysterious Sphinx of Persia had for a life time bestowed upon him. Was it a dream, or the hallucination of a distempered brain?

CHAPTER XIII.

IKE a palace of El Dorado, with its white-vaulted ceiling illumined by the light of a thousand lamps of gold, burst upon the dazzled eyes of the commander the glories of the subterranean *treasury* of Cyrus. The mountain had been a hollow cone of rock ; the great king had cased its sides and inner roof and floor with snow-white marble, until it resembled a vast basilica dedicated to the worship of gold. Fluted columns of white marble sustained the entablatures, above which, circled round the sides of the cone, until they formed an octagonal figure upon which were standing (one over each column) angels of ivory, with solid golden wings and sceptres of gold. Near the apex of the cone, a circle of ivory angels, with crowns of gold and expanded wings, looked down upon the angels of the entablatures, or rather beyond them, to the vast golden bowl which stood upon the centre of the marble floor below. This golden bowl, full fifty feet in diameter, was covered with battle scenes in *alto relievo*, and was sustained upon the heads of marble genii. It was heaped full of golden coins stamped with the images of ancient princes. It was the accumulated treasure of many kingdoms, which Cyrus brought away from the plunder of Babylon. That famous city had been enriched by the spoils of Nineveh, Jerusalem and Egypt. Between every two of the fluted marble columns stood side by side, and facing inward to the great central bowl, two horses of the size of life.   One was of solid gold, with flowing mane and tail.   The other was of ivory, with bridle and surcingle of pure gold.

On either side of the dazzled officer, and as if disputing his further advance, stood two immense tigers of solid gold, with eyes of priceless Budukshán rubies.   An ominous red fire seemed to play in these eyes from the brilliancy of the many swinging lamps.   In the rear of the horses, and between the colonnade and the wall of the treasury, stood a procession of solid silver camels extending round the entire circuit of the subterranean basilica.   They were loaded with golden baskets heaped full of precious gems of every hue and quality, which blazed like the sun in the flood of light flung upon them from the lamps.   The topaz and beryl of Mourzinsk, and rubies, garnets, and diamonds from the Urals, glistened on every side.   On a pedestal of marble stood candelabra nine feet high, formed of the rich jasper porphyry of Ravennaja Sopka.   A magnificent vase of the same precious material was heaped full of rubies, lapis lazuli, and turquois from the Kwan-lun chain of mountains.   Between every two of the silver camels was a marble platform or table, on which were spread the golden vessels and drinking cups taken by Cyrus when he surprised Belshazzar in the midst of his great feast.   Here, too, was displayed a statue of silver of Belus, the national divinity of the Chaldeans and Assyrians, with a crown blazing with jewels.   Shields of massive gold, with bosses of large emeralds and rubies, jewel-hilted swords and daggers, and armor polished and enriched with gems, were suspended from the marble columns.   Grouped upon the tables were silver jars hermetically sealed, containing gallons of the precious ottar of roses.   Here, too, was the elaborately wrought harp of gold presented to Cyrus by the Hebrews, in grateful acknowledgment of his kind release of them from the Babylonian captivity.   The lamplight reflected from a heap of talents of gold flung into a corner of the treasury —.no doubt a portion of the treasure with which the two queens Semiramis and Nitocris enrcihed the coffers of Babylon.   At one side stood sculptures of the former queen on horseback throwing her javelin, and her husband, Ninus, piercing a lion.   Here, too, were hung against the walls splendid vestments of the Jewish high priests, rich in jewels, and part of the plunder of Jerusalem at the period of the captivity.   The arts and sciences, driven from Phœnicia and Egypt, centred in Babylon.   And here were precious samples of the purple and wine colored fabrics of those lands, enclosed in gold-banded chests of cedar. Crystal jars full of red and yellow wines, of immense antiquity, were seen on every hand. Mellowed by time, no doubt they would flow gently and pleasantly across the palate, like the celestial waters of the fountain of Salsabil. In a heap at one side were cast bracelets of emeralds, girdles of beaten gold studded with rubies and pearls, and ancient saddles and bridles encircled with gold and gems.

With a throb of exultation the officer crossed and recrossed the marble hall, peering with wonder at each new object of splendor that attracted his attention. His joy was almost frantic. The wild, heated blood coursed through his veins as he examined and touched each object, to assure himself of the reality of the scene. All was true, real solid gold, marble, silver. He climbed to the bowl in the centre of the treasury, and grasping a handful of the coin flung it high away into the air. The golden missiles fell upon the marble floor with a clear musical ring, which caused his heart to thrill with rapture. He was indeed the wealthiest citizen of Persia ; aye I more, he had the means for luxury and splendor that would make the superb gardens of the Shah at Negauristan dwindle into insignificance. He sprang from the rim of the golden bowl down at one leap upon the marble floor. In his half-crazed excitement he had miscalculated the distance, and for a moment he was painfully reminded that he had once been fearfully wounded. The jar of his fall was severe, and at the clank of his sabre upon the marble he heard the voice of Zenayi in warning at his rashness. He had forgotten his benefactor, forgotten that he was not alone. All memory, care, apprehension had fled for the moment, and in the wild exultation of his grand fortune all thought centred upon his gold.

The accents of alarm from the Ghebre recalled him to the sense of danger and caution, and to the consciousness that he was observed. The voice of the mysterious priest reverberated through the subterranean hall. The owner of all this wealth turned at the sound, and found the astrologer standing near him and leaning upon the side of an ivory steed. The dark, inscrutable eyes of the learned sphinx were steadily regarding him. The elbow of the white-robed *savant* rested upon the back of the horse, and the palm of his hand supported his head. In this easy attitude of calm repose, he stood contemplating his pupil, his heir, his beloved commander of horse. It seemed to the officer as if those mysterious eyes had never glowed with so profound meaning ; they seemed to search out his very soul, to read all the hidden thoughts, intentions, and aspirations which crowded upon his brain at the realization of the immense treasure which had become his own. Then, as their *chatoyant* light settled into that wonderful expression of far-off mystery, of fathomless intelligence and profound, ever expanding extent of consciousness, the officer experienced a sense of awe. He seemed to realize in that look, that there was indeed, as the Ghebre had said, another and greater secret yet to be revealed — something more valuable than all this hoarded wealth of Cyrus. Was it the power or knowledge of transmuting all substances into gold? Was that occult lore of transmutation, which had engaged the attention of the learned and studious in every age, realized in that representative of an outlawed faith ? A second glance into those dark eyes beside the ivory horse dispelled this conjecture. There was something deeper, more valuable, known to the astrologer than this. An instant earlier the officer had seemed to realize that all the dreams of youth were realities within his grasp, The unbounded usufruct of wealth had been granted him, and with his clear military perceptions and his inordinate soldierly ambition he saw before him armies equipped, and magnificently equipped for battle and conquest. The sinews of war were spread before him in the ancient treasury.. He felt seething in his own brain the military genius to embody those unequalled resources into *actions*. The consciousness of his own abilities to make the most of means was ever present to him.

But now, true to the maxim of human experience in all ages, the present possession did not satisfy in the knowledge that there was something higher still to attain. That something higher, more precious, more difficult of attainment looked out from the eyes regarding him. What that greater altitude of wealth or power might be, the mysterious eyes did not communicate. But they seemed in their sphinx-like consciousness to regard the officer with an expression of calm superiority, as if he and his treasure were still far behind the *summum bonum* of life. And this unruffled calmness of the Ghebre, and his mysterious contempt of the wonderful treasure he had so carelessly relinquished, served to obumbrate the glitter of the gold in the sight of its new possessor. The ambition, apparently the moment before satisfied by its firm grasp upon the elements of power, now stood irresolute, abashed, and expectant. It had surmounted the long-discerned obstacle to its triumph only to ascertain that a higher cliff impended above.

"Why do you look disconcerted, Alfonso? You seem to hesitate in your inspection of your treasury. Is it not ample for all your wants?"

The officer started at this reading of his unsatisfied soul on the part of Zenayi.

"Are you wizard or *deev*," exclaimed the officer, " that you can read discontent in me?"

"Neither one nor the other," calmly responded the Ghebre. "But an instant ago you were revelling in your wealth. Your eyes beamed joy. You were exhilarated. Suddenly you relinquished your investigation, and your brow lowers. Then, when natural wonder induced my question, you demand if your friend is wizard or *deev*."

"Forgive me, Zenayi. But you have wrought a marvel before my eyes, that all the genii of Ginnistan could not surpass. You cannot wonder that I am bewildered, and speak inconsistently before my friend. I know and believe you to be a true *man*. But you seem so calmly defiant of the glitter of gold, and your eye seemed to say "come up higher," so that my recollection reverts to what you have said to-day. Tell me again, have you a secret worthy the attention and the effort of manhood to attain — a secret that transcends all this?"

"I have already said it, Alfonso. I would not exchange either of my two remaining secrets for a thousand such as this."

"And how may I hope to obtain the mastery of the greater secrets?" inquired the officer.

"You are not satisfied, then, with my gift, Alfonso?"

"No," was the prompt response.

"Oh! the immortal mind, the immortal mind!" exclaimed the Ghebre. "Nothing satisfies its longings. Each new height gained suggests a higher." After a moment's silence he resumed: "It *may* be possible for you to know in time what still remains locked in my breast. But to attain this ineffable knowledge the first requirement I shall make of you is this: You must devote your energies to the honor and glory of my Persia. You must be foremost in her battles, studious of her best military development, and never allow your individual aggrandizement to overtop the best interests of the Empire. Be a firm, unselfish, heroic defender of my Persia; use the wealth I have given you, not in the gratification of sensuality, not in the display of personal vanity, but in earnest efforts to advance my people in everything that makes a nation happy and great. This will cost you great self-denial. You will have to trample upon your passions. For to be a great soldier you must long accustom yourself to the hardships of camp and field. This great wealth, which tempts so powerfully to effeminacy and self-indulgence, you must employ in the interests of Persia and the army. You must not display your wealth, for this engenders the jealousy and enmity of princes. Wisely and cautiously under my advice you must use these resources when needed, and in a manner to divert the attention of the Shah and his satellites from their existence. This self-denial and this unselfishness will react upon your own character, and make you really great of soul. Then this treasury, instead of proving your ruin, will advance you to real greatness. I desire you to start in your career as a commander as a prince starts, with an inborn consciousness that wealth is one of the meanest objects of human pursuit. I know full well the almost inevitable result of a life-long grapple for wealth. It narrows the heart and contracts the character. The qualities essential to success in hoarding gold are parsimony, incessant attention to the saving of trifling sums, impenetrability to the demands of the poor, and constant dwelling of the mind upon the one pursuit which fills the coffer. In nearly all men these things are detrimental to magnanimity. The habits of economy become a second nature. The habit of holding on firmly to small sums and eagerly watching every trifling expenditure, warps the judgment and the heart. The agony of taxation in the owner of a *tumán* of gold is equally great when he has accumulated a million. I desire you to start divested of the eagerness to accumulate. I know that possession often paralyzes energy and exertion. But because I recognize in you kingly qualities, I have determined to flood you with gold. Believe me, however, that your self-abnegation in regard to the manner of employing this treasure will result to your great advantage. For the second secret is far more valuable than the treasury of Cyrus."

"And the *third* secret, Zenayi ; how shall I acquire that?" inquired the officer, his vaulting ambition already winged for higher flights.

The astrologer, steadily regarding the questioner, replied,—

"It will require a heroic life to win the second. The struggle for that alone may cost you years in the field. It may cost you your life in battle."

"But the *third*, Zenayi — tell me the means of winning the *third* secret."

Some powerful emotion seemed to cross the countenance of the astrologer. His eyes dimmed with moisture ; his lips quivered ; his voice trembled as he spoke.

"When you have mastered the *second* secret, come to me. Tell me then of the woman you love beyond all created things — the woman who holds the highest and purest place in your heart, and then and only then can I tell you how you can become the owner of the ineffable, *the great third secret of Zenayi.*"

"Then, and only then, Zenayi ?" inquired the amazed commander.

"I have said it, Alfonso."

The commander, after a moment of silence and reflection, standing before the sphinx, and vainly reading the changes of his wonderful eyes, turned slowly away to look upon his treasures. The first object that met his renewed gaze recalled vividly the memorable scenes at Negauristan. They were the magnificent dresses of women. There were nuptial garments of crimson velvet, embroidered with gold and enriched with pearls and diamonds ; cinctures of gold, strings of pearls from the Persian Gulf, necklaces of emeralds from Egypt, and ornaments of turquoises from Iran. There were tunics for women of buff-colored ground, interspersed with flowers of blue, white, violet, and gold. There were heaps of ear-rings and bracelets of gold, pointed golden crowns worn by brides, Syrian nuptial veils embroidered in gold and silver, jewelled crescents, and Persian tiaras heavy with diamonds. All these recalled the mysterious beauty, the veiled woman of the garden of Negauristan, the woman to whom he had vowed eternal constancy, and upon whose face he had never looked. With all this resource of wealth he could no doubt tear her from that *anderoon* of the Shah, and clothe her with everything that her heart could desire. He could erect for her a paradise unequalled in Persia. He could do for her all that an ardent heart could conceive within the power of wealth. She loved him and mysterious as she was he knew that every hour her influence deepened upon him. His long absence from her had confirmed his affection for her. That single interview had made her mistress of his heart. Could he now consent to divert from her use this wonderful treasure. To attain the higher secrets, he must use none of this wealth for his selfish

purposes. All must be employed in the interest of Persia.
He could give her nothing but his heart, and what ·his own
good sword might gain.

But the greatness of the astrologer's mind was working upon
his own. The unbounded generosity of the great priest of
the Magi who gave him without stint his whole treasure, that
he might thus reward his trust and love, and perhaps win him
to a boundless heroism and devotion to the interests of his
native land, awoke in his heart such a yearning to exhibit
qualities worthy of such a noble friend and patriot, that he was
already hesitating between his affection for the unknown and
his love for the known. She might await the triumphs of his
sword. Zenayi ought not to wait for his triumph over himself
and his passions. He had already caught the inspiration of
the soil made sacred by the memories of noble Cyrus. The
nobility of character of the Ghebre came upon him like a
magnificent storm. It touched the depths of a generous,
thrilled heart. He turned his back upon the accumulations
of Cyrus, and placing his hand in that of the Ghebre, swore to
devote every coin and every article of value to the interest of
his friend's native land.

The breast of the Ghebre heaved with violent emotion. The
sacrifice seemed too stupendous for a young man, and as if the
words of the officer had been misunderstood, he inquired seriously again,—

"Do you really mean to say that you will relinquish all this
treasure for my Persia; that you will voluntarily descend from
the position of the most affluent man in this empire to that of
one receiving only the pay of a commander of horse?"

"I do mean it. Your word has indicated a more valuable
secret to be wrung from you by manly exertion and self-denial.
Your word to me is as pure and exalted as the stars of heaven.
I believe you, I love your country, and I relinquish this treasure
to its interests. Why should I deny the wisdom and fidelity of
my friend. I renounce all this wealth to my belief in the integrity and sincerity of Zenayi. I would rather be a true hero
in your eyes, than to revel in twice this wealth."

The astrologer wound his arms about the officer, and drew
him tightly to his breast, while tears streamed from his eyes in
the intensity of his emotion. Calming himself at length he said
exultantly, —

"In all the annals of the "City of the Violet Crown" was
never known a sacrifice for country or for friend like this. Boy,

soldier, hero, friend, you have made a noble choice. If the
sword of battle spares you, you will never regret this bold, blind
leap into the dark. You will look upon halls beside which this
treasury of Cyrus is a mole-hill. I cannot express in words
my admiration for you."

"I shall await your revelation, Zenayi, with patience, and
until my sword cuts the way to fortune. But now I would like
to probe one mystery of the present which you created for me
upon my journey to this place. How could Cyrus, never having seen this subterranean hall, and never hearing of it, know
of its existence? Why did he tunnel his way to the heart of
this mountain to find a cavity to adorn for his treasures?"

"I will satisfy that curiosity of yours at once," replied the
astrologer. "I will bring the moon from heaven to show you.
Come on."

Advancing to the genii which supported the central golden
bowl, the Ghebre passed under it, and brought out a large
wooden vessel containing water.

"Mount," he said to the officer, "to the edge of the golden
bowl, and I will hand up to you this vessel of water. Go to
the centre of the bowl and place the vessel there carefully
upon the coin. Place it there as near the centre as your eye
can judge, and then wait there until I extinguish all these
lamps."

His amazed companion obeyed these instructions, placed the
vessel of water in the centre of the golden bowl, and then, sitting in the midst of the rattling coin, watched Zenayi extinguish
all the lamps by a pressure upon a rod which ascended one of
the fluted columns. Instantly all was darkness impenetrable,
save in the centre of the wooden vessel of water. There, to
the astonishment of the commander, quivered the full moon of
heaven. The water grew at length perfectly still, and in the
centre of it lay the calm, full, silver image of the moon. The
spectator remembered then that Canidia the sorceress made
the moon descend from heaven by her enchantments, and so
he told the Ghebre.

"Look up, Alfonso," said the mysterious priest from the
midst of the darkness, "and you will see how the adventurous
boy, Cyrus, discovered the existence of what he could not see,
and never heard of. He was a splendid climber among the
mountain rocks, and you will see where he dropped stones into
impenetrable darkness."

The officer, looking up through the circle of ivory angels, detected a small aperture at the summit of the cone through which the moon was shining.

CHAPTER XIV.

" His brandished sword did blind men with its beams ;
His arms spread wider than a dragon's wings ;
His sparkling eyes, replete with awful fire,
More dazzled and drove back his enemies,
Than mid-day sun fierce bent against their faces.
What should I say? his deeds exceed all speech ;
He never lifted up his hand, but conquered.".
Henry VI.

 DESERT boundless, where the sky is fire, and the soil a sea of flaming sand. Not a tree, or shrub, or blade of grass breaks the surface of the interminable waste. The summer air, glowing with the intense fervor of Solomon's fountain of molten brass beats upon the head of the unlucky traveller, until he sinks to earth a helpless, wilted thing, devoid of energy or hope. To augment the agony of his eyes and brain, the desert is radiant with the effulgence of lichen-like tufts of salt. These at intervals widen into miniature lakes of white dazzling salt an inch in thickness, upon which the full blaze of the sun pours, until a glare is reflected which pierces the eyes of the beholder like the points of myriad daggers. The slightest puff of wind raises the volatile dust in clouds, until it blinds the eyes and fills the nostrils almost to suffocation; and the ill-fated victim, falling upon the sand, covers his head in his mantle to breathe until the stifling agony has passed away. The streams which cross at long intervals the desert, are so salt, that the animals even refuse to drink. The yielding sand beneath the feet is so hot in the ardent glances of the sun, that the bare hand shrinks from touching it. The heat which floods downward from the red orb of day, appears to come in successive pulsations, each one hotter than the last, until at length the brain reels as from excessive intoxication, and the vitality for further advance dies out. If in the moment of this extreme prostration no water for the lips and forehead is near, the man dies in stupor. Such is the fearful desert of Khorassan.

The order was peremptóry, and the army marched. The reluctant commander dared not disobey his sovereign. But he knew full well an enemy at the court had gained the royal ear. The army was in the highest state of efficiency, and he had only awaited the subsidence of the summer heats to cross the desert. The soldiers murmured, not at their commander, but at the court far away and safe under the shade of their luxurious garden trees and in the cool recesses of their baths. Men who had never flinched before the onset of the mounted enemy were appalled at the remorseless foe which awaited them in the sands and the sky. But the magnetic influence and energy of the young commander were equal to the emergency. He addressed the troops in words of fire, applauded their skill and discipline, and promised them double their usual allotment of plunder in the enemy's country. He purchased out of his *secret resources* a large number of camels, and loaded them with skins fashioned in the form of jars. These replenished with water from the mountain springs would suffice for the painful desert journey. Then, with every precaution taken for their subsistence on the march, he led his troops out of the fertile plains and valley of Mourg-Aub, passed through the towns of Aberkouh, Deh Shaheh, and Yezd, and entered the suffocating atmosphere of the desert of Khorassan.

Halting by day and marching by night, according to the Oriental custom, the army were protected by their tents from the full violence of the summer sun. The moonlight glistened upon the moving columns arrayed in all the bright colors and flashing armor of Asiatics. With their Arabian steeds superbly caparisoned, their sabres and spear-heads polished to unusual brilliancy, and their camels' and asses covered with scarlet cloths, the five thousand cavalry moved on through the moonlit and bewildered Persian towns in mysterious magnificence and discipline. When at length they reached the treeless desert and their horses' hoofs sank into the yielding sand in which the heat of the day still lingered, they were cheered on in their arduous march by the voice and ever-present watchfulness of their commander. The inflexibility of his character came out in the midst of the fearful ravages of the *simoom*, which soon added its horrors to the heats and dust of the desert. It came at length, as he had apprehended, whistling with great violence over the volatile sands, and pouring its torrents of furnace heat through the clouds of dust it raised in the path of the horrified army. He caused the kneeling horses and their riders, together

with the asses and camels, to be covered with the tent-cloths
which he had stripped from their poles. Thus they were in
part enabled to keep from their nostrils the fiery atmosphere
which swept over their prostrate forms. Thus were most of
his troops and their animals saved, rising at length to their
feet, dusty and dizzy from the hot tornado which had passed
on in its deadly career. The dead were buried under the
desert sands, and the survivors marched on.

At length, as the army advanced near to the frontiers of
Toorkomania, there arose from the monotonous sands of the
desert huge barriers of naked rocks, standing like dark spec-
tres amid the arid wastes. The number of these mountain
ridges increased with every night's march, until one morning,
as the troops were about to halt, and pitch their tents for the
day, they saw before them a vast barrier of rocky cliffs, with
an intervening gorge which they must cross to gain the territory of the enemy on the plateau above, and level with the
summits of the barrier. Across the gorge in one spot alone
was there a passage, and that was a natural inclined plain
of rock, some three hundred feet in breadth, and rising from
the level plain of the desert with a gentle ascent to the very
level of the overhanging cliffs. Solid columns of cavalry could
with easy pace ascend the inclined plain to the plateau on the
cliffs, and look down on either hand into the gloomy depths of
the gorge as they passed across and upward. But an unmanageable steed might easily back himself and his rider off
either edge of this rocky crossing to instant death. The guide
to the territory of the Turcomans, employed by the commander
of this superb body of horse, had notified him of the existence of
this romantic crossing at the enemy's frontier, had expatiated
upon the wild grandeur of the locality, and aroused his curiosity
to view the place. At the same time he had warned the commander of the dangerous character of the position should the
foe learn of his advance and seize it for the purpose of disputing the passage. There were other less difficult means of
access to the Turcoman territory, but they would necessitate a
longer delay in the burning sands of the desert. The commander, secure in the secrecy with which he had veiled his entire
plans, anticipated no resistance on the border, and was determined to see the natural bridge over the gorge. What was
his amazement, then, upon glancing up the inclined plain and
running his eyes along the edge of the plateau, to discover that
both were densely crowded with the dark masses of the enemy,

like scowling thunder-clouds awaiting the advent of the sun-light, to pour down upon his little army with overwhelming fury. An older and more experienced soldier might well have been appalled. His force was outnumbered four to one. The advantages of the ground were in their favor, whether they chose to dispute the passage or to advance in overwhelming force down upon his command. His own troops had been upon the march all night; how fresh the myriads of Tur-comans on the ascent and cliffs might be, was enigmatical. They were there to crush him, and the chances were in their favor. Perfect and matchless discipline seemed alone in favor of the young soldier. Ha! another favorable indication burst upon the ear of the Persian commander. It was the yell of defiance from his troops, who caught a glimpse of the reality of their danger. As the morning sun flushed the eastern sky, the Persian horse, looking up, saw the enemy, whose lances gleamed through the clouds of dust raised by their horses like fire be-hind a dark curtain. The Turcoman horsemen returned the yell of the Persian cavalry. From cliff to cliff their war-cry was taken up, and the successive peals of mortal defiance told plainly enough how greatly the royal horse were outnumbered. But to this grander demonstration the Persians again hurled back their contemptuous defiance.

The superb courage of his troops thrilled the heart of the young commander, and his orders were then delivered with great rapidity and clearness. The bugles cheerily sounded for the evolutions, the squadrons of horse wheeled swiftly to the front, and the baggage was sent far away to the rear.

From his rocky altitude the Turcoman chief had looked down and maintained an ominous silence. Secure of his prey, and with his swarms of lancers massed for a terrible charge down the rocky hill, he had remained passive. Confident of the speedy annihilation of the little army below him, he had awaited the first manifestation of their terror and panic and consequent flight. The Oriental horses are cultivated with an especial eye to their powers of endurance in long flights, when victory has become impossible for their masters. By the speed of the Persian horses alone could the plans of the Turcoman chief be frus-trated. Thus he reasoned, and was watching for the disorgani-zation and flight of the little army confronting him. What was his amazement then to hear their defiant cry, and to witness the instant rapidity of their movements in some novel and orderly plan of battle. Three thousand horsemen were thrown forward

in column, confronting the inclined plain, and the remaining
two thousand, who were regiments of lancers, were wheeled
away to the right and left of this solid column, and facing its
sides. It was evident enough that if these lancers maintained
their position, they would be possessed of the power to strike
his Turcomans on either flank, when they had charged far
enough down on to the desert. He was not prepared, however, for the next movement of the young commander, who
rode to the head of the solid column of horsemen armed only
with sabres and pistols, raised his sabre vertically to the full
length of his arm, and gave the command, *march*. The bugles
sounded fearlessly, the horses approached the enemy at a trot.
The heroic Persians were advancing to attack. The green
and red banner, stamped with golden crescents, was rashly and
madly ascending the hill, which barely could hold the densely
crowded lancers of Toorkomania. Soon the clatter of hoofs
sounded upon the rocky ascent, the dark visages of the Turcomans began to come out distinctly from the late confused
mass of their high fur caps, the blue and red stripes of their
long *baronnees* became more clearly marked, their steel spear-
heads with four flutes glistened close at hand, and their glittering, vengeful black eyes were seen full of hate for the hos-
tile "*Kuzzilbashes.*" Within eighty paces of the Turcoman
lances the command, "*march, march,*" was given; the bugles
sounded the *charge,* and the Persian horse, with the *élan* of
tigers, and sabre in hand, dashed into the ranks of their foes.
Their pistol balls fully compensated for the disadvantages of
the rising ground, and every shot that missed its object told
with fearful effect upon another man or horse behind and higher.
But many a Turcoman lance bathed in Persian blood, and the
narrow, rocky battle-field grew more cumbersome at every cut
of sabre Amid a confused clashing of arms and the sharp
report of pistol shots, "*Sunnites*" and "*Sheeans*" fought each
other with the genuine fury of religious partisans. The followers of the Arab Prophet slaughtered each other without mercy,
and fell together ghastly and dying under the trampling hoofs
of horses. There was no soil to suck up the blood of the stern
conflict, and the red rivulets ran down the sloping rock and
added horror to the fallen faces of the dead below.

Destroyed by a false estimate of their own strength, the advanced squadrons of the Turcomans found their centre pierced
by the energetic, heroic, and indomitable commander, who held
his cavalry firmly and steadily to their work. Pushing, cutting,

trampling ahead in a compact body to the one object in view, namely, to secure a central point in the huddled masses of the foe whence he could push them on either side back to the edge of the precipice, the commander led his horsemen. They had been instructed to cling closely together, and to follow the flash of his sabre. He cut his way thus steadily onward and upward through the masses of the foe, who could not fall back towards the summit from the crowd of horsemen who impeded their retreat. Attaining, after heroic combat for an hour, the centre of the inclined plain and of the enemy huddled upon it, his column parted through the middle, the upper half pushing still onward and upward, while the lower half, dividing into two parties, wheeled to the right and left, and pushed the enemy towards the edges of the horrible gorge. Backward and still backward the indomitable Persians now pushed the enemy in three directions, as they had often done in their mock battles on the plain of Mourg-Aub. Their own ranks were fearfully decimated, but their ardor grew with their success. Discipline and their pistols, with which they had been abundantly supplied, gave double victory to their sabres, which outweighed the long lances of the enemy, crowded together as they were, and unable to bring them into effective use. The Turcoman horsemen near the edge of the gorge felt the backward pressure of their comrades upon them. The scattering bullets wounded their horses and rendered them frantic and unmanageable. Steed pressed against steed, and rider shouted to rider; but still a greater and more terrible pressure came upon both from the centre of the battle-field, where the Persians were cutting down rank after rank and still pushing the solid mass backward slowly but surely. At length a pistol shot cut the neck of a Turcoman horse standing near the gorge. The animal plunged madly to one side, and drove the next horse and rider over the edge. The hoof of the beast's hind leg slid over the edge of the chasm, he lost his balance, his flank sank downward, his head and neck swung backward, and with a scream of mortal terror the rider fell with his steed through space into the unknown depths. In his frantic struggle to regain his foothold the lost steed had frightened other horses. They plunged, reared, and screamed in their terror, and in their mad struggles drove other horsemen over the edge. Hoarse words of command to the frantic steeds, oaths and yells of despair from the lost riders poising for an instant on the edge of the chasm, ere they fell forever, blended with the clash of sabres and the crack of pistol shots. Every instant the situation grew more appalling, for with fierce yells of triumph those disciplined and heroic bands of Persian horse hewed their way onward and outward from the centre, cutting down the Turcoman riders and sending their wounded horses trampling and terrified, backward into the surging masses of the foe. The rear ranks of the lancers, unable to fight or to flee, were pushed by inches towards the gorge, struggled like demons for an instant on the edge of death, and then were flung by the pressure, heels in air, down into the horrible void, a flying, shapeless mass of heads, hoofs, hands, lances, striped garments, and human trunks of writhing flesh, falling downward through space, to be crushed in pieces on the rocks below as in the Mohammedan "Al Hotama" of hell. The Turcoman chief from his commanding position saw this terrible catastrophe result on both edges of the gorge, and the shapeless masses of his troops falling through space. And still remorselessly pressed onward the two divisions of the Persian horse, pushing the remnants of his lancers towards the edge. Unable to advance fresh bodies of his troops to the assistance of those at the front, so encumbered with his own horsemen was the narrow way, he saw no hope of ultimate triumph, save in the exhaustion of the little body of horse that were fighting stubbornly up the hill straight for his centre. Under the immediate eye and leadership of their commander, and some fifteen hundred strong, this division of horse were fighting their way steadily up the rise. The sabre of the Persian commander once dazzlingly bright like Colada, the gold-hilted sword of the Cid, was now crimsoned with blood. Wherever he struck, death followed ; his path was strewn with the fallen, and terror rode with him on his fierce career of destruction. In the magnetism of his onset and his ringing voice of encouragement, his followers faced and trampled down every obstacle, and the terrified foe would have fled had there been an outlet behind them at the summit. But the Turcoman chief held steadily and persistently in their place the riders whom he could not advance to the succor of their fellows. Trusting to the exhaustion of his foe by the sheer opposition of numbers, he watched the stern conflict, saw his horsemen at last entirely cut down or hurled over the edges of the gorge, and the victorious squadrons with shouts of triumph ascend the hill to the assistance of their commander.

The victorious detachments were not a moment too soon.

The commander had fought his way nearly to the summit, and they had to reach him over ghastly heaps of the slain. Their exultant cries as they leaped the piles of the dead and dying, and sprang up the slope to the rescue, awakened fresh enthusiasm in the ranks of their friends. The Turcomans, by their failure to avail themselves in the first instance of their superior position, and to charge down upon the ascending foe when momentum was everything to their cavalry, had now to fight on nearly equal terms. They fell like sheep before the fierce riders of Persia, who seemed to be fired by the personal heroism and dash of their commander. Wherever the fiery Al Borak and his rider dashed into the crowded ranks of the enemy, there was a shrinking back of the Turcomans, rapid flashes of a sabre, ghastly wounds, and a flight of riderless horses that plunged and floundered away upward amid the solid mass of troopers, or, springing into the air, attempted to force their way over the necks of the Persian horses. Balisardo, the enchanted sword of Ruggiero, cut no more deadly swaths than the blade of this terrible leader. His energy and skill cleared a broad path for his followers, and pouring in behind him, they widened the breach, and neared the summit of the hill. Then came that terrible order again. The column parted into three divisions, and a second time were the Turcomans hurled headlong off the sides into the gorge. The commander of the Persians now discerned that one bold, impetuous push alone was required to gain the level plain at the summit. Braining with his sabre the Turcoman immediately opposing him, he turned in his saddle, and glanced back over the plain. Then followed a word of command. The trumpeter who clung close to him sounded a call for the lancers at the foot of the hill. They came dashing up the slope with alacrity. They gained the summit at the instant their commander reached it in triumph, and saw the baffled chief of the Turcomans dash forward to intercept the advance with a fresh body of lancers. But the impetuosity of the Persians knew no bounds. They cut their way again to the centre, shot down the commanding chief, and routed his lancers. Then came a brilliant running cavalry fight over the plain, the Turcomans striving to escape, the Persians determined to slay every man. Far away over the new desert scattered the combatants in the full blaze of the Oriental sun. Long bamboo lances drank the blood of men and horses. Steeds and riders fell headlong in their swift career, quivering in the agonies of death, or like frantic demons held on their course to escape, shaking off every impediment, and flying onward through clouds of dust and over glowing wastes of sand.

When evening came (for they had fought all day) the Persian commander reined in his steed and recalled his scattered forces. His victorious troops were almost agonized to death with fatigue, and thirst, and heat. But a superhuman strength of endurance was conspicuous in their chief; and when the recall was sounded, he dispatched messengers with orders to hurry up the camel train with water for the suffering and exhausted. Superintending every movement for the resuscitation of his men, he rode amongst them, and gave orders for the encampment, and for the night. At length the baggage-train arrived upon the conquered field, and gradually order and silence reigned where battle and blood had held high revel.

As the shadows of the night settled upon the camps and obscured the watchful sentinels, the commander rode forth alone to the scene of his heroic struggle at the cliffs. Backward to the gorge he slowly moved upon the back of his faithful Al Borak, knowing that the moon would ere long illuminate the battle-field with almost the clearness of day. Yielding a free rein to his horse, he rode on in profound thought. That eventful day had been a grand day for him and his friends. His jealous enemies at the court had been baffled. They had urged upon the monarch this premature advance to ruin the aspiring officer. He had triumphed over a prepared enemy. Some one had notified the Turcoman chief of his advance. He was satisfied that the officers who were his foes at Teheran had dispatched a secret messenger to Toorkomania. Zenayi, who learned all the court intrigue from Irene, had warned him of the cabal against him, but advised him to obey the sovereign promptly, and march. Now, the noble heart of the Ghebre would be thrilled by the splendor of his victory. Persia would ring with his name. The brilliant Irene would be proud of the young commander whose cause she had so enthusiastically espoused. Aye! more. The mysterious beauty of the *anderoon*, to whom he had vowed eternal affection, and who had secured his appointment to the command of the expedition, would rejoice as only a lover could at the laurels won by her idol. The fame of his skillful generalship would ensure him high consideration with Abbas Mirza, and consequently with the Shah. It had been his hard task to conquer difficulties as well as foes. He had gathered an army, formed it into a well-trained and thoroughly equipped corps, fit for active and dis-

6

tant service, and had accomplished this glorious victory under adverse and discouraging circumstances. The plan he had projected for bringing the campaign to a brilliant close had been obliterated by the new plan which he had conceived and executed like lightning, when the unexpected contingency and opportunity arose in his path. His troops would bear the knowledge of his prompt and efficient military skill to their homes. His own self-knowledge had been suddenly augmented. He had demonstrated his ability to grapple with unforeseen obstacles. And he knew this power of eagle-eyed discernment and lightning execution, was an attribute of military genius. It was with emotions, then, of pride and exultation that he reined his steed to a halt upon the summit of the cliff, and endeavored to penetrate the gloom below him.

Darkness for a few seconds lingered with its sceptre. Then its realm was invaded. Far away above the horizon a light appeared. It grew clearer, larger, brighter, Then in full effulgence burst forth the *Evening Star.* So pure, so majestic, so lovely, so peaceful, glowed the heavenly light, that the commander was entranced. He clasped his hands above the neck of his steed, and gazed upon it, while memories sweet, bewitching, and tender floated up from the past. Persia and its passions were forgotten. The sweetness of his boyhood, with its young hopes, and the tender kindness and sympathy of one face that had pleaded for him in his despair, were all he remembered, and burying his face in his hands he sobbed aloud, "'Tis *Madeleine's star ;* ah ! 'tis *Madeleine's star.*"

<hr>

CHAPTER XV.

HE had not eaten of the lotus ; he had not forgotten his country. Years had passed away, and his intellect had become the intellect of a man. But amid the turmoil of camps and the engrossing objects of ambition, the memory of Madeleine had ever come to him with the advent of the evening star. It was like the distant music of a dream, the recollection of the lovely girl who had interceded for him in the hour of ignominy. When his proud, boyish heart was on the point of being crushed by inexorable fate, this radiant being in her purity had espoused his cause, and then cheered and stimulated him forward in the path of ambition. He remembered her, girl as she was, as a passionless, pure, self-sustained, and self-dependent being — a princess in whom all the virtues centred, and whom exquisite beauty crowned. But in the bewildering transformations of his career since he had parted from her the memory of his boyhood's queen had become dim, and he thought of her only at intervals, when in silence the evening star glorified the night.

But now, in the hour of his great success, when he had gained the distinction she had years ago predicted for him and urged him to, this lovely star, arising in matchless brilliancy upon his own great battle-field, recalled the boyish dreams in all their fervor, and he wept at the sweet thoughts of Madeleine. The poor outcast and friendless convict boy had shivered all the opposition of fate, and created his own destiny of power. Great thoughts had usurped the throne of his heart, he had trampled upon boundless wealth, his soul was enlarged, his ambition was more exalted, and great intellects were already leaning towards him in admiration. The wonderful Ghebre had condescended to admire him, and the brilliant Irene had deemed him worthy of her high-toned, aristocratic regard. The worthiest master minds of Persia regarded him as essential to the glory and triumphs of the Empire. Where would he have been upon this glorious night had Madeleine and her kindred passed him by in scorn, as the world had done? The convict's cell and the prison lash would have been his destiny.

As he gazed upon the star he wondered at his own heart. It was beating at this moment, not for the lovely unknown of the royal *anderoon* to whom he had pledged his eternal fidelity, but for a long-forgotten and distant child. How vividly he recalled now those dark, glorious eyes, and the wonderful shower of her golden hair, and the tender sympathy of that face which had smiled upon the deserted and outcast boy in his agony and his loneliness of soul. And with that memory came a vague consciousness that she was purer, that far-off child, than any woman he had encountered upon Persian soil ; that she would frown upon what Irene approved in policy, and would bid him cast aside as pernicious and unworthy all counsel that savored of deceit and secret ways. And as he pondered on her distant loveliness he wondered if she had grown beyond his power to identify her, if she were alive and radiant in the more mature loveliness of womanhood. And while he dreamed thus of his boyish love and the unaccountable conviction in his mind of her superior purity and exaltation of character above Oriental women, he was seized with a sudden sense of shame that he was proving for the moment disloyal to her to whom he had given solemn vows. He shook off then the dream of Madeleine, and vowed anew his allegiance to the veiled charmer of the *anderoon,* the unknown beauty who loved him and had gained for him the separate command which had immortalized him before the world. He longed once more for the hour when he should lay his sword and honors at the feet of his lovely mistress, and plead for the withdrawal of the mysterious veil.

While he exulted in the thought of his secret and exalted mistress, the moon arose and illumined the ghastly faces of the battle-field, and upon his ear broke the low moans of the wounded and the dying. So terrible had been the exhaustion of the long conflict, that he had forbidden his troops to succor the wounded or bury the dead. The victorious army had fallen to the ground in dreamless sleep. The commander alone reviewed the dead and the mangled victims of the conflict.

As the wondrous effulgence of the Oriental moon waxed more powerful with every moment's flight, objects became more clearly visible, and he rode slowly down the declivity to view the scene of the more stubborn conflict. His horse's hoofs necessarily trod upon the dead, so densely were they piled about upon the sloping rock. But he avoided the wounded, many of whom recognized him and called to him. He bade them keep heart, and wait patiently, if they could, for the morning, when their exhausted comrades would come to their aid. The poor mutilated wretches often hushed their piteous cries for help when they realized that they were not deserted. Persia had triumphed, and for many of them there was hope on the morrow. They knew that their beloved commander alone had returned to them in consequence of his more firmly knit constitution of iron, and his unbounded watchfulness and tenderness for his crippled heroes. He was there alone, self-denying, and thoughtful for them, and planning for their relief on the morrow. But the scene was ghastly in the extreme, and now that the light of battle had died out in his eyes, they wore the expression of gentleness and pity. There were heaps of the dead and the dying mingled promiscuously with the slightly wounded, the latter too weak from loss of blood to extricate themselves from the superincumbent mass of dead flesh which suffocated them. Many of these he drew out from their torture and laid more comfortably upon the pillowing bosoms of the dead. Frantic steeds of the desert, in the agony of their wounds, plunged about, unable to rise in their crippled condition, but rearing partially upon their fore-legs, and dealing death with their crushing hoofs upon the heads of the wounded. And ever and anon the foam of their gasping fell upon the pale faces of the fallen troopers as they turned over and around in their brute agony. And there were fearful sounds of brute and human agony arising at intervals from the depths of either abyss, where man and beast had fallen off to destruction. The moonbeams fell upon masses of quivering flesh, severed arms, bleeding stumps, eyeless sockets where the bullets had travelled on their destructive mission, and skulls cloven to the brain by the sabre, or transfixed with the bamboo lance. The spots of rock untenanted by prostrate masses of flesh were slippery with blood and gore. The commander, already smeared and spotted with the red stains which had dripped and spattered upon him from his own uplifted sabre in the fury of the combat, now slipped in the pools of blood upon the rock as he led Al Borak over and amid the heaps of the slain.

"And this is the penalty of glory," he muttered, as he slowly made his way over the rock. But then there came to him the memory of the horrible outrages upon men, women, and children committed upon Persian soil by these lawless invaders. "It is human justice," he added, solemnly. "According to the testimony of the wise and good in every age and country, merciless invaders must be terrified by the retaliation of wholesale slaughter. The brute in man must be restrained by brute retaliation. Murder has become sanctified by usage and exalted to the dignity of patriotism, heroism. Christian and Mohammedan alike sanction the code of slaughter. So upon their joint creeds I shall mount to the pedestal of glory."

He paused at length in the middle of the inclined plain of rock, with the mutilated corpses on every side of him, and looked out upon the dim sand desert at the foot of the declivity. Distant lines of shadows seemed to lie along the plain below. He started in amazement after a moment's steady gaze. The shadows seemed to draw nearer. He looked more narrowly, to satisfy himself there was no optical illusion. He caught the glisten of steel running along the lines of shadow. The moonbeams were his friends. They revealed the shimmer of spearheads. The shadowy lines were approaching, surely and stealthily. The star-points crowning the dark lines grew in

number and distinctness every instant. He saw they were
sweeping down upon the gorge. They were heading for the inclined battle-field. His camp would be surprised. With the
quickness of his military instinct he detected the night strata-
gem, turned the head of Al Borak up the hill, sprang to the
saddle, and vaulted upward over the heaps of the slain as best
he could. It mattered not now where the steed's hoofs fell,
whether upon the face of Turcoman or Persian, friend or foe.
The military instinct was predominant, and his sleeping troops
must be saved.

Al Borak seemed to scent the danger and share the alarm of
his master. With fearful leaps he cleared the piles of the slain,
trampled over the helpless countenances upturned to the moon,
and sped away upward with the activity of a demon. Without
a moment's sleep or rest the commander must fling himself into
the toils of another battle. Fresh bodies of the enemy, fierce
masses of desert riders, were sweeping forward to surprise his
exhausted and slumbering forces. He cleared the battle-field
with the swiftness possible only to the superb steed of Khorassan he rode, he reached the cliffs, he flew away over the sands
of the upper desert, he darted through the line of the watchful
sentinels, flinging to them the pass-word as he bounded into the
camp, and then his clarion tones of command aroused the sleeping squadrons. Exhausted as they were, they grasped their
weapons, the horses were rapidly turned out into the plain for
battle, the lines were formed with marvellous rapidity, the bugles
sounded the orders clear and startling in the moonlight, and
order ensued from the confusion of the first alarm. Fortunately
for the Persian commander, his troops had been thoroughly disciplined at Mourg-Aub for surprises. He had tried them often
and persistently with the midnight alarm. They were soon in
battle array, and their celerity of movement was marvellous.
Scarcely had they slept an hour; but the routine of discipline
was triumphant, and the royal horse were ready.

As they sat motionless in their saddles awaiting the foe, and
relying with unbounded confidence upon the skill of their commander, who appeared to them now the very impersonation of
invincibility, they could detect near at hand a sullen *thud*, as
of hoofs trampling upon human flesh. The desert riders of
Toorkomania were mounting by thousands the inclined rocky
passage over the gorge, and were crushing under foot the masses
of fallen humanity. The brother of the fallen chief had met
a fugitive from the disastrous battle-field, and was hastening

onward to surprise the victors with a fresh body of Turcomans. He had been scouring the desert in search of the Persians while they were, in fact, engaged in battle with the main army commanded by his brother. Fierce for revenge and confident of surprising the camp of the Persian commander, the fresh army swept over the desert in the form of a huge crescent after they had gained the level of the cliffs. On they came, with every precaution for silence pre-arranged, like a shadowy fate from which there was no escape. Suddenly upon their astonished ears burst the notes of a bugle sounding the evolutions. They fancied it the first signal of the alarmed sentinel who guarded the sleeping camp, and onward they dashed to make the surprise complete. They saw before them the tents of the Persians glistening in the moonlight and at once their crescent line of approach extended into a circle which closed in the foe, that none might escape. With terrific yells they dashed into the camp from every side, but found no enemy. The Persian commander had anticipated their manner of advance and withdrawn his squadrons to a distance on either side of his camp, awaiting the moment of confusion which must ensue. The great circle of Turcomans closed in upon the camp, rapidly enveloping their intended victims and pressing in from every side upon the centre. At the moment of their greatest disappointment, and when their own horsemen met face to face amid the deserted tents, they heard behind them on three sides the yells of the advancing Persians as they dashed in upon them and sabred them to the earth, where they stood in inextricable confusion. They were taken wholly at disadvantage; their lines already broken by the confusion at the centre, were rent into fragments by the disciplined charges on three sides which trampled them to the earth in the glare of the camp-fires. Some fought long and with desperation; but the greater portion of the Turcomans discovered the truth that resistance was only destruction, and surrendered themselves prisoners to the royal horse, which had entrapped them so adroitly and so effectually in the midst of the camp. Six thousand Turcoman lancers laid down their arms at the feet of the Persian commander, and among the number was their chief. The victory was complete, and hostages enough of high rank were sent to Teheran to secure the good conduct of Toorkomania for the future.

On the ensuing day the dead were buried, the wounded cared for, and the prisoners sent away under guard to the Persian cities. Then the young commander led his troops

into the unprotected country of his enemies, burned the dwellings, scattered or carried off the herds of cattle and camels,
and inflicted such terrible destruction upon the property of the
foe as he had promised when he assumed the separate command.
The terror of his name lived long among that lawless tribe of
plunderers and assassins, and Persia was freed for years from
their dreaded inroads.

CHAPTER XVI.

SNOW-STORM in Persia !
The season was winter; the scene the province of
Iran-Ajemi in the north-western section of the empire
and adjacent to the Caspian Sea.

The cavalry camp at Kasbin had been broken up and the
troops were ordered to march in the direction of Sultania, to
meet the Prince Royal, and escort him to the residence of his
royal father, the Shah of all Persia, at Teheran, the capital.
The cavalry selected for this honorary duty were the heroes of
the Turcoman war, and their commander was the young officer
with whose exploits all Persia had rung. At Kasbin Alfonso
had continued the admirable discipline which had rendered his
troops so efficient against overwhelming numbers on the Turcoman frontier. At the conclusion of the war, which had given
him the opportunity he so coveted for renown, he had been
stationed with his troops at various posts adjacent to the Caspian Sea. But never since the period of his Turcoman distinction had he looked upon the countenance of the Shah, or of
his illustrious son, Abbas Mirza. Neither had there been formal recognition by the sovereign at any time of his eminent
military services and merits. He had, indeed, been notified by
Zenayi that the Shah was pleased with his young general, and
would in time honor him. Though chafing under the apparent
neglect, he maintained a dignified silence, and wisely devoted
himself to the greater perfection of his troops in the art of war.
Every request that he addressed to the headquarters of the army,
regarding the equipment and comfort of his men, was listened
to, and promptly responded to. He was furnished with every
means of making his command the most perfect and efficient

in Persia. In this acquiescence were encouragement and hope that his services would yet be properly recognized and compensated. His heart throbbed exultantly when the order arrived at Kasbin to join the Prince Royal. He was now about to pass under the eyes of royalty at Teheran. His greater joy was that the Shah's son, Abbas Mirza, the idol of Persia, the statesman and soldier, would now have an opportunity to witness the admirable discipline he had introduced into the corps entrusted to him.

The scene as the young commander advanced at the head of his cavalry on the road leading north-west from Kasbin to Sultania, was one of wintry desolation. The whole valley in which they were marching was covered with snow, and the mountains which towered on either hand wore the same spotless mantle. Along the cliffs at the left, and crowning their very tops, were vague outlines of fortresses and towers, guarding the dangerous pass. Here a score of resolute warriors could dispute the passage safely with ten times their force of invaders. The plastic snow had rounded the angles of the deserted fortifications and given a certain smoothness to the adjacent crags. This had been the fastness of the great and mysterious chief of that terrible religious sect whose atrocious deeds had for two centuries aroused terror and superstitious reverence throughout the land. Even the ranks of the Crusaders in the neighboring Syria had been decimated by the cavalry of this monstrous empire of violence, as they swept down from the heights of Mount Lebanon, with their terrible war-cry, and with sabre in hand. The name of this remorseless fanatic sect was Assassins, and from them has the world derived the designation for all who treacherously and in darkness slay their enemies. Their founder and chief was called Sheik-ul-Jebal, or lord of the mountains.

Shivering in the wintry blast, and half blinded by the flying snow-flakes, which were whirled capriciously about by the keen sweep of the gale through the mountain pass, the commander of the Persian horse heard with surprise the cheery notes of a bugle amid the desolation. Then came the rattle of sabres, the sound of human voices, and the tread of hoofs partly muffled by the snow. A cavalcade swept into view, at intervals toiling slowly among the rocks, and then bounding forward at a fleeter pace when the widening and more level road allowed. Their novel Oriental costumes, their horses caparisoned in varied and brilliant colors, and with bridles covered with bands

6*

of silver and adorned with silken tassels, and the strange dialect
which passed to and fro between them, indicated that they were
treading the territory once ennobled by the rule of the heroic
and magnanimous Cyrus, the Persian.

They were the advance guard of the superb Abbas Mirza,
heir-apparent to the crown of Persia and in their midst were
five ladies of his royal highness's *anderoon*, dressed in scarlet,
with magnificent shawls from the looms of Tabreez over their
heads and faces. These royal beauties, selected to attend their
lord on his visit to Tcheran, were riding *astride* on the most
beautiful and spirited horses, which they managed with ease and
grace, even amid the violence of the storm. They were guarded
by twelve powerful eunuchs whom the royal cavalry hemmed
in on every side. The troop of horse swept by, riding into the
very teeth of the gale, and then followed the baggage train of
the royal ladies, covered with scarlet and blue cloths. A *tack-
i-ravan* followed after, resting upon poles between two white
mules. This royal litter and the mules were arrayed in scarlet
cloth with golden fringe.

As the *tack-i-ravan* passed the horse of Alfonso the scarlet
curtains were thrust back and a veiled lady looked out, steadily
regarding him. She appeared to recognize him, for her hand
was waved to him three times, and yet so adroitly, that her
guard did not see the movement from their position in rear of
. the litter. The curtains instantly fell, the brilliant and storm-
wrapped pageant disappeared in the gorge of the mountains,
and all was still again, save the muffled sounds of the horses'
feet in the snow, marching on to Sultania. Who was she ?
Could it be the mistress of his heart, to whom he had vowed
eternal constancy ? Why should she be travelling with the
ladies of Abbas Mirza ? The recognition set the heart of the
young commander in a flutter at once. The freshness of his
love for her in the Shah's gardens returned to him. He felt
that he loved her with redoubled vehemence. How fortunate
that she was going in the same direction which he must soon
wheel about to, and pursue with his corps. The chances of
seeing her again upon the long winter journey were by no
means improbable. All things are possible to the Oriental girl
when outside the latticed enclosure of the *anderoon*. He exulted in the thought of meeting his mysterious mistress as he
rode on towards the main body of Abbas Mirza's household
troops.

Back over the rocky road the royal ladies had just traversed, moved the young commander's splendid cavalry. The wind whistled past them and the snow beat in their faces; but up and down the mountain sides they rode, now rushing past towns and villages whitened by the storm, and each with its little embastioned fort rising amidst the most romantic sylvan scenes where one could picture to himself the beauty and loveliness of the far-off summer, when it should resume its sway over the hills and valleys; now passing the ruined mosques and walls of the old Persian city, Abhar, where once the captive children of Israel were settled on their removal from Jerusalem; and then sweeping through Kurumdara, with its circle of neat and lovely Satellite villages, watered by numerous rills from the adjacent mountains. They skirted the sequestered village of Sian Kala, sheltered in a valley, and finally ascended a great hill, upon whose summit they paused, and looked down upon the ancient city of Sultania, with its domes and minarets rising in all the majesty of the old eastern architecture.

Upon this elevated ground where they were formed in line to await the advent of the Crown Prince a Kurdish peasant at work once found a royal sarcophagus containing the skeleton of an ancient queen of Iran, whose name and identity are lost. A golden diadem encircled her brows, and in it were set precious stones of wonderful size and lustre. On her wrists and ankles were bracelets of pure gold. A string of lovely pearls, of the most perfect color, was resting upon her breast. All were taken to the Shah of Persia, and to this day the wise men of Iran cannot name or conjecture what ancient female sovereign was their owner. Perchance ages before the foundations of the great sepulchral mosque of Sultan Mahomed Rhoda were laid in Sultania, this ancient queen was entombed here under a marble canopy whose ruins have, ages ago, been borne away.

While the cavalry stood expectant upon the hill in the storm, the thrice-repeated blast of a bugle announced that the foot of Abbas Mirza was in the stirrup, and the royal cavalcade were leaving Sultania to follow the advance guard and the muffled ladies of the Prince's *anderoon.* They were upon the road between Tabreez and Teheran. The former was the capital of the Crown Prince of Persia, who was coming southerly to attend the great feast of *Nowroose* at Teheran, the capital and residence of his royal father, the Shah. They were far away in the north-western corner of Persia, in the worst season of the whole year; and yet in summer this quarter of the kingdom is lovely and salubrious. They would soon, however, reach warmer lati-

tudes; and this reflection yielded the troops some consolation
as they shivered in the terrific and icy gale which swept over
the elevation where they stood looking down upon Sultania.
At length they were diverted by a grand flourish of trumpets
which announced the advent of the Prince Royal and his escort
of nobles and royal cavalry. With alacrity they dashed out
from Sultania on their fiery steeds, and resolutely faced the
gale, riding swiftly up the rise toward Teheran and the troops
of Alfonso which awaited them. A company of one hundred
and fifty cavalry came first, in all the glory of Oriental splendor, and bearing aloft long bamboo lances. The fury of the
snow-storm could not entirely disguise the richness of their garb
and the silver and gold trappings of their horses dashing on in
all the fiery impetuosity of their Asiatic blood. Then came
the noble soldier and enemy of the Muscovites, Abbas Mirza.
The superb black steed of this great prince kept side by side
with that of his son, Mahomed Mirza, and his brother, Malek
Khassum Mirza, both dark-eyed youths of twelve.

Trained to the saddle from his earliest youth, like all the
Persian boys, Abbas Mirza was one of the most daring and
graceful riders in the kingdom. He rode now swiftly up the
rise, attended by his illustrious Khans, who followed close behind him. The young hero of the Turcoman frontier watched
his advent eagerly. In the rear of the Persian nobility came a
splendid body of five hundred *goolams*, the *élite* of the national
cavalry, armed with long guns, swords of Ispahan, pistols, and
daggers. The silver chains upon their horses' necks rattled at
every step as they rode at ease, now wandering away from the
line of march, and then regaining it swiftly and at will. The
peshkidmats followed after, upon powerful horses, bearing the
kaliouns of the nobles and officers, with kettles of burning coals
swinging from the saddle-girths, with cans of water, Turkish to-
bacco, and all the appliances necessary to put in operation
those complicated Oriental smoking mediums. Heavily laden
as they were, the steeds of the *peshkidmats* were expected to
keep up with the most rapid pace of the cavalcade over plain
or valley.

As the Prince Royal reached the summit of the hill, and his
dark, searching eyes took in the whole line of Alfonso's splendid troops, his thoughtful countenance lighted with animation.
The soldierly instinct in him was aroused. He was delighted
and amazed. Turning in his saddle he raised his right arm in
signal to one who rode behind him. A black steed, such as

Alexander might have deemed worthy of a king's bestowal, dashed immediately to the side of Abbas Mirza where one of the young princes made room for him. His rider was clothed in a garb of pure white. He was the royal astrologer, whom all Persian princes consult when undertaking a journey and upon the march.

"Zenayi," he said, when the Ghebre had reined his steed to the Crown Prince's pace, "you have not told me half this young officer's merits. The Czar of Russia has no finer squadrons in all his army."

"They are modelled upon the Russian horse," replied the Ghebre. "Your royal father assented to Alfonso's request, that the Muscovite discipline and drill should be adopted for his Turcoman expedition."

"And these are the heroes of the Turcoman war?" inquired the Prince.

"They are, every man of them," replied Zenayi; "and yonder is their commander."

He pointed far down the line of motionless horsemen to the spot where Alfonso, on the back of Al-Borak, awaited the moment when his cavalry should receive his order to salute the Prince.

"When we have passed on to the plain below," said Abbas Mirza, "and his men have fallen into the line of march, summon the commander to my side."

The astrologer signified his approbation of his royal master's purpose and fell back then to his former position among the Khans. As the royal cavalcade rode past the hero of Toorkomania, the eyes of Abbas Mirza gave him a searching glance. Alfonso, as the prince courteously returned his military salute, gave him a look in return which burned into his royal recollection for a lifetime. Two noble soldiers had met for the first time, and the younger saw in that one glance that he was appreciated by the potent head of the Persian army. His orders soon rang out clear and distinct amid the whistling of the storm and the whirl of the snow. His cavalry fell in behind the royal cavalcade to the music of the bugles. The augmented train of Asiatics moved on grandly toward Teheran, passing down on to the plain whitened by the snow.

When at length the Ghebre rode back to execute the command of the Prince Royal, he said, after greeting his pupil:

"You have made a favorable impression upon the Prince by your discipline. He has summoned you to his side. Speak freely to him now upon your ideas of army matters. Fear not to notify him of the abuses in the army. He is honorable and just, and your complaints will be heard and buried in his royal soul. He will remember every sensible word you utter, will honor you for your candor, and will reward you for every valuable hint on military subjects you may proffer. Go on now to his presence, and may Ormuzd assist you."

The young commander, with a single word of excitation to Al-Borak, was off like the wind for the front. He dashed through the snow which whitened the wayside, passed the *goolams*, flung salutes to the Khans as he flew past, and reined in his steed beside the man who, he believed, more than any other, held his military future in his hands. He was with the great soldier and favorite of Persia at last. With that winning suavity which had won him thousands of hearts, Abbas Mirza greeted his young general. In the splendor and self-possession of his ripe manhood, being apparently about half way between thirty and forty years of age, the Governor of Tabreez impressed all who approached him with the idea that he possessed the ancient principles of truth, simplicity, and general interest for the welfare of his country. Mental power was traced upon his brow, and in the gleam of his dark eyes. He uttered now a few words of the most gracious welcome. His smile put Alfonso at ease in a moment.

"Persia is indebted to you, brave soldier, for her present tranquillity. Your name is reverenced already by her patriots Upon our arrival at Teheran, your services will meet with proper recognition. Our noble Zenayi has often mentioned your military merit, and your fitness for command. Your own acts have now justified the eulogy of your good friend. What are your wishes and your wants, that I may present them to the Shah?"

Seeing that Alfonso was silent, he said again, "What are your wishes? Speak boldly, for you address a soldier and lover of Persia."

"The permanent command of my present corps, that I may perfect them for our day of vengeance upon the Muscovites."

The clear, bold, manly tones seemed to touch the Prince in the hidden depths of his nature. His eyes lighted with a kindred fire. He turned warmly to his companion, as he said :

"Our generals who distinguish themselves expect and receive gold from the treasury, and promotion to more extensive commands."

The young commander, with his piercing gaze directed to the Prince, reiterated simply his request.

"I desire only the present command."

"Has money no charms for you, young man ?"

"No, your Royal Highness. I am a soldier of Persia, and the empire needs every *touman* in the treasury. The army chest should be filled with the self-denials of the officers who love Persia better than gold. The Muscovites can only be defeated at last by the sacrifices of the Persian people."

"Noble words ; young soldier. I would that Allah would put your words into the mouths of all our Khans. Your demand is modest, and our earnest effort shall be directed to obtain it from the Shah. I owe to you gratitude for preserving my brother from the desert robbers. I now owe to you a higher gratitude, as one who falters not in his offerings of blood and treasure for my Persia. You have suffered for her : you will suffer again. From this hour, Abbas Mirza is your friend. Ask anything from me in the name of my country, and you will be heard. You shall have your present command over your troops, but it shall be extended. If you can make five thousand men good soldiers, you can properly be entrusted with the drilling of double the number. I shall ask that five thousand cavalry be added to your command, and that your pay be doubled."

"I decline the additional pay before it is offered," was the response.

"What if it is forced upon you ? "

"Then I shall present it to the army chest, to be reserved for the Muscovite war."

"Is your purpose firm ?"

"As iron, your Royal Highness."

The Prince Royal smiled, as he watched the intense interest his son, Mahomed Mirza, was manifesting in the young commander. The boy seemed to be thrilled with his admiration for the handsome face and deep enthusiasm of the hero of the Turcoman war.

"What would *you* do with this obstinate soldier, my son ? " he said jocosely to the youthful Prince.

"I have no power, your Royal Highness," was the prompt response.

"And if you had ? " continued the father.

"Then I would put all the Shah's body-guard under this

officer, and have them drilled to keep in line, and fight to some purpose when the Cossacks come down upon us."

"The idea is not a bad one, my son," replied Abbas Mirza, with a laugh. "We must think of this. The highest discipline will be demanded for a northern war, sooner than many suspect."

After a brief silence he resumed, addressing the commander of cavalry :

"You may now return to your troops. Upon our arrival at Tehcran, you will find that tents have been provided for your corps outside of the walls. But at the feast of *Nowroose*, when the Shah receives the homage of his subjects, present yourself in full uniform in the spacious area, shaded with trees before the palace. Do not fail to be there, for it will be the hour of your long-expected recognition."

After these words, he waved his hand in token of dismissal, and the commander, turning his steed out of the line of march, rode back along the long array of troops to his own command. Scarcely had he reached his men, when the word of command was heard by the advance guard. They spurred on, and soon the whole cavalcade were flying like *deevs* towards the capital. The air was growing softer with every mile of progress ; the snow was thinning out ; the sky was growing clearer, and the flat-roofed houses of the towns were coming more clearly into view.

CHAPTER XVII.

AT length, after a tedious march, they reached a latitude where the snow had all vanished. The air was balmy like spring, and the great plain spread out so level before them, that with one accord the whole cavalcade extended their front into one great line, each horseman, prince, and private contending for the mastery in speed. On they spurred, shouting in glee, brandishing their bamboo lances, firing their pistols, and racing like madmen. Abbas Mirza took the lead at length upon the superb stallion which had borne him unharmed through many an encounter with beast, and human foe. The princes of the East rely upon their steeds for flight when the battle is adverse. The royal stud of Persia is un-

matched for beauty and speed. Arriving at length upon a
great hill, he paused alone to await the coming up of his escort.
What was his amazement to see that Alfonso and his troops
had not joined in the wild sport of the *run*, but lingered far
behind the disordered *goolams*, maintaining perfect discipline.
They had deployed from close column by squadrons upon
reaching the great plain, and were now seen in the distance
advancing with the precision of veterans. The sight was imposing, and Abbas Mirza remained motionless upon the eminence and allowed the *goolams* and Khans to come up with him
and pass on towards Teheran, while he tarried with his astrologer to watch the evolutions of the young commander's cavalry.

It was evident enough that the advancing line, with their
drawn sabres flashing in the sun, and the wings extending far
out to either side in dazzling array, was under the guidance and
discipline of a master mind in the art of war. Suddenly the
glittering line appeared to hear some talismanic word, for with
a mighty shout which arose evenly and grandly upon the distance, they quickened their pace and dashed onward towards
the Prince and the Ghebre. Nearer and nearer came the
glittering line of sabres, not a horse lagging behind his fellows,
not a wavering indication in any section of the array, but all
dashing on in such perfect uniformity of carriage and pace that
at times the sabre points gave the illusion of a single bar of
glittering steel advancing broadly through the air. The Ghebre
anxiously scanned the face of his royal master. It wore the
immobility of Saladin. But the dark eyes were blazing with
delight and appreciation. Some storm of emotion was waking
up in the great patriot's soul, for his cheek was flushed as he
sat there motionless upon his panting steed and gazed upon the
glorious charge which seemed to come forward with the invincibility of destiny. He was thinking of Russia, his foe, the unrelenting scourge of his father, and the future scourge of himself and his children. He was thinking of his Persia, with its
naked crags, and its flower-enamelled valleys, of its temples of
the Present, and its glorious marble monuments of the heroic
Past, of the people who looked up to him in entreaty and unbounded faith, of the mothers who held aloft to him their infants
and begged from him the integrity and the safety of the land
where they had first drawn breath. And as his soldierly eyes
observed the method and the blended power of the advancing
men of Persia, his very soul flushed as his cheeks flushed with
pride and hope and the consciousness of coming power.

Suddenly within gunshot of the height upon which he stood, and while his ears had just begun to catch the thundering *thud* of the thousands of hoofs upon the earth the dazzling line of steel shivered and broke, sweeping away in regular masses of glittering stars which the parting squadrons seemed to bear away to the front and rear upon the upturned points of their sabres. A single voice, of strange distinctness and thrilling power, arose at intervals upon the air, guiding the squadrons which swept away to their new positions. It was the voice of the hero of Toorkomania giving the preparatory commands of the general commanding. They passed away then to the right of the Prince Royal in close column, their commander being on the directing flank of the leading subdivision of his command. As the compact masses of horsemen moved on towards the capital following the route taken by the *goolams*, Abbas Mirza, and the Ghebre turned their horses' heads towards the southeast and followed after.

It was long before the Prince broke silence, and the Ghebre was unable to fathom the mysterious abstraction of his master. But he knew instinctively that Alfonso had passed already into high favor. Skilled himself in the science of war, as he was in every other science, the unfathomable Zenayi had realized now that his pupil had brought his men to the highest perfection of physical and moral discipline. His royal master must, with his keen perceptions, have remarked it too. Quick to recognize excellence in any department, the Prince would now advance Alfonso. Suddenly the silence was broken.

"Zenayi, the whole army of Persia, excepting only the artillery, must be reorganized at once."

"Your Royal Highness reiterates my own idea of last year."

"I remember your suggestion, my faithful Zenayi. I realize now its value. You never advised me to my detriment or the injury of Persia."

"Ormuzd grant I never may!" was the fervent ejaculation.

"You never summon Allah to your aid, Zenayi," said the Prince, with a smile.

"No, my beloved master. Zenayi calls only upon the *oldest* God of Persia. The Parsee and the Ghebre name him Ormuzd (great king), "*the luminous*," "*the brilliant*," a manifestation only of Zerwan (without beginning or end), "*the incomprehensible*."

"But Allah is the God of the world as well as of Persia," replied the Prince, pleasantly.

"Aye, your Royal Highness; Ormuzd rules the universe by whatever name he may be called. Even the African boy, from the borders of the great Karroo desert, points to the heavens, and calls him *Utika,* " the Beautiful."

"We will not contend about words, my good Zenayi. By whatever name Allah may be called, we owe him the allegiance of a good heart and a good life."

"That is the essence of truth and of religion, my royal master. But seè! we are approaching Siahdan."

He pointed out the town ahead of them, and putting spurs to their horses the two dashed on, passed the orderly squadrons of Alfonso, and overtook the *goolams* and Khans, and with them passed in full career the town of Siahdan, where a new cavalcade, commanded by the Prince's brother, Ali Nackee Mirza, dashed in behind them, all hurrying on to the great feast of *Nowroose.* At the walled town of Casvin a great multitude poured out to salute them as they passed. Armed with guns and lances, the crowd were ranged in double lines, and greeted the cavalcade with music, athletic games, and silken banners of blue, on which were blazoned the lion and the sun. At every town new accessions came to their ranks of gallant Asiatics on fiery steeds. When at last the towers and walls of Teheran appeared before them in the plain, with its huge background of towering mountain peaks, overshadowed by the still loftier peak of Demewand, a grand pageant of troops, nobles, and elephants, the latter clad in scarlet and gold, came forth from the gates to meet them and welcome them to the great yearly feast.

The force of cavalry under the command of Alfonso was halted a mile and a half outside of the walls of Teheran. Here a camp had been provided for them as Abbas Mirza had said. The young commander was not long in ascertaining the localities and distances about him. He soon discovered that Negauristan, so memorable for him, was between his camp and the city. It was only a mile from his tent to the gardens where he had met the mistress of his heart, and whispered to her his vows. His magnificent hospital, where he had been so tenderly nursed, and where intrigue had secured him the command of the Turcoman expedition, would be passed by him whenever he entered Teheran. He could see from his camp the luxuriant trees and the walls of the royal palace above the enclosure of the luxurious *anderoon.* In passing the place on his way to the city, it was possible for the lovely inmates of

Negauristan to recognize him through their latticed windows. But to his eyes they were as effectually veiled as if they were in their graves. Nevertheless it was pleasant to dream, as he rode along daily to the city on the back of Al-Borak, that the sweet eyes of his mistress were looking forth upon him, and her tender heart beating itself like a bird against the walls of her prison. What had become of the lady who signalled him from the curtains of the *tack-i-ravan*, he could not discover. He was convinced of her identity with the mistress of his heart, but he could only ascertain from the officers of the *goolams* that the ladies and their special guard had always kept in advance of Abbas Mirza, from the time of leaving Tabreez until their arrival at Teheran.

He was bitterly disappointed at having no opportunity of being near her on the journey, for well he knew that once she was within any *anderoon* he might as well expect to be in contact with the moon as with her. The probabilities were that he would never again be honored with apartments in the *anderoon* of the Shah. The extraordinary combination of circumstances which had given him a hospital there once was not likely to occur again. With all these discouraging reflections mingled surmises as to who she was. He felt satisfied from her own words in the garden that she was the wife of no man. She was not Ayesha. Then who was she? He was perpetually propounding this question to himself, and as frequently recollecting that Irene was the only living being who was likely to solve the enigma for him. But to this brilliant schemer he dared not mention the subject. She was ludicrously enough entangled in the misunderstanding regarding Ayesha. But friend as she was to his ambitions, it was questionable if she would forward his love affairs. There was just enough of instinct in his composition to teach him that the lovely Irene (herself a mystery) had manifested extraordinary interest in the young officer herself. There was sufficient reason for believing that she would not repulse rudely any tenderness shown to herself on the part of Alfonso. And added to his own self-conceit in the matter were the suggestive cautions of the Ghebre. "Be careful, Alfonso," said this wise friend, "that you do not mar your projects in life by permitting this brilliant girl to gain the ascendency over your heart. Irene is beyond your reach, and any attempt to gain her love may cost you your head. I do not doubt that your personal fascinations would go a long way with so appreciative a being as she is. She may be above love-making. But whether she is or not, *you* can never gain her, and the attempt is too hazardous for you even to think of it. Were you even known to harbor the hope of winning her hand, you would be strangled without delay. She must remain to you as a mystery of the Persian Court, whom Abbas Mirza and myself are forced to employ in the interest of the empire. Do not jeopardize her happiness and your own success by any heart follies."

He dared not, therefore, expect any light regarding his unknown mistress from Irene. The latter beauty, if jealous, had the power of inflicting death both upon his mistress and himself. If utterly indifferent to him in matters of the heart, she still might be enraged by the knowledge that another woman had baffled her intrigues, and by her superior power with the Shah had assumed into her hands all the management of Alfonso's military fate. He decided for these reasons to allow Irene to live under the delusion that the old woman, Ayesha, was the heroine of the love scene in the gardens of the Shah. But how, when, or where he should ever again meet either Irene or his mistress, was the difficulty of his present condition.

In the midst of these perplexities of the young officer the spring advanced, and the great event of the year, the feast of *Nowroose,* was at hand. He could not look upon this festival with indifference. The Prince Royal had notified him that it would be the occasion of his military recognition at court. How valuable this recognition might be to him he could only conjecture. He found his friend, the Ghebre, who often visited his camp, reticent upon the subject. The Crown Prince would certainly endeavor to secure him the command of five thousand more cavalry. This was certain, as the Prince had promised to use his influence with his royal father to this extent. When the designated time had arrived, Alfonso donned his full uniform, and sought the dread presence of the great potentate of Persia, whose word was the life or death of the subject.

The feast of the *Nowroose,* or that *of the commencement of the new year*, was instituted by the celebrated Jemsheed, the sixth in descent from Noah, whose ark alighted upon Ararat, an ice-clad mountain on the boundary line of Persia and Turkish Armenia. Tradition designates him as the fourth sovereign of Persia of the race of Kaiomurs. This festival has been alike observed by the ancient Magi and the followers of Mahomet. It continues six days. On the first the king bestows marks of his favor on the humblest class of his subjects, addressing the throng from his throne. On the second, he rewards his counsellors and ministers of state. On the third, he recompenses the learned and skillful. On the fourth, he receives his royal relations and the great mass of the nobility. The last two days are devoted to rejoicings, feasting, and horse-racing. It is called also "The Feast of the Waters," in commemoration of the subsidence of the deluge. It corresponds to the Saturnalia of the Romans. During the festival, eggs, dyed or gilded, are mutually presented by the citizens. On the evening preceding the day of its commencement the king sends abroad his *kaalats*, fine shawls and similar gifts as badges of honor to the persons highest in his consideration, who are expected to don them during the festive time. With the Persians the new year commences with the opening of spring, in the last of March. From this festal day, therefore, look for the rapid swelling and bursting of the bud, the sudden upshoot of the grass, the wonderful development of Oriental flowers, and the luxuriance of foliage coming like enchantment.

Passing through the streets of Tcheran, which were thronged by the crowds making their way to the palace — Alfonso slowly and in the full splendor of his military uniform entered a spacious area, shaded with trees and intersected by water, in the centre of which appeared the splendid edifice where the Shah receives the homage of his subjects. About the fountains were china plates loaded with fruits, and pyramids of oranges, pears, apples, grapes, and pomegranates, alternating with vases filled with flowers. Here also were regular rows of the finest china bowls filled with delicious sherbet. In two parallel lines stood the *Khans* and officials, arrayed in costly attire of gold or silver brocade, some wearing the royal *Kaalat*, a pelisse lined with fine furs and covered with the richest embroidery. Their heads were bound with Cashmere shawls of every hue and value. They were all assigned their positions by the grand marshal of the palace. This official was preceded by a Persian bearing before him an enamelled wand surmounted by a golden eagle, which Xenophon declares was the early ensign of Persia.

Then the royal procession made its appearance ; the numerous sons of the king marching in advance and superbly habited in the richest brocade vests and shawl-girdles, from the folds of which glittered the jewelled hilts of their daggers. Each wore a robe of gold stuff lined and collared with delicate sables, falling a little below the shoulder and reaching the calf of the leg. Around their black caps they had wound the finest shawls of Tabreeze. Each wore bracelets of the most brilliant rubies and emeralds just above the bend of the elbow. The personal beauty of these princes was extraordinary, the infusion of Circassian and Georgian blood in the harems having perfected the original Iranic stock till they have become a race of the handsomest men on earth. With fine features, large, dark eyes full of lustre, and possessing graceful stature and noble mien, they advanced to the vicinity of the throne.

At some distance, near the front of the palace, appeared a crowd of *moullahs*, astrologers, and other sages clothed in their more sombre garments of religion and philosophy, every person standing quietly in his place and awaiting the monarch.

A sudden discharge of swivels from the camel corps without, with clangor of trumpets and shouts of the people, announced that the Shah had entered the gate of the citadel. Then came the appalling roar of two royal elephants trained to announce the king. The Shah entered, advanced with the indescribable air and step of the genuine sovereign, easy and graceful in perfect majesty, and seated himself on his throne with ineffable dignity. He was one blaze of jewels which literally dazzled the sight. A lofty tiara of three elevations was upon his head. It was composed entirely of thickly-set diamonds, pearls, rubies, and emeralds, so exquisitely disposed as to form a mixture of the most beautiful colors. Several black feathers and a heron's plume were intermixed with the resplendent aigrettes of this truly imperial diadem, whose bending points were finished with pear-shaped pearls of immense size.

His vesture was of gold tissue, nearly covered with a similar disposition of jewels; and crossing the shoulders were two strings of pearls, the largest in the world. His dress sat close to his person, from the neck to the bottom of the waist, exhibiting a shape as noble as his air. From the waist it descended in loose drapery and was of the same costly materials as the vest. Nothing on earth could exceed the splendor of the broad bracelets round his arms above the elbows, and the belt which encircled his waist. They blazed like fire when the sun's rays met them. The jewelled band on the right arm, called " The Mountain of Light," and that on the left, called " The Sea of Light," were the superb diamonds placed in the Persian regalia after the sack of Delhi. The conquests of Nadir Shah had secured them for the monarchs of Iran. Of the sixty millions of *toumans* of treasure carried by this chief to Persia, nothing was so highly prized as these transcendent stones.

The throne brought forth for this occasion was a platform of pure white marble, raised a few steps from the pavement and carpeted with shawls and cloth of gold, on which the king sat in the fashion of his country, while his back was supported by a large cushion encased in a network of pearls. The spacious apartment in which this seat of majesty was erected was open from the roof of the building nearly to the earth, on the side opposite to the assembled people, and was supported in front by two twisted columns of white marble fluted with gold. The interior of the saloon was profusely decorated with carving, gilding, Arabesque painting, and looking glass, which latter material was in a manner interwoven with all the other wreathing ornaments, gleaming and glittering in every part from the vaulted ceiling to the floor. Vases of flowers and others filled with rose-water were arranged about the apartment, though they could scarcely be' seen from the close ranks of the young princes who crowded near to their royal parent.

CHAPTER XVIII.

WHILE the great King was approaching his throne, the whole assembly, with one accord, continued bowing their heads to the ground, till he had taken his place. A dead silence then ensued; the whole presenting a most magnificent and indeed awful appearance; the stillness being so profound among so vast a concourse, that the slightest rustling of the trees was heard, and the softest trickling of the water from the fountains in the marble canals. The face of the Shah seemed exceedingly pale — of a polished marble hue; with the finest *contour* of features and eyes, dark, brilliant, and piercing; a beard black as jet, and of a length which fell below his chest over a large portion of the effulgent belt which held his diamond-hilted dagger.

In the midst of this solemn stillness, while all eyes were fixed on the bright object before them, which sat indeed as radiant and immovable as the image of Mithras itself, a volley of words, bursting at one impulse from the mouths of the *moullahs* and astrologers, made one start, and interrupted the gaze. This strange outcry was a heraldic enumeration of the great King's titles, dominions, and glorious acts, with a panegyric on his courage, liberality, and extended power. When this was ended, with all heads bowing to the ground, and the air ceasing to vibrate with the sounds, there was a pause.

Then his Majesty spoke. The effect was even more startling than the sudden bursting forth of the *moullahs.* For this was like a voice from the tomb, so deep, so hollow, and at the same time so penetratingly loud. Having addressed the people he looked toward Zenayi, who stood at one side, robed as usual in white, and raised his royal arm, beckoning to him to advance. The Ghebre took the hand of the commander of cavalry, who stood near him, and informed him that he was expected by the sovereign, to advance to the foot of the throne.

Totally unprepared for this summons, Alfonso advanced with the astrologer, while thousands of eyes were bent upon him. After proceeding a few paces the two paused, and bowed. They then advanced into the centre of the court, or open space, and bowed again. They then disengaged their feet from their slippers (having red Kerseymere socks, a kind of boot without sole under them) and drew still nearer to the throne. They then made a third bow. Proceeding then to the foot of the throne, they paused and saluted the monarch the fourth time. The Shah then uttered a few words of the most gracious welcome, and made a sign for them to be seated. A luxurious divan of silk was awaiting them, and upon it the two were at once seated in the fashion of Persia, with their eyes fixed upon the King. Then a herald advanced, and in a loud tone, which thrilled the multitude, enumerated the services of the young officer of cavalry, from the rescue of the Shah's son until the conclusion of the Turcoman war. He announced the gratitude of the royal family, and of all Persia for the valuable and heroic services of Alfonso, and proclaimed that from that hour he was invested with the command of ten thousand troops, to be practised in the cavalry drill, which had rendered the five thousand Turcoman heroes so effective. His refusal of additional pay was also announced, which caused a murmur of applause to run over the assembled thousands

When silence again reigned, the monarch of all Persia arose to his feet and descended the steps of his throne, pausing upon the lowest tread. An attendant advanced, bearing a large golden tray, upon which rested a magnificent sabre of Ispahan, whose gold sheath and handle were glistening with jewels. With his own hands, the Shah invested the officer with the costly weapon, amid the murmurs of approbation from the crowd, and then bidding the two to be reseated, he returned to his original posture on his throne.

Then a noble and commanding figure came to the foot of the throne, majestic and beautiful. His advent seemed to electrify the multitude, for their faces lighted with enthusiasm, and many eyes filled with tears of joy. They could apparently scarcely restrain their exultation, at sight of that countenance, to the decorum proper for the presence of royalty. Then a profound silence ensued. With breathless interest, they saw their favorite, Abbas Mirza, the Prince Royal of Persia, hold aloft something which glistened like a star, turning it about in the air, till every eye was fixed upon it. They knew it then right well, and they knew that by the usage of the court decorum was for the moment abolished. Wild cheers of thousands of excited soldiers and citizens rang out upon the air, and swelling away over the city were caught up by the people outside the court of the palace, and re-echoed until the thunder of cannon from the walls shook the air. The great honor of Persia was to be given to the hero of Turcomania. Pale and agitated, Alfonso knelt upon the embroidered cushion placed for him. The limbs which had never trembled in the horror of deadly battle, trembled now. The Ghebre was obliged to give him an arm to steady him upon the cushion, and Abbas Mirza, placing the point of his own royal sword upon the officer's shoulder, in the ceremony of investiture, felt the blade tremble in his grasp. The words of the ceremony were soon over, and the Prince Royal, bending over to the kneeling officer, secured to the breast of his military coat, and over his heart, the magnificent badge of the *Order of the Sun Lion.* Alfonso arose to his feet, and was led away, the happiest and most excited man in all Persia. He was now before the nation. In times of great public danger, he might be summoned to the war councils of the Shah, and his badge of honor was the pledge that his advice would be patiently listened to, and treated at least, with respect. He was by this investiture, in fact, created a military councillor of the Shah, an honor shared by few of the noble Khans of the empire. The grand marshal of the palace met him a few paces away from the throne, accompanied by the bearer of the golden eagle, and first bowing low to him, stepped forward, and flung upon his shoulders

a pelisse of scarlet silk, lined and collared with costly white
furs, upon which was embroidered in gold the likeness of the
badge of the *Order of the Sun Lion*, with which he had just
been invested.   If summoned at any time to a war council by
the Shah, this would be the garment he was expected to wear.
Alfonso and the Ghebre then fell back to their original places
in the audience, and were instantly served with bowls of most
delicious sherbet.   Then came an attendant, and held before
them a large silver tray, on which lay a heap of coin, silver
shy and gold *tomauns*.   Imitating the action of Zenayi, he
held out both hands, according to the custom of the great festival of *Nowroose*, to be filled with this royal largess.

As the ceremony of rewarding different meritorious citizens
went on before the throne, in accordance with immemorial
usage, Alfonso had leisure to compose himself and familiarize
his sight with the scenes and faces about him.   Looking up to
one side of the open court he detected what he had failed to
notice before — the lattice of an *anderoon*. 'He felt confident
that this screen must hide the faces of the Shah's women, from
its similarity of construction to others he had seen.   He whispered his surmise to the Ghebre, who assented, and informed
him that the place was crowded with the loveliest women in
Persia, the property of the monarch, who were allowed every
year to congregate behind the lattice and witness the ceremonies of *Nowroose*.   He asked the Ghebre if other ladies than
the Shah's wives were peering out there ; and was gratified to
learn that female relatives, daughters, and friends of the royal
ladies were without doubt looking down upon him at that moment.   The heart of the young officer warmed at the thought
that perchance the mysterious beauty of the Shah's garden was
looking upon him in this moment of his supreme triumph.
His eyes were often turned up to the lattice ; but not a thing
could he discover but an occasional color of some bright silk
against the cross-bars of the wood, as some unknown beauty
pressed more closely against the lattice, in her eagerness to
peep through.

While he stood there watching the *anderoon*, and cursing the
fate which probably would debar him from ever again folding
his mistress in his arms, he was surprised to find himself touched
upon his hand by a *moullah* who had crowded up close to him
in the throng.   The action was repeated, until it was evident
the priest was endeavoring to attract his attention.   The
moullah, seeing that his object was attained, put his finger to his

lip covertly in token of silence, and then, unseen by the Ghebre, slipped into the officer's hand a fragment of paper. When he could do so without observation, Alfonso looked upon the paper and read these words :

"In the name of Persia, give me the password to your camp to-night. I will send a messenger to you there. IRENE."

With immediate acquiescence, the officer whispered in the ear of the *moullah* three words, constituting a single name. The man smiled, and soon after made his way slowly out of the throng. Seeing that the multitude were commencing to leave the court, and that the Shah had gone out by another passage, Alfonso and the Ghebre walked slowly out into the streets of the city, conversing upon the happy termination of all their schemes to gain a footing at the court. The astrologer had been in incessant communication with his pupil by trusty messengers from the first planning of the Turcoman expedition until the cavalry camp had broken up at Kasbin. The resources of Zenayi in the matter of trustworthy agents and facilities for obtaining early knowledge of court intrigues appeared to be inexhaustible. He informed Alfonso that it was the purpose of the Government to establish a permanent camp near Teheran, and that his present camp would be the site selected, and he would be retained as its commander. After mutual congratulations upon the satisfactory shape Persian military matters were assuming, the officer remounted Al-Borak near the gate of the city and rode out to his camp, Zenayi remaining in the city.   .   .   .   .

The midnight moon sailed away in unveiled loveliness above the Persian camp. Although so near to the city and in the midst of the great festival of *Nowroose*, the tents were noiseless, the troops were sleeping. No belated stragglers were coming in to arrest the attention of the watchful sentinels, whose sabres flashed occasionally in the moonlight as they moved. The sentinels were as alert as if the war was still going on and they might at any moment be aroused for battle. There was no other indication of life abroad save the occasional stamp of the cavalry horses as they stood in long rows, each fastened by the right forefoot to a picket rope on the ground. It was wonderful that among so many thousands of troops such quiet and order should reign. But the soldierly spirit of their commander had worked like a wizard's spell upon the men. Something seemed to whisper to them that in imitating him were safety and future

advantage to each of them. They were already recognized
and treated by the people as heroes; the Shah had presented
to them a handsome sum of money for their families, and future
rewards were promised if their soldierly perfection should continue. They knew that no Persian troops had ever before
received such careful and considerate attention from a commander. From admiring the skill and courage of their chief
they had now come to love him for the unfaltering kindness
and watchfulness for their individual interests he ever manifested.
His face was familiar in every tent, and they anticipated from
his leadership in the future great renown and spoils. He had
excited their rivalry with other corps of the army, and promised
to place them as far ahead of the other troops as the other
troops were ahead of the keepers of the bazars. His wonderful magnetic influence was upon them, and they were ready to
die for him, and for the Persia he extolled to them in such eloquent language. Some enchanter's wand surely had fallen to
him, so silent and orderly was the great camp, stretching away
in the full glory of the moon.

One tent alone, a huge circular pavilion, exhibited signs of
life. It was illumined by a lamp, and before it was a sentinel.
A superb carpet from Tabreez covered the ground within;
and in the midst of a pile of cushions, which were both bed and
table, was stretched the young chief, busily studying a number
of maps of North-western Persia. The brilliant lamp was
suspended from the top of the pavilion by a long silver chain,
and hung low, nearly touching the officer's dark hair, as he
reclined there at ease, but intensely thoughtful. He had
spread the maps on the cushions about him, and turned from
one to another from time to time. There were maps of the
provinces of Iran-Ajemi, Azerbijan, Ardelan, Ghilan, Mazan-
deran — all in North-western Persia, or touching on the Caspian Sea. There were two or three maps also of Armenia and
Georgia, and these appeared to occupy the greater part of his
attention. His eager, handsome face was bent low to these
maps, that he might trace out the minute subdivisions, and the
route of the smaller streams, which are always so unsatisfactorily
traced and defined on maps. His long, black moustache nearly
drooped upon the maps as he studied them. He seemed determined to make himself master of the subject before he
dropped it, and recurred again and again to the maps after
long periods of reverie.

His studies were interrupted by a sudden challenge just

before his tent. The hour was so late, that the interruption aroused his curiosity. He listened to the voice of the intruder, giving the password, "*Futteh Ali Shah.*" He had selected the name of the sovereign of Persia, in honor of his condescension in bestowing the jewelled sabre with his own hands. He heard then a slight altercation between the sentinel and the stranger, regarding gaining admittance to the tent. In another instant the curtains of the pavilion were thrust apart, and the head of the sentinel appeared. The soldier announced a messenger who had received the password before the throne of the Shah.

"It is right. Admit him," said the commander.

The soldier saluted his chief and withdrew. Alfonso fixed his eyes upon the entrance to the pavilion, expecting to discover the figure of the *moullah*, to whom he had entrusted the countersign. To his surprise, a soldier of the royal artillery, then under the efficient command of British officers sent to the Shah from India, appeared at the entrance, gave him the military salute, and advancing a few paces into the pavilion, halted respectfully. The young Persian was handsome, but slender, and his eyes dazzling in their softness and beauty. He was evidently a son of some Khan, and might be serving in the artillery with a view to a future lieutenancy in that superb and renowned corps of the army. The English officers had raised the Persian artillery to an efficiency equal to the best in the English service.

"Advance and deliver your message!" said the commander.

The soldier came nearer into the fullness of the lamp-light, and halted again. Standing there in the splendor of the artillery uniform, and with the light shining full upon his fair, Georgian face, his lustrous eyes, and dark, drooping moustache, he seemed to the cavalry chief as handsome a young soldier as his eyes had ever rested upon.

"I come from Irene," was the response, delivered in a low, cautious tone, as if fearful of being heard outside.

"I was certain of that," replied the chief, noting the anxious glance the soldier cast towards the direction of the sentinel. "But come nearer, and be seated upon this cushion. Then we can converse without hazard of being heard."

The handsome Persian advanced, and occupied the cushion in the fashion of his country. Alfonso gave a searching glance into the messenger's face, and then exclaimed, "It is Irene ! Woman, are you mad?"

"No; not mad," she replied, with intense feeling and earnestness; "but there is terrible danger to Persia gathering fast, and for this alone am I here, at the hazard of my life and my honor."

"I tremble for you, Irene," he said. "You appreciate your danger."

"Yes, yes," she said, with a gesture of impatience. "But you do not hear me. *Persia, Persia* is in danger!"

She emphatically pronounced the name of her country as if that one word caused every other consideration of life or death to sink into insignificance.

"Do not heed my peril or your own," she added, fixing her beautiful eyes upon him. "Perils lie thick and varied before us both, to which this risk of mine to-night will be as the fire of a *caleeoon* to the home of Eblis. Listen to the danger of Persia and hush every other apprehension."

"I am attentive," he replied, raising himself from the recumbent position in which the girl had surprised him and seating himself upon a cushion opposite to her.

"You comprehend, do you not," she said, "the difficulties and disputes which have arisen between Persia and Russia from that wretched treaty of *Gulistan?*"

"I do," he said, amazed to discover that she was about to speak of the very subject upon which his thoughts were engaged when her arrival was announced. "Look at these maps," he continued, pointing to the cushions about him. "I was studying this boundary question when you entered. Go on."

"Did you know," she responded, "that the Emperor of Russia had sent Prince Menzikoff, as ambassador extraordinary, to the Court of Teheran, to reconcile the differences regarding the disputed territory?"

"I did. The Ghebre told me that the ambassador of Nicholas would soon be here."

"Menzikoff is here," she exclaimed, with startling earnestness. "He is here in the city, and he has been *insulted* by the Shah. There will be war if some of these madmen are not stopped."

Her eyes glistened with terrible earnestness. Her listener was fully aroused now.

"*Insulted*, Irene?" The government surely is in the hands of the prudent and the wise."

I thought so too a few hours ago. The Ghebre concurred

with me that there was no serious danger of rupture between the two powers. But there has been an undercurrent of madness which we had not detected, and now war is imminent. Listen to me. Menzikoff has been granted an audience to-day. When he presented the Emperor's letter to the Shah, the latter, instead of taking it in his own hand, the usual mark of respect to a foreign potentate, *made a sign to the Prince to lay it upon a cushion,* a mark of contempt and insult to his royal master."

Alfonso sprang to his feet in the thrill of excitement and apprehension. "There *will be* war. How unfortunate for Persia! We are not half prepared. Why do you come?"

"Simply because *you know* that we are not prepared. You will be summoned to the war council. Your tongue is fire. It will eat into the hearts and brains even of madmen. Go! and denounce this war as only *you* can. I trust the safety of my Persia in your hands. Go to the war council and stop this madness. The blessing of every Persian woman and child will attend your success. Go, and the blood of Irene will flow for you at any time and at every time."

She was wild with excitement, and she had not overrated the danger. He regarded her for an instant, splendid even in her strange garb, pleading for her country.

"How stands Abbas Mirza?" he said.

"For *war!*"

"You know this?"

"Yes; Abbas Mirza is at the bottom of the whole affair."

"And I will have to oppose my counsel to his?"

"You will," she said, steadily regarding the expressions of his superb face. She could read his secret thought like a book. He remained silent in reflection.

"The struggle is going on in your mind between your ambition and your sense of wisdom," she said.

"How can you know that, Irene?"

"By a woman's insight, when she knows that what is dear to her is at stake. You regret to lose the friendship of Abbas Mirza. You *will* lose it; but that loss will only be for a time. Your great qualities will lead him back to you. Oppose him now, and wisdom will be on your side; Zenayi will be on your side, and one other who is potent to help your advancement."

"And who is that other? Ayesha?"

"No. Ayesha will go with Abbas Mirza."

"Then who is that other," he asked.

"*Irene!*" she replied, as she eagerly regarded him.

The commander, whose decisions were rapid and prompt in emergencies, answered her thus:

"I will go on the side of *Irene.*"

The eyes of the girl were full of light, exultant, joyful light.

"Is this decision irrevocable, Alfonso?"

"Irrevocable," he answered firmly.

"And you will denounce the war in the council of the Shah?"

"With all the power that Allah has given me."

CHAPTER XIX.

BEFORE proceeding to detail the stirring scenes which followed rapidly upon the midnight interview between the commander of cavalry and Irene, it is due to the intelligent reader to sketch enough of the historical facts connected with the war of 1826–28 between Persia and Russia, to afford him an idea of the real points of the controversy. The reader's own experience and knowledge of nations will teach him that a brave people are capable of displaying the noblest heroism and self-sacrifice when their country is in danger, no matter what pretences or misrepresentations or errors of the government have involved the nation in the horrors of war. The mysteries of diplomacy are so tortuous in questions of boundary, that the masses of the people may well be pardoned for not comprehending the details of the controversy which terminates in battle. But it is safe to hold that when a people see their territory torn from them gradually and by successive encroachments of a huge, overshadowing power, they must possess some instinct of right and of self-defence when they rise and heroically struggle to prevent that power from despoiling them still more.

The following may be regarded as a fair statement of the grounds upon which Russia based her claim of right to carry on her second war with Persia. No admirer of the former power would be likely to demand for her a more favorable statement.

When Russia in 1812 and 1813 was collecting all her resources to oppose the invasion of Napoleon, and disentangling herself from every embarrassment which might hamper her exertions in a contest in which her existence was at stake, she put an end to the war, then existing between her and Persia, by the treaty of *Gulistan.* In that treaty the boundary between the territory of the two countries on the north-west, toward Georgia, had not been marked out with sufficient distinctness, no other line of demarcation having been assumed than the positions occupied by the belligerent armies, not following either any natural limit, like that of the mountains and rivers, or any succession of artificial works, such as towns and fortresses. The Khanats of Shirvan, Karabun, and Noucha had been ceded to Russia ; but they were still governed by their ancient Khans, who, acknowledging the Emperor Alexander as their sovereign lord instead of the Shah of Persia, still retained their ancient laws and customs, were separated by their religious belief from their Christian superiors, and, while paying formal homage to Russia, preserved their attachment to Persia, cemented as it was by conformity of faith, similarity of language and manners, and ancient recollections. The disputes about the frontier were perpetually renewed. Russia alleged that Persia had taken possession of a tract of country expressly ceded to Russia in the treaty of Gulistan ; while it was certain that Russia, certainly without authority from that treaty, had taken possession of part of the Persian territories on the Lake of Goktscha.

These differences had long been the subject of negotiation between the two courts, and Russia had, in the meanwhile, continued to occupy the disputed ground. No threat or appearance of hostilities had as yet occurred on either side. Russia had offered to restore the territory in question upon the district belonging to her and occupied by Persia being given up in return ; or to exchange it for another tract described to be of far less value, and whose dry and arid soil offered no compensation except the vicinity of the lake. At length it was agreed between General Yermoloff, the Russian commander in Georgia, and Abbas Mirza, the Prince Royal of Persia, that it should be retained by Russia, and that Persia should receive in return a tract of land between the rivers Kapan and Kapanatchy. The sovereign of Persia, however, never ratified this agreement.

Nicholas, immediately on his accession, despatched Prince Menzikoff as ambassador extraordinary to the Court of Teheran, to announce his accession to the throne, and put the finishing hand to the arrangement regarding the line of demarcation; authorizing him, if it should be necessary for the final settlement of the matter, to give up to Persia, in addition to the district of the Kapan, part of the neighboring district of Talyschine. Prince Menzikoff, on his arrival on the frontiers, was treated with the highest respect. Abbas Mirza himself received him at Tauris, and expressed to him the most friendly assurances.

But *Abbas Mirza*, who was heir-apparent, having been named by his father to succeed him, and whom, therefore, Russia had bound herself by the terms of the treaty of Gulistan to recognize as successor, was not favorable to a peace which left so much of the spoils of war in the hands of his adversary. Whether from uncalculating ambition, national antipathy, distrust of Russia, or mere precipitate folly, he had been watching a favorable opportunity for recovering from Russia by force part, at least, of the spoils which she had secured to herself at the peace of 1813. He thought that he had now found it, and that the occupation of the disputed territory by Russia would furnish a good pretext for war, while the discontents of the new subjects of Russia would both be useful instruments in prosecuting it and render it popular at home. The Mahommedans of Georgia were averse to the rule of an infidel; the petty chiefs were dissatisfied with a power which abridged their own prerogatives, and, by its greater strictness in comparison with the supremacy which had been exercised by Persia, compelled them to remember that they were subjects in reality as well as in name. In some places the violence and misconduct of the Russian soldiery and of some of the inferior Russian agents had produced general discontent among the lower orders of the people. In the Persian camp near Sultania a Chousk of Karabang made the following speech to the Shah: "Man, do you call yourself the King of the Mohammedans, and idly pass your time in the harem when Mussulmen are daily abused by infidels? I was obliged to look on while five Russian soldiers violated my wife in Karabang. *I spit at your beard.*"

All these circumstances, exaggerated and enforced by the *moullahs*, the Persian priesthood, had produced a general belief in the country that Georgia was eager to rise in arms against its northern oppressors, and that now was the time for Persia to drive back the neighbor before whose advance she had hitherto been compelled to recede. A solemn appeal in defence of the suffering believers in the Prophet was made to the people by the *moullahs* and despatched to the provinces, to be read in all the mosques; calling into action religious prejudices which are such powerful motives to popular action everywhere, and in the East rise so easily to fanatical enthusiasm.

Abbas Mirza was assisted by the prime minister, Alaiar Khan, who was likewise his brother-in-law; and supported by the public wishes, they prevailed over the pacific dispositions of the King, representing to him how much he would gain in the opinion of all true Mahommedans by standing forth as the champion and avenger of their religion and to what degradation of character he must submit if he refused to listen to the prayers of his brother-believers, groaning under the oppression of an infidel yoke. . . . . .

The above sketch of the historical situation will enable the reader to comprehend the violent passions which agitated every class of society at the Persian capital, and indeed throughout the empire, and crushed to the earth at length the counsels of the wise and the prudent.

Before consenting finally to a declaration of war, Futteh Ali Shah, the Persian monarch, who possessed little independence of character, a mere Bibulus in the conduct of affairs, and ruled by Abbas Mirza and by his favorite women, called a council of war, secretly hoping that the moderate men would prevail, and his reign continue to the end in peace. He knew that a few of his leading generals were disposed to advocate a postponement of hostilities to a future period when all the forces of the empire would be in a more efficient state for war. These sagacious chiefs of his army were all summoned to the conference. But Abbas Mirza, by his own expostulations and by his influence over Ayesha, the Shah's favorite wife, contrived to have a large number of his own adherents among the officers of rank summoned also. The consequence was that the war council in the audience hall of the Shah was more numerous and stormy than any which had assembled within the century. Zenayi, the favorite counsellor of the Prince Royal, was not summoned for two adequate reasons. He was a well-known adherent of the proscribed religion of Zoroaster, and the religious character the war party was rapidly assuming would create a prejudice against his counsels. Orthodoxy was rampant, and true believers alone should guide the counsels of the Shah. Again Abbas Mirza was the only man who wielded influence sufficient to induce the monarch to summon the Ghebre. Zenayi had boldly notified the Prince Royal that he was decidedly antagonistic to his war scheme as being premature and detrimental to the best interests of Persia. Words had run high between these warm friends, and Abbas Mirza determined not to have the Ghebre summoned.

With regard to Alfonso there was a conflict of opinion among the advocates for war. The young hero had risen like a meteor in the regard of the Persian people. His recent brilliant achievements, his powers of fascinating the soldiery, and his precocious talents, coupled with the late public recognition of his military merit, made it hazardous to refuse him admittance to the war council. He unquestionably, by usage, had the right to expect a place in the council, since he had received the decoration of the Order of the Sun Lion. Moreover, certain influential *moullahs* demanded his admittance. He had won their regard by his courtesy and by his strict observance of the regulations of their faith ; and they predicted for him a glorious career in his battles for the true believers.

They justly imputed his splendid successes to his military superiority. They therefore publicly advocated his claim to be heard in the council. The Prince Royal, apprehensive that the gallant cavalry commander would view the war through the eyes of the Ghebre, his friend and instructor, had announced to Ayesha his purpose of having him excluded from the council. To his amazement this favorite wife of the Shah pronounced a brilliant eulogium upon the young commander, and declared that if his wisdom and military discernment were not allowed to be heard in the council she would personally influence the Shah to exclude some of the Prince Royal's adherents also. This decided the question. Ayesha was a power, and her wishes were not to be trifled with or neglected. Alfonso was formally summoned, and Irene and the Ghebre, when they met, as they often did, in secret exulted over their unseen and unknown triumph over " the power behind the throne."

Danae was not more amazed when Jupiter visited her in the form of a shower of gold than was the commander of cavalry to receive this brief note from Irene by the hands of the Ghebre :

" You will be summoned to the war council by the direct interposition of Ayesha. Abbas Mirza was moving to have you excluded. Never hesitate again to tell an old hag she is beautiful."

Alfonso turned the contents of this note over and over again in his mind. Who had interposed this time in his favor? Was it the genuine, *old* Ayesha, or the beautiful substitute of the garden? He was astute enough to know that the Ghebre and his confederate, Irene, were the real movers in his behalf. But upon which woman in the *anderoon* were they working, and were they really conscious that he had a young and beautiful advocate always pleading his cause in the harem, and whose name never appeared? Sometimes it occurred to him that perhaps Ayesha and the unknown beauty were acting in concert in his behalf. Perhaps the veiled beauty was the daughter of Ayesha, and the mother had connived with her to have her receive his admiration with reference to a future marriage. Mothers are ambitious for their daughters as well within as without the walls of the harem. If this supposition were correct, how exasperated Irene would be some day at the discovery. The more he reflected upon this solution of the mystery, the more plausible it appeared to him. If Ayesha, with all her influence over the Shah, was indeed pushing his claims to preferment in the hope of marrying him to her relative what rapid progress might he not make if only he could contrive to be brought into immediate communication with Ayesha herself! How superior a woman must she be, if she were strong enough to turn over to another the flattery which he had sent to herself! He resolved that he would move heaven and earth to secure a personal interview with the Shah's old, but favorite wife. But upon further reflection, he remembered that once discovered in a secret interview with a wife of the monarch, his ambitions would be thwarted and his head fall into a basket.

In the midst of his bewilderment, and while tortured at the fate which separated him even from a glimpse of his unknown mistress, he received a peremptory order to present himself at once at the *citadel* to participate in a council of war. Girding himself with the sabre presented to him by his sovereign, and flinging over his shoulders the scarlet silk pelisse of the Order of the Sun Lion, he summoned a *dehbáshi* or decurion of cavalry to attend him, and mounting to the back of Al-Borak, dashed off toward Teheran. Entering at the Casvin gate, he made his way through the narrow and *crowded* streets, for the festival of the *Nowroose* still continued, and reached the court of the citadel, where his *dehbáshi* took charge of his horse, while he proceeded to the presence of the king. It chanced to be the morning when a review was to take place in the court of the citadel. On his way to the grand saloon, he passed through the great *meidan* where the artillery were stationed. It was crowded with military, infantry, and cavalry, the latter being in readiness to march individually, man and horse, before His Majesty. Their arming was curious, hardly two alike: some bearing muskets; some long spears; others shields, sabres, and pistols; their costumes varying with their weapons. Some were in shirts of mail, with the high black cap of the country. Others wore iron skull-caps, with the scarlet dresses of the country. There were others in warlike garb from top to toe, being completely arrayed in chain armor, with lofty helmets gallantly plumed and wrapped round the frontlet with shawls. Alfonso smiled at the lack of uniformity. It contrasted oddly enough with the long lines of his own superb corps, habited every man alike.

An elevated building overlooking the south side of the *meidan* contained the open chamber whence the Shah was to review the assembled troops. A clangor of trumpets announced His Majesty's entrance, when the cavaliers immediately set forth to gallop singly across the square, flourishing their arms, shaking their spears, and going through all the accustomed exercise of firing, charging, *et cetera*, at full speed. These desperate chargings were performed before avenues of grandees and populace, by the finest horsemen in the world. The Shah was seated at a large open window, and looking with marks of approbation on the dexterity of his troops. His head was covered with the cap of his country, a black lambskin, worn alike by prince and peasant. His robe was of fine gold brocade, having a deep cape of dark sable falling on his shoulders. His under garments were composed of *red* Kashmere shawls of the richest work. Another shawl of deeper hues, but of greater value, bound his waist, in which was stuck a curved dagger, blazing with diamonds, rubies, and emeralds, and hung with a tassel of the largest pearls, with which he occasionally played while he discoursed. Behind him was placed one of his magnificent cushions, totally covered with Oriental network of pearls, and tasselled also at its corners with bunches of the same costly ornaments. Two Persian noblemen stood a few paces from him, one bearing the royal mace or sceptre, the other the shield and sword, each insignia of empire being thickly studded with every kind of precious stone. The boss of the shield was *one entire ruby*, which for size, color, and perfection is not to be matched in the world.

Alfonso had taken his station in the saloon during the

review, standing some distance from the King, and amid a group of military officers, some of whom knew and recognized him. When the review was over, the Shah turned from the window, and after receiving the homage of his chiefs, and addressing a few words to each of them, requested them to be seated upon the divans about him, as the conference would be long. While Abbas Mirza was having a private conversation with his royal father, the hero of Toorkomania had an opportunity to study the face of the King. He traced His Majesty's features line by line, ascertained every detail of his physiognomy, and felt new interest in the varieties of its expression. His complexion was exceedingly pale ; but when he spoke on subjects that excited him, a vivid color rushed to his cheek, but only for a moment, it passed so transiently away. · His nose was very aquiline. His eyebrows ·were full, black, and finely arched with lashes of the same appearance, shading eyes of the most perfect form, dark and beaming ; but at times, full of a fire that kindled his whole countenance, though in general its expression was that of languor. His beard was black as jet, ample and long, and tapering to a point considerably below the hilt of his dagger. The almost sublime dignity which this form of beard added to the native majesty of his features, can scarcely be conceived by an Occidental ; and the smile which often shone through it, ineffably sweet and noble, rather increased than diminished the effect. Yet the enervating style of his life was evident, both in the languid movement of his eye when he sat quiescent, and from the usual hollow tone of his otherwise sonorous voice, but which, like the occasional flashes from his eyes, became powerful when under the influence of animating discourse.

When the private conference between the Shah and his son had terminated, Abbas Mirza took the first place of honor, on a divan near the sovereign, and the council of war was formally opened. The Prime Minister, Alaiar Khan, who sat next below the Prince Royal in the line of dignitaries stretching down the saloon, arose to his feet, and bowing toward the Shah, proceeded to read aloud a document, detailing the grievances to which Persia had, for many years, been subjected by Russia. The gradual absorption of territory by the ·latter power, under one pretence or another, from time to time, and the military struggles that had ensued, were ably portrayed in this State paper, and the dissimulation of Russia in her statements of her case before the world were severely animadverted upon. Her encroachments upon Persian territory on the Lake of Goktscha, notwithstanding the treaty of *Gulistan*, were clearly stated, and the belief expressed that she would never relinquish her hold, unless by force of arms. The same master hand that had traced the lines of this State paper exposed, in language calculated to thrill every patriotic heart, the outrages in their persons, property, and religion, to which Persians had been subjected by the Russian officers and soldiery. Redress had been demanded, but no indications had Nicholas manifested of removing his brutal agents or granting pecuniary indemnity.

The document further recited the universal indignation of the Persian people, and their demand for a war which should hurl back the invaders, and restore the honor and glory of the Empire. Then came an appeal directed to the religious prejudices of the council. Should the infidel forever be allowed to encroach upon the domain of the faithful, until the name of Mahommedan became the synonyme for cowardice and ignominy?

Amid a murmur of applause, faint, but indicating the smothered passions ready to flame out, Alaiar Khan resumed his seat. The Shah was deadly pale. He saw, as every chief present saw, that Persia had a good excuse for war, and that her reasons had been summed up and presented by a superb intellect. Few present doubted regarding the authorship of the document which demanded blood. It was the work of Abbas Mirza, the heir-apparent to the throne of Persia, and the man who had the greatest interests at stake. The favorite of the people demanded war.

CHAPTER XX.

*" For Pleasure and Revenge
Have ears more deaf than adders to the voice
Of any true decision."* — TROILUS AND CRESSIDA.

AMID the profound silence which ensued upon the reading of the document, was heard the faint rattle of the pearls as the Shah played nervously with the tassel of his dagger. At length the startling hollowness of the monarch's voice sounded through the hall, requesting an expression of opinion from any chief who had aught to say to strengthen the statements just presented in favor of a war with Nicholas of Russia. Then one by one the advocates for war arose to their feet, and urged further reasons for hostilities, or suggested specific plans and arrangements for the campaign. Respectfully they waited for each other, no one among that intensely agitated throng appearing hasty, or anxious to precede his neighbor in rising to his feet. At length all the advocates for war had spoken, save only the commander-in-chief of the Persian army, Abbas Mirza, upon whose shoulders must rest all the responsibilities of the campaign. The Shah, turning to the silent chief, requested his opinion. The Prince Royal arose to his feet, and with ineffable dignity pronounced calmly the following words, and then resumed his seat :

"Your Majesty, I *favor* the war, for the reasons so ably advanced by my brother soldiers."

The effect was superb.

Who now would have the audacity to assert an opposing opinion to the great weight of military authority cast on the side of war? The keen eyes of Abbas Mirza darted glances into the faces of the few military leaders who had refrained from speaking, and ominously had remained quiescent upon the divans. The Shah looked anxiously and nervously in the same direction. Would any able expositor of the necessities for peace arise from those silent divans? He hesitated a moment before he would summon them, one by one, to utter the irrevocable words which would become a part of the annals of the empire. And while the fearful silence reigned, ominous sounds ascended through the great open window which looked down upon the huddled masses of troops and citizens upon the grand *meidan.* With the instinct of people upon the eve of some great civil commotion, they surmised what was going on in the royal hall above. Their wives, their children, their country, their religion, their homes were all involved in what was going on *there.* At any moment dove-eyed Peace or bloody, hideous War might beckon to them from that royal window. And they were agitated, heaving from side to side like waves of the sea, and still eagerly gazing upward for a signal. They were growing impatient, and cries were beginning to break over the throng. "*War, war, war*" was the tenor of the sounds — at first the individual cry of the bolder men, then waxing louder, wider, fuller, until the whole multitude took up the thrilling cry, and the thunder of their united clamor burst over the *meidan,* and rolled upward to the royal council in majestic power and startled the councillors upon their seats.

"Does Your Majesty hear that?" inquired the Prince Royal with a smile, as the Shah remained silent, and still delayed to summon the remaining chiefs to a show of hands.

"I hear it all, Abbas Mirza," was the dignified response, "and it is the voice of my people. But I am the *father* of my people, and will do nothing rashly. Young commander of horse, *hero of Toorkomania*, what say you to this cry for war?"

The cavalry officer was upon his feet in an instant. His eyes brilliant as an eagle's — the soldier in every look and attitude. The badge of the Order of the Sun Lion glistened upon the breast of his military uniform, the scarlet silk pelisse falling gracefully from his shoulders. All eyes were upon him. Fresh from the theatre of glorious achievement, there seemed a propriety in his voice being heard. The listeners soon realized the magnetic character of that voice and mien, which carried the soldiery with him as the autumn wind carries the leaves. His expression, lucid and energetic, fell upon all like a spell.

"I am for the war in the future: I am against the war *now* — earnestly, decidedly, *utterly* opposed to the war. I *shall* oppose it until the decision comes. When war is declared, my sabre leaps from its scabbard for relentless destruction upon the enemies of Persia. I am the Shah's soldier while Allah grants me strength to ride or stand. But I cannot and will not ignore the reason which Allah has planted in my brain. Persia is not ready to cope with the Muscovites. One arm and one alone of the service is thoroughly equipped and drilled. The artillery *is* ready. The infantry at Sultania is *not* ready. Their guns are unserviceable. Half of them will have to be flung aside, or converted into better arms. Why did not General Malek tell you this in his speech? He is too good a soldier not to know it. Before Persia can remedy this deficiency of weapons, her ranks will be decimated by the foe. The troops are not clothed for those higher latitudes, where the contest must be carried on. My own troops, even as low down as Kasbin, were suffering and sick from the cold a week ago; and to conduct this war with vigor we must strike at once into Georgia before Yermoloff can concentrate his troops. The war will be a long one. The whole power of Russia will be hurled against us, and splendidly equipped as is every branch of her service, we cannot stand long the shocks. It is madness to fight now. In a year we *can* be ready. And with all the earnestness and the emphasis which can come from a soldier's heart I entreat Your Majesty to delay. Negotiate, procrastinate, quibble — do anything to gain time for more perfect organization. We will slave ourselves, Your Majesty, to prepare your troops that they may not be sacrificed uselessly upon this altar of blood.

"The women of Persia, who relinquish fathers, and sons, and husbands at your call, have a right to demand this ; to demand time, equipment, and weapons, that the brave hearts they push to the front may have a *chance* to live.

"The spirit and courage of the Persian army are superb. Give us but the time and the money, and we will make that army triumphant.

The fortress of Abbas Abad is not ready. Heavier guns must be mounted, and to effect this we must have time, for it is near the frontier. The fortresses of Erivan and Ardebil are not ready, and they will be attacked early in the campaign. I *know* they are not ready ; and this document (in the handwriting of your best engineer) which I hold in my hand tells you plainly how long it will take to make them impregnable; now they cannot stand a siege of *ten days*.

"You are initiating a war with the colossal enemy of all small kingdoms and states, That enemy adds to her overwhelming numbers the marvellous potency of *drill*. Her myriads move, wheel, charge, *die*, by the magic of a single will. The wizard, *unity*, triumphs in war. Meet, then, this detested foe as equals. Drill triumphs over numbers.

"We are not ready. Hence I entreat Your Majesty to pause. I feel all the exultation of the combat with this detested plunderer of nations that all Persians feel. But a cruel reality incessantly dissolves the enchanting vision of victory, and recalls my attention to realities, to the suffering and wretchedness which must alight upon tens of thousands of brave men who march out unprepared. These brave hearts so willing to die are Your Majesty's hearts. I entreat you in the name of humanity to give these hearts a chance to live and to triumph.

By the flowery and seductive path of transient glory and by the impetus of lofty courage have Your Majesty's able generals here assembled reached this immature decision for immediate war. Reason and the permanent glory of great Persia are arrayed upon the side of present peace. Yield but to a year's delay and preparation, and our great chief, the Crown Prince, shall find an army worthy of his skillful command and his great genius. The transcendent vigor of his powers shall then act upon the marshalling of *soldiers*, not upon a patriot *rabble.*

"If this madness of precipitancy shall go on, and our swords be drawn against our military judgments, mark the prediction. Persia will be stripped of other territory. Her sons will be further humiliated, and her widows mourn uncalled-for slaughter. I am earnest and strong in my speech, because I love the lives of my soldiers and the honor of the flowery land. And when upon my grave you drop the comrade's tear, remember that I deprecated this war *now* with my whole soul, my whole power, and the whole energy of my tongue.

"Listen to me, and heed not the shouts of the unreasoning populace without. They speak from the heart. Our duty is to speak from the head. Listen to me for the last time. There is in the sandy desert towards the Persian Gulf a shrub which the people call *gul-bad-samoun* (the flower that poisons the wind). This plant impregnates the warm breeze of the Persian summer with a quality so deadly, that it kills those who inhale it. Such a deadly plant now poisons the moral air of Iran. All who inhale its noxious vapors are poisoned, and thus is the life of Persia poisoned too. This plant is *passion* and its exhalation death. Military chiefs and monarchs are truly great when they bury passion and wield the destinies of a great empire by godlike *reason.*"

With his dazzling eyes fixed upon Abbas Mirza at the concluding sentence, the eloquent commander stood an instant in silence, as if watching the effect of his shaft upon *the* statesman of Persia. Then he slowly resumed his seat. A thrill of admiration at his boldness and eloquence passed over the Prince Royal, but he remained silent. Occasionally he would raise his dark eyes and study the cavalry officer as if he was one whose nerve and power must be remembered in the future. How deep the shaft had penetrated none could tell, for he remained in the same attitude and awaited the result. But other commanders, thrilled and encouraged by this intrepid leadership of the opposition, arose successively to their feet and added further details to his statement of the insufficiency of Persia's preparation. One gray-headed general of horse took occasion to pay a glowing tribute to the splendor of Alfonso's discipline, and to declare his conviction that the Persian cavalry, now equal to the Cossacks, would surpass them, if all were subjected to the drill of the young commander's heroes just outside the walls of Teheran.

The conference continued, the Shah still hopeful that the eloquence of Alfonso might turn the tide of opinion to a year's delay. But the spirit of revenge, so difficult to allay in an Oriental when once aroused, triumphed over every prudent consideration. Arguments were futile. The great majority of the chiefs had entered the hall predisposed for war, believing that Russia might be surprised and taken at disadvantage. They were, moreover, under the influence of the religious frenzy aroused by the *moullahs* or unwilling to incur the displeasure of Abbas Mirza. When, therefore, all the military and other officials had individually expressed their views, it was evident that three-fourths of those present were in favor of immediate war. The Shah was convinced from the manner in which this earnest controversy had been conducted, that the great preponderance of intellect and wealth in the nation had pronounced for hostilities. He at once, then, without divesting himself of the dignity that was innate to him, arose and declared that war should commence at once, and ordered Abbas Mirza to march the troops as soon as practicable to the frontier. The excitement outside continuing unabated, the sovereign advanced to the window, attended by his nobles, bearing the insignia of the empire, and announced to the assembled thousands that war was declared. Scarcely had the cheers died away which greeted this welcome announcement when the booming of cannon shook the air. The people were wild.

The King returned to his seat and a strange scene ensued. Alfonso held aloft his arm as a signal that he desired to be heard. The Shah signified his assent, and the commander of cavalry immediately left his divan and advanced towards his sovereign. Pausing and bowing at intervals he saluted for the *fourth* time at the foot of the throne. Then he drew the magnificent sabre which the monarch had given him at the public audience of *Nowroose*, and kneeling before the king laid it at his feet, and announced that he craved the honor of dedicating that weapon to an unrelenting war upon Russia. The excitement was fearful. Every chief in the saloon leaped from his divan and crowded behind him, with drawn sabres flashing in the sunlight, and united in the same request. The emotion of the Shah was visible. He could scarcely speak.

"Noble hearts!" he said at length, "you that know the hazzards and the horrors of war, ask your sovereign to accept your blood. The Persia that we all love, the land of glory and of heroes even from the very cradle of time, gives you her thanks.

May Allah bless you and return you safe to your homes and those you love! I cannot speak, for the grandeur of your eagerness to sacrifice and suffer for my Persia, and your Persia, overwhelms me. But you go to this war with the heart of your sovereign linked with each of your noble hearts as steel is linked with steel. I accept every one of you, and, as Allah is my judge, you shall every one of you receive a king's reward. Rise, now, and sheathe your sabres. Nicholas shall know how an outraged Persian king and a noble Persian people can fight for their country.

.   .   .   .

As Alfonso was about to leave the Casvin gate with his *dehbáshi*, on his return to camp, he encountered the Ghebre, who beckoned to him to halt. Zenayi was one of a group who were seated near the gate listening to one of the professional story-tellers seen everywhere in the East, and who are never at a loss for an audience. The commander obeyed the signal, and waited for his friend to come up with him.

"Dismount and come with me," was the Ghebre's first salutation. Seeing that the commander hesitated, he continued: "Leave your horse with the *dehbáshi*. You can be spared sometime yet from the camp. This is public business and you must know it — come."

The tone was peremptory, and admitted of no parley. Alfonso surrendered Al-Borak again to his attendant and followed Zenayi. As they entered once more the narrow streets of the city he said to the Ghebre:

".You know that war has been declared?"

"Yes, I know what all Tcheran knows by this time. You will soon see that we propose to be prompt and early in this trying time. What I am about to show you is to be entirely confined to yourself. Speak of it to no one."

They passed on to the second street, filled with the excited populace discussing the war topic, and entering through an arch a small courtyard of a private residence, paused before a door upon which the Ghebre rapped with his knuckles. A fountain was playing in the courtyard, and for a moment they heard only the plashing of its waters. Then the door flew open, and they followed the servant who appeared into a large room elegantly furnished in the Oriental style. Directing Alfonso to be seated on a divan, Zenayi, who appeared to be familiarly known in the place, passed on unbidden with the domestic, and disappeared in an apartment beyond. The officer, left to himself, awaited the Ghebre's return. At length, when his patience began to be exhausted and he moved uneasily upon the divan, wondering what public business could find shelter in this private dwelling, the door slowly opened from within and a solitary figure closely veiled entered the apartment and paused before the divan. He could see that the female was elegantly attired in the costliest materials of the East, and that elegance was her birthright. She held him in suspense for only an instant. Then she drew aside her veil, entirely revealing the loveliest face upon which he had ever looked in Persia. It was Irene. Lovely and beautiful as he had deemed her before, she was transcendently dazzling now. Some excitement had flushed her fair cheek with roses, and there was a subdued lustre in her dark eyes, as if some holy emotion had usurped the place of the sparkling merriment or fire which was wont to play in those perfect orbs of light. She looked like a queen-martyr, as if she had divested herself of everything like selfishness, and was going forth to make some great sacrifice. And her looks did not belie her purpose. Irene was going forth to encounter whatever of death, or torture, or mental agony, or shame, or ruin, or despair Fate might hold for her in his iron hand. She was going forth *alone*, ready to incur any evil that her loneliness might entail. The woman nurtured in the midst of affluence and protected by the hand of imperial power was going out as a solitary, unprotected girl upon the world, and *such* a world!

And as she stood there in her superb beauty, and told the young commander how willingly she made the sacrifice, how she exulted in the opportunity of proving at last that great love she had always borne for her country, he felt the tears gather in his eyes, and his voice falter. At last he pleaded with her, with all the eloquence God had gifted him with, to abandon her purpose.

"Ah! brave soldier," she responded, "you know that *some one* must go in every war. And why not I, who deem it the noblest act the patriot can do for his country. Some deem the loss of blood and of limb the highest sacrifice. But there is the halo of glory for *that*. The world *may* hear of that and applaud. But for my mission, no matter how successful and valuable the service rendered, there is no reward but an ignominious death, or the sneers of men, if life is spared. Seek not to move me. My Persia has at last found something valuable for me to do. A girl can help her, and the girl will go."

"But there are others, Irene," he pleaded again, "who can be more efficient and useful than you. Your sex will impede you in the most critical hours when speed and punctuality are vital. Abandon this to those who are competent."

"None are more competent than I. Reason with your own judgment and knowledge of me, and tell me candidly if you believe there is a Muscovite who can outwit Irene?"

"Not one. I must speak the truth to such a woman as you."

"Then I shall go, and go gladly. But I summoned you here, Alfonso, to bid you farewell. I may never return. And there is something in my heart and brain that tells me you are true of heart and noble — that your soul can appreciate what I am about to do. It is this yearning for sympathy in my mission, from a noble and heroic heart that induced me to inform you of my purpose. Remember me kindly when I am gone, and if ever there is an hour, at any time, in this war, when one more struggle, one more heroic effort may turn the tide of battle for my Persia, remember that I am *a spy in the Russian camp*, that I have sacrificed *all* for love of my country, and let that thought nerve your arm to that effort, and strengthen your voice to shout that order which shall give us victory."

She pressed the hand which he extended to her, and before he could restrain her, she darted through the door and he saw her no more.

CHAPTER XXI.

THE luxurious Persian spring awoke suddenly to life and beauty, like Psyche at the touch of Cupid's arrow. Upon the great plains encircling the walls and citadel of Teheran, the bare earth as by an enchanter's power was covered with a carpet of rich green. Even up the slopes of the adjoining mountains on the north the emerald carpet was spread, one peak alone refusing to don the spring color, and standing high above his fellows clothed in his eternal mantle of snow. The majestic mountain, Demewand, never changes at the touch of spring, but in his spotless white ever overlooks his fellows and the plains around the Persian capital, as if his antiquity dated back to an epoch when all nature

knew only the eternal reign of white. "Demewand among the
Elbrooz mountains," mused the commander of horse, as he lay
stretched at ease upon the grass of the plain, "is like the Ghebre among the green-robed *moullahs*, always clothed in white,
and in the majesty of his intellect towering above them eternally. Who can he be? What caprice of the Eternal Ruler
of the Universe has planted this matchless intellect in the
guise of man upon the surface of this flowery realm? Zenayi
comprehends all learning, and has it classified and ready for
immediate ·use. He does not know the future ; he does not
know the events to-day transpiring in Persia beyond the limit
of his senses. But in the past he is a master. The knowledge
of all lands in all ages of the world seems to have passed into
his intellectual grasp. Where, how, and when has he mastered
the science of war with the same ease that he has mastered as-
tronomy? In the details of each branch of the military service
he is as learned as if his days had all been passed in camps.
How can the human intellect master all science in the limit of
a lifetime ?"

Thus meditating after the fatigues of a morning passed in
marching and counter-marching five thousand new troops ·
raised for the war, Alfonso was stretched beneath a tree already
rich in its spring foliage. The scene spread out before him in
the warm light of the sun was varied and beautiful, and the
heat of the Oriental spring came to him freighted with the perfumes of countless roses pendent from the walls of the royal
anderoons on both extremities of his camp. On the right was
Tackt-i-Kajer, with its enclosures overtopped by luxuriant shade
trees, and looming up from its foundations on a detatched and
commanding hill on the great southern slope of the Elbrooz mountains. The palace within its walls, lofty and fairy-
like in the delicacy of its outlines, was distinctly traced against
the pale-blue sky and drifts of downy-white clouds beyond.
The stateliness of this royal structure was enhanced by the
superb ranges of terraces connecting the spacious gardens as
they diverged from the base of the palace downward towara
the bottom of the hill. On his left was the peerless *Negauristan*, buried in luxuriant sweets, where Irene and his veiled mis
stress had communed with him. And beyond *Negauristan* was
the city, with its outworks bristling with cannon, and beyond
all were the Elbrooz and the white-browed Demewand guard·
ing the horizon for miles away upon the north. From the sum·
mit of the knoll where his pavilion was pitched and his solitary

tree stood, he overlooked a startling array of military camps covering the green plains about the capital. And as his eyes ranged over the thousands of tents, and the banners of Persia flying everywhere to the breeze above the luxuriant carpet of grass, he could not forbear to remember how soon the lovely young velvety grass would be stained with the bright heart-blood of thousands !

And as he rested there with his elbow deep in the grass supporting his head, and with the varied scenery of the springtime contrasting with the blue and white of heaven, as his dark eyes roved far and wide, the thought of his own singular destiny came to him. By what an extraordinary combination of circumstances had he gained influence and wealth. He was the most affluent man in the empire whenever he chose to divest himself of his word of honor to the Ghebre. Most men, he knew, would violate any promise to secure the enjoyment of so vast a treasure. He did not deny to himself that he was often tempted to forget his vow, to ignore his honor. But he had always shaken off the temptation. He shook it off now, when the glimpses he caught of the luxurious gardens and the stately palaces aroused his passions, and suggested to him that to enjoy the ease and sensuality of a prince he had but to violate his vow to devote the hidden wealth at Mourg-Aub to the exclusive benefit of Persia. He said to himself, " I am surely under the spell of Zenayi. When I am tempted, that noble countenance seems to rise before me with the smile of an exalted friendship changed to a look of reproach. I am ambitious as Cæsar. I know it. I intrigue with the harem to secure my military advancement. I succeed by means of the intrigue. Doubtless I would not hesitate to intrigue again to gain my purpose. I have been advanced in the army simply because I played a double part at the suggestion of that master of intrigue, Irene —that wonderful being whose beauty and heroism are in contradiction to her craft. She is artful, but she is superb. She tempted me to write that false letter, and yet she has gone upon a mission which proves her to possess the grandest patriotism in Persia. She hazards her honor, her life, her all. I trample upon wealth, and choose toil before ease, poverty before palaces ; and yet my ambition is rampant still. Has the mysterious Zenayi placed us both under a spell of enchantment ? Is there something God-like in the manifestation of noble qualities which can influence and lead two such unscrupulous intriguers as Irene and Alfonso ? Before the God of Heaven, the Christian's God, I believe there is nobility of soul and true integrity lurking somewhere in me yet. It is weak, but it *must* be there. I thrilled with a certain intensity of triumph when I trampled on that gold. Would that my life was *full* of such noble thoughts as moved me then. Why, when this better nature comes to me, as it comes now, do my thoughts revert to that golden shower of silky hair, those dark eyes and that girlish face beyond the sea? My boyhood's dream, my Madeleine, my first defender, the convict's friend, why do my thoughts wander to you when the *grand* in my nature struggles for supremacy? Why did Irene in her grand sacrifice recall you, and stand before me with a radiant beauty she never seemed to have before? Are you the essence of nobility and grandeur, that everything pure and heroic, everything unselfish, recalls the memory of your sweet face? Where are you now, Madeleine? Has the perfection of womanhood set its seal upon you, or are you sleeping under the grass? Ha! what is this?"

The commander raised himself to a sitting posture, and looked upward in amazement. He had been looking toward the blue sky while thinking of Madeleine, and his sudden ejaculation was caused by something falling swiftly as if from that sky. Down, down, down the small object descended toward him, and yet by regulated stages, as if there was intelligence guiding its perpendicular fall. Nearer and nearer it came, clearer and clearer was it defined against the blue of heaven, and still its descent was regulated by some law of nature or of art. With amazement he watched it come, and something in its shape or movement told him it was not of Persian origin. In that land of wonders he had never seen its semblance, and with an eager curiosity he retained his eyes upon it as it grew larger and more defined above him. Had he not been gifted with a power and reach of vision such as is ascribed to the author of "Vathek," he never would have descried that object so far aloft. It was so minute, and came so swiftly and perpendicularly downward. But once those eyes were concentrated on a distant object in field or sky, there was no evading their tenacity of vision. A field glass for that officer of horse would have made him smile. He required no such aid. When a sailor before the mast, his range of vision had been deemed wonderful by his messmates and officers. In this he exulted over Zenayi, who was a marvel, and whose very eyes suggested the idea of immeasurable distance. But he could not distinguish distant objects with the power and clearness of Alfonso. This gift of vision served him now, and down out of the immensity of upper air he detected the object, falling, falling, falling towards the tree where he was seated. Nearer, nearer it came, until he could identify it with objects that have a name on earth.

It was evidently an immense bird dropping out of the empyrean, and if the descent continued in that line the immense creature would reach the earth in his immediate vicinity. He had never seen its like, and so rapidly now it seemed to approach the earth, and so wonderful was its size, that he naturally enough laid his hand upon the hilt of his sabre, anticipating a combat. What clime had sent so immense a winged creature to Persia? Nearer and still nearer it came, its dusky wings now plainly visible and stretching wide from its body as it hung apparently for an instant a motionless shadow against the sun, and then dropped swiftly lower, lower, lower towards the expectant officer, who had now risen to his feet and stood watching it, sabre in hand. Then the details of its body, head, and talons were manifest as it approached the ground, and he realized that the bird was immense beyond any winged creature in his experience, and was likely to make him trouble if he encountered it single-handed. This apprehension only whetted the edge of his desire to possess himself of the huge stranger, and as it lowered at length just above his head, and fell like a dark cloud upon him, he grappled it by the neck, and a struggle ensued which veiled him for a moment in darkness. The huge wings folded about him and covered his face, and in the struggle both man and bird fell to the ground together. The contest was brief, for the man regained his feet, and dropping his sabre put both hands to the creature's neck and by his iron strength of arm bore it to the earth and held it there, amid a beating of huge wings, which flapped upon his head like blows from human arms. When he had reduced the stranger to submission he held it down with one hand, while with the other he disengaged his military sash, and giving it two or three turns around the bird's neck, he knotted it and dragged his prey away in triumph to his tent. There he secured the prize by a rope halter fastened about one of the legs and tied to the pole of his pavilion. Upon examining and measuring the bird he found that it was probably the famous king-vulture (condor) of the Andes. It measured *fifteen* feet across the expanded wings. There were indications of extreme exhaustion about the huge wanderer, as if from an immense flight through space ; and doubtless the last struggle with the man was unpremeditated, as the bird descended exhausted to the earth. The great Humboldt is authority for the statement that the *vertical* flight alone of the condor of the Andes exceeds *twenty-three thousand feet* above the level of the sea. Where had this traveller of the skies made his start? Why had he changed hemispheres?

As the commander sat in his tent eying his prize, he detected suspended from the neck of the king-vulture by a black ribbon a large oval object, perhaps half the length of his hand, and covered with black leather. He soon cut the ribbon, and detached the startling evidence that the condor had once before been captive to man. What was his surprise to find that the oval leather was a locket, and within upon an ivory plate was painted an exquisitely beautiful face and bust of a young lady with golden hair, fair face, and dark eyes. He knew it instantly, It was *Madeleine* developed into a woman, her beauty ripened and intensified, and her power of fascination quadrupled. She was smiling upon him. Her image had dropped to him from the skies or he was dreaming. He looked at the luminous eyes of the strange bird, regarding him. They seemed in their wild, startled lustre to be the eyes of a demon mocking him. He knew that only a lunatic could fancy that the image of a girl had cleaved thousands of miles of upper air, above seas and mountain peaks, to flash its loveliness in his eyes and warm the hidden depths of his soul. But there it *seemed* to smile that exquisite illusion, and in the study of it the veil of past years was rent, and he was the boy again, with the boy's thoughts and dreams and hopes. Why did this charming *illusion* bring back also that shudder of the olden time? He surely saw once more that cold, leaden sky, that broad chilly river, those iron faces of the officers who dragged him towards the solemn walls of heavy masonry, and felt that cold hand of ice upon his heart which man calls despair. Surely that hour had returned when the boy realized what it meant to be utterly *alone* in the world, to see the faces of men and of all men leering like demons at a boy's agony. Aye, the death struggle had indeed returned, and the young heart, crushed by the cruelties and wrongs of men, was turning in its fierceness and its despair to rend like a wild beast its torturers. Aye! the mother's face was whitening as she caught the clanking of chains fastened upon her boy, and she was fainting at the receding vision of a convict marched away to shame.

He seemed to see it all again, that agony on the Western

hemisphere, which had rendered him frantic so that men fell dead before his levelled musket ; and at the terrible memory he buried his face in his hands. The old agony revived ; the intervening years shrivelled up like a rising stage curtain, and the scenes of blood and flight, and struggles with the freezing waters of the river — all were manifest. Then he looked once more upon the picture which had come from the sky. It was no dream. It had form and weight, that ivory miniature, and the strange messenger that had brought it was that moment flapping his huge wings in his futile efforts to escape. Perchance Madeleine was in South America, and by some strange chance her picture had become attached to a captive condor which had escaped from his prison and mounted to the skies. But she lived ; she was a lovely woman ; the grave had not claimed his boyhood's dream. Madeleine lived, and he counted upon his fingers how many years had been added to the girl's life since the seas had parted them and he had become a leader of armies. Did she remember him, or had he passed from her recollection as one of the follies of a girl's fancy that now appeared to her childish indeed? She was a woman now, with beauty to enthrall the loftiest, and mature intellect to make her the centre of a charmed circle. She doubtless had no time now to think of the escaped convict. But her image, by some strange fatality, had crossed seas and hovered over mountain peaks, risen above the clouds and traversed thousands of miles of strange climates, and its wonderful history would surprise her, entertain her, no matter how she might now be engaged. Was it probable that the lovely Madeleine would ever know the fate of her picture? For the first time in years the thought flashed upon him that he would write to her, notify her that her property had strangely fallen upon Persian soil. Would there be danger in that? This startling question recalled vividly the fact that he was a convict. A *convict* in one country, a *hero* in another. In one land the citizens would hunt him as a wild beast. In the other thousands blessed him as the benefactor of their country, the protector of their families from tribes who would enslave and maltreat them. In one land honored, in the other a felon. In one land clothed in garments of shame, that he might not escape from prison walls unchallenged ; in the other, honored with a pelisse of scarlet silk and fur, and entrusted with the leadership of ten thousand troops, and a favorite general of a king.

But as he pondered his actual condition he shook his head

at length.   No ; it would be unwise to entrust his name or
writing to a fragment of paper.   Falling into government hands
beyond the sea, by any natural chance, it might compromise
his present, his future, his all of hope and ambition.   Silence
regarding his past beyond the sea, utter isolation from all he
had known or cared for in youth, brave, persistent efforts right
onward into the future — these were the true lines of conduct
for the soldier of destiny.   He would not swerve from these.
He would not cumber his pathway to glory with unnecessary
hazards.

Until in the dim future a safe method of restoring Madeleine's
property might become manifest, he resolved to retain that image of loveliness, too pure and bewitching for. earth.   He would
study it in the intervals of military duty, and bestow upon its
contemplation all the ardor that was consistent with the vows
he had given to his veiled mistress of the garden of Negauristan.   And thus the hours wore away in his tent under the mild
spring atmosphere of Persia, and still he sat absorbed in study
of the marvellous miniature and the marvellous messenger which
had not faltered on his mission over thousands of miles of sea
and land.

From that day the messenger condor became the commander's companion.   He bent every energy of his potent will and
employed every suggestion that the sphinx, Zenayi, could offer
to the one purpose of taming that king-vulture to treat him as
a friend.   He fed him with his own hands, caressed him,
watched him in pain and applied remedies, until at last the
huge bird would run after him, obey his commands, perch upon
the top of his pavilion, and fly above his head like an omen of
terror when he bounded away upon the back of the fiery Al-
Borak.   The Persian soldiery, ever ready to believe in prodi-
gies, auguries and omens, looked upon this huge bird of their
chief, which sailed away high above the head of Al-Borak and
his master with dark, gloomy, widespread wings, as the em-
bodiment of some destructive spirit the mysterious Ghebre had
conjured up to aid the conquering onset of the fearless battle
hero, his friend Alfonso.   At length the king-vulture became
well known to the Persian army, and when at last patience and
training had taught the bird to distinguish a Russian from a
Persian uniform, and it was found that the commander's condor
would feed only on the Russian dead, the troops were confirmed in their belief that a friendly demon fought for Persia
and cast his baneful spell upon the advancing Russian columns.

The king-vulture bore among the troops the title "*Boshran*" (good tidings), and his advent on the battlefield was regarded as an omen of victory.

CHAPTER XXII.

UNRISE seen from the summit of ice-clad Ararat! What a vision of grandeur to the startled eyes that first looked down upon it! *Three miles and a quarter* above the sea and nearly *two miles and three quarters* above the plain of the Araxes, the ice-clad peak of great Ararat glistened like a brilliant phantom in the morning sun. The north-eastern slope of the mountain stretched away downward fourteen miles. The north-western slope was *twenty* miles in length. From the summit downwards for nearly two-thirds of a mile perpendicular, or nearly three miles in an oblique direction, it was covered with a crown of *eternal* snow and ice. The *silver head* of Ararat glistening in the sun! What millions of eyes from the earliest ages to the present hour have looked up to it from valley, plain, and hill in wonder. The traditional resting-place of the Ark, the starting-point of the post-diluvian races of men, has attracted countless glances from below. How few feet have trodden its summit and *looked down* upon the panorama of valleys, plains, rivers and mountain peaks! Adventurous explorers, inured to hardships and familiar with upward toiling, have turned back from the arduous ascent, disheartened. Bolder men, gifted with iron purpose, have overcome the obstacles and stood in triumph on the summit.

Two of the successful few stood upon the glittering peak, when morning flung open the golden gates of the East, and with tongues of admiration greeted the chariot of the sun. The elder of the two seemed adapted to the spot by the robes of white he wore, the sacred garments of his priestly office seeming to harmonize with the eternal crown of snow. The younger was in striking contrast with the scene, the bright colors of his military uniform coming out clearly in the increasing effulgence of the sun. *White* from the earliest ages of Persia was sacred to the sun. Hence the priests of the magi were habited in white. White was also the peculiar mark of royalty. Hence the great Cyrus wore a vesture of purple half mixed with white, and tradition traced his royal descent to the sun. One of the ancient line of priests who followed the religious faith of Zoroaster, and whom modern religious prejudice has styled *fire worshippers* or worshippers of the sun, on this superb morning on ancient Ararat fell upon his knees and with outstretched arms greeted the sun, the *symbol* of his overruling God, Ormuzd. His companion of another faith respectfully withdrew a few paces, and, while the Ghebre prayed, feasted his eyes upon the magnificent spectacle spread out on every side, miles below him.

Passing the lower extremity of the snow-cap which eternally covers the summit, his eyes wandered down over the wooded slopes of Ararat, on one of which stood the lonely Armenian monastery of St. James, at the entrance of a chasm whence issued a cool stream of water purling and flashing its way down the mountain side to the far-off Araxes. Then his startled eyes looked off over hundreds of miles of valleys and mountains, lakes and rivers in dreamy distance varying the scene. Accustomed at length to the fearful reaches of scenery the eye covers to the verge of indistinctness, the spectator resumed the study of objects immediately below Ararat and along the curving silver line of the Araxes river. The Kour river winding off to the Caspian Sea, the Arpachai and Abarane rivers pouring their mountain waters into the rapid current of the Araxes, the serrated head of *Alághés* rising majestically in the northwest, with the Pambak summits and other peaks of the great circular sweep of the *Saganlúg* chain, and the Armenian towns and villages and monasteries in the arid and level basin of the Araxes, overlooked by the north-eastern mountains, — all came under his raptured gaze, and he stood motionless as marble in his amazement. Then with a start he appeared to recognize a beautiful, dark-blue lake on the north-east, beyond the Araxes. It was behind high mountains, which enclosed its shores abruptly and close; but still the loftier summit of Ararat commanded its tranquil waters, and he saw it glimmering in loveliness amid its guarding mountains. This view alone of the Lake of Goktscha enabled him to realize the awful altitude of Ararat.

No wonder that the commander gazed with renewed interest upon the blue waters of Goktscha. There, upon the lake's shores, had Russia violated the treaty of *Gulistan.* There had Nicholas laid his iron hand upon Persian territory, and for this act armies were gathering for battle. The inviolability of those lovely blue waters Persia would maintain with her best blood. Crimson was to be the fearful price of *blue.*

Glittering like a *bazubend* on a prince's elbow, suddenly appeared the far-off spires of the Cathedral of *Echmiadzin.* The glorious sunburst had reached the famous Armenian monastery where the Patriarch of that religion resides and oft officiates in his jewelled robes in the ancient cathedral. This monastery and church and grounds are surrounded by a wall thirty feet high, with loop-holes and towers at the angles. The distance around the walls is a mile and a quarter. *Echmiadzin* is the religious centre to which the eyes of all Armenians turn. It is particularly memorable in the annals of the Persian and Russian war of 1826–1828 as having given the name to a bloody battle, between those two nations, fought near it. *Echmiadzin* was itself occupied during that war as a military post, and was besieged by the Persians under *Abbas Mirza.* As the country north of Ararat, over which the eyes of the officer were looking, was destined to figure in the military campaign upon which he had entered, he studied *Echmiadzin* and its surroundings with intense interest. From the summit of Ararat he looked directly north over the vast plain of the Araxes to the walls of the famous monastery standing upon that plain. To the north-east of the walled monastery lay the blue *Lake of Goktscha,* surrounded by mountains, and to the west of the monastery extended a chain of mountains called Saganlug, with the river *Abarane* sweeping down along their rocky sides and emptying into the plain of the Araxes. Armenian villages were scattered upon this plain in the midst of groves of walnuts, Italian poplars, mulberries, willows, and gloomy oleasters. Some eighty miles north of the Lake of Goktscha lay Tiflis, a great rendez-vous of the Russian army, and situated near the southern slope of the Caucasus mountains. The great theatre of war was to be located, then, between Ararat and the Saganlúg mountains on the south-west and the Caucasus mountains on the north-east. Standing upon Ararat and looking over the plain of the Araxes towards the Caucasus on the north-east, the commander was facing the great posts of the Russian army from which the Muscovite troops would be hurled down upon the great plain of the Araxes, if the Persians were not able to check their advance at points farther north in the mountains by pushing on over the Araxes and meeting them in the mountain roads north and north-east of the *Lake of Goktscha.*

While from this awful ice-clad peak the commander of ten thousand Persian horse eagerly fixed in his mind the map of the theatre of war, the Ghebre had finished his devotions to Ormuzd, and approached the side of the absorbed officer.

"You see now, Alfonso, why I brought you up to this glorious peak of Ararat. Your eye is the eye of an eagle. You cannot take in a superhuman range of objects, but you can here sketch a good map of the Araxes basin, and the mountains on the north and north-west, with the rivers and roads which lead from them. Sketch also the mountains on the north-east, for Russia *may* push armies down upon us in that direction also. Spread your cloak upon the ice and let us seat ourselves. While you draw the map, I will give you the distances from point to point from *memory*, will show you the curves of the roads and the mountain passes, for I am familiar with this country. Abbas Mirza will push your cavalry ahead there to the northward in advance of the army. . You can make great havoc in Georgia, because Russia will be surprised and will not be ready for months yet. You will thus also strengthen the hands of our disaffected people there, and enable the chiefs to rise and organize against Russia. Unroll the papers now, and let us make an excellent map for your use. Afterwards I wish you to make a fine copy of it, and present it to our Chief, *Abbas Mirza.* He will be amazed at your skill and energy, will appreciate the map, and you will rise still higher in his military estimation."

Alfonso produced the materials for constructing the map, which he had brought on his back up the difficult ice-cap of the mountain. Their horses were secured at the monastery of St. James, on the wooded slope of Ararat, below the eternal snow, and were in charge of a detachment of Persian cavalry. The two friends were hours at their work, and the result was an admirable topographical view of the country immediately north, north-west and north-east of Ararat. The Ghebre, as usual, knew everything regarding distances on Persian soil. When their task was completed they regaled themselves upon bread, dates and the golden wine made at the foot of Ararat, and which, tradition has it, is pressed from the grapes of the species of vine which Noah planted there after leaving the Ark. The cavalry commander was not exemplary enough Mohammedan to refuse that luscious wine of Ararat. When their repast was completed, and before they commenced their difficult descent of the icy peak, Zenayi recalled his companion's recollection to the historic character of the ground just below Ararat.

"You are looking down upon the valley of the Araxes, upon whose banks Hannibal sought refuge, after having paid the penalty of his superiority on the plains of Italy. Here, too, was the ancient Artaxata, the rich and mighty capital of Armenia, where the Parthian Tiridates assumed the kingly crown which Rome had presented to him. Here he sought to annihilate the first seeds of that fruitful religion, Christianity. And marvellous transformation was that of the persecutor. Gregory, '*The Enlightener*,' before his death instructed him in the Christian faith. And yonder is *Echmiadzin*, the ancient episcopal seat of the Armenians. How persistently has Christianity maintained a habitation there, despite uninterrupted persecution and unceasing contests between Parthians, Romans, Persians and Turks for the possession of the soil. This is memorable battle-ground, Alfonso. See to it that your sword reaps a harvest worthy of the crops that have been reaped here before. Experience has taught me that war is to be deprecated. But the passions of men are still too strong for their reason. Negotiation, compromise, concession, should amicably settle questions that destructive war will not adjust in years. But, Alfonso, as long as war is the fashion of nations, I must confess that I relish the settlement of accounts with hateful Russia by the sword. But we are not prepared for this war now. Nevertheless, do not allow that reflection to influence your activity and energy in the approaching conflict. For we *may* get the better of the Muscovites. But look where I point you now, and do not forget the place if ever you see or hear that the Russians will attempt to march by that road. Aye! more. *If ever you can by your spies or by your stratagems entice the Muscovites to march by that road, seize that opportunity and allure them that way. If once we can get them into that trap they are lost.* Now mark the points I give you."

The Ghebre turned the attention of the commander to the north of Ararat, pointing across the Araxes directly to the Armenian monastery and cathedral.

"There is *Echmiadzin* directly north. Continue your gaze right on over the cathedral still north. There lies *Tiflis*. It will be the base of the Russian operations. Their army will march south, some day, on *Echmiadzin*. They cannot come directly to the monastery on account of the dividing mountains. The *main road* from Tiflis to *Echmiadzin* makes a great curve to the south-west to avoid the mountains of the *Saganlúg*, and finally reaches the monastery from the west, crossing the Abarane river a few hours before doing so. It is a short march from the cathedral to the Abarane on the west. Now mark that serrated head of *Alaghés*, that lofty peak, just north of where the *main road* crosses the Abarane, going towards the monastery. At the foot of *Alaghés* a shorter road, but a mountain road, comes down south and parallel with the main road but farther to the east, *follows* the southern flow of the Abarane, and is close beside that river. Just before the short road coming south cuts the main road coming east, it passes through a *rocky gorge* close beside the bank of the *Abarane*. The Russian army if they take the short road can be defeated in that gorge. The place is fearful. Visit it if you ever have a chance ; keep your mind upon it through this entire war. In the fluctuations of the campaign, some army may attempt that passage. It is safe but difficult, if not contested by a foe. But *woe to the army that is led into ambuscade there*."

"And what is the fortress I see a few miles east of *Ech-miadzin*?" inquired Alfonso ; " there appears to be a river between the two."

"That is our fortress of *Erivan*, which you will see by referring again to our map. You will soon familiarize yourself with these points. The river which you see is the Zanga. The Russians, coming down from the north-west, may cross that river and attack Erivan, if they are successful farther up in the north-west. Now look away here, to the north-east, over the basin of the Araxes. In this direction the Araxes flows away to the Caspian Sea, constantly widening and deepening. When you were looking to the north-west at Echmiadzin, and the *dangerous pass on the Abarane river*, you were facing the mountains of the Saganlúg chain, that furnish the head waters of the Araxes. Now in the north-east you are facing the Caucasus mountains, whose southerly slopes contribute small streams to the Araxes, before it falls into the Caspian Sea, away there to the east. On these slopes you will also have work for your cavalry. For the foe will advance upon us from the north-east also, seeking to cross the Araxes near the Caspian Sea, and lay siege to Ardebil, and our other fortresses toward that sea."

At length the Ghebre succeeded in making his thoughtful companion comprehend the theatre of war, as seen from Ararat, and by frequent reference to the map he had drawn under

Zenayi's instructions, Alfonso possessed an admirable preliminary and general view of the military position. Time and familiarity with the roads would make him a more perfect master of details, during the progress of the campaign.

As they took their parting view of that matchless panorama, seen from that icy peak by so few human eyes within the century, the commander, ever observant, pointed out to Zenayi a black speck upon the face of a white cloud above Ararat. The Ghebre failed to see it for a time. But as the speck grew larger as it lowered in the sky, his eye caught it, and he inquired:

"Is it Boshran?"

"Yes, that strange bird never loses sight of me now," replied the officer. "I saw him hovering high above us as we rode up to the monastery of St. James. He will be just over my head before we are half way down the mountain."

"He is not unfamiliar with snow," said Zenayi. "I have seen them flying high above Cotopaxi when that volcano was robed in snow."

"You have been a famous traveller, Zenayi," said his companion.

"Aye, and hunter, too," was the response. "The *Stut Ozel* of the woods of Germany has spread his dusky wings before me in the chase, as surely as before the rush of the wild huntsman. Not very surely, then, you think, eh? Well, I have shot chiguires at the mouth of the Cano de la Tigrera, just to fling to the Zamuro vultures, and watch how much like men the ravenous creatures grasp their prey. I have travelled far, and witnessed strange sights, Alfonso. Few men have been greater wanderers. I have seen on the Apure little white herons walking along the backs of crocodiles, and I have seen Persian kings and warriors almost trodden upon by the dainty feet of favorite girls. Ha! ha! what a world of contradictions and absurdities is this. We write flaming panegyrics upon great men, and yet they all possess some *littleness* that dwarfs our demigods. All, all have made some egregious mistakes. Even our splendid Abbas Mirza has made a war now, which is not dictated by the highest wisdom. Listen to me, Alfonso, for in you centre some of my most precious hopes for the future. Pertinaciously adhere on all occasions to the dictates of moderation and prudence. In the long run they confer upon nations the *permanent* benefits. The *ignis fatuus* of error has led off our brave crown prince this time. Ormuzd grant his

temerity do not prove fatal to Persia. Come, let us descend.
We have little enough time to return to the camp, and I wish
to diverge from the road a little after we pass St. James.
There is an object I will point out to you on the way down,
which may be of great service to you hereafter, if any accident
should happen to me during the war. It is a landmark I would
have you remember, as a guide to you in the future."

"Is it of military importance, Zenayi?" inquired the commander, as the two resumed their travelling packs, and grasped
their steel-pointed staffs preparatory to the icy descent.

"No, Alfonso. But *for you it may prove some day to be of
vital importance to your fate.*"

"Does it relate to one of the *three great secrets*, Zenayi? is
it one of the remaining *two* you have not revealed to me yet?"

"How quick you are, Alfonso, to surmise my thoughts," replied the Ghebre. "It does relate to one of the *three secrets*,
and to the one which I deem the greatest of the three. I may
never reveal this one to you; but something may prevent my
ever returning to this mountain. If then I exhibit to you the
landmark now, you will be able to find the secret hereafter if
I should deem it expedient to reveal it to you before my death.
Beware the edge of that icy ledge when we pass it again, and
fix your steel firmly in the ice. Come on, now."

Thus cautioned, Alfonso followed his guide down the slippery side of Ararat, taking the same circuitous route by which
they had ascended the icy peak. After a tedious descent of
several hours they reached the monastery of St. James, where
their horses and escort awaited them. Resuming at this point
of the descent the command of his detachment of cavalry,
Alfonso led the way on Al-Borak, down the rocky path.
Reaching at length the Armenian village of Arguri, the only one
upon Mount Ararat, and having about one hundred and sev-
enty-five families in all, they halted at the rivulet, which has its
source in one of the glaciers of the mountain, for the purpose
of watering their horses. Leaving this settlement and diverg-
ing to the right, the Ghebre led the cavalcade a half of a mile
out of the path, and over the rocks, until they reached a huge
boulder of dark porphyry, resting upon smaller blocks of the
same volcanic material. The Ghebre pointed out to the commander this misshapen mass of rock, and bade him remember
its appearance and location during all time. They then resumed the descent of Ararat.

CHAPTER XXIII.

IN the month of September, 1826, on the southern declivity of the Caucasus, a Circassian scout was posted on
the rocks overhanging a defile. The position was admirable, commanding a wide extent of the Georgian
territory between the mountains and the Koor river. The watchful soldier was one of a company of Circassian light cavalry in the
service of Russia. His glistening steel armlets, from wrist to elbow, wee polished to marvellous brilliancy, and the steel rings of
his coat of mail seemed to undulate upon him like soft silk at every
movement. His helmet was pointed like a spear-head at the
top, and from it a veil of mail fell backwards, protecting his
shoulders and the back of his neck. There were divisions
for cartridges sewed upon each of his breasts, while a sabre
swung from his belt, in which were thrust his pistols and dagger. He was armed, also, with a bow, and a quiver was secured at his left side. The bow and arrows are used to pick
off the enemy's sentinels without giving the alarm to the main
body. His boots were of soft morocco, laced up at the sides
with silver cord. There was a light, airy effect in his costume
and movements, suitable for the swift partisan warfare in which
he was engaged. The Persian and Russian cavalry were making daily raids upon the neighboring settlements, and upon
each other's outposts, and constant vigilance and rapidity of
movement were demanded. The quick advance or the sudden
flight were daily experiences to this young Circassian. His
raven-colored steed was hidden in the shadow of a huge rock
behind him.

Occasionally the scout looked down upon the magnificent
valleys below him, with their groves of palm, fig and pomegranate trees, and their mountain streams fertilizing and tortuous, with appreciative eyes. But constant espionage was
demanded of him upon the rocky defile over which he was
perched, and upon a similar defile, parallel with the first but
lower down the slope of the Caucasus. He could see far
away to the southward a point where the road forked, one road
entering his defile, and the other the defile parallel with it. He
had been intrusted with two flags, one *yellow* and the other
red, which lay upon the rock beside him. His instructions
were to keep a sharp lookout upon the fork of the road where

a body of Persian cavalry were expected to make their appearance on their way to invade the Russian territory. If the Persian horse entered the defile upon whose summit he was posted, he was ordered to raise the *red* flag, which could be seen by the Russian general at his camp some distance to the northward. The Russian commander would thus be enabled to post his artillery in a position to annihilate the advancing cavalry before they were aware of the trap set for them. If the Persians entered the lower defile, the scout was to raise the *yellow* flag, and a different disposition of the Russian batteries would be made to surprise them.

After a long vigil in the warmth of the mid-day sun, the eyes of the scout were rewarded by seeing in the distance a body of two hundred Persian cavalry approaching the fork of the road. He was evidently familiar with the appearance of that portion of the regular Persian cavalry which were causing the greatest havoc in this campaign, for he said aloud:

"Ha! ha! the regulars of *General Alfonso Debaena.* How fortunate Abbas Mirza has sent *them.* The flower of the Persian horse will give a strange report at headquarters to-morrow."

As the scout watched their advent, he appeared to be thrilled with exultation. There could be no further question of the division of the army to which they belonged. Their uniform, their *style* betrayed their commander-in-chief. The two hundred reached the fork of the road and immediately advanced upon the upper defile. The *red flag* waved the signal to the distant Russian general, and immediately an answering *red* flag was raised to signify that Russia was on the alert, and would be ready for the foe. Then ensued a remarkable manifestation of anxiety and subsequent joy on the part of the Circassian scout. Without appearing to take any interest in the further movement of the two hundred horse which were on the point of entering the upper defile, he looked away down the distant road as if in eager expectation of a further arrival. ·They came at length, as he had anticipated, another body of horse full *five thousand strong,* and wearing the same uniform as the two hundred who had preceded them. Arriving at the fork of the road, they moved directly on to the *lower* defile, entered it at a rapid trot, and disappeared from the sight of the scout. The Circassian made no movement to raise the *yellow* flag, but left the Russian forces to their error caused by the elevation of the red flag. The Russian commander would concentrate his military energies upon the destruction of the two hundred, while the *five thousand* would pass unharmed and unnoticed by another route. The scout did more than neglect his duty. He fell upon his knees, and trembling with joy and excitement, exclaimed in the fulness of his heart, "Great Allah! I thank thee, oh! how fervently I thank thee, that I have struck so deadly a blow into the bosom of detestable Russia."

Then rising to his feet, and securing the two flags, he mounted his steed and sought the Russian lines over a circuitous mountain road. He had flung open wide the Russian gates for a disastrous Persian inroad. While this traitor to the Russian cause was flying away to the lines of the army he had betrayed, secure from arrest from the fact that the two hundred horse which were expected would be found in the upper defile as he had signalled, the five thousand horse, under the command of General Alfonso Debaena, were advancing rapidly through the lower defile, and approaching by a circuitous route the rear of the Russian camp. The two hundred horse, acting in concert with Debaena's command, were advancing through the upper defile slowly and cautiously, having received orders to retreat upon the first indication of an enemy, and if possible draw off a portion of the Russian cavalry in pursuit, which portion would inevitably fall into an ambuscade prepared for them by the remainder of General Debaena's horsemen, who had been left behind. The Circassian scout was a confederate of Abbas Mirza, who had instructed General Debaena how to take advantage of the information sent by the friendly scout. So perfectly familiar was this Circassian with the details of the upper defile, that he had sent to the adjutant-general of Abbas Mirza a drawing of it, marking the spot where the artillery of Russia would inevitably be posted to sweep away the two hundred Persian horse. A small ravine connecting the two defiles was also indicated, by which a portion of the cavalry in the lower defile could penetrate to the rear of the Russian battery and capture the guns, which might then be turned upon the Russian camp.

General Debaena had with him in the lower defile two pieces of light artillery, with which he proposed to entice a portion of the Russians from their entrenched camp when he should have gained their rear. Swiftly and unnoticed his immediate force made its way through the lower defile, and gained the woods about two miles in rear of the enemy's camp. Not dreaming that so large a body of Persian cavalry had been concentrated upon the Koor

river so early in the campaign, the Russian commander anticipated no attack, and was merely calculating upon entrapping
a small detachment of horse that were out marauding. His
favorite and active scout had brought him intelligence from
Elizabethpol that about two hundred of the enemy's cavalry
were advancing. His plan was laid to entrap them, and his
guns were admirably placed. Presently his ears were greeted
by the discharge of his artillery, and, after an ominous cessation of the reports, word was brought him that the enemy's
cavalry had fled at the first discharge, having discovered the
artillerymen before they were fairly in the trap. An angle in
the defile had prevented the effective discharge of the guns.
He immediately dispatched cavalry in pursuit, and ordered one
of his aids to bring back the artillery to camp. What was his
amazement to discover that his aid did not return in due time.
He dispatched another aid to ascertain the cause of the delay.
Presently this second messenger returned at full speed, with the
appalling intelligence that his artillery had been captured by a
small body of Persian horse. The guns were now posted at
the summit of the defile, a few rods from their former position,
and were pointed in the direction of his camp. They could
only be retaken by infantry. He immediately ordered a
chef-de-bataillon to advance with 800 infantry and capture the
guns, moving cautiously, however, as it was evident there were
more Persian cavalry stirring than he had been notified of.

It was not long after this body of infantry had vanished from
his sight, before the thunder of the artillery and the rattle of
musketry announced that the cavalry would not give up the
guns without a struggle. Scarcely had this contest fairly commenced, when the Russian commander found his entrenched
camp attacked from the rear by two pieces of light artillery,
which advanced from the woods and took position upon a
knoll. The pieces were well served, and for a few moments
inflicted severe loss upon the infantry, who were totally unprepared for this sudden firing into their camp. The Russian
artillery, however, soon compelled the Persians to retreat with
their guns towards the wood, into whose shadows they disappeared, leaving several dead upon the open field. Confident
now of capturing the two pieces of light artillery, Russian infantry were pushed across the open field, but were met half
way by squadrons of Persian horse, which charged furiously
upon them from two roads leading out from the forest. A
terrific struggle ensued; many a wild horse of the Persian

mountains died upon the Russian bayonets, his rider falling headlong to the earth. The clash of the sabre and bayonet was terrific as the Persian horse plunged frantically through the stubborn masses of the foe, but the wild riders of the mountains were invincible, and trampling under foot the infantry, they dashed on to the artillery which was being hurried up in the rear, and sabred the artillerymen at their guns. Fresh bodies of infantry were advancing to the field, but the Persian cavalry, augmented every instant by fresh squadrons of horse emerging from distant parts of the forest, charged like demons upon them, unheeding the cannon shot which played upon them from the intrenchments. The Persians in numbers far exceeded the Russians, weakened as the latter were by the absence of their cavalry and the 800 infantry sent away in the opposite direction towards the upper defile. The horsemen of Iran, under the leadership of the skilful Debaena, swept onward in frantic and bloody charges, tearing and scattering the ranks of the Muscovites, and covering the field with heaps of the dead and the dying. Onward, right onward, they poured like their own mountain torrents, till every opposing square was rent and the fugitives were streaming off over the plain. Few escaped that fearful massacre, and the pursuers only drew rein when the grapeshot from the fort commenced to play into their squadrons. As they were about to withdraw from their exposed situation, General Debaena, with the light of battle in his eye and a figure towering above his fellows, dashed out to the front of the advanced squadrons, shouting, " They are ·weakened beyond redemption. Charge into the fort." He rode straight up the rising ground, followed by squadron after squadron, for his voice and manner were electric. He leaped the dry ditch amid a shower of grape and bullets. Many horsemen also cleared it in safety, and the others crossed upon the dead bodies of their comrades who soon filled it up. Like a whirlwind the Persian horse swept through the blaze of the guns, and the charge was successful. The Russian commander surrendered to Alfonso Debaena his sword and the small force he had retained within the intrenchments. He had been utterly surprised by numbers, and his forces were divided.

The contest was still raging in the distance, where the Persians were maintaining an obstinate defence of their strong position with the captured artillery. General Debaena pushed on to their assistance with his victorious cavalry and attacked the Russian infantry in the rear. Taken by surprise, they were cut down or scattered into the woods on either hand, and soon gave up their arms. The heroic band that defended the rocky height with the artillery were fearfully decimated and could not have held their position a half hour longer.

As General Debaena had anticipated, the Russian cavalry sent in pursuit of the two hundred Persians who had fled through the upper defile, followed on so far beyond the fork of the road that they fell into his cavalry ambuscade, and were surrounded and cut down by the Persian horse which were the remainder of his command of ten thousand. When night set in the Persian commander knew that his victory was decisive, and that the survivors of the Russian force were all his prisoners. He sent back on the following day to Abbas Mirza beyond Elizabethpol his report of the battle, together with the captured cannon, guns, military stores and all the prisoners. Providing for the wounded as best he could, he remained upon the field awaiting further orders and the arrival of the army surgeons. With promptness Abbas Mirza responded to his demands and sent him the brief order :

" Push on rapidly into the enemy's country and carry terror to the foe by the celerity of your movements. Issue manifestoes as you advance to our delivered friends, calling upon them to take up arms in the name of Mahomet and in defence of their religion. The eyes of all Persia are upon you. The splendor of the manhood with which you opposed me in the council of the Shah is only equalled by the splendor of your military genius. Push on."

With alacrity the commander of horse obeyed this injunction of his chief, whose military abilities he had learned to respect from the day he assumed command of the army of invasion. As he advanced, the Russians at the posts on the frontiers fell back, being too weak to withstand him. Great quantities of military stores, cannon and horses fell into his hands, and his name became the terror of Georgia. The tramp of his steeds was heard in every town and hamlet, and thousands of the oppressed Mohammedans arose in arms behind the glitter of his sabres.

Having driven the scattered detachments of the enemy (which were totally unprepared for this.sudden invasion) before him to Tiflis, where General Yermoloff, the Russian commander, was endeavoring to concentrate his troops, the victorious Debaena received orders to march his cavalry across the country to the west, and pursue a similar career of conquest in that section of the country beyond the Lake of Goktscha. This new field of operations gave him an opportunity to become personally familiar with the roads described to him by the Ghebre on the summit of Ararat, and particularly with the one leading through *the dangerous rocky pass beside the river Abarane* and near to the mountains of the *Saganlúg* chain. After inspecting the fortress of Erivan he passed on west toward *Echmiadzin* and dividing his cavalry into two parties near this monastery, sent one off toward Tiflis by the north-western road. The other he led in person north toward the same Russian headquarters by *the difficult road up the Abarane river*. Then did he realize the force of the Ghebre's suggestion, that upon the rocky banks of the Abarane the Russian army or a portion of it should be entrapped if possible.

So vividly did the image of the astute Zenayi rise before him as he traversed this rocky pass, that he whispered to himself: "How that patriot priest watches over Persia! This is indeed a trap for the enemies of the Shah. How shall it be arranged with our spies in the Russian camp? They must be wntten to at once to bear this pass in mind during the whole war. I have it. *Irene!* Of all our secret agents, that patriot loveliness is the only competent spy at Tiflis to arrange this snare."

After mature reflection as he rode on northward through the pass he determined to write to the beautiful schemer himself. Irene would redouble her activity in the secret service if she knew that he was personally anxious in any particular scheme. The Ghebre had informed him of this partiality of the girl for his military opinions. He had also given to the commander of horse the secret cypher arranged at the headquarters of the Persian army, by means of which he could write with safety to any of the secret agents at the northward.

At his first encampment, therefore, on the slope of the Saganlúg mountains, he addressed a letter in cypher to Irene, known in the secret service of Persia by the title "*Coadjutor.*" He could not omit writing to her also concerning her personal safety. He cautioned her in terms of earnest entreaty to value her own life in the enemy's camp as he valued it, and as the Ghebre and the adjutant general of the army valued it, and notifying her that he had heard she was too reckless in the audacity with which she penetrated to the highest councils of the Russian army. He requested her to commune freely with the Circassian scout when opportunity offered, and make this fearless friend of Persia an accomplice in the plan to entrap

the Russians some day in the rocky pass of the Abarane river.
He desired her to return his earnest thanks to the scout whose
skilful management at the defiles beyond Elizabethpol had
given success to his arms, and secured him the especial commendation of Abbas Mirza in the official report of the battle
forwarded by a horseman to Teheran.

"I deprecated your dangerous mission," he wrote, "as you
well know. At the same time I must confess that I experienced exultation at the thought that your transcendant
powers of intrigue and diplomacy were secured for Persia.
I know that the same prompt and active display of intellectual
resources that you have ever manifested will continue, even
when you daily move with a Russian halter about your neck.
But in the name of Persia, in the name of all that is tender in
friendship, in my name, spare yourself any unnecessary hazard.
You are the soul of audacity, but remember that your innate
elegance and the stamp of high birth that is unmistakably
yours, may cause you to be suspected by the officers of a hard,
harsh nationality. I know that you appear as a *Georgian
nurse* in the hospitals, but I warn you to curb your wit, your
satire and your brilliancy, or they will betray you to death.
But whatever befalls you rest assured I trust you utterly,
and whenever you write me that your judgment demands of
me to place my cavalry in any strategic position, or myself in
any personal hazard, I will obey you. Can trust in a woman's
tact, talent and patriotism go farther than my promise? I
have told you before that you are an eagle among butterflies.
I make this strong promise to you now, that you may understand how perfectly your noble sacrifice is appreciated by Zenayi and by me. There is something so heroic in your love for
your country that it is contagious. It arouses in me a holy
zeal to be worthy of your friendship, to equal you in great
thoughts and sacrifices for that which is grand.

"The commander is emulous of the greatness of the girl.
There are moments when I believe firmly that my towering
ambition melts away in the desire to be unselfishly *sublime.*"

CHAPTER XXIV.

EWARE the immense cloud of the Cossacks! Yermoloff has concentrated *twenty thousand* of them in the rear of General Madatov. Make no stand north of the Araxes unless you can effect a junction with General Debaena's cavalry."

These words were read aloud to Abbas Mirza and the adjutant-general of the army, as they reclined in a tent near Elizabethpol. The cipher of the secret agent was interpreted to the commander of the Persian army by the white-robed Ghebre, who added to the warning of the spy his own urgent counsel, that the army should retreat towards the Araxes until reinforcements could come up. Abbas Mirza, in a military undress, listened patiently to the letter, which had also apprized them of the day General Madatov would advance upon them from Tiflis. At the conclusion of Zenayi's remarks he puffed away vigorously for a moment at his *Kaleoon* and the smoke arose in clouds above him, circling away toward the top of the tent. Then the Prince Royal calmly opened the discussion of the letter thus, turning slightly as he addressed the adjutant-general.

"Who is your informant?"

"She is known to your royal highness by the name of '*Coadjutor*,'" responded the officer.

"That is a woman of discretion," replied the Prince Royal. "If I mistake not, Zenayi, she is the same who gave us such reliable information of the movements of the Russian *pulkoonick* and his light horse."

"The very same, your Royal Highness," responded the Ghebre. "To *Coadjutor* are we indebted for the utter defeat of his four thousand horse."

"You know the woman, personally, Zenayi?" inquired the Prince.

"I know *all* the secret agents personally. I would employ no one on such important service for whose skill and integrity I could not personally vouch. Your Royal Highness should know me well enough for that, after all my years of service."

"I intended no impeachment of your sense, noble friend," replied the Prince, amid the dense clouds of smoke which were blending together from his own *Kaleoon* and the Turkish *narghillés* of his two companions. "We are too much indebted to

9

you to withhold the highest encomiums for your discretion and forethought. But this is a question which involves the safety of an entire army. Is *Coadjutor* ever inclined to exaggerate numbers? *Twenty thousand* Cossacks are a great number to collect upon so short a notice as Nicholas has had."

"I will pledge my word, your Royal Highness," responded Zenayi, "that when the cool hand of *Coadjutor* penned the words, *twenty thousand*, she was copying from Russian *official* papers."

"Your faith in her, Zenayi, is only equalled by your estimate of her power of gaining access to the headquarters of Yermoloff himself."

"*Coadjutor*," replied the Ghebre, "is a *military secretary* of Yermoloff."

"Impossible!" ejaculated the chief of the army; "moreover you notified me that she was employed by the Muscovites as a hospital *nurse*."

"So *was* she, your Royal Highness, but *Coadjutor* has the brilliancy and beauty of Statira. If Alexander was once magnanimous on the banks of the Issus, why may not beauty again overpower a general of so much inferior ability as the Russian Yermoloff."

"And you have pushed an agent into the Muscovite service itself, even to the table of the Russian commander?" exclaimed Abbas Mirza, half rising from his cushion and eying the Ghebre in amazement.

"And how would Your Royal Highness otherwise defeat the great dominant terror of the North?" inquired Zenayi. "We undertook this war as I understand it to *defeat* the Muscovites. Then we must defeat them by every method of strategy that occurs to us. If our noble people are ready to hazard their necks in the camps of the foe shall we not accept their services? *Coadjutor* has exquisite beauty, tact, perseverance and zeal for our cause. Knowing her rare gifts, I could not refuse her offer of service. She is naturally enough mistaken for a full-blooded Georgian. She has intrigued her way from the hospital to the headquarters. Yermoloff hopes to make her his wife. Step by step she has won his respect and confidence. The witchery of her beauty and grace have not enslaved him half as much as her abilities and conversational brilliancy. She writes me that two of his staff officers have offered her marriage. She is adroitly keeping them in suspense, and thereby gaining military favors and privileges which yield her valuable information for our headquarters. As you trust my judgment trust Coadjutor's, or rather, I would say, trust im plicitly the truth of the *details* which she sends. She *knows* that unless Your Royal Highness effects a junction with Gen eral Debaena your army will be overpowered. She tells us in this letter that the regular army of General Madatov exceeds yours in numbers, and now behind him Yermoloff is pushing ahead to the front *twenty thousand* Cossacks. I know how those wild horsemen can travel. Their horses are small but swift. When they do not move in compact bodies and carry little or no baggage, they can without difficulty advance from fifty to seventy miles a day for several days in succession. I apprehend that when Your Royal Highness is actually giving battle to Madatov they will dash in upon us and neutralize, aye more, destroy utterly your most skilful combinations. The army here may by superior handling and by choice of position defeat Madatov, whose force outnumbers us. But the Cossacks will prove too much for the small cavalry force at our disposal. I earnestly counsel Your Royal Highness to fall back behind the Araxes now at your leisure to meet our new army from Sultania, rather than to await the time when we shall be driven across it in confusion. The Cossacks are fearful upon the flanks of a retreating army. Their lances are then irresistible."

Again silence ensued and the smoke of the *caleeqon* indicated the energetic brain that was working behind it. Huge puffs of it issued rapidly. Then the mouth-piece was withdrawn from the depths of the heavy black imperial beard, and Abbas Mirza smiled as he spoke :

" Why, Zenayi, the hearts of the Persian people would sink if they saw us retreat from the first opportunity for a general battle."

" Hang the people everywhere," interrupted the adjutant-general, who removed from his mustaches the mouth-piece of his *narghillè* just long enough to utter his military opinion of the sense of the masses. Zenayi dropped his *narghillè* from his lips and laughed immoderately. The Prince Royal was soon laughing as heartily as the Ghebre. The adjutant-general only smiled grimly.

" Zenayi," exclaimed Abbas Mirza, intensely amused at the pithy sentence of the officer, who was one of the ablest soldiers in the army of Persia, " this council of war is manifestly against *me*, and I must add that the grand title, *the people*, is greatly undervalued here."

"The adjutant-general is right," exclaimed the Ghebre firmly. "The people, the wretched, vacillating, unreasoning, treacherous, ungrateful people; always persecuting and hating those who love them best; never recognizing the noble, fearless defenders of principle, but everlastingly lauding to the skies the men who flatter in order that they may rob them. *The people, the people!* oh! what a farce are the opinions of the people. There is but one way to deal with them, and that is to treat them as we treat children. Love them, work for their best interests, but ignore their clamor as one ignores the senseless remonstrances of children."

"And how about the opinions of the *soldiers*, Zenayi?" interposed the Prince Royal.

"The soldiers must be deceived," responded the Ghebre. "Their ardor must be stimulated by the report that some remarkable strategic snare is about to be laid for the foe. They must be promised an extra compensation in *toumauns* for the silence and secrecy with which they withdraw from the line of the enemy's advance."

"And what does my silent adjutant-general say to a retreat behind the Araxes?" said Abbas Mirza, after a long interval of silent smoke.

The *narghillé* was reluctantly relinquished for an instant for the utterance of the sententious advice of the old veteran.

"Order it to commence before daylight."

"To-morrow?'

"Ay."

The monosyllable and the returning mouth-piece jostled each other in passing.

"I thought my adjutant-general was anxious to smell gun-powder," continued Abbas Mirza.

"Too great odds," were the prompt words that usurped for an instant the place of the *narghillé*.

"You have not forgotten Mingrelia, General Hassam?"

The veteran smiled grimly. In the war of 1813, he had seen two-thirds of his command swept away by Russian grape and would not surrender to five times his own number. He was scarred with eleven wounds, all from grape-shot, and his last act before he fell senseless was to hurl his broken sword into the face of a Muscovite officer of artillery, a *pulkoonick*.

Abbas Mirza remained long after this reference to past heroism in silent meditation. His companions awaited his decision and puffed away with their *narghillés*. Once only they exchanged glances, when after an ominous silence of several minutes their chief inquired of the Ghebre how many days it would take General Debaena's cavalry to march from the lower Abaranc to Elizabethpol. They realized then how firmly their chief was bent upon offering battle in his present position at the north. Zenayi gave him the distances by the different roads to the camp of General Debaena, and an estimate of the time in which Debaena could join them if not encountered by the enemy on his way.

After another prolonged silence the chief announced that he would not retreat, but would await the advent of General Madatov and give him battle. Then turning to his adjutant-general, he directed him to summon General Debaena from the west with all possible dispatch and order him to bring with him six thousand of his cavalry, leaving four thousand to watch the enemy in the west and harass their advance if they should make a forward movement.

Soon after this indication of his purpose to meet the foe near Elizabethpol the conference broke up.   .   .   .

In the middle of September the advance-guard of the Persians was encountered by General Madatov, who attacked a body of them amounting to about ten thousand men under the command of a son of Abbas Mirza. After a severe contest the Persian cavalry took to flight, and the infantry, being thus left unsupported, were broken by the regular cavalry of the Russians, and after a desperate conflict completely routed. The Persians lost two thousand men in killed and wounded. Amur Khan, the uncle of Abbas Mirza, was killed while endeavoring to rally his troops. The young prince, son of Abbas Mirza, was taken prisoner by a Russian horseman, but was rescued by one of his officers and escaped from the field. The Russians promptly advanced after this disaster and took possession of Elizabethpol without opposition. Abbas Mirza having effected a junction with the forces of Alaiar Khan advanced against Madatov, who was surprised by the rapidity of his adversary and was driven from the field with heavy loss. As the Persians were about to convert his defeat into a route the Russian commander was relieved by the appearance of General Parkaewitch with his forces, who immediately charged the victors with such vehemence that the tide of victory was turned. An obstinate contest, lasting through the entire afternoon, terminated with the fall of night, the Persian army being driven at all points a mile backward. At daybreak the battle was renewed, both armies displaying the most determined courage and every inch of ground being fiercely contested. Abbas Mirza commanded in person, and by his admirable generalship twice turned the Russian left, driving it back in confusion upon the centre. The artillery of the Persians, brought to the highest perfection by the training of English officers from India, inflicted frightful loss upon the enemy. But the stubborn heroism of the Russian infantry prevailed after several hours of bloody conflict, and by noon the Persians were slowly falling back at all points. Inch by inch did the heroic sons of Iran contest the ground, winning the admiration of their foes, men scarred with the bullets of hard-fought European battles. The Muscovites pressed forward flushed with the confidence of the coming victory; but their exultation was of brief duration. Abbas Mirza, fruitful in devices, had planned the apparent retreat of his men to entrap the Muscovites, and now as they fell back beyond the limit of a dense wood the Russians discovered their motive. It was to allow their concealed cavalry, the *goolams*, to strike the Russian flank. The first astonishment ·of the surprise, the unearthly yells and the furious onset of the *goolams* struck dismay and disorder into the Muscovite ranks. They were speedily broken and scattered, and those who escaped with their lives were soon huddled in confusion under the protecting guns of the Russian batteries. Overwhelmed with the confusion of the field, and fainting under the intense heat and burning thirst of the climate, the weary and despairing Russians endeavored to regain some degree of order for a retreat before the general advance which it was manifest the indomitable Abbas Mirza was organizing. The Persian light artillery was flying over the adjacent hills with marvellous rapidity to secure favorable positions to throw their enemies into confusion. The Russian light artillery-men had been sabred beside their guns by the wild *goolams*. The only cannon that remained to the Muscovites were the heavy guns which they had rallied under after their terrible decimation. It was manifestly the duty of Madatov to commence a retreat at once, and he had already ordered it when his eyes were greeted by a vision which filled him with joy, at the same time that it appalled the victorious Persians, who were already advancing to intercept the Russian retreat.

From every hilltop, plain and ravine on either flank of the Persian army a *swarm of Cossacks* was advancing. Their lances glittered in the sunlight and were carried upright by means of a strap fastened to the foot, the arm, or the pommel of the saddle. They were armed also with pistols, sabres and bows and arrows Each *pulk* had two silken banners adorned with images of the saints. By thousands they poured in on either flank of the advancing Persians, and the Ghebre was the first who rode up and called the attention of Abbas Mirza to his danger.

"*Beware the immense cloud of the Cossacks!* See yonder, Your Royal Highness, the accuracy of *Coadjutor*." Zenayi pointed on either side to the glittering spear-heads of at least *twenty thousand* of the irregular flying cavalry of Russia. On they came, a fearful array of fresh, fearless riders, eager for battle and plunder, and moving on steadily upon the exhausted ranks of the heroic patriots who were gathering their last energies for the *coup de grâce* to Madatov's defeated regulars. The hearts of the bravest might well be appalled at the danger of this immense flank-movement. *Pulk* after *pulk* they advanced, each under command of its *ataman*. Cossacks of the Don, Cossacks of Malo-Russia, Volgaic, Terek, Grebeskoi, Uralian, and Siberian Cossacks blended their Polish and Oriental uniforms in one overwhelming horror as they swept forward upon the doomed flanks of the Persians.

Abbas Mirza was mounted upon a superb black steed whose swiftness equalled that of the black-maned Arcion. He was surrounded by a brilliant staff, some of them slightly wounded. From the rise of ground whence he was overlooking and directing the advance upon Madatov the danger from the sudden approach of the Cossacks was fearfully manifest. Ever prompt and brilliant in sudden emergencies, he issued his orders now with rapidity and clearness. His aids dashed away over the field and the advance upon Madatov was countermanded. The light artillery came scampering back to avoid being cut off by the Cossacks, and the infantry were soon in retreat, while the adjutant-general was intrusted with the important duty of massing the artillery to protect their flight. The *goolams* were assigned to the fearful duty of meeting the Cossacks. Every moment of time that they could delay the huge masses of this irregular cavalry of Nicholas was vital to the safety of the Persian army. Right gallantly did these fiery Asiatics dash forward to the unequal combat and meet the Cossacks. Their light bamboo lances drank blood, and with the *élan* of tigers they forced their way over heaps of dying men and horses, for the life of their Persia was at stake. Against immense odds they forced their way on both flanks of the retreating Persians, and Abbas Mirza watched their prowess with intense interest, for the fate of his army depended upon the duration of their resistance to the immense horde of Russian cavalry. Each Persian *goolam*, with the soul of a Codrus in him, thrust his lance and met his death, or dealing fearful havoc with his sabre, lined his path with the dead and the dying, and then escaped from the crush of the Cossacks only to whirl a swifter flight upon another part of their advance. The slaughter at these flanks was terrific and the Cossacks bit the earth by hundreds. The *goolams* fought like incarnate fiends, and for a time the skill and desperation of their onset were successful. The Cossacks were retarded. Seconds, moments, *an hour* passed by and still the Persian heroes held them back and met their death one after another, until their small force had dwindled to a dozen knots of horsemen enveloped by huge crowds of the frantic and enraged foe. A few of the *goolams* broke away from the throng and escaped death and capture. The fatal hour had been passed, and the Asiatic light horse had saved the army of Abbas Mirza from annihilation. The infantry were passing away down the road beside the Koor river, and the adjutant-general, the veteran of 1813, had planted the artillery at the entrance of a pass so that Madatov hesitated to push ahead with his veterans, who had rallied and followed the retreating Persians upon the advent of the Cossacks.

All of that afternoon and the following night Abbas Mirza continued his retreat towards the Araxes, and when morning broke he halted his dispirited troops, hopeful of a day of rest. His adjutant-general soon joined him, having brought off in safety the artillery, which had not been molested by the Cossacks. This extraordinary forbearance on the part of these fleet horsemen was soon explained. Upon looking to the southward, where the road led up over rocky hills, it was discovered that the Cossacks held the heights, having by a circuitous and rapid advance *cut off the Persian retreat.*

CHAPTER XXV.

"——front to front
Bring thou this fiend of Scotland and myself;
Within my sword's length set him. — If he 'scape,
Then Heaven forgive him, too.

MACBETH.

ABBAS MIRZA had selected his camping ground with the eye of a great commander. Forced to halt his army by reason of their extreme exhaustion from continuous fighting and marching, he had at the first glance proposed to occupy the height now held by the Cossacks. But he fortunately recollected before the enemy's horse appeared upon this eminence that the position could readily be flanked by the Russians, whose combined armies now so far exceeded in numbers his own force. Riding in the van with his staff he found when day dawned that the road upon which he was retreating descended abruptly into a great amphitheatre several miles in width from east to west, but from north to south (the direction he was marching) only two miles across. At the southern extremity of this amphitheatre were the heights now occupied by the Cossacks, who could only descend into the plain of the amphitheatre by the narrow road which was flanked on either hand by an impenetrable morass. Should their horse attempt to charge down on to the plain they would be exposed to a murderous fire from his artillery when about half way down the descending road. This artillery, and indeed his entire army, he posted at once upon a rocky mountain standing alone in the midst of this amphitheatre, which commanded the road he had just come as it descended into the plain, and also the road through the morass down which the Cossacks must attack unless they consumed a fatal length of time by taking a tedious and rocky circuit of many miles. .

The artillery which the Persian commander was enabled to place in position for the defence of this central rock mountain was formidable indeed. In addition to his own admirably handled field-pieces, he held the cannon captured from the Russians when they were routed by the charge of the *gœlams* on their flank in the late battle. If Madatov made his appearance on the high ground at the north he would be exposed to a destructive artillery fire from Abbas Mirza's loftier position. On the south the Cossacks would meet a similar fire if they approached half way down the heights where they would come within range. While Abbas Mirza made this disposition of his forces, the Cossacks looked down upon the movements of the Persians, but made no effort to interfere with them. Doubtless they had received their instructions from Madatov, who expected to capture the entire army of the Shah. Along the rocky heights the Cossack line extended, plainly visible above the morass. No indication of the coming of Madatov was to be seen on the north, and Abbas Mirza congratulated himself upon the rest which his weary troops would secure. His central rock mountain was bristling with bayonets flashing in the sun, and the brass field-pieces on every side were visible, ready to sweep every approach up to his citadel, should the Russians succeed in eluding his first artillery fire and attempt to storm the heights.

The morning wore away and still none of the enemy had appeared on the north. The forces of Madatov had been too badly cut up and disorganized to pursue with vigor, and that general, doubtless, trusted to the Cossacks to hold the retreating army in check until he could come up. The Persian commander was confident that if he could maintain himself for two days in his present position, ten thousand infantry from the camp on the Araxes would come to his relief. Towards evening all speculations as to Madatov's movements were silenced by the appearance of the Russians at the north. Along the winding, rocky road they moved in solid column, a splendid spectacle, with their bayonets glistening in the red light of the setting sun. Even the small green *yaschicks* or waggons of the companies were visible by the aid of field-glasses, each containing sixty rounds of ball cartridge for each man in addition to those he carried in his pouch. Arriving at the point where the road widened out, just before commencing to descend to the plain of the amphitheatre, the advance regiment was received with a discharge of Persian artillery, which inflicted frightful havoc, so admirably were the guns handled ; the balls ploughing their way through the solid mass of infantry crowded upon the road. Unable to retreat from the broken nature of the ground and the impeding regiments in the rear, this regiment was well nigh annihilated. The well-directed shot swept every yard of the highway, and the enemy's advance was for the time effectually checked. When night fell, the Russians were evidently falling back out of range of this destructive fire, to await the light of the ensuing day.

When midnight came silence brooded over the three armies. Mystery magnifies danger. The ominous quiet which everywhere reigned in the camps of his adversaries, the possibility that at some point of the compass they might be stealing a circuitous march upon him, the knowledge that in the direction of Madatov's left were a few prominent rocks, *apparently* inaccessible, which genius with her marvellous hands might crown with artillery which would overreach his guns, all tended to keep Abbas Mirza upon the alert during the entire night. He was watching at midnight upon the apex of his rock mountain-every mile of the surrounding country. The moon was at the full and the stars were luminous over the entire expanse of the heavens. His staff were stretched upon the rocks about him in heavy sleep, with their horses secured near them ready for instant service. His only watchful companions were the adjutant-general, reticent but irresistible as Tydeus, and the white-robed Ghebre, who stood apart upon a broad platform of level rock with all the implements of astrology, taking an observation of the stars. As court astrologer of Abbas Mirza it was his duty to ascertain on the eve of great events or the commencement of a journey if the great lights of heaven portended fortune or disaster. The Persians from the earliest ages of their history have been devotees of the occult science. It was then with delight that the mysterious Zenayi returned with the astrological calculation to his master's side, and announced that the stars favored the cause of Persia on the morrow.

"Will it be victory, Zenayi?" inquired the Prince Royal.

"No," was the response.

"We shall effect our escape?" continued the anxious commander.

"So the lights of Ormuzd indicate to their servant," was the reply of the Ghebre.

The Prince Royal laid his hand affectionately upon the shoulder of his great friend and *savant* as he said :

"Why does your zeal and love for Persia equal the persistency and tenderness of a mother's love?"

"Persia is my child," replied Zenayi, and as he spoke he looked full into the eyes of the Prince. And in that unfathomable and far-off look of the Ghebre's eyes Abbas Mirza saw again that peculiar expression of immensity of knowledge, or measureless consciousness, which awed all who encountered it and set them to dreaming of their earliest recollections. In that look all men felt themselves to dwindle. Their power of memory, of intellectual grasp, of analysis, seemed to grow feeble by contact with that singular intellect whose acquirements stamped him *master*. Who could dispute with that being whose memory of facts, whose immense study, had provided him with an ever-ready torrent of comparisons, illustrations and figures. Zenayi was no sciolist. What he knew he knew thoroughly, and like a deity he seemed to know *everything* of the past. Men would have pronounced him a god had not his power been limited to the past. The future to him was as hidden as to all men. But what *had been* he was master of, and when one looked full into those deep, thoughtful eyes he seemed to behold an intellect which had been a contemporary of the earliest knowledge that existed from the foundation of the race of man. The thought suggested was, "That being commenced with the cradle of knowledge and has existed down to the present moment, always studying, always acquiring, and his memory never fails him." But if in any one department of knowledge Zenayi appeared to men to be more perfected than in another that department was Persia. He knew every detail of its history from *Kayomurz*, the first man, to Futteh Ali Shah, the present sovereign. Dynasties, wars, *savans*, topographies were all known to him. Could he have indeed visited every foot of ground in the empire? Sometimes it appeared so. For when men accosted him for details and distances in Persia he answered promptly and to the point. There were no inaccuracies in Zenayi's statements. Could any man without a personal visit know every corner of Persia as well as the local natives of each place? Many a map had lost credit simply because this illustrious scholar pointed out inaccuracies from his memory of distances and the peculiar formations of mountains and plains and rivers. There was no professional story-teller of Persia who could hold an audience in raptured silence and attention as this priest of the proscribed religion of Zoroaster could do when he was betrayed into an argument at the gate of a town or city. For then the doors of the great and wonderful past seemed to fly open at his magic touch, and consultations with historic books all confirmed his statements.

He would portray with the eloquence and accuracy of Aristarchus the ancient sculptured royal tombs of Nakshi Roustam or the "Mountain of Sepulchres," coeval with the splendor of Persepolis, until the patriotic enthusiasm of his listeners was aroused to the loftiest pitch at the memory of the lost glories of Iran. And every visitor to the place would return with encomiums upon the accuracy of the Ghebre. The fluted columns of Persepolis, the equestrian carvings upon the ruins of the ancient and famous city of Rhey, made by artists two hundred years before the deliverance of the Jews by Cyrus, and the sculptured wonders of Mourg Aub, were so vividly portrayed, with all the details of the surroundings, that the listeners were oft induced to believe that the narrator was some mighty wizard who had had personal knowledge of these cities when they were in the perfection of their architecture and glory.

But never in an unguarded moment had mortal man been successful in drawing from the Ghebre the *secret* of his matchless knowledge and memory. He always responded in this manner :

" Patience in study, and a judicious use of our time, will compress the recollection of many things into the ordinary lifetime of a sound, healthy man."

Nothing further could be gleaned from the Sphinx. The listeners would shake their heads and whisper to each other of Eblis and the infernal powers that deity could manifest on earth. The Jews in Persia of the cultivated classes styled him " *Azazel,*" a demon of the pre-Mosaic religion. But whatever he was, or from whatever power, human, infernal or divine, he gained his wonderful knowledge, no man could charge him with evil acts. His life was exemplary, his charity proverbial as his honesty, and his love for Persia the admiration of the patriotic. In just proportion to his powers of intellectual perception was his ability to read the true characters of men. The subtleties of logicians he unravelled with ease. He penetrated to the secrets of hypocrites on wings of lightning; he drew close in tenderness to the pure of heart and motive. He manifested no resentments. His most vigorous denunciations of the bad were ever coupled with recognition of the inherent good in them. Hence men who desired an unbiassed opinion sought the counsel of Zenayi. His sterling and intrinsic merit early recommended him to the attention and friendship of the heir-apparent to the crown of Persia. Abbas Mirza had received much of his early education from the Ghebre. He would quarrel at times in mature life with his friend on matters of judgment. But with rare sense this patriot Prince ever returned to his friend, and avowed his own error when cool counsels at length prevailed. He had commenced this war with Russia contrary to the advice of the Ghebre. But when the horrid gauntlet of blood had been raised from the earth by Russia he hastened to restore Zenayi to his former confidence.　He needed this friend, and the great patriot priest never hesitated when he could serve Persia.　The inexhaustible resources of Zenayi's intellect and his thorough knowledge of military details proved to be of inestimable value to the Persian commander.　The magnanimity evinced by the Ghebre in ignoring his expulsion from the council of the Shah won so upon the heart of Abbas Mirza, that he secretly vowed eternal fidelity to the priest to the end of time; and now in the critical hour for Persia, the Prince, the Ghebre, and the able adjutant-general stood upon the summit of the rock-mountain in perfect accord, mutual respect, and undying zeal for their beleaguered country.　In this hour of danger, those three hardy and valorous soldiers stood watchful through the entire night.　They could not sleep when the Persian army perchance rested on its last battlefield.

When morning broke, as the adjutant-general had predicted, the Russian artillery opened upon the Persians.　The foe had, during the night, with incredible toil and persistency, succeeded in dragging (by means of wooden platforms, made of their baggage wagons and tent-poles), several brass field-pieces to the summit of the rocks, which had been deemed inaccessible. From an equal altitude, then, with some of the Persian batteries, at dawn they opened their fire.　The upper Persian batteries commanded these rock-summits, and returned the fire with rapidity and accuracy.　The cannonade continued for hours, the Russians obstinately continuing their fire until every one of their field-pieces was disabled.　In the meantime the infantry and artillery, lower down the mountain, had suffered severely from the cannonade.　The Muscovite infantry had remained concealed by the turn of the road.　Now they appeared, rushed forward in the face of a terribly galling artillery fire, and descending the road to the plain, pushed forward to the assault of the mountain.　Gallantly they advanced until they were within range for musketry fire.　Great gaps had been torn through their ranks by the artillery, but onward they came, and stormed the mountain with indomitable resolution.　The Persian infantry swept them away rank after rank by the most deliberate and deadly fire.　Simultaneously the Cossacks attempted to descend the hill through the morass-flanked road. The Persian artillery piled them in dead heaps upon one another, until corpses of men and horses blocked up the way. The attempt of these wild riders to cause a diversion in favor of Madatov's troops was a complete failure; after a time they withdrew up the hill, and rejoined their companions on the summit. At this sight the Persians on the southern slope of the rock-mountain yelled with exultation. Their comrades on the northern slope, hearing their cries, joined in until the whole mountain was alive with human voices blending with the roar of the cannon, and the rattle of the musketry, which were dealing death to the soldiers of Madatov. The charge of the Russian infantry was repulsed, and they retreated in confusion under a galling fire of artillery, not by the road they had come, but away off over the open plain of the amphitheatre towards the west. Abbas Mirza having lost his *goolams* in the former battle, was unable to pursue with cavalry, which he earnestly desired, but sent immediately a portion of his admirable flying artillery and four regiments of infantry after the fugitives. The fire from the rock-mountain now ceased entirely. All upon its sides were either spectators of the movements of their comrades on the plain, as they pursued the foe, or watched the Cossacks on the distant hill. The eyes of Abbas Mirza were fixed upon the road to the north, where he believed the reserves of Madatov were concealed behind the turn.

Moments passed by, and still all was quiet at the northward. Only on the distant plain was the battle raging. Then the adjutant-general rode up to the black steed, upon which his chief was mounted, and directed his attention to the Cossacks, whose dense masses of spear-heads were leaving the heights, and disappearing behind them to the southward. It was doubtless the purpose of this immense force of cavalry to seek the plain by some tedious circuitous route, which was the only possible method of their rendering any assistance to Madatov's forces. Soon the last man of them had disappeared from the sight of the Persians, and the result was awaited with intense interest.

The contest on the plain was now being conducted with great determination and skill. The Russian infantry had reformed upon a slight eminence and were making stubborn resistance to the Persian infantry and light artillery, when, to the amazement of the Persian commander, a heavy force of infantry and artillery appeared in the rear of the Muscovites and marching to their assistance. The entire reserves of Madatov ·had evidently discovered a new route by which they could descend from the hills and reach the plain of the amphitheatre, unmolested by the batteries of the Persians on the rock mountain.

Without a moment's hesitation Abbas Mirza directed the evacuation of the mountain and pushed his remaining force of artillery and infantry, the bulk of his command, forward to the battle on the plain. He trusted to the spirit and zeal of his troops to defeat a second time Madatov's army before the Cossacks could make the circuit of the hills. He rode along the lines of his army as it was reformed upon the plain, and cried to his troops in his clear, magnetic voice :

"Persians, can you fail to defeat yonder army of Madatov which you have already defeated only two days ago? Forward upon the dogs of Russia !"

With yells of exultation the army moved forward to the assistance of their countrymen, who were already hard pressed by the reinforced ranks of the Russians. The junction of the formidable reinforcement under command of Madatov, in fresh, firm and ardent array, infused new life and hope into the sinking energy of the Muscovite infantry. They rallied and charged with desperate valor upon the Persians, driving them slowly backward until they encountered the bulk of the army of Abbas Mirza. The entire forces of the Prince Royal and of Madatov were now engaged in deadly conflict upon the plain. The tide of battle surged back and forth for hours. Neither commander would for an instant flinch from the terrific slaughter of men, which now seemed inevitable whichever way the final victory might move. Hour after hour the artillery sounded its thunder tones of death, and the musketry poured its leaden hail into the breasts and brains of foemen who had resolved never to yield.

In the midst of the death harvest an aid rode up to Abbas Mirza with the startling intelligence that the *twenty thousand Cossacks were advancing over the plain* from the southward, and would strike the flank of his struggling army. "Let them come," was the reply of the chief. "Persia will die pushing boldly on upon the ranks of Madatov. It is our only hope." And the battle went on without cessation. The Ghebre and the adjutant-general, as they listened to these words, knew that the Prince Royal had chosen the desperate chance. A retreat to the rock mountain was feasible, but he had abandoned the mountain forever. Unless the Russians were speedily routed there was no hope for Persia. And speedily were they routed. For Abbas Mirza, knowing full well that every moment was precious, dashed to the front into the midst of the hottest fire, and led the charge of infantry upon the stubborn

Russians with the gallantry of a Boemond. Seeing the recklessness with which their Prince exposed his person, the Persians, as by one magnetic impulse, rushed forward with fixed bayonets, and by the fury and impetuosity of their charge crushed in the Muscovite line. For a time the enemy struggled desperately to reform their line, but they soon were forced into utter confusion, and fell away in every direction to the northward, leaving twelve pieces of artillery in the hands of the Persians. The cheers of the victors rang over the plain, and for a few moments exultation was in every heart.

But Abbas Mirza restrained the victors as they pursued the retreating foe, and rapidly changed front, for a fearful array of Cossacks were advancing at a brisk trot to overwhelm his army. He had little time for preparation. He formed his infantry into squares to resist the charge of twenty thousand cavalry, whose tactics he well knew were repeated dashes from every side until their foes were harassed to death by the frequency of their assaults. What was his dismay to learn that the shot for his artillery were entirely exhausted. This arm of the service was therefore useless. But with the ingenuity of despair he ordered the gunners to stand with lighted fuses beside their pieces after they had loaded them with the pebbles which strewed the plain. This extemporized grape-shot was reserved for the last minute of the doomed Persian army. With the royal standard of the Sun Lion unfurled beside him, and with his gallant staff and the white-robed Ghebre on their superb Khorassan steeds around him, Abbas Mirza awaited death. The huge cloud of the Cossacks in another instant would burst into charging fragments around him. Hundreds would die on the Persian bayonets, but the doom of the crippled army a few minutes later was beyond question. The Prince Royal of Persia was superb in his death struggle. His own sabre was unsheathed for some Cossack's brain. Every man in the kneeling ranks was superb as he clutched the musket which would deal death to an enemy on its glittering bayonet before the overwhelming rush crushed it to the earth. A silence as of death reigned. Every patriot hero's eye was fixed for the advance of the wild horse, the clatter of whose hoofs already sounded on the plain.

Hark! a shout so loud, even-toned and quick as the near thunder crash rose over the plain, that every Persian knew it was *hope*. They had heard that even-toned, short, disciplined shout too often upon the parade ground not to know who was coming like lightning to the rescue. *"Debaena ! Debaena !"* The glad shout broke from every heart in the beleaguered army. From the road through the morass, abandoned by the Cossacks hours before, the regular cavalry were advancing. They were already down upon the plain from the hill, and in five divisions they were dashing forward like the wind for the Cossacks. Leading the central division, whose coats of mail glistened like a silver river in the sun, was Al-Borak. His master's sabre was flashing in air above him. And twenty feet above all was the huge king-vulture, *"Boshran"* (good tidings). His wide expanded wings swept forward with the frantic onset of the horse, as with the yell of victory they pierced at five points the Cossack array trampling and sabring everything before them, and then issuing in wonderful order on to the open field beyond. Without a pause the five divisions wheeled, and returning upon another portion of the Cossack flank, cut their way through a second time, leaving horses, men and lances scattered in wild confusion upon the plain. Again and again they charged. The hero of Toorkomania was in his element, and nobly did he respond to the trust the Persian army reposed in his skill. With resistless impetuousity he fell upon the sanguinary hosts of the hirelings of Nicholas and by repeated assaults scattered them in every direction. The weight and compactness of his Asiatic cavalry overpowered the loose order and desultory tactics of the Cossack horde. They bent and wavered and broke at every charge, and rising to their feet the Persian army yelled in exultation to see Debaena chasing them from the field. They broke and fled at last in every direction over the plain, and were pursued until the close of day with incessant slaughter. The plain was strewed with horses, lances, sabres, bows and quivers, and thousands of bleeding and dead Cossacks. Of six thousand Persian horse only five hundred saddles were emptied. Debaena had saved the army of Abbas Mirza, and with this matchless cavalry hovering upon their flanks and rear, the Persians continued their retreat towards the Araxes, followed by the inevitable Madatov, who speedily reconstructed his veterans and collected his routed Cossacks.

CHAPTER XXVI.

ILLIAM the *Conqueror* was thrown from his horse and killed. Frederic Barbarossa, the great monarch and still greater commander, the first horseman of the Third Crusade, was flung by his steed into the torrent of the Calycadnus and died from the fall. It was then. no marvel that General Alfonso Debaena, the most fiery and accomplished horseman of the Persian army, should be flung crippled to the earth by Al-Borak. In a skirmish with Cossack cavalry in the valley of the Araxes, after Abbas Mirza had crossed that river with his army in his memorable retreat, a Persian standard-bearer was shot beside General Debaena. As he fell from his horse the standard escaping from his grasp struck the eyes of Al-Borak. The frightened steed plunged and threw his master as he was. on the point of braining a Cossack with his sabre. His troops fought desperately over the body of their fallen chief, and the king-vulture, ever hovering over his master's head, fell upon the Cossack, who had confronted Debaena as he raised his lance to transfix the fallen man, and tore his eyes from their sockets. Satisfied by this manifestation of his devotion to his master, he rose again in air and followed the course of the horsemen who were bearing away their crippled chief to a place of safety.

The consequences of this disaster proved how largely his cavalry had been indebted for their success to the splendor of his personal qualities. The Cossacks, who had hung upon the flanks and rear of Abbas Mirza's retreating army even down to the banks of the Araxes, recovering from the terror inspired by the skill and daring of Debaena, renewed their assaults upon his cavalry with increased vehemence and recklessness, which insured them many advantages. The regulars of Debaena fought well and heroically, but the *esprit* and confidence evoked by his presence and dash, and which had rendered them invincible, had departed with his fall, and they fell back more frequently before superior numbers.

When Abbas Mirza established himself in winter quarters at the fortress of Ardebil, south of the river, and the Russian army sought for the winter a post north of the Araxes, the disabled commander of horse was, by the advice of the army surgeon, sent in a *tackti-ravan* to the residence of a wealthy khan

of the empire upon the shore of the Caspian Sea. The distance from the winter quarters of the Prince Royal to this luxurious hospital was some fifty miles. The Persian noble who
had offered this asylum to the disabled officer was on the staff
of Abbas Mirza, and his son was a *yuzbashi* or centurion of
horse in General Debaena's cavalry. The Prince Royal was
particularly gratified by this offer on the part of his staff officer,
as, in addition to his own tender sympathy for the misfortune
of the able soldier, he had received a letter from Ayesha ex-
pressing her regret at the great loss her country had received
in Debaena, and imploring him to see to it that the sufferer
received such rare attention and nursing as were due to one who
had rescued a son of the Shah from the horrors of Turcoman
slavery. Such powerful interposition from Teheran, coupled
with the entreaties of the khan and his son, could not fail to
influence the commander-in-chief of the Persian army to send
Debaena with all tenderness of conveyance to the shores of
the Caspian. During the winter the Prince Royal himself
visited his officer in his retreat, and Zenayi found more than
one excuse for stealing away from headquarters and tarrying
beside the couch of his *protégé*. To insure the most assiduous
attention and kindness for · Debaena, the Persian noble and
his son wrote letters imploring the mother and daughter of
the khan to treat the sufferer as if he were a member of their
family.

The winter season wore away at last, and when the shores of
the Caspian were clad in the luxuriant foliage and the marvellous flora of that voluptuous clime in May, the commander of
horse was notified that he might with safety leave his bed and
enjoy the sensuous delights of the open air in a short stroll
every day. His internal injuries had yielded to the touch of
science, and he would in time be an efficient soldier once more.
"*Mens sana in corpore sano*," said the Ghebre to him when
the attending surgeon pronounced the words of hope. "Does
not that thought come to you now, my hero, my hope, like the
gift of a new existence from Ormuzd? Ah! my life has been
bound up in yours. I shall go back to the army now with the
lightest heart that ever man bore. And Abbas Mirza! How
his noble heart will tremble with exultation at the tidings.
And the troops; how they will cheer before the citadel of
Ardebil. Boy, is it not a reward for suffering and toil and
heroism that brave hearts exult over your recovery, that patriot

eyes brighten at glad news from your bedside, and the mothers and daughters of Persia bless your name?"

When the Ghebre walked forth with the invalid leaning upon his arm and accompanied by the lovely daughter of the khan and her grandmother, who had watched the couch of the soldier for many months as only patriot women can watch over strangers crippled in the service of their country, the view of the great estate stretching away to the shore of the ochre Caspian was like a dream of *Jannat al Ferdaws* (the garden of paradise). In the broad limits of the Persian noble's *charbagh* were seen the most beautiful trees of Persia. On the slopes of the hills were luxuriant oaks, elms, sycamores, beeches, ash and walnut trees in the fulness of their May foliage. To the right were lowlands with a dense growth of enormous alders, willows and poplars. To the left were thickets of wild pomegranate, plum, blackthorn, orange and lime trees. Near to the shore of the Caspian was a great marsh, where wild vines festooned the giant trees and the grass was enamelled with flowers. As the soldier wandered on in the warm, tropical sunlight and listened to the gentle sound of the voices about him, calling his attention to some new beauty of the landscape, he espied a long stretch of green meadow which went rolling gently on before him till its emerald freshness was cut abruptly by the waters of the sea. This wide reach of verdure had ever been his delight, and now his languid eyes dwelt upon its unbroken extent as its green waves undulated gently away without a tree to the Caspian. He paused at a seat upon its border that he might enjoy it at his ease. Drooping branches of the willows above his head sheltered him from the sun's rays, and his seat was at the verge of a spouting spring whose sparkling spray he loved to watch and listen to the gurgling of its waters. Seeing how entranced he was by this particular locality, and how his appreciative eyes preferred to dream in silence over the wide-reaching view, his companions withdrew for a few moments and left him to enjoy it alone. So adroitly did they leave him, one by one stealing gently away with noiseless tread in consonance with his dreamy mood, that he did not realize their absence until his eye encountered after a time the white robe of Zenayi some distance to the left, beneath the shade of a cluster of orange-trees, where he had seated himself to look upon the plain which spread far away towards the mountains, the blue dome of heaven rising like a pavilion above him. He knew they would all return to him ere long,

and he resumed his reverie. His thoughts wandered on and
on, beyond the green meadow and far across the Caspian in
the distance. There over the waters directly to the east lay
Toorkomania, bordering on that sea. There had he by one
energetic campaign won eminence in his profession. He had
there arisen like a meteor to the uplifted eyes of a nation.
He had there immortalized his name in Persian annals. Was
he satisfied with fame? He asked himself this question, now,
seated alone. Would any height of military command ever
satisfy that yearning which strengthened with every new acquisition, with every new post of honor? The Ghebre had told
him over and over again that a man's only happiness on earth
arose from the consciousness that his efforts, his hazards, his
sufferings were accomplishing ends which would render humanity happier and better; that an etire abnegation of self
for the purpose of rendering others happy was the true philosophy of life. Was this true? Had that marvellous sphinx of
Persia, from his immense erudition, his profound readings in
history, deduced the real secret of happiness? Sometimes the
ambitious soldier fancied that the Ghebre was right; that
power, fame, rank had no essence of joy within themselves, but
derived their sole value from the consciousness in a man's soul
that he was using them to make others smile and be at peace.
He was now one of Persia's favorite commanders. The success which had crowned his efforts was due in part to his secret
appropriation of some of the hidden treasure to the perfect
equipment of his troops and to their better arming with modern improved weapons of war. Their saddles, sabres, pistols,
lances had been imported through the port of Balfurosh from
European factories by the medium of his paid secret agents.
The entire expense had been borne by himself out of the secret treasury. Had this sacrifice of his treasure been made for
himself or for Persia? Was it to further his own ascent of the
ladder of fame, or was it to render the Persian people happier
by securing to them what was their right? Was it to shield
the Persians from plunder and disgrace, or was it to render
clearer to men the military superiority of General Alfonso Debaena, that they might the more readily assent to his clutching
of power and be ready to submit to his future ambitious as-
sumptions? Sometimes he believed that he was disinterested
as the Ghebre would have him to be. And when that impression took firm hold of him there was an exultation in him that
thrilled heart and brain. Upon the earth his feet seemed to

tread with a more kingly elasticity, and he warmed with the thought that the Ruler of all things was pleased with his life because it was devoted to the good of the Creator's children. This feeling, while it lasted, seemed to bring him a vast exultation, a wonderful satisfaction, and he earnestly desired that this sublime joy might continue. It seemed to bring him nearer to Zenayi, to make him worthy of that great patriot's esteem. The truth was that a noble being was influencing a spirited, generous heart by contact and by example. The power of man over man arising from mere contact and example is one of the unfathomable mysteries of creation. A bad, unprincipled man daily, in the experience of mortals, leads the naturally generous, impulsive, noble-hearted to such familiarity with evil thoughts and words that they do to-day what yesterday they would have revolted from. Zenayi's atmosphere was an atmosphere of grandeur, of heroism, of self-denial. It was working, had always worked good for this noble-hearted, ambitious, fiery Alfonso Debaena. Intensely aspiring, the soldier still could not shake off this grand influence.

In the midst of dreams of armies, palaces, power and glory, a vision or suggestion of something grander than them all had been placed before the heroic youth and the victorious commander. Could he with his great soul and his towering ambition stop short of the *highest* pinnacle? It was a grand struggle, a superb conception of the venerable Ghebre to place before Debaena the choice of the world or of something in the world but loftier than the world. It waked a great soul up to reflection. "I shall go to the top if *I live*," said the convalescent soldier to himself by the Caspian. "But if I gain all power that soldiers ever gain and yet lose that mysterious *something* which is above armies and their commanders, and which is in the growth of the soul itself, what have I to boast of? I crave power, but I must attain the greatness which the Ghebre believes me capable of. I must have the highest or none."

In the midst of his reverie the trio returned to him, and he found himself attended also by two slaves with white dresses and scarlet turbans, who had brought with them silver waiters loaded with viands for a repast under the trees. They placed these upon the grass, where the officer was seated on a Khorassan rug. Similar seats were spread for the others, and the whole party were soon sitting at ease in the fashion of the East, and eating from the china bowls on the waiters, with the spring bubbling beside them. The females, being strict Mohamme-

dans, refrained from the use of the wines.   But the officer was
not debarred from this luxury, being rather enjoined to use
them by his surgeon.   The Ghebre was a fearless opponent ot
the faith of Mahomet, and praised the wines in his appreciative way, offering during the repast more interesting information
upon the fruit of the vine in all lands than the others could have
dreamed the subject possessed.   The elegant meal spread in
the shade of the drooping willows was likely to tempt even the
palate of a poor, wasted soldier, debarred so many months from
the exercise of his limbs when he had all his life been a marvel
of activity.   There was lamb, fed on the aromatic slopes of the
mountains, fish from the Caspian port of Astrabad, and wild
honey from the hollow of some ancient oak on the crescent of
mountains which shut in the southern shores of the Caspian.
In green baskets skilfully made from the leaves of the cactus,
were the dates of Dalaki, the apricots of Armenia and the pis-
tachio nuts of Aleppo.   The golden wine of Lebanon, the fragrant juice of vineyards in the far-off islands of the Cyprian Sea,
the wine of Shiraz extolled by the Persian poets, and the wine
from the hills of Engaddi, in stone jars, were there in profusion,
and testified at once to the affluence of the noble Persian who
owned the estate, and his appreciation of what was due to his
country's defender in his hour of suffering.   The transcendent
personal heroism of Alfonso Debaena, and the martial qualities
by which he was pre-eminently distinguished, had won the admiration of the noblest and best of the chivalry of Persia.
He was held now, in this day of agony for the patriotic, second
only to the people's favorite, Abbas Mirza.   At evening, in the
skirt of the woods or in the deep ravine, whilst the camels
drank together at the lonely spring, even the common muleteers
and grooms of the horses, who, in Persia salute the passer-by
with exquisite quotations from Ferdusi or verses from Hafiz,
had caught up snatches of the songs composed by the soldiers
in camp, in honor of Debaena, the terrible rider and *sabreur*,
and they sang them to the evening stars with hearts trembling
for the future of their beloved flowery land.   And in all the
anderoons of the empire of Iran, the beautiful wives and maidens
sang triumphantly of their hero and his Azrail, *the angel of death*,
who flew as a huge bird above him to foreshadow the fate of
the Muscovite invaders who crossed his path.
     What wonder then that the aged mother of sons slain by
Russians in 1813, and of sons now in arms against the same
detested foe, should gaze with tenderness and pride upon the

handsome soldier before her, from whose recovery Persia had the right to expect so much? What wonder that the large dark eyes of the maid should linger with interest upon that face, and her heart listen for the tones of that voice which had led her brother, the *yuzbashi*, on over the dead and the dying, to Persia's victory? The Bakhtiaris, the Turcomans, the Cossacks, the Caucasian dragoons, and the Russian regular horse, the cuirassiers and cavalry of the line, were all the same to Debaena, and where he charged their equal in numbers they all inevitably went down, or scattered before him. So rapid and furious was his onset, so overwhelming the force and weight of the shock he centred at a single point, that nothing had yet been able to endure it. What wonder, then, that the khan's daughter, reared in seclusion, should become intensely absorbed in this gallant soldier of her country, who had been sent to her to be nursed, and restored to usefulness? Over his couch she had leaned and soothed the fevered head, the lips compressed in pain had arrested her gazelle eyes in pity, and the reviving strength and elasticity of the hero's spirits had filled her with patriotic joy ; and now, in this moment of festive enjoyment, when his old fascination of manner and of tone had returned upon him, and the balmy May was opening the gates of a new life to him as he sat there upon the Khorassan rug in the splendor of his returning beauty, it was not possible that this lovely girl could see him suddenly perish when her own life could avert the blow. And so, in the midst of hilarity and feasting, they saw her by a spasmodic motion of her fair hand, strike away from Debaena the head of a venomous serpent that had raised to bury its fangs in his arm. Quickness could alone have saved her country's hero, but the fangs penetrated her own flesh, and with the deadly reptile clinging to her hand, she sprang to her feet, and carried the serpent far away from *him.* It was as true a heroism for Persia as the tented field or reckless battle charge ever knew. Alas ! for the khan's daughter, beautiful as Psyche, heroic as Leæna of the Acropolis ! She shook the reptile from her hand, and the whiteness of death came over her; too well she knew her fate. In the horror of the scene one alone was calm. *Zenayi.* Rumor had it that this mysterious being knew *everything.* Fortunately for this lovely heroine, the Ghebre was ever an observer of what Ormuzd had planted around him. As he sat a short time before the repast, beneath the shade of a cluster of orange trees, he detected near him the plant, *uvularia grandiflora.* It bore a general resemblance to "Solomon's seal." The height of the wonderful plant was two feet, leaves alternate, smooth and perforated by the stem, which was forked near the top. This plant, early in May, bears two drooping liliaceous yellow flowers. It was a labor of love for this lover of humanity to hasten to the spot and pluck up the plant by the roots. He followed the poor girl as they bore her to the house, and immediately gave her a decoction of the roots and leaves. Then he chewed some of the roots and leaves, and bound them upon the wound made by the fangs; the girl recovered with no other remedy. The serpent was the deadliest in all Persia; but Zenayi, with his shield of plants, was a match for the most venomous reptiles of both hemispheres. He smiled the sweetest of smiles when the khan's daughter revived, and whispered, as he turned to Debaena, "We must look to our heroic laurels, boy; two Persian *girls* are already ahead of us."

As the two walked together in the *charbagh*, later in the day, the Ghebre, pointing away to a low ledge of rocks on the shore of the Caspian, said to his companion :

"In the shelter of that ledge I have made an appointment for you to meet and consult with a spy, sent into our lines by the enemy; the spy is really acting in our interest, and it is desirable that you should know what is transpiring in the Russian camp; ponder well what you hear, for it requires caution and great deliberation to act wisely in this matter. You will find Al-Borak secured to this willow to-morrow night, and saddled. Ride at the hour of eight to the ledge, and clap your hands *thrice;* if you hear in response the word "*Zenayi*," all is well; if not, return."

CHAPTER XXVII.

T HE hush of the night, the glory of the full Oriental moon, the music of the low, gentle waves plashing upon the pebbly shore of the Caspian, and the odor of plants, floating upon the warm air of the May evening, lulled the senses of the convalescent soldier as he rode slowly on to the place of the secret interview. The hoofs of Al-Borak, *crunching* the pebbles of the beach, as he skirted the sea, caused the only discordant notes to that dream of harmony. Debaena checked his steed, at length, and dismounting secured him to a dead tree which had floated ashore; then he paced slowly on alone, unwilling to listen to aught discordant in that scene of enchantment which lured him on. In a few minutes his steed was hidden from his view by an interposing angle of rock, and the officer found himself near to the low ledge the Ghebre had indicated as the place of interview. No human being was in sight, but shadows amid the pile of rocks doubtless concealed the figure of the Russian spy who awaited him. As he advanced along the shore, he heard voices between the sea and a row of rocks which shut him out for a moment from a view of the water; he started at the sound, and laid his hand upon the hilt of his sabre. The strangers were conversing in the Russian dialect. He understood it perfectly, and stopped to listen to the discourse of the foe; he soon discovered that they were sailors discussing the peculiarities of the coast; they were hidden from him, as he passed behind the rocks, and he feared to approach them any nearer. His suspicions were aroused; he moved on cautiously and stealthily, until he reached the ledge indicated by the Ghebre; all was distinct before him now in the moonlight, save only the extreme end of the rocks where they seemed to sink to the level of the sands of the beach. Finding himself far enough away from the Russian sailors to be unheard, he clapped his hands *thrice.* The name of the Ghebre was called out to him in return from the end of the ledge in familiar accent; he advanced in surprise, and there beheld, seated on the rocks on the Caspian shore, *Irene.*

"*Coadjutor!*" he exclaimed, in astonished delight, as the matchless loveliness of the Persian heroine greeted his sight.

"Alfonso Debaena," was the response, as she arose from her reclining posture, between two rocks, over one of which her arm and hand had hung gracefully as she sat at ease. "Praise be to Allah for this moment; never did the damned know a greater wall of '*Al-Aráf*' between them and Paradise than the distance which has parted me from your hero-face."

"Irene," exclaimed the soldier of Persia, as he bent reverently on one knee, and pressed his lips to the fair hand she extended to him in greeting, "I am not worthy to touch your hand; you are the star of Persia to us all; and as the night of Iran deepens, and her hour of gloom comes on, we look up to you, for your cheering light never fails; you are bright and beautiful above us when defeat and slaughter crush us to the earth. Oh, Eternal Creator and Ruler of men, give us fortitude to struggle and hope on like COADJUTOR."

She raised him from his kneeling posture as he trembled with emotion, and bade him be seated beside her, as she dropped again to her seat between the rocks. The moonlight was full in her face as she regarded him, and he thought her never so beautiful as now. Her dark eyes so full of tender light were studying him. The face of the martyr to Persia was holy in the flood of the moonlight. The entirety of her offering to her country had given her a radiant refinement of beauty which had stamped itself upon her features in unmistakable lines. It had given her an exalted look, and he remarked it to her in warm, earnest words.

"Happy am I, indeed," was her response, "if the glory of my Persia is reflected ever so feebly in my face. My heart is warmed for my country, and it is not strange that that warmth should find its way to my face when, for the first time, I can freely speak to a soldier of Persia. Ah! the bitterness of this separation from my sunny land and the wild exultation with which this night I planted my feet again upon her soil. I have waited here for you, General Debaena, and breathed the perfumes of those flowers yonder as they came to me in greeting, until my heart was full to suffocation with rapture. Oh! my Persia, how I love you! How light a task it is to endure hardship and pain for you!"

"Noble girl," was the response, "your devotion, your skill, your valuable information are appreciated at headquarters. Abbas Mirza desired me if ever you came within the lines to conduct you to his pavilion, that he might in person express his admiration at your noble conduct, and thank you in the name of Persia."

"Never," was the startling response.

"What can you mean, Irene? I have heard you express unbounded enthusiasm for the Prince Royal."

"Never, never will I face him in his camp," she replied, with emotion. "You do not know my relations with the Crown Prince, or you would never speak of this again. I cannot tell you now who I am. My identity is merged in the cause of Persia. If we both live to the end of this war you will know my history: but never, by word or suggestion, allow the Prince Royal to expect he will ever encounter me. He knows me only as *Coadjutor.*   So let it remain to the end.   But my time is short here.   The business I have with you is important."

"Go on, then," said the officer.

"You remember your promise, General Debaena, in your letter?"

"To place myself or my cavalry in positions of hazard when you demanded it?"

"The same, brave soldier.   How much better you remember promises than most men.   I have come to demand the fulfillment of that promise as regards yourself alone."

"You will find me truthful, Irene; your judgment I will trust."

"I was sure of it, General Debaena.   But my demand will startle you.   You must go with me within the Russian lines."

"A spy?" exclaimed the officer.

"No, no, I do not demand that.   You must die by the lance or sabre.   Allah has qualified you for that, and your sword is too valuable to Persia.   But in fulfillment of your promise you must go with me."

"How?" was his response.

"As a *prisoner entrapped.*   I have given my word to General Yermoloff that if he would send me as a spy within the Persian lines I would not only bring him information, but you also as a prisoner."

"And is not my sword valuable to Persia?" inquired the amazed commander of horse.

"Of the first importance is your sword, General Debaena, and you know it.   But it is of vast importance to the armies of my country that I should send them the highest information.   I must convince Yermoloff of the value of my services, that I may secure more confidence for myself and have access to the adjutant-general of his army.   I must have their utmost confidence, and thus shall I send to Persia information which will thwart their best-laid plans.   To be a great schemer for them I must bring them the best sabre in the Persian army. Listen to me: I am only a woman, but I have contrived to bewitch that old Yermoloff till he scarce knows whether he stands on his head or his heels.   He is a splendid officer, but he is weak where a woman is concerned.   He thinks I have great abilities and he trusts me.   But his adjutant-general laughs at his fondness for me, and is so reticent that I might as well attempt to pump intelligence of army movements from a stone.   Give into my hands, General Debaena, but the power to say to the adjutant-general, 'Here are my practical services. *Here* are posted such and such regiments of the Persians. *There* is a battery which the Cossacks may surprise.' Do you arrange for me, General Debaena, to post troops just long enough at places to establish my veracity and then withdraw them to safety just in the nick of time, and you will see *Coadjutor* forward you in cipher information of the Muscovite movements which will insure you victory. But first of all allow my Russian sailors yonder to seize you and carry you to Tiflis. Rest assured that I have the means to aid your escape within two days. Then will the Georgian girl, Yermoloff's secretary, rise to unbounded confidence at headquarters, and I shall have my hand upon the vitals of our accursed enemy. Trust me, trust me this once, and I shall save Persia."

Seeing that he hesitated to reply, she continued:

"Your escape is beyond question. A fool on the staff of Yermoloff has charge of the prisoners. He is so silly about me that he will dance for joy if I condescend to ask him a favor. He is a nobleman's son and ranks as a *pulkoonick*. Oh! he is such a *goose*, and they have decorated him with Alexander's badge of St. George. Why this has been given him, the wisdom of Allah alone can determine. Why, General Debaena, I can wheedle this man's prison keys out of his hands. Come with me to Tiflis; you will soon escape, and then *Coadjutor* will be so established at headquarters that she cannot be shaken off. They need good spies: Yermoloff told me that, and then I persuaded them to send me. Come with me and I assure you I will in the end place Muscovites in such positions that your cavalry will reap a harvest."

"I have given you my promise, brave girl. I will not break it. Does the Ghebre approve of this?"

"Perfectly," was the response.

"And would you have yonder wretches seize me to-night?" inquired Debaena.

"No; return to the Ghebre and dictate orders to your officers to dispose of their troops as I have marked down for you here." She gave him a map of the Araxes valley with the posts he should establish, and the length of time that he should retain them, and then withdraw the cavalry in time to escape capture. She named to him the posts she had arranged.

"The Ghebre has aided you in these details," said the amazed officer.

"Certainly. Zenayi knows everything," was her reply.

" I will allow myself to be seized by your deluded Russians," he said ; "do with me as you like. After I have dispatched my orders to my officers, what then ? "

" Then return here to-morrow night and make a show of resistance when my sailors spring upon you. The officer in command of the boat on the shore yonder knows that I have come here to entrap an officer of the Persian army. He will be astounded when he learns who you are. Your name and exploits are in every Muscovite's mouth. I will make some excuse to him for the delay, and the boat will hover on the coast until to-morrow night. Do not fail me ; everything depends upon my giving a good account of myself at headquarters. But let me once have access to the adjutant-general's confidence and you all will find *Coadjutor* of some real service to you then."

" Did you deliver my thanks, Irene, to the Circassian scout who was the cause of my victory over the Russians at the defiles beyond Elizabethpol ? "

Coadjutor laughed her merriest laugh at this inquiry. Then she said :

" Your generalship was the cause of that victory."

" No, Irene, that Circassian is entitled to the credit. He should receive a sword at least from the Shah after the close of the war."

" They never give swords of honor to women, General Debaena."

" The Circassian scout a *woman !* Impossible !" exclaimed her companion.

" Everything is possible in war, General Debaena, to those who have nerve, The Circassian *is* a woman, and feels flattered by your high commendation."

" Who is she ? You amaze me," said the officer.

" Has not Zenayi told you ? "

" Never. The Ghebre does not tell me his whole mind at any time."

" I will tell you, General Debaena, provided you will not name her to any one."

" I will never speak of her, then," said Debaena, "unless to you."

" *The Circassian scout is Coadjutor.*"

" *You ?* Irene ! I am amazed. You have made my fortunes so far as Abbas Mirza is concerned. *You* the Circassian ? "

"I am or *was* the Circassian before I was promoted ·to Yermoloff's table. He took me from the hospital, and does not know that I was the scout who was *mssled* by the Persians entering both defiles. Ha! ha! how my heart throbbed when your gallant band broke into their camp. I watched you all in the fight. I was hidden in the woods, and at every charge of your horse my blood warmed. I saw the standard of my country fall, then rise again, caught up by another Persian hand, and my heart went up in gratitude to Allah. Then came the last fearful, madcap charge into the fort, right into the blaze of the cannon; I gasped for breath, holding on to a tree for support. I knew *you* could not escape from that terrible fire; then came the smoke blowing over to the woods. I could see none of you. I clung there half dead with anguish and terror and despair. Then the smoke lifted and curled away. There was silence. The guns ceased. I listened with beating heart. Then the cheers burst forth. Oh! Allah. They were Persian cheers, my countrymen, my Persia. Then I knelt down by the tree and prayed for Debaena, my hero, my beloved Persia's hero. Then, praise to Allah! I saw Al-Borak coming. I knew his stride. I knew his rider. I fell on my face and wept, oh! such tears of joy. The whole of my powers of joy seemed to centre in that thrill of that moment when I knew you were safe. May Allah bless you where you ride, and deal such terrible death for Persia. Don't interrupt me now. Let me speak and unburden my heart. I have for months lain with a gag on my lips and an iron weight on my heart in the camp of our deadly enemies. I have forced myself to smile when my heart was breaking over our disasters. I had to sing for joy when those wretches triumphed over my countrymen. I had to look dejected when Persia won glorious advantages over the Muscovites. Oh! General Debaena, no tongue can tell my anguish when I heard the *tramp, tramp, tramp*, of reinforcements passing under my window at Tiflis and moving on towards Abbas Mirza, and I had no means of counting them and no way of sending a messenger to warn him of his danger. At all hours of the night thousands upon thousands tramped by. I thought that dull, heavy *tramp, tramp, tramp* would never cease. Every tramp seemed to fall upon my heart and upon the grave of my country. And I would lean upon my window in the dull starlight and see the dark, ominous mass moving on solemnly towards Persia, until I was ready to scream in agony because I had no power to

warn or to help. But then I learned to distinguish the different arms of their service, and I listened to every word that fell
from the lips of the men on Yermoloff's staff. They danced
attendance upon me and I smiled upon them, and jested with
them about their army, and flattered them, until I caught up
precious words which they had heard at headquarters, words
of intended movements, of numbers marching to particular
points, and I learned to distinguish *vital* information from
trivial details until I knew what my Persian commanders
craved to know. And when at last I was able to glean *vital*
intelligence and send it by our agents through the lines, my
whole girl's nature seemed to expand, to grow higher, better,
brighter, at the thought that *I* was serving Persia and serving
her with *vital* news, *vital* to her salvation. And now I fear
nothing. I will go anywhere, will wring out of their confidence and their gallantry to me the life of my country."

"Yes! and be hanged for it at last like a dog," exclaimed
Debaena.

"Hush! the death of a dog is a death of glory to one who
loves Persia as I love it. Strangle me with a rope for my service to my country, and I will kiss that rope as the pilgrims
reverently kiss the *black stone* of Al-Caaba."

"Allah give you a safe retreat from the Muscovite camp at
last," said Debaena. "But I tremble for you at the same instant that I am filled with admiration for you. Noble girl!
you have served your country with the most valuable service
that a human being could render. But tell me of a matter
which you have doubtless forgotten. Zenayi hinted to me that
something was transpiring in the Russian camp which I should
know."

"I have not forgotten it, General Debaena. Only my
heart needed an outlet after my forced silence so long among
our foes. I have spoken to you Persian words. My whole
life before this night has been Russian. I have identified myself with them and their thoughts for months that I might the
better slay them in the end. If they triumph, my Persia will
be a hall of Eblis. Hence I cling close to the heart of Russia
that I may stab it at last, that my country may live. I feel
relieved now since I have spoken my heart to my hero. The
matter to which Zenayi referred is mysterious, but must be approached cautiously. I have discovered at headquarters that
some officer of the first Tabreez regiment of Abbas Mirza's
army is corresponding with the Russians. That regiment is

stationed at the fortress of Abbas Abad. You know how valuable that fortress is to Persia. If it is betrayed into the hands of our foes or exposed to successful assault by its weak points being communicated to them, it will be very disastrous to our cause."

"Treachery at Abbas Abad!" exclaimed the commander. "Are you certain of it? I would rather that Persia lost the fortress of Erivan than Abbas Abad."

"So says the Ghebre," responded Irene. "But there is the difficulty. I cannot define what the correspondence has been or discover the name of the officer of the Tabreez regiment. But I overheard Yermoloff when drinking heavily with his friend, and when both were under the influence of the liquor, boast that he knew everything which transpired at Abbas Abad. An officer of that Tabreez regiment had opened a correspondence with him, he said, and he boasted that he would some day surprise Abbas Mirza by the facility with which he would march into that fortress."

After a moment of troubled reflection General Debaena inquired, "Has the Ghebre notified the Prince Royal of this mystery?"

"He has, for I wrote to him early regarding it. Abbas Mirza promised to move that regiment into the field and put a detective officer into its camp. All this has been promptly attended to. But since this change, I have heard a staff officer of Yermoloff say that the Surhungs of Nuckshiwan were writing to headquarters something about Abbas Abad. To this news the Ghebre answered me that I must talk with you, as you knew the particulars of a difficulty in that quarter."

"So do I know," exclaimed Debaena with sudden emphasis. "I believe, moreover, that I can put my hand upon the very man who is disaffected. I will probe this matter, Irene, rest assured. If the Surhungs are mixed up in the matter I know the traitor."

CHAPTER XXVIII.

ON the right bank of the Araxes and some sixty miles south-east from the towering peak of Ararat, stood the Persian fortress of Abbas Abad.   It was defended by twenty-eight cannon, was well supplied with provisions and munitions of war, and had a strong garrison of the best troops in the service of the Shah.   The governor of this strong-hold was accustomed during the heats of summer to pitch his tent outside of the walls and toward the bank of the river. There being no immediate apprehension of an attack from the enemy, whose lines were many miles away, it was deemed per-fectly safe to allow the tent to remain outside of the fortress during the greater part of each day.   The intolerable heat of Abbas Abad drove the governor out to this pavilion for fresh air and repose several hours out of the twenty-four.   Sentinels were stationed in every direction to apprise the garrison of the approach of danger, and thus the commander enjoyed his *calecoon* and his shady retreat in perfect repose, his steed stand-ing picketed near him.   The site selected for the daily nap and smoke was the depth of a grassy ravine in a little grove of olives, poplars and date trees.

One day the governor of the fortress was reclining in this pavilion, smoking and reading.   He was alone.   The sentinels were dozing at their posts.

The only sound that met his ear was the occasional and rest-less stamping of hoofs, as his steed contended with the swarm of annoying flies.   A letter was in his hands which deeply in-terested him, though he had already perused it several times. He crumpled the paper in his hands and then sat looking through the tent door at the sky in profound thought.   To his amazement a stranger rose as if from the very ground and con-fronted him.   He would have given the alarm to the sleeping sentinel had not the stranger entreated him to be silent.

" Hush!" said the man, " I come to you from Yermoloff with a message.   Look at the mud upon me and my torn gar-ments.   I have worked my way through the lines with great dif-ficulty."

" What can the Muscovite have to say to a faithful soldier of Persia?" was the stern response of the governor.

" Only this," replied the stranger, producing a letter and presenting it. " Yermoloff says that the governor of Abbas Abad should enjoy an easy mind regarding his correspondence. Hence he returns you your letter to quiet your fears, and sends you in advance part of your promised reward. Here is a draft upon the treasury of Russia for the amount, which Yermoloff will quadruple when the business is complete. He begs that you will manifest equal courtesy and confidence by signing this receipt for the amount."

The draft and receipt both were passed into the hands of the governor, who exclaimed —

"And who are you?"

"An officer of Yermoloff's staff," was the composed response.

"Why, the draft is for more money than I was promised in all."

"Such is the usual liberality of my chief," was the staff officer's reply. And then he added, "Russia does nothing niggardly by her friends in need!"

The governor studied the stranger's countenance, and then, as if reassured by the investigation, said —

"I will sign the receipt, but fear to have you carry it through the lines. It might cost me my head."

"No fear. Here is a secure place between the soles of my, shoe," said the Russian officer, exhibiting an ingenious spring which opened and closed a recess in the shoe large enough to carry two or three letters.

The governor laughed at this device, and turning to his writing materials signed the receipt, which he returned to the officer.

"What does Yermoloff say," he inquired, "about his capture of our famous cavalry officer?"

"*General Debaena has escaped,*" was the startling response.

"Great Allah!" exclaimed the governor. "Yermoloff must be insane to allow so dangerous a foe to elude him. Why did he not send him to Russia?"

"He escaped when on the road to Russia. He drugged his sentinels."

"And where is he supposed to be now?" demanded the anxious governor. "Come, be seated beside me and tell me everything. I will pass you out of the lines in due time and safely."

The staff officer, in his filthy disguise, seated himself beside the governor and proceeded to detail the particulars of Debaena's escape. In the course of this description he took up a military scarf from a divan and passed it around the neck of the governor to explain how the great cavalry officer had been tied to the neck of his guard. In another instant the commander of the fortress of Abbas Abad was choked by the scarf and then securely gagged by hands which clutched him like an iron vise. In a moment more he was bound hand and foot. The stranger then left the pavilion with the same stealthy tread by which he had entered, passed the sleeping sentinel unobserved and escaped down the ravine, but in the direction of the fortress.

Scarcely a half hour had elapsed before the tramp of soldiers under the command of the second officer of the fortress was heard by the prostrate governor in his tent. They entered, released him from the fetters and gag, and upon searching his person discovered the draft of Yermoloff and his own letter to that commander. He was then informed that he was arrested upon the representation of General Alfonso Debaena, who stood before him at that moment in the disguise of the Russian staff officer, and with the receipt which the governor had given him open in his hand.

In five days from that startling occurrence the traitor governor was shot by order of a court-martial.

CHAPTER XXIX.

IN a rocky ravine and close by the waters of a shallow river three Persian officers were seated upon their horses and earnestly discussing the details of a military ambuscade. They formed a picturesque group in their bright-hued uniforms and seated upon steeds possessing all the fiery and graceful beauty of Oriental thoroughbreds. They had halted in a narrow road running parallel with the river and divided from its waters by scarcely three feet of earth. Occasionally they looked upward to the barren rock mountains which hemmed them in on every side and stood eternal sentry over the tortuous and murmuring river. The trio were soldiers bronzed by exposure to the burning sun of the Orient, and though possessed of strong and independent wills were respectfully and calmly listening to each other's military opinions regarding the proper disposition of troops for the approaching

battle   Across the river, which was fordable, were large cavities
in the rocks, sufficiently level on the bottom for the posting of
artillery, and where the guns would command the river road for
several rods north and south, or deal a deadly flank fire upon an
enemy directly across the river.   The range of vision on every
side was limited, and the foe would encounter a galling fire
almost at the instant of seeing their adversaries, and from the
distance of only a dozen rods.   The trio, with little discussion,
decided upon selecting these cavities for their artillery, or
rather that part of it which was to contest the enemy's advance
at the opening of the battle.

They looked in vain, however, for any foothold on the cliffs
where supporting bodies of infantry could be posted, and
finally they rode slowly down the river southward, looking for
more advantageous situations for battle.   Under the barren
and impending crags they moved on until they were gratified
by discovering an amphitheatre amid the mountains sweeping
away to the west and east on either side of the river, and on the
south terminating in a bold mountain which divided the waters
of the river into two channels which laved its base and united
in a single stream again behind it.   The river flowed directly
south through the centre of this amphitheatre, until it was rent
in twain by the opposing mountain.   The road followed the
western channel as it swept away around the mountain.   As
the road rose gradually at this point to the southward, they
determined to post the army on both channels of the river and
defend them both from the Russian army advancing from the
north.   Both channels made their way through deep and frightful ravines, and though troops might readily march in the
shallow water when unopposed, they were almost certain to be
destroyed when artillery and infantry were galling them from
the heights above.

When the officers had at length arranged the details of the
ambuscade to their satisfaction, the one who appeared to be
the highest in rank from the deference exhibited by the others,
turning to the youngest soldier, inquired :

"Now, General Debaena, what shall we do with your cavalry?   It would chafe your lion heart out of you to hear all the
music of the battle and have no part or lot in the matter.   You
see there is a place for every arm of the service but the cavalry.   If your horses had wings now we could post them on
the mountain tops, to the east and west of the river.   But as

it is I fear we shall have to send you all far to our rear to smoke your *caleeoons* and listen to our guns."

"My horses *have* wings, Your Royal Highness," was the calm response.

"Ah! you would scale those pyramids of rocks and with your horsemen view the battle?"

"Undoubtedly, Your Royal Highness. The view of a battle is the next best thing to a participation in it."

The Crown Prince looked at the gallant commander of his cavalry in surprise. He was not wont to take so coolly a proposition to be cut off entirely from the opportunity of glory and battle.

"I would desire no better position," continued General Debaena, "than yonder mountain-tops, provided Your Royal Highness will stipulate that, in the event of your defeat and surrender, I and my idle horsemen shall not be included in the terms. We can escape by the easy slopes on the back of those mountains, and may live to render you valuable service on other fields."

"I can see no other way to dispose of the cavalry," replied Abbas Mirza, thoughtfully. "Your fidelity and valor are already immortal. I will grant your strange request, and you shall, like eagles, watch the battle, and our defeat shall not involve the surrender of the Persian horse."

"Farewell, Your Royal Highness," replied Debaena, turning the head of Al-Borak towards the north. "May Allah grant you victory!"

In another instant he was bounding away along the river-road and in the direction of the advancing Russian army. The other two rode away southward towards Echmiadzin, near which the Persian army were encamped and engaged in the siege of that place. . . . .

The setting sun was gilding the peaks of the Saganlúg mountains as General Yermoloff, with a brilliant staff, rode down the passes of the Abarane river on his advance from Tiflis. For miles in his rear stretched the disciplined masses of his superb troops, who were advancing with high hopes and in the gayest of spirits to reinforce their comrades on the plain of the Araxes river. The sunbeams flashed from their bayonets as they crowned the crest of a hill, and then they were hidden in premature night as they descended into the gorges and shadows adjacent to the river. With Yermoloff in the advance rode a lovely girl upon a spirited horse, which she managed with ease, having been an admirable horse-woman almost from the cradle up. She was one of the military secretaries of the Russian commander, and was treated with the highest respect by all the staff officers, who had learned to admire her intellectual qualities and acknowledge the power of her personal attractions. It was understood at headquarters that she would eventually become the wife of Yermoloff. She wore a military jacket over her dark dress, and her raven-colored hair was surmounted by a military cap. She was unusually pale, which gave to her dark eyes an intense brilliancy. But she was in the merriest of moods and her wit and laughter were contagious as she jested with every one about her.

"When shall we be clear of these gloomy defiles?" said Yermoloff to her as they rode low down into a gorge beside the Abarane. "I confess to an ever-recurring apprehension that some of the enemy may learn of our advance and contest the way with us."

"I have at times felt a similar apprehension," replied the girl. "They surely could cause us much trouble here if they learned of our movements. But there is no human probability that they have, and by to-morrow night we shall be beyond the defiles and safe upon the plain of the Araxes."

"You have traversed this road before, I believe you told me?"

"Twice," responded the girl; "and I noted every mile of the way. There is but one locality along the entire river where a considerable body of the enemy could be posted to advantage. That is just at the point where we leave the river and march out upon the slope which leads down to the Monastery of Echmiadzin. They can make no stand on this side of that gorge. Regarding that locality I am a little apprehensive myself. By this hour to-morrow evening we shall be beyond danger, without doubt."

During that entire night the Russian army, weary as they were by their long march, held on their way. Yermoloff's anxiety would admit of no proposition to halt. The Abarane must be left in his rear, before rest and sleep were to be indulged in. Through the entire warm, sultry night, the everlasting *tramp*, *tramp* of the infantry was heard, and the rumbling of the artillery wagons and the clatter of hoofs. The stars looked clearly and solemnly down upon the marching thousands, and the river murmured over its pebbly bed beside their gloomy way. But on and on their shadowy columns moved, half awed by the .

majestic, barren rocks which towered above them on either hand.

When morning broke at last upon them they discovered that the defile had grown more gloomy, wild and startling still. The ragged summits of the mountains seemed to meet the sky, the road was narrower, the way more broken. But in the brilliant sunlight which glittered from the peaks above them they took heart and toiled on along their difficult way. At length the advance reached a point where the Abarane parted into two channels in the midst of an amphitheatre ; and here the Russian Yermoloff, the indomitable soldier, looking up and around him, discovered *the entire army of Abbas Mirza* posted to intercept him. The scene was fearful, but majestic and brilliant. On every lofty rock and available foothold for men the flash of bayonets was seen in the full effulgence of the morning sun. The Persian infantry in three lines extended from mountain to mountain across both channels of the Abarane and the road. Their cannon frowned on every side. On the mountain-tops east and west, which from the river bed looked inaccessible, were posted the entire cavalry of General Debaena's command. The most superb body of horse in all Asia were at an altitude where the sun's rays had full play upon their steel coats of mail, which shimmered and flashed like long silver serpents, stretched along the windings of the opposite ranges of mountains. On the summit of the mountain which confronted Yermoloff's advance and divided the river, was floating the banner of Persia, surrounded by glittering masses of bayonets. Here was the Prince Royal with his staff overlooking the scene.

Taken completely by surprise, the Russian commander was fully sensible of the danger of forcing a passage by a road thus defended. But the fear of losing the fortress of Echmiadzin determined him in his purpose to advance. The fire of his artillery apparently drove back the first line of the Persian infantry, and he gained possession of part of the ascending road and their advanced positions. His columns moved onward in exultation. But just at the moment they and their cumbersome baggage were involved with great confusion in the defiles on either side of the central mountain, the Persians charged on all sides, and their admirable artillery opened at the same instant a destructive fire. Only the superior discipline of the Russian troops saved them from utter destruction. They rallied and recovered their order. A sanguinary contest ensued which lasted from seven o'clock in the morning until four in the afternoon. The Persian infantry attacked with obstinate impetuosity up to the very mouths of the cannon and points of the bayonets. The Muscovite veterans encountered at last their equals. The river ran down its channel stained with streaks of blood, for the contending masses of infantry were frequently fighting in the water ankle deep. The bodies of the slain would not float away from the shallowness of the stream, but lay there and rocked back and forth impeding the footsteps of the charging foemen, who were alternately advancing and retreating with the fluctuations of the combat. The echoes of the thunder of the artillery pealed from cliff to cliff in the narrow defile, and the heavy shot came plunging down into the masses of infantry struggling in the river, or dashing into the water, flung high in air the spray and sands of the bottom. The obstinate courage of the Russians cost them a fearful sacrifice of life. Their infantry were stretched in heaps upon the road and in the river bottoms, their artillery was disabled and the gunners one by one slain. The staff of Yermoloff with their horses were nearly all killed or disabled. Two only remained to him, and with them appeared the beautiful girl who refused all solicitations to retire to the rear. The female secretary remained beside Yermoloff, eagerly watching the battle and listening to every word that fell from the commander's lips. She noted every order issued to the aids, who dashed away but returned no more. Her whole soul was bound up in the various evolutions directed by Yermoloff. She seemed to be looking anxiously for some event to occur which yet lay hidden in the future of that terrible day. She refused the proffered canteens of the officers. She refused the offer of bread. She never dismounted to relieve the posture or soothe the agonies of the dying. She refused to wheel her horse aside into the shadow of the cliffs, though the August sun of the Orient beat upon her with intolerable fierceness. She was utterly absorbed in the conflict, and though pale as a corpse, was apparently beyond the reach of fear. *The battle, the battle.* That seemed to be her only thought. How goes the battle? At length a Persian battery succeeded in securing a position which gave a direct range with the spot where Yermoloff was watching the progress of the battle. In another moment, the last man of that commander's staff was slain, and his horse dashed wildly away up the road to the north. The girl turned her brilliant eyes upon the chief, with the remark:

"You will have to accept my services now. You can no longer refuse. Do you still hold to the opinion that General

Krassousky will have to retire from the opposite side of the river and reform his men."

"I do. But I will never send you. Look at the cannon shot cutting the air on the route to him a messenger must travel. I will send an officer of the infantry to him."

"No, send me. Nicholas will make a countess of me if I come back safe. That would just suit his fancy." The words were calm as those of a veteran.

"No, I cannot expose you on any terms, and then your secret services are invaluable to us," was Yermoloff's reply. ·

"I will abandon you forever," was her firm answer, "unless you send me."

"You cannot mean that," he said.

"I do, and on the instant, too. Suffer me to go, I entreat you. I will be at your side in a few moments again. I will tell him you order his immediate retreat up the river to reform. Let me go to him, or I leave your presence forever."

"Then go," he said petulantly. "You have the will of a deity. Go, and may God return you safe."

In an instant she turned her horse toward the river's edge, plunged into the stream, and galloped across to the opposite bank with the Persian cannon shot plunging through the air on every side of her. Her teeth were clenched, her eyes terrible in their brilliancy ; every nerve was braced for the emergency. She would retain the mastery over the natural timidity of her womanhood until her purpose was accomplished, even if she fell dead under the unnatural strain the next instant after it was effected.

She reached the opposite bank, bounded up its easy slope to the plateau where Krassousky, superbly mounted, was inciting his men to stand firm until they were reinforced, and flying directly over the heaps of the dead and dying, accosted the chief thus, as she drew rein before him :

"General Yermoloff has lost every officer of his staff. He sends me to say to you, '*Charge instantly with every man you can rally, and drive the enemy's infantry down the river to the first bend in the stream.*' He has discovered that the Persians are retreating. Order also your artillery down to the position now occupied by your infantry."

"Strange order !" exclaimed the officer. "Am I left no discretion ? "

"None," she ejaculated. "Yermoloff bids me say, 'The battle depends upon a prompt execution of the order.'"

The general knew her too well to doubt the authority vested in her, and though the order seemed to him an insane one, he acquiesced, and she rode off. Pausing upon the river's brink, she saw an aid dispatched to advance the artillery from its commanding position, where it was inflicting frightful havoc among the Persian infantry, to low ground where its range would be intercepted by the Muscovites themselves. Then she witnessed the organization of a desperate infantry charge, which proved successful, the enemy slowly giving way before it, and falling back upon the first bend in the Abarane, south. The artillery occupied the ground just vacated by the Russian infantry, and behind them stretched the commanding ground or slope from which they had inflicted so much havoc with their cannon. While the artillery were assuming their new position, the isolated girl upon the river bank was enveloping her entire figure in a *snow-white shawl.* Yermoloff, who was darting anxious glances across the stream at the singular result which had followed his order to retreat, caught a glimpse of her and beckoned to her to return. She paid no attention to him ; her eyes were riveted upon the mountain tops to the east of the river, while the cannon shot ploughed the ground and the stream on either side of her. Presently she gave a start, and clutched her reins convulsively. A bugle sounded close at hand. The sound seemed to issue from the solid rock-mountain on the east. Tears burst from her eyes ; she was thrilled by some intense emotion. The tension of her nerves was unloosed. Words trembled on her lips, inaudible, but struggling for utterance. The woman so calm amid all the lengthened horrors of that day, so rigid, so ice-like in her composure amid shot and shell and dying men, was weeping and laughing and exulting at the sound of a bugle. It came again, nearer and nearer that martial music came, and the girl burst forth into a loud cry of joy, choked again and again by tears, but again finding utterance.

"My Persia ! my country ! *victory ! victory !* Debaena is coming ; Debaena is here. Fly, Russian dogs, the sword of great Allah is here."

In another instant a horseman issued from a cleft in the rock-mountain in the rear of the Russian artillery. Another and another followed at rapid pace, until the rising ground was covered with thousands of them forming for battle. The girl's eyes were fixed upon one alone. Over his head was hovering the King-vulture, *Boshran* (good tidings).

CHAPTER XXX.

THE Russian artillery wheeled in their disadvantageous position to meet this unexpected enemy. Their rapid fire with round shot and grape emptied many saddles, riders falling headlong to the earth, and steeds plunging madly to the rear in agony, or gasping foam as they lay stretched upon the earth. For a few moments confusion reigned amid the forming squadrons of Persian cavalry. But Debaena's men soon yelled their terrible war-cry, and like the wind charged upon the artillery, sabre in hand. The gunners were slaughtered as they were in the act of applying the match, and though their last fire was fatal to many horsemen, the irresistible legion swept on to rapid victory. All the guns fell into the hands of Debaena, who immediately dashed on to the attack of the infantry.

Abbas Mirza had been notified early in the day that a gorge had been discovered in the eastern wall of mountains through which a descent could be made by the cavalry to the Russian rear, in a certain contingency. That contingency had been accelerated by the heroic "*Coadjutor*," who had discovered the critical moment, and by delivering a false order of Yermoloff cleared the coveted knoll of the Russian artillery. Her *signal shawl* had been seen from the cliffs, and Debaena hastened down to participate in the conflict. The instant the Crown Prince of Persia discovered from his elevated site the advent of the horse in the enemy's rear, he ordered a general charge. The Russians were taken at disadvantage, but fought with marvellous courage and resolution, and the carnage became appalling. Nobly did the veterans of European battlefields struggle to retain their military *prestige.* They died in their tracks, unyielding, heroic and hopeless. The Persian patriots, burning to avenge their brethren slain on so many fields, and confident that the enemy was at last within their net, with exultant yells saw the ranks of the foe decimated and thrown into confusion by the artillery, and charging with impetuosity broke and routed the Russian lines on every side, and bayoneted the stubborn veterans who refused to surrender.

Before sunset all hope for the Muscovites had fled. Their generals massing a small body of horse and infantry forced the Persian line at the western channel of the Abarane and fled towards Echmiadzin, pursued by Debaena and his fleet cavalry. The Persian horse charging upon them at every favorable opportunity cut them down all the way to the walls of the beleaguered monastery. The batteries of the Russians fell into the hands of the victors, together with the stores and ammunition intended for the besieged of Echmiadzin. The victory was decisive, and is deemed the most glorious in the annals of modern Persia. Before the shades of night fell, the victors were cheering by thousands from the cliffs, and amid them sat upon her horse a wounded girl, supported by two soldiers, waving her *white shawl* in air while tears of joy streamed down her cheeks. It was *Irene.*

.   .   .   .

In a hospital tent near Echmiadzin Abbas Mirza was bending over the couch of Zenayi, severely wounded in the arm. The Ghebre had participated in the cavalry charge led by Debaena, and while dealing death with a sword of antique pattern was struck by a bullet and fell from his horse. Debaena with the light of battle in his face was cutting his way through the Russian infantry when his friend was stricken down at his side. Clearing a circle about the wounded man by a few desperate charges of his horsemen, he gave the command into the hands of his junior officer, and while the cavalry pushed on, dismounted from Al-Borak, kneeled beside his friend, and by a skillful pressure of his finger upon an artery of the shoulder saved him from bleeding to death until a surgeon came up. Then remounting he pushed on after his men.

"I shall recover, Your Royal Highness," said the Ghebre. "Persia shall have my services and counsels for many a day yet. But I should have been a spirit had not Debaena's recollection of a simple remedy for bleeding saved me for sublunary affairs."

"Allah be praised for saving you both," fervently ejaculated the prince. "To you and Debaena and *Coadjutor* are we indebted for this glorious victory. Would that I might look upon the face of that heroic girl who has proved to us a protecting angel."

"Your wish is of easy accomplishment," replied the Ghebre. "Yonder, on that couch, she lies, near the wall of the tent. Go to her. Forgive her. Bless her as you hope the forgiveness of Ormuzd."

"Forgive her!" exclaimed the amazed prince. "I shall

rather crave her forgiveness that I have so long suffered her services to go unrewarded."

Passing across to the couch of "*Coadjutor*," Abbas Mirza gazed for an instant with intense pity upon the pale face of the poor girl. Then as her large, lustrous eyes opened upon him with their irresistible light, he started, looked again, and with a cry of anguish flung himself upon his knees beside her, and folded his arms about her with ineffable tenderness.

"*Irene*, my darling *Irene*—light of the East," he murmured, amid his sobs and tears and uncontrollable emotion, and then laying his head upon her breast he wept long and violently. The fingers of the girl twined in his dark hair while a smile of exquisite beauty played upon her lips, and she murmured softly, " My *brother*, my *brother*, my darling *brother*."

.   .   .   .

The subsequent events of the Persian war may be delved out from the archives of the years 1828 and 1829. We discontinue here the line of historical events and dismiss them with brief mention. The final result of the war was disastrous to Persia. The armies of Abbas Mirza were gradually vanquished and driven across the Araxes river, which eventually became the boundary between the two empires. The important fortress of Abbas Abad was surrendered to Russia by a traitor. The execution of its former governor had not eradicated all the treason lurking behind its walls. This defection led to the surrender of the fortress of Ardebil, with its cannon, valuable stores and rare library of Oriental works. Abbas Mirza, finding the contest hopeless, sued for peace. By the final arrangement made between the two powers, Mount Ararat became the point in which Persia, Russia and Turkish Armenia cornered.

.   .   .   .

At the termination of hostilities Zenayi and Debaena stood higher than ever in the public esteem. It was well known that both had opposed the war *ab initio*. Their subsequent heroism and devotion to Persia in the field, where they incurred every hazard in what they believed to be a hopeless cause, gained them the devotion of the entire Persian people. Honors and emoluments were heaped upon them both by the Shah, who had originally leaned strongly to their anti-war opinions. The generous Abbas Mirza, the moving spirit in instigating the war, was the first to propose that Debaena should be honored with the command of the entire cavalry of the empire. His

suggestion was adopted, and the young officer was invested
with this dignity and all the emoluments pertaining to the command.   The Shah presented him also, in recognition of his distinguished services, with one of his palaces.   True, however, to
his promise to the Ghebre, Debaena employed none of the secret resources at his command to his own aggrandizement or
pomp.   The treasury of Cyrus remained intact, save only when
the efficiency of the army intrusted to him required the use of
the hidden gold.

But what had become of the *heart* of the young commander
now seated at the zenith of power and military glory?   He
lived in his luxurious palace with his military friends alone.   No
woman was ever permitted to enter the inclosure of its walls.
This mystery became a common topic of conversation in all
the *anderoöns* of Persia.   It was known that several lovely and
affluent beauties of Iran were dying or sighing for the love of
Debaena.   Songs composed in his honor were heard throughout the land.   He was the pride, the favorite of the nation.
But woman was to him apparently a myth.   He ignored the
sex.

Finally a strange rumor was heard throughout the empire.
A brother officer had rallied Debaena upon his neglect of
women, and received in response the following quotation from
the Persian poet, Kasim Al Anwar :

"*Fate is a hand that exercises its five fingers on its victim.
Two are placed on the eyes, two upon the ears, and one upon the
lips, saying ' Be forever silent.'* "

The women of Persia now extended to Debaena the honor
of their pity.   The solution of the riddle was manifest to them.
It was of easy interpretation.   The young commander was
hopelessly in love with some hidden beauty of the harem.   He
could neither see, hear or speak to her.   Hence all hope was
gone.   Poor Debaena !   The *savans* of Persia, however,
laughed at this solution, and maintained that the gallant officer
was only strongly tinted with *Sufi* mysticism.

But notwithstanding all the sage conjectures of the day
Debaena was dreaming of woman and of more than one.   One
day he sat in his voluptuous gardens beside a fountain, with two
miniatures in his hands.   One was *Madeleine,* the other was
Irene.   The latter was the gift of Abbas Mirza, her brother.
His thoughts were divided between the two lovely faces before
him and the veiled face which he had never seen.   The trio
were the only women that ever occupied his attention.   While

the soldier was thus engaged Zenayi entered the garden and accosted him.

"Dreaming of women still! Alfonso, heed my advice. Shun them all. I have in reserve for you an *immortal beauty*, whose ravishing charms will fill your soul to satiety, a mistress of whom you will never weary, who cannot grow old or change. You have made giant strides in the path of true heroism. I have the power to wed you to a bride worthy of the real nobility in you."

"And yet, Zenayi, the penalty of winning your mysterious beauty, you have said, is no less than an utter abandonment of the sensual in love."

"Aye! To win her of whom I speak you must never live with mortal woman, either as wife or mistress. You must be entirely pure."

Alfonso answered, "Suppose, Zenayi, that I have contracted the habit of loving a mortal woman, and cannot shake that habit off. Can I still win your immortal beauty?"

"Without a doubt," responded the Ghebre. "The *ideal* love for a mortal woman is eminently pure. Beyond the *ideal* you must never go. The instant that the *sensual* is indulged you become unfitted to be the companion of the immortal beauty, and you lose her forever."

"I may love a mortal woman, then, but never wed."

"Those are the terms, Alfonso. A total abandonment of the sensual in love qualifies you for the possession of the immortal beauty."

The Ghebre calmly contemplated the eloquent face of his young friend, and witnessed the fearful struggle going on. And as the eyes of Zenayi, the Sphinx, brightened in gazing, Alfonso saw again that mysterious, far-off look of immensity which awed and fascinated all who encountered his full, steady gaze. And then he fell a-dreaming of his own vague, earliest recollections. After a pause the Ghebre spoke again :

"The time is limited within which I have the power of bringing you in contact with the immortal beauty. In a few months the opportunity will be lost to you, and if lost, *lost forever*."

The last words seemed to boom like a distant funeral bell, filling the soul of the listener with a vague apprehension that something of priceless value was passing from the grasp of man forever.

Again the mysterious being addressed his friend, who sat absorbed in profound contemplation.

11

"I have promised to reveal to you the second of the three great secrets. Now I am forced by gratitude to offer you the last and *third* also. In saving my life at Echmiadzin, you con·ferred upon me the greatest boon that man can give. Hence I offer you the *third.* Ponder well the terms, and when I bring you face to face with the awful responsibility of a decision you will tremble at the glory, honor and power that waits upon the utter abandonment of the *sensual* in your love for women. *Your love for woman, no matter how intense and strong, will fade away in the inestimable value of the immortal beauty I shall offer to your arms.* Prepare yourself by contemplation for the trial day."

With tenderness the Ghebre kissed the forehead of his favorite pupil and walked solemnly away through the *charbagh.*

For hours the commander sat there silent. The miniatures had fallen to the ground neglected. He knew not that they were lying beside the fountain. He was absorbed in dreaming of that vague, inestimable gift which would compensate man for the loss of woman. At length he started from his reverie, raised the miniatures from the earth, placed one upon the rim of the fountain, and walked away with the other in his hand. And as he strolled on and on amid the shrubbery and flowers of that Eastern paradise, he was dreaming of a woman's face that haunted him, and wondering if her soul was indeed as beautiful as her face.

CHAPTER XXXI.

HE Ghebre and his pupil stood once again together in the cave. Here had Debaena first learned the rudiments of science and of military lore. From this subterranean school had he emerged, a meteor upon the air of his adopted country. And now with the honors of the empire fresh and bright upon him, he had returned to the rude cavern of the sage beside the sea, to be initiated in the mysteries of that mysterious *second secret* so long promised by the Sphinx of Persia. The Ghebre had conducted him to a corner of the cavern veiled in shadows, and bade him remain motionless until a light was struck. Presently a scarlet flame sprang up from the rocks, at first no larger than the flame of a lamp, but flaring wider and brighter every instant as Zenayi poured a dark powder upon it from a flask. At length it had risen to the height of twelve inches, and in its scarlet brilliancy flowed away down the rock upon which it had been lighted, until the whole cavern glowed with its brightness and every object was revealed.

Then Debaena discovered before him a horrible, yawning pit in the floor of the cave, fifty feet in diameter, above which was suspended a silk balloon inflated with gas. A car was attached to the balloon, in which Zenayi bade him be seated. He found also that this car was surrounded by lamps attached to it by wires. The Ghebre lighted these lamps one by one, and then seating himself beside Debaena loosened the cord which held the balloon to the rock, and the two slowly commenced to descend into the yawning pit. Gradually the Ghebre, by means of a cord, allowed the gas to escape, and Debaena realized that he was swiftly descending into the bowels of the earth. Down, down they sped, silent and thoughtful, into the depths of blackness, and the unknown. The soldier knew too well the reticent character of Zenayi to question him when in his silent and mysterious moods. He therefore only held his peace and watched the regular, rocky walls of the shaft down which they sped. Seconds, minutes, hours passed by, and still no indications of the end of their journey appeared. Finally the Ghebre looked directly at his companion and said:

"You are drowsy, Alfonso. Sleep if you can, for the journey is long."

The soldier without a word stretched himself in the bottom of the car, which was covered with an elegant carpet, placed his head upon the side or rim of the car, and in a few moments slept as soundly as he had ever done in camp.

When the commander of all the cavalry of Persia awoke, it was at the touch of Zenayi's hand upon his head, and the loud words of command:

"Arouse yourself, take this lamp and follow me."

Debaena with a start looked up, saw the mysterious eyes of his friend regarding him, and noticed that the Ghebre had detached two of the lamps from the car, and was offering him one of them. He arose at once, and taking the proffered lamp, stepped from the car in imitation of Zenayi, and followed him. His feet instantly felt the firm resistance of rock, and he followed the Ghebre's lamp into the impenetrable darkness; walking on and on into pathless gloom. Turning once he looked behind him and saw the lamps which had been left in the anchored balloon dwindling away into indistinctness in the darkness. After a time he looked back again. Their light had vanished. The consciousness that a fearful extent of rock, doubtless the thickness of many miles, was above his head and between him and the surface of the earth, appalled the hero of a hundred fights, and he followed on in amazement and curiosity that at length became painful. He could see nothing above his head. His lamp light was inadequate to give him the details of his surroundings. His whole life and hope of escape from this natural prison rested in the person of the white-robed being who walked on and on before him with a lamp.

He discovered inequalities in the path or way he was travelling. Sometimes the bottom was apparently as level as the floor of a dwelling, then it seemed at intervals to be ribbed or channelled. But there were no serious impediments to his advance, and he realized that they must be making rapid progress. Finally his guide paused and said to him:

"Be patient. You will soon be amazed, and forget the tediousness of your journey."

Even as Zenayi spoke, Debaena fancied that he discovered far ahead a faint light as of the early dawn of day. Nevertheless he remained silent, so completely had the Ghebre's habits of silence and self-control influenced his own conduct and become a second nature to him when alone with this mysterious friend. The Ghebre had resumed his advance and Alfonso followed in the same thoughtful mood as before. He was slightly awed, but kept this emotion to himself. Curiosity soon usurped the place of every other emotion, for the subterranean dawn was surely increasing in brightness. As they advanced it lighted up the gloom, and presently Debaena saw far above his head a wonderful net-work of white stretching away on above and on either side of him, like a subterranean forest of white, interlacing graceful branches. The coming subterranean day waxed clearer, whiter, brighter before them. Everything was becoming visible and distinct about them, and the amazed soldier recognized the white, graceful net-work above him as a forest of coral, white as the driven snow, and of immense extent. The floor upon which he was walking was also coral, and soon his guide led him away to one side of this vast subterranean chamber, where their way passed amid trees of coral, standing erect upon the floor and stretching their branches above their heads as they walked. The brightness ahead augmented, and seemed at length to develop into a golden light which tinted all objects around, and in whose effulgence the soldier discovered that his path was now covered with a wide waste of tiny pink shells. Away, away on before him spread this wonderful carpet of pink, and above him twined the branches of the snow-white coral, and around him clustered at intervals the trunks of the coral trees. Was he indeed within the realm of a fairy queen, and was Zenayi a magician, gifted with the power of revealing to him the haunts of these supernatural beings? This idea strengthened as he advanced, and leaving the white forest behind him entered one where the trees were pink and the floor covered with golden shells, dotted with specks of white.

To the ejaculations of surprise and delight which broke now from the lips of his companion, Zenayi exclaimed :

"Come on, now, to the coral treasury from which I pilfered my chair you have seen so often in my cave. It is just before us."

Hastening on in excitement and rapture after the Ghebre, Alfonso came to a great amphitheatre or vast circle of red coral trees, a hundred rods across, whose branches, interlacing and exquisite in their details, were illumined by a brilliant golden light issuing like a river from the floor beyond, and

which the Ghebre informed him was a vast body of burning
gas, which had doubtless for ages been flowing up from the
bowels of the earth and illumining this wonderful fairy spectacle.   The fire worshippers of the earliest days had known of
this subterranean fire, and to their chief priests had been intrusted the knowledge of the locality of its existence, until the
secret had been lost by the sudden death of the one who should
have passed it down to his successor.   Zenayi had known of
the ancient tradition regarding it, and by accident discovered it
when experimenting with his balloon in the pit of his cave.   As
the amazed soldier gazed upon the gorgeous spectacle, ever
varying with every turn he made from right or left, and witnessed the vast extent of this precious treasury, he exclaimed :

"Could this valuable coral be transported to the light of
day it would make a fortune for its owner before which the
treasury of Cyrus would dwindle into insignificance."

"It is yours, Alfonso," replied the singular man in white.
"I have given it to you.   One chair alone has been transported to the cave above.   All else is yours.   Time and
science may enable you to transport vast quantities of it to a
market.   If the love of wealth still lingers in your heart you
may make the attempt to turn this coral into the gold of men's
traffic.   But if you value the counsel of your friend Zenayi,
you will leave all this wealth, too, behind and push on to the
acquisition of that *immortal beauty* which alone can satisfy the
human heart ; that *immortal beauty* which will enrich you far
beyond the treasury of Cyrus, far beyond all this wilderness of red coral, trafficked into gold.   In the possession of
that transcendent wealth, these two treasuries, these *two secrets* intrusted by Zenayi to you will seem trifling and of little
value."

That transcendent secret again.   What could be more valuable than this wilderness of coral, red and beautiful for the
markets of the world ?   Ages on ages could not exhaust the
resources of this subterranean coral mine.   With this wealth at
command he could overwhelm and conquer empires.   What
the splendor of the sword could not effect, the power of the
inexhaustible riches would.   "Relinquish this certain wealth,
Zenayi, for an uncertainty ?   I should be a madman," he exclaimed.

The Ghebre looked upon his eager, beautiful face, lighted up
with the glory of the subterranean flames, and his magnificent,
dark eyes brilliant in the enthusiasm of his new acquisition.

Then he smiled one of his mysterious, dubious smiles, which seemed to Debaena to signify so much superiority, so much knowledge of the great *unrevealed.*

" Tell me, Zenayi," he said, annoyed by the calm superiority of the man, " shall I find in the *third* great secret greater wealth than this ?"

The priest of the Magi abandoned his usual calmness of manner and tone, and burst forth into eloquence as if the theme engrossed the noblest and best qualities of his heart and brain.

" Aye ! greater wealth than a thousand secrets like to these I have given you. Greater power than these can ever buy : power to face princes, to contend with *savans,* to read the secrets of men and of nature, to be great in that mysterious, but awful auxiliary to success, *learning.* Seize the prize I offer ! Abandon the *sensual* in love ; accept the arms of my *immortal beauty,* and you shall have the *greatest gift Ormuzd ever bestowed on mortal man."*

As he spoke his eyes seemed to flame for an instant with a *chatoyant* light. Then came that gaze which awed and fascinated all men, but now conveyed to Debaena the impression that the Ghebre ardently yearned to bestow upon him his own mysterious power and knowledge.

The soldier was buried in profound thought. A struggle was going on, and he remained silent.

" You are harassed by love for a mortal woman, I fear," said the Ghebre.

" I am," replied the soldier, startled by the mysterious intelligence which seemed to read his thoughts.

" Then abandon the hope or desire to make her your wife, and love her with the calm, holy veneration we have for the pure, distant star of evening, whose loveliness we love to gaze upon, but can never approach."

" Can I attain to this lofty summit of self-control ?" inquired Debaena.

" Aye !" was the response. " When you realize the loveliness of the immortal beauty I offer to you."

Debaena was again thoughtful and silent. Finally, raising his eagle-eyes to the face of Zenayi, he said :

" I am human, but I will try."

" Your answer is noble, Alfonso, and worthy of a being guided by reason. After a time, I shall bring you face to face with this mystery, and rest assured your devotion to the mistress of your heart will be sorely tried. Let us abandon the subject now. Do you know that you are very near the sea?"

"I have believed it, Zenayi, and do not know how it could be otherwise, as your cave is near the sea. The coral formations alone would tell me that."

"Once the sea flowed where we now stand," replied the Ghebre, "but volcanic upheaval has doubtless barred it out."

Thus conversing, they wandered on and on, exploring the marvels of the place, until Zenayi warned his companion that it was time for them to return. They regained the locality of the balloon and the shaft once more, where Debaena witnessed the process of inflating their balloon from the apparatus carefully placed there by Zenayi. Mounting the car again, the two were wafted in time to the upper cave, and regained the light of day. . . . .

When Debaena returned to the capital of Persia, he found that the court of Teheran were engrossed by the discussion of a foreign beauty, who had arrived with her father from England, in company with the ambassador from that nation. She was said to be an American lady travelling for pleasure in the East: her name was Madeleine Delaplaine. Her attractions of person and intellect were reported to be marvellous, and it was said that she was a great favorite in the royal *anderoons* which she was visiting, and that the Shah had treated her with marked courtesy. Debaena, upon receipt of this startling intelligence, was thrilled with pleasure and excitement. His boyhood came fresh and clear upon his recollection in an instant; and with strange emotion, he hastened away to the palace of the Shah in full uniform upon the reception day, when it was understood that the beautiful foreigner and her party would be present in the costumes of their own country. Abbas Mirza had sent a messenger to his favorite commander of horse, urging him to be present by all means, as the stranger was transcendently lovely.

At the appointed hour the gallant commander, standing near to the person of his sovereign in company with the other dignitaries of the empire, witnessed the entry of the English ambassador and his suite, accompanied by the American lady and her father. The Shah, with infinite dignity, courtesy and grace, directed the party to be seated in his presence, and so near that conversation was readily carried on in the English tongue. The voice of Madeleine, unheard for so many years of adventure and battle, fell upon the ears of Debaena like the music of a dream.   He stood erect before her, a few paces distant, and for a time she did not see him, so bewildered was she by the array of princes, nobles and dignitaries, who thronged the apartment.   Presently the splendor of his attire as a member of the Order of the Sun Lion caught her attention.   Her eyes ran over its details, then mounted to his face, gazed for an instant, and brightened with the joy of recognition.   She knew the escaped convict, and was delighted. He saw it all — her surprised look, her pleasure, her smile of recognition.   He bowed slightly in return, as became the reserve and caution of the Persian court; but his eagle eyes full of joy told her that his heart was still the heart of the boy whom she had befriended and loved with her innocent girl-heart.   With admirable self-control, this superb loveliness betrayed to the court no further evidence of her acquaintance with the favorite commander, but sought occasion, by her frequent look, to notify him that he was the only being present whom she deemed worthy of her admiration.   There was no opportunity for him to address her during the royal reception. It would have outraged the decorum of the Persian court. But as she passed out at length with infinite grace from the presence of the Shah, she bestowed upon Debaena a look so long, eager, and full of interest that every nerve in him seemed to thrill.   Her style and beauty, as she swept away from the brilliant scene, were well calculated to make princes uneasy upon their thrones.   She was an empire in herself.

All that night the commander of horse was restless upon his couch.   Madeleine had come.   The dreams he had cherished of her growing loveliness — of her beauty maturing into perfect womanhood, had been realized.   His miniature was a truthful likeness of her.   She was faultless in form, face, movement — a dream of Paradise.   Aye! and there was a tremulous joy in his heart that she was unchanged in soul.   She had predicted distinction and glory for him.   And in that proud moment of his life, when her eyes had said to him, "*You have won it,*" he exulted with a heroic joy, that her thoughts had never ceased to dwell upon his career, all unknown and distant though it had been.   Her faith had been firm.   Her memory of him as constant as "Madeleine's star."   And then the thought came to him — "Is the regard of that superb woman friendship, or is it love?"

On the following morning, a note came to him in all the delicate chirography of a refined, educated woman.

"Alfónso Debaena! come at once to the palace of the English embassy. I told my father that I recognized you, and with him and me your secret and early history are safe. It appears that you are the lion of the Persian court, and the hero of the Russian war. I knew you would attain the summit, wherever your path in life carried you. You have been in my thoughts constantly, all these long years. You will not delay your visit to your earliest friends, but come at once to see

"MADELEINE."

CHAPTER XXXII.

"Let us boldly, in pursuit of our ambitious wishes, place our foot on the head of empire, or in manly bravery sacrifice our lives at the shrine of courage." — SULTAN AHMED.

IN the hush of the summer evening a lady was seated upon a divan, in the palace appropriated to the use of the English Embassy, anxiously awaiting the advent of the great cavalry commander of Persia. The soft air of the night fanned her fair cheek as it whispered in at her open window, and the moonbeams fell upon her delicate hands, and her white dress fashioned in the style of a far-distant clime; she was pensive, anxious, on the alert for the sound of footsteps, and filled with a vague apprehension that some dream of her life was on the eve of dissolution. Was his heart already gained by some one of the lovely beings who, she acknowledged to herself, were the most perfect women in the world? The exquisite women of Persia had arisen upon her consciousness as a new creation. From the moment she had entered the land of roses and heavenly nights, the surpassing loveliness of Oriental women had been her constant surprise and study. With that dash of Circassian and Georgian blood in them which gave them their fair, soft complexions, and with that willowy grace peculiar to them, and unknown to any other race of females, they walked and danced before her in the gardens and halls of the *anderoons*, until they seemed meet companions for the countless roses and flowers of Iran. What man could withstand the fascination of eyes, lustrous and tender with the soft passion of love, and the red lusciousness of lips, which sang with such exquisite pathos the songs of their native land? She had seen in one day in Persia more beautiful women than in England and America in a month. Unlike the great mass of females of the last two countries, these Orientals had voices modulated like gentle falls of music, and she knew how powerful was this charm of voice upon the hearts of men. The rapid, nervous step of Occidental women, so repugnant to all refined sense of the graceful, was here never seen; even the mother who bore her child in her arms across the *anderoons*, seemed to lull the little one to rest and quiet by the gentle, airy movement of her body alone. About the couch of the nervous invalid the Oriental woman moved like a spirit of grace and noiseless tread, and her presence conduced to peace and sleep. Discordant sounds, loud laughter, and harsh voices among women were unknown, and even in their mirth and glee these Orientals charmed, but never startled. What wonder, then, that the white-robed stranger with the golden hair and dark-brown eyes should fancy Alfonso Debaena had been ensnared by charms which the stern and hardy so intensely relish?

A firm tread sounded in Madeleine's ear, a slave quietly pushed aside the drapery, and Debaena entered. His eyes were full of the joy of greeting, but he was slightly pale, which gave a darker effect to the long military moustache, which was parted evenly and smooth upon his lip. He was very beautiful; the same classical, manly beauty, which had first charmed the intellectual Irene in the gardens of the deserted village; his short, raven dark hair was silky and smoothly brushed. Every detail of his military undress was scrupulously clean and orderly; his features were delicately chiselled by nature, and retained their spiritual type by that abstinence and mental study which render faces delicate and intellectual to the close of life. Something of the majesty of Zenayi's intellectuality seemed to hover over his features, for the Ghebre had trained him to a habit of daily intercourse with books, which he sought eagerly in the pauses of military duty. Like a born prince of the empire, Debaena approached and touched his lips to the hand the lady extended to' him in greeting; then seating himself upon the divan beside her, the gates of the past were flung open, and they were once more the convict boy and the pitying girl of the far-off continent.

"You knew me, then, at once, Alfonso?" she asked, after a long recital of the events in her native State, which interested him as being connected with his final escape by sea.

"I could scarcely fail to know you," he replied, "having in my possession a likeness of you as a woman upon which I looked so often that every lineament was burned into my brain."

"As a woman? impossible!" she said; "I never had but one likeness taken of me."

"Is that it?" he replied, producing from his breast the miniature brought to him by "*Boshran.*"

With a cry of amazement she took it, examined it, then looking at him, inquired:

"And when did you become a wizard? This is mine, and the only picture ever painted of me."

He was contemplating her loveliness with eager curiosity, and the glance of a mountain-eagle; his admiration was manifest, and a flush stole over her cheek, and her eyelashes fell.

"Tell me," she continued, looking up at those magnetic eyes again, "by what supernatural messenger you gained possession of this."

"A bird brought it to me, and since that day he has never left me, but soars above me wherever I ride or walk."

"Was it a condor of the Andes?"

"It was; but how should you know this? It was a condor, which fell upon my camping ground as if from the very heavens. Did you send him to me?"

"No, Alfonso; a sea captain gave him to my father; we kept him in a cage, and one day an officer visiting us, who proved afterwards to be insane, tied my miniature to him, and set him free, saying 'Go like the eagle to Memphis, and make Rhodope's fortunes.'"

"How startling this wonderful flight!" he exclaimed; "over thousands of miles of seas and mountains, and high in heaven through the clouds, the little picture of my friend and advocate sped on to me. Oh! I have lain upon the battlefield, and, too weary to sleep, have looked up to the stars and thought of Madeleine. I have wondered if she had forgotten me; if she remembered the predictions she had made of my success and the high ideal of heroism she had presented to my youthful mind, and when victory perched upon my standards I have longed eagerly that she might know it, but fear restrained me. I knew that when a girl develops into a woman the tastes and friendships of her early life often pass away and are supplanted by others. Still I hoped that amid all who worshipped your beauty of heart and mind, that amid your

throng of admirers, sometimes the face of the convict-boy
might rise before you, and you dream again of the heroisms to
which you sought to arouse his soul."

He paused, overcome by the emotions and the gratitude of
his early years.

Madeleine looked for a moment upon his bowed head,
bowed to conceal the emotion which he would retain within
his control. Then she spoke, and her words were very low
and gentle, falling upon his ear like music.

"Alfonso, I am one of those who never forget the friends
of my childhood. In early life the friendships we form are so
much more unselfish and disinterested. We have not then
learned to select from motives of policy and self-interest.
Hence our purest and best ideals are formed then. You were
the ideal of my girlhood. I looked upon you as noble of heart,
and yet a martyr ; as bowed beneath a load of unmerited shame
and anguish, and yet waiting only the opportunities which God
gives to assert your claim to the highest of honors. I thought
of you often when you were gone. I knew not that you were
alive. And yet when I came to know so many men of culture
and of intellectual strength, I said to myself, 'These have not
suffered the anguish of the innocent, tortured Alfonso. They
may have struggled up from poverty to eminence, but they
never bore so painful a cross as he. If he shall surmount all
obstacles with this reproach of the prison upon him, and with
this anguish of shame rending his heart, then is he greater than
all these.' To me you have been ever the *star rising from
the gloom of the dungeon.*"

He raised his bowed head, and looked upon her face radiant
with her earnestness and her imperial beauty. Never had he
seen a face rivalling that, save only the exquisite countenance
of Irene. Even in this moment of renewed admiration for his
boyhood's friend, he could not forget that "*Coadjutor*" was
the most beautiful woman in Persia. He was fully conscious,
too, that this lovely sister of Abbas Mirza exercised upon his
life a potent spell. The very brilliancy of her beauty and
talents recalled the attractions of Statira. And now in the
hour of his exaltation and glory, with beautiful women by
scores looking after his receding form, and longing for converse
with him, he remembered with profound gratitude that in the
critical hours of his life both Madeleine and Irene had rendered him invaluable service. He would in return gladly
recompense them by every means in his power. How should

he reward them ? What would these beautiful women desire from him above all else ?

But he was looking upon Madeleine, and the longer he contemplated her, the more was he impressed by the air of purity and spirituality which enveloped her. Something seemed to say, " This lovely woman is guided by the purest and holiest principle. She will parley with wrong under no circumstances. She has a link binding her to God and Heaven, which no temptation can shatter. She will suffer, sacrifice herself and all her selfish interests, rather than forfeit the favor of Heaven." And this light which enveloped her, this purity which seemed to rise and fall with the undulations of her breast, was the same which had given her the charm of her girlish life, the same which had lingered upon his memory during the long years of separation, and had seemed to find expression in the steady, luminous light of " *Madeleine's star.*"

In the soul of the ambitious man, who tramples over every barrier of moral and physical restraint to gain his purpose, ever lingers the consciousness of the superior beauty of *right*. The turmoil of the worldly contest, the delights of the successes which attend a career of unprincipled action, and the ebullitions of the energy and will necessary to victory, may often deaden and obscure the sense and appreciation of pure *right*. But the lucid intervals of conscience return, and the soul, created in the image of God, bows in reverence to the truth. So did the soul of Debaena, resolute as it was, trampling over everything which blocked the way to victory, ever return for a draught of pure water at the fountain where Madeleine was priestess. Whenever in the turmoil of life he encountered a pure spring, a serene star, a glimpse of the innocent and untainted, he thought of her, and the purest emotions of his boyhood came winging their way back to him like heavenly birds.

Thus influenced by the pure and the ideal was he now, seated beside her and looking into her exquisite face. He saw that her nature leaned toward his nature, that in some way she identified him with herself, that she trusted and believed in him, and perhaps at his suggestion and proposal would follow him to the ends of the earth. Should he make to her this proposal ? The thought agitated him. There was so much of sweetness in the very idea of folding this pure loveliness to his breast forever, that his heart warmed and his blood glowed like fire within him. Then with sudden revulsion of feeling he recalled the Ghebre's mysterious warning, that he could only worship woman as the far-off star, that he could never fold Madeleine in his arms if he hoped to gain the *immortal beauty*, that mysterious loveliness which was in fact the acme of human power. But as he looked upon this lovely Madeleine, he realized that the struggle was becoming fearful between the human and the ideal within him. Could he pass an entire lifetime near this woman and never approach her? Could he for a lifetime forbear to clasp her hand in his, fold his strong arm about her waist, and draw those lips to his in tenderness? This was essentially sensual. This was forbidden to the aspirant after the *immortal beauty*, and for the Ghebre's third and last great secret his ambitious soul was already uplifting itself in the earnestness and determination of a man who grasps with avidity " the highest good."

Something in his look attracted her attention in the midst of their delightful intercourse, as they warmed towards each other in the magnetic sympathy of conversation and kindred natures, and she said :

" A troubled expression has come into your eyes, Alfonso. Something discordant is crossing the current of your thoughts. Tell me, tell Madeleine with the freedom of years ago what troubles you."

" I am dreaming of *power*, the old, old *ignis fatuus* of men in all ages," he replied ; " andstrangely enough your presence, which charms me to excess, suggests to me that I cannot have all power."

" Why cannot you have all the power that a reasonable man desires?" she replied. " You cannot own a hemisphere, but you have won an empire of hearts. You are the idol of Persia and your resources for pleasure are great. The women of Persia worship you, the men honor you, and the Shah would rather lose his right arm than you. So he said to me, and with deep feeling he made that remark."

" I would have the power over a woman, and fate withstands me. I would win her love, but a mountain looms up between me and her."

" Not if her heart is free, Alfonso ; no woman on earth *knowing* you would refuse you if her heart was free."

It seemed at this response as if the heart of Debaena would burst every restraint and he would kneel at the feet of the superb woman before him. He arose, paced the apartment, and returned to her in deep agitation, entreating her pardon for his strange conduct and restlessness.

"I cannot sit calmly beside you, Madeleine. Your presence has aroused a storm within me which neither you nor I can quell. Oh ! ambition, ambition ! you are an eternal agony. In your following hearts go down, the calm joys of life are wrecked, and a nervous clutch is placed forever upon the heart that feels. I cannot win the woman. Ambition stands before me beckoning, and I must follow. Pity me, Madeleine."

The woman before him was bewildered, and seeing it, Debacna exclaimed :

"Mystery attaches to me in all that I do from this hour forward. Believe me when I say to you that to be near you is happiness and agony, rest and unrest, hope and despair. I will seek you often. I will fly from you capriciously. I crave your society at the same moment that I fear it. Now, if you think me a madman, dismiss me from your presence forever. But if you value an immortal soul do not send me away."

Madeleine was amazed, then thoughtful. At length she said, "I will do anything to render you happy, Alfonso. And since mystery must hold its veil between us, suffer me to say once and forever that your happiness is of inestimable value to me. If in any way I can promote it I am your friend, ever ready at command. Whenever you will be happy by coming to me, *come*. Whenever you will be happy by leaving me, *go*. I will not strive to penetrate your secret. But whenever my presence and my conversation can even for an instant cheer your heart or your life, ask them, and they are yours."

"You are sublime in your friendship to me, Madeleine, and I accept your gift, which is priceless, your gift of your society and time to me on demand. Perhaps in time a holier influence than ambition will gain the mastery over me. Then will I speak to you the naked truth, then will you know the struggle through which I am passing now. Then shall you judge the Alfonso of other days ; and perhaps the magnitude of the interests which are involved in my present mental struggle will then plead with you for me. You first aroused in me ambition. If that ambition has become inordinate, you will forgive me if I, in this trial hour, am wavering, undecided and unlike myself."

Again the low, sweet voice of the woman fell upon the soldier's ear :

"I would rather stimulate you in a noble ambition than impede your way. So unbounded is the faith I have in you, that I know unhallowed ambition is not in your thoughts. That

to which you aspire is, in the sight of Heaven, a legitimate object of pursuit, I doubt not."

" It is, it is," he exclaimed ; "I firmly believe it to be such.
He who holds up to me the beckoning hand is one who has always led me right, one whose faithfulness to me I cannot question, one whose counsel has made me a purer man, a more self-
denying man, a better friend of humanity than I should otherwise have been."

" May I ask the name of the counsellor who has gained such
veneration from you ? "

"Oh, yes ; that man, that benefactor, that friend, is Zenayi.
You have heard of the sage of Persia ? "

" Abbas Mirza told me of Zenayi," she replied.   " In his estimation Zenayi is one of the purest patriots and one of the
most cultured intellects the world has ever known."

" He is more than that, Madeleine ; he is a firm believer in
the goodness and mercy of God, the Creator and Ruler of all
things.   Ormuzd is the title applied by him to God.   But that
matters not.   The same pure, holy overruling Being whom the
Christian denominates God, Zenayi worships.   When the morning sun lifts in the east he falls on his face and adores his Maker
and dedicates the day to His service.   In the name of that Being
he pardons his enemies and strives to live justly with all men."

" Then are you safe in his counsel, Alfonso," she replied,
"for the essence of truth lives in him.   Shall I see you to-
morrow ? "

" If you desire it.   I would gladly see you every day during
your sojourn in the East.   The freshness of my life has come
again with your presence, and though a beautiful woman has
supplanted the girl, I am bold enough to call you only *Madeleine.*"

" And to me you are only my poor, dear hero-boy, Alfonso.
Come to see me when you can.   Farewell."

She pressed his hand at parting.   Her smile lingered upon
his memory when he was alone, like that of a pure angel of
Paradise.

CHAPTER XXXIII.

ENAYI drew aside a curtain of scarlet silk, and exposed to the view of his companion a large hall paved with white marble. The walls were covered with books. It was a royal library, and every book was bound in red morocco, and lettered on the back in gold. The accumulated lore of the East for ages was here exposed to the privileged few who gained admittance. A silence as of the grave reigned. One might well fancy Harpocrates was standing at the entrance with his finger on his lips. Divans covered with scarlet velvet were scattered here and there for the convenience of students ; but one only of them was occupied. The hall was deserted, save by the solitary reader.

"Let us advance and confront the student," said Zenayi.

With their feet in scarlet velvet slippers which had been provided for them in the ante-room of the library, they moved noiselessly down the marble pavement and stood before the princess, who was deeply absorbed in the small volume in her hand. The startled reader looked up in all the splendor of her unveiled loveliness, and saw her instructor, whom she cordially greeted ; but at sight of his companion she felt the warm blood mounting to her cheek, and her voice slightly trembled as she addressed him :

"General Debaena, your presence is an honor to me. The idol of my country is as welcome as a prince of the royal blood. Be seated on this divan with Zenayi."

"No. I am about to retire," said the Ghebre. "Alfonso sought an interview with you, and Abbas Mirza bade me conduct him to your presence. I shall retire. Farewell."

Thus speaking the sage withdrew and left them. For a moment Debaena contemplated his companion seated beside him. He was manifestly embarrassed, while she sat with her eyes cast down and awaiting anxiously the announcement of the cause of the sudden intrusion upon her privacy.

"Irene," he said at length. The Princess detected at once the tremor in his voice, and that he paused at that single word, unable or hesitating to speak further. She remained silent, with her eyes still bent upon the marble pavement.

"Irene," he said again, "what is the greatest mystery of life ?"

"The human heart," were the simple but startling words which came in response. They were the echo of his own thoughts.

"You amaze me by the utterance of my own secret thoughts. Are you wizard enough to tell me also what problem is before my own heart waiting a solution?"

"I can try," was the response, as she still sat with her eyes cast down.

"Then tell me," said Debaena.

"You love three women, General Debaena, and you cannot decide between them."

"By the Eternal God!" exclaimed the commander of the Persian horse. "You are gifted with supernatural discernment. You have spoken the truth. Now answer me once again."

"Well, General Debaena."

"If the three women knew that I was undecided between them, would they value my love at all? Would not the dilemma of my heart disgust each of them with me forever?"

"No," was the monosyllable that came calmly enough in response.

"And why not, Irene?"

"Because a man who is worthy of a woman's love for the inherent qualities in him, is worthy of her love through all the struggles, dilemmas and contradictions of his life."

"And could you, Irene, love a man who could not decide between yourself and two others?"

"I could, General Debaena." Then she added, "But do not give me credit for supernatural powers that I do not possess. I have contrived to draw out from the superior discernment of your friend, Zenayi, that you love three women, and that you love each of them from the same motive, *gratitude.* This is not singular. It is a common experience among women. I have known many women wed whose love has been built up upon that same foundation, *gratitude.* The little kindnesses, one by one and oft repeated, have not only won the hearts of women, but of men also, — have not only won the hearts of the feeble-minded, but won also the hearts of the strong-minded."

"And tell me, Irene," said Debaena, "what is the greatest test of a woman's love?"

"To marry her rival," was the instant response.

"Will not her love then die gradually out and be forever lost?"

"*Never,*" was the emphatic response. "There is little true

love on earth, General Debaena.   It is a priceless pearl.   Its counterfeit is everywhere."

"Then true love burns on like an eternal lamp.   Do you believe this, Irene?"

"With all the earnestness of my nature I believe it.   True love is unselfish, eternal, craves the happiness of the object, no matter in whose arms he may be folded."

"You answer differently from other women.   Is this your firm belief, Irene?"

"I *know it* to be the truth," was her response, as she for the first time looked up, and he caught the lustre of her eyes, the most glorious eyes in intellect and beauty in all Persia.

A tremor passed over Debaena.   Some mighty emotion was aroused within him, and he hesitated to speak from the inadequacy of words to convey the full import of his soul.   Then he bowed his head and meditated profoundly and long, while the Princess Irene regarded him with intense interest.   At length she said :

"I would not have the anxiety upon my soul that you have now, General Debaena, for worlds."

"And why not?" he said, still sitting with his head bowed.

"Because the love you will give to a woman will be blind as superstition, as eternal as fate.   You have not yet passed under the absolute control of love.   But when you do, you will surrender all.   Wealth, empire, glory will shrivel up in the fire of your love, and be forgotten.   Therefore you do wisely to meditate and meditate long.   What is glory, power, affluence, in comparison with the love of a human soul, — a soul that is a prisoner here in the flesh, but beyond the stars shall be of the untrammelled nature of Allah?   If you win a true woman's soul it goes to the stake with you.   It lives with you forever, after the period of life's sufferings, in the eternal paradise.   Love, love, sweet love !   It is the *undying* attribute of Allah."

With such sweetness of tone and intensity of feeling did she utter these words, that as he looked upon her radiant countenance he was impressed with the conviction that this woman would love with the same *abandon* of herself as had distinguished her patriotic services in the Russian camp.   The very idea of possessing the heart of a woman who could thus vehemently and eternally love, seemed to him at that moment to be the loftiest eminence a mortal could ever reach.   The soul of the princess seemed to be on fire.   Brilliancy and softness alternated in her dark eyes ; her bosom heaved with emotion, her lips took on a riper, richer color, and then her eyelashes drooped at his gaze, as if she had betrayed too much of her inner life.

"Irene," he said, "could you indeed love without hope, love forever without hope?"

"I could, General Debaena," was the response, as she again looked down upon the marble pavement. Then she continued: "The words of Wasaf, the poet, haunt me when the eternity of true love is mentioned. Listen to the music of them:

"'The impression of the happy moments passed in thy loved presence will never be obliterated from the tablet of my heart whilst the world revolves and the heavenly bodies continue their course. The pen of intense love has so vividly written *Eternal Affection* on the page of my soul, that if my body languish, nay, even if my life expire, that soft impress will still remain.'"

At the delivery of these words, given to the silence of the place with all the pathos and melody of the Oriental tongue, Debaena was filled with tenderness and would have cast himself at the girl's feet had nót one thought restrained him.

"Irene," he said, "tell me, and tell me truthfully, out of the deep convictions of your heart, to what extent you hold a lover to be bound by his vows of eternal affection when he feels that his affection is passing away, that in a moment of hasty decision he has vowed, aye! *sworn* eternal constancy, and he knows that he has been precipitate, and that he has not really loved and does no longer love."

"It would be madness to wed, General Debaena, one who did not possess the heart. It would be wrong to her, wrong to yourself, wrong to society. Tell her the truth and bid her go. It will be mercy to her, true mercy."

"Your counsel, Irene, chimes in with my own purpose. I will seek her and tell her the truth. Then will I return to you, with your gracious permission, and speak to you further and clearer upon the matter which has brought me hither."

"Wisdom is swiftly coming to the aid of the hero of Persia," she said, with one of those ringing laughs which had so often greeted his ears in the days of their earlier acquaintance. "Go, General Debaena, and free yourself that you may the better grasp the inestimable pearl of true love wherever you may find ·it. The learned have said of the excellence of Zehir's poetry, '*If you find the Diwan of Zehir Fariabi even in the holy Kaabah, hesitate not to steal it.*' But I say to you that if you can catch a glimpse of true love to which your own heart responds, trample upon every intervening object to clutch it, and when you have it, part not with it until death."

"Farewell, then, Princess Irene," he said, rising to depart. "When I seek your presence again I shall bring you unexpected tidings."

She watched him as he passed noiselessly away and then whispered to herself the sneer of Zehir : "If with fine and magnificent dresses, a common woman may become a respectable person, then dress a wolf in satin, an alligator in Abbasi."

.   .   .   .

At the request of Zenayi, Debaena had retired to a part of the garden remote from his palace, the present from the Shah. The Ghebre had given him a rose and desired him to inhale its fragrance until he should send a messenger to him. The flower by Zenayi's chemical art was drugged, and the soldier fell asleep upon a divan in the shade of the *chinar* trees, with the murmur of a rivulet beside him. As he slept, a lady, veiled but graceful as a sylph, approached gently, and stood for a moment riveted to the spot by the charms of the enchanting· sleeper. Then she seated herself upon the divan, and softly placed his head in her lap. The unconscious soldier still slept on, but in his dream saw the most perfect beauty his eyes ever beheld, and believed her to be a princess. In ecstasy he started at length from sleep, but awoke to the real and exquisite happiness of beholding a being hanging over him with the attitude of unspeakable fondness, and recognized her figure at once as that of the mysterious veiled lady of the *anderoon*. Expressions of love, transport, amazement and delight followed each other in rapid succession, as he half arose from his place and beheld *attached to her veil the badge of the Order of the Sun Lion with the broken point.* With rapid movement he tore the veil from her face and gazed upon her. What was his amazement and delight to discover the loveliest face upon which he had ever looked. Dark-blue eyes, large and tender, with long, dark eyelashes, and a mouth that seemed to plead for a lover's kiss, cheeks fair and tinted with the delicate flush of a rose, and features all so delicately chiselled, that she seemed a pure, fresh creation that instant dropped from the gate of Paradise. Her hair, rich in its brown lustre, was wavy, and adorned with delicate and tiny white myrtle flowers with their green leaves. The eyes of the two for an instant timidly contemplated each other, then with a simultaneous impulse and instinct they pressed their lips together and indulged in a long, long, tender, exquisite kiss of love. Rising entirely then from his reclining posture, Debaena threw his arm about her waist, drew her head to his shoulder and gazed long and tenderly into the blue eyes, which looked up to him in utter *abandon* of love and devotion. Again and again he drank the nectar of those red lips which denied him nothing in this banquet of love, but seemed only eager to yield up in those tender kisses the offering of a woman's soul.

The dreamy hours of the Persian day sped on, but the lovers knew not the flight of time. Utterly and passionately folded in each other's arms they alternately murmured of love in words ever varying and ever sweet, or drank from each other's lips the dew of young, passionate hearts. For them was the perfect harmony of nature, for them the magnetic thrill which passed from breast to breast as they pressed each other, and which called forth from both the exclamation, "*A spark! a star!* a *something strange but beautiful* has passed from your breast into mine." And still as the roses shed their fragrance on the air, and the rivulet murmured, and the soft atmosphere trembled with joy they clung to each other, kissed passionately each other, and whispered of that endless day of tenderness and trust which now had dawned upon them both. Heart whispered to heart, soul vowed to soul, or tenderly they pressed cheek to cheek in that silence which, more potent than the sweetest utterance of the tongue, tells that at last two ardent hearts have found *peace, perfect rest, perfect isolation* from the world, its cares and its discordant sounds, and bathed in the fullness of each other's love, realize no existence, no intelligence foreign to themselves, save that serene face of God which smiles upon their union from the star-girdled throne above.

And the birds of the air, wheeling their musical flights through the garden, came to listen to the whispered words of the lovers, and swaying upon the branches of the rose-trees near, bent their little heads to hear the sweet sounds of love, and catching the heavenly notes from the warm lips of the 'enraptured pair, trilled them forth that their mates might come and listen too. But closer and closer Debaena drew her to himself, and more dreamy grew their tenderness and more abandoned were their kisses to each other, until a half-unconscious languor overcame the girl, and her head fell back upon

his shoulder, and her eyes closed, while a smile of exquisite
beauty lingered on her half-parted lips, and she seemed to
dream, then feebly roused herself, then fell back upon his arm
again, and slept the lover's sleep, sweet, innocent and peaceful
as the repose of a babe.

And thus her lover watched her in manly tenderness and
joy in the delicious silence, or bending his lips to hers touched
them gently and withdrew them again to hold his love-watch
over her.

And once a face looked out upon them from the depths of
the fragrant shrubbery, and with eager eyes seemed to study
this mystery of nature, this realization of perfect harmony, this
utter isolation of two beings from the interests of mortals. And
as the splendid eyes grew fixed in the intensity of their study
one might have detected an uneasy, dissatisfied look upon the
face to which the eyes belonged, an expression which seemed
to say : " An element of resistance has arisen against the *great*,
which may overpower the *great*. The finite may wage successful war with the infinite. The mortal may grapple successfully ·
with the immortal." And still as the day lulled itself away in
the Persian voluptuousness of clime, and the evening hastened
and the shadows lengthened from the occident, the spectator of
this glimpse of paradise held the shrubbery parted in the earnestness of his curiosity, and watched the lovers as if they were
his offspring, which inexorable fate was about to rend from him.
And thus he lingered regarding them until the night fell, and the
luminous stars became watchers also of the lovers at peace.
Then he fled noiselessly away, and was seen no more by the
nightingales. It was the Sphinx of Persia, *Zenayi*.

CHAPTER XXXIV.

*" How sweet is love ! how bitter is the sigh ! how distressing is absence ! But
alas ! how easily is the beloved reconciled to it !" —* AAXIL KHAN.

WILL not offer to you the *immortal beauty*, Alfonso,
until you realize perfectly what you reject, and what
you accept. The gift I offer you must be chosen after
mature reflection. All illusions, all false impressions must
be eradicated from your mind. You must *know* what you are giv-

ing up; what you shall gain. Your heart is vacillating still. You have not yet decided between the three women, although you fancy that the loveliness you have folded to your heart in the garden is your final choice. I believe that I shall now free you from the intensity of that passion. You shall at least have the opportunity to form a cooler judgment. Come on now."

Thus speaking Zenayi led the way into the royal gardens of *Negauristan.* He exhibited the ring of the Shah to the armed eunuch who guarded the portal, and the slave, bowing low, flung open the gate for them. They passed into the enclosure, and were instantly embraced by the branches of the rose-trees, which grew luxuriantly along the wall. Strange emotions coursed the heart of Debaena at entering once more the scenes of his early military promotion to the important rank of *Sarkardah.* Here, too, had he met the lovely being who was now unveiled to him and whose hand he might any day claim. But something in the Ghebre's words troubled him. Could the intensity of that sweet passion ever cool? The question itself he felt to be an infidelity to the lovely girl who adored him. But as they crossed the royal garden and entered the rear of the palace, curiosity supplanted for the time every other emotion.

The Ghebre found ready access for himself and companion, by means of the talismanic ring. Doors flew open for him, sabres fell with their points to the pavement, and slaves everywhere bowed reverentially to his white-robed dignity. At length they arrived at an apartment whose walls were draped with lavender-colored silk, the curtains of the windows of the same color, looped back with slender chains of pure gold, the carpet white with a broad gold-colored border, and the walls covered with oval picture-frames of gold, containing portraits of the beauties of the royal *anderoon.* Here they seated themselves while slaves divested them of their heavy clothing, and put upon them robes of white silk embroidered in lilies of gold. Slippers of the same material and pattern were put upon their feet, while slaves were bringing them bowls of sherbet on salvers of gold. Thus lightly clothed, and after leisurely refreshing themselves with the cooling sherbet, the two friends were left alone. Then the Ghebre addressed his wondering companion thus:

"By the connivance of the all-powerful Ayesha, your friend, but whom you have never known, I am enabled to present to your eyes a scene which will live in your memory. What you see will influence you despite yourself. But I entreat you to remember the teachings I have given you, that the pure and

12

the ideal are alone worthy of the truly great man, alone worthy of you whom I have destined for the possession of the *immortal beauty.*   I implore you to remember that I hold in reserve for you, upon the terms I have mentioned often, a wonderful, surpassing and exquisite gift.   Control yourself by the aid of Ormuzd and resolve to win the *immortal beauty.*"

The Ghebre then advanced to a curtain of lavender-colored silk, with a white-silk divan pressing against its lower folds.   He bade his companion be seated, and uttering the following words departed, and left him alone : " Draw the curtain when I am gone and study the scene at your leisure."

Debaena sat for a moment in silence, inhaling the luxurious air of the early summer which entered the open windows laden with the perfumes of flowers.   Then he turned to the curtain behind him, and drew it aside.   He first saw the lattice of wood which filled the window opening ; then peering through this he beheld an apartment whose top opened to the sky.   It was paved with pink-colored marble and its walls were painted in arabesques of pink and gold.   In its centre was a large circular basin of marble filled with clear water, around whose margin large rose-trees filled with flowers were drooping their heads. Scarcely had he taken in the quiet scene, when merry laughter, ringing laughter, which he recognized at once, sounded upon his ears.   Then he heard the voices of girls conversing near at hand.   Then a song was heard, and a sweet-toned harp accompanied the voice.   While he listened to the song, the laughter he had recognized drew nearer.   Then he heard the same voice talking gayly, so that every word was clear and distinct to him. Nearer and nearer she came, but he heard no footfall.   Then a vision of loveliness burst upon his view, noiselessly approaching the marble basin.   It was the form of Madeleine Delaplaine, perfectly nude, but brilliant in her perfection of beauty and grace, and with her golden, luxuriant hair gathered in a knot at the back of her head.   She paused an instant upon the rim of the bath, plucked a rose from its tree, inhaled the perfume, and then placing the stem of the flower between her pearly teeth, plunged into the water like an accomplished diver, and rising to the surface, swam around the basin with the graceful, easy movement of one long accustomed to the art.   After a time the exquisite creature, faultless in form as mother Eve, climbed to the rim of the bath, and drawing to her a cushion of pink which lay near, stretched herself at ease upon the marble pavement, and with her elbow on the cushion, and her slender hand supporting her head, watched the movements of some one to whom she was talking, and who evidently was preparing for a bath also.

The instant Debaena looked upon the faultless girl he wondered at the brillancy of her beauty. Then he murmured to himself, "Dear, dear Madeleine, you are lovely as an angel. Face, form, soul, all perfect. There can be no *immortal beauty*, no gift of the Ghebre equal to you." Then he bowed his head upon the lattice, and closing his eyes dreamed of the purity and sweetness of this girl's attachment to him, of the long, long years her thoughts had clustered about him, and idealized him, and of the trust she reposed in his nobility and honor. And then he looked at her again, and found her still reposing, with the glamour of innocence and purity enveloping her. "I *could* love her in the ideal way indicated by Zenayi," he whispered to himself. "Nay, more, I do believe I so love her now. My heart rests, seems to rest in the physical sweetness of my mysterious love of the royal *anderoon*. But about this Madeleine my inner soul, the royal in me, seems to hover, and I long to be as pure and lovely in my soul as she. Is she the queen of my better nature? Is she the angel from heaven who is sent to guard me, and in the form of perfect humanity appears before me to remind me of the superiority of the spiritual over the material? Is not the Ghebre right? Is not the perfection of true love utterly ideal? Ha! what approaches now?"

Another girl was approaching the bath, shorter than Madeleine and with darker hair. The type of her beauty was fuller and more sensual. Her form did not fulfill the expectations aroused by the exquisite loveliness of her face. Debaena recognized her, too, and was amazed, startled, pained. As she stood hesitating upon the brink and looking into the water he experienced a sensation akin to that which the true horseman feels when looking upon the formation of a steed he exclaims: "That is not a thoroughbred. The symmetry of perfect blood is wanting." Alas! alas! This was the being he had clasped in his arms in the garden and from her lips had drunk such rich draught of kisses. This was the lovely face which had in languor fallen to sleep upon his arm, and over which he had watched that delicious watch.

"Strange, mysterious Zenayi," he murmured to himself. "How well you know the depths of a man's heart! I am indeed free of my illusions now. And *she* is the girl I fancied a dream of Paradise. Why did the inscrutable Maker of our

race join such a lovely face to such a sensual body.   Alas! the
surpassing loveliness of Madeleine, now that they appear
together, unfetters my heart from this unknown girl, and it is
free again, pleading for an owner.   Oh! how I crave to be
loved, loved by an exquisite being all light, all tenderness, all
angelic in her beauty."

And as Debaena watched the two alternately bathing in the
limpid waters and resting upon the marble pavement, he caught
again the tenderness he had once felt for Madeleine.   She
must be the wife of his body, and the wife of his soul.   At her feet
must he plead for her hand.   Naught in the realm of true loveliness and worth could equal this Star of the West.   His love
for the unveiled girl of the *anderoon*, his intense passion for
her, was passing away.   Something in her form told of mixed
blood.   A low type had blended with a higher type, a poor with
a richer blood, and this girl recalled to him now, as she had to
the discerning Irene in the library of the Shah, the words of
Zehir the poet: "If with fine and magnificent dresses a common
woman may become a respectable person, then dress a wolf in
satin, an alligator in Abbasi."

Presently other girls, perfectly nude like the two who had preceded them, approached and entering the bath swam about, or
seating themselves in every posture of grace and ease upon the
rim of the basin, jested and laughed together, or in frolic dashed
the water over each other.   Beautiful and graceful in every
limb were many of them, and like the Oceanides, the nymphs
of the sea, they seemed to be the spirits of the crystal element
in which they sported.   Several of them clustered about Madeleine as she reclined, admiring her foreign and rare type of
beauty.   All had the dark hair of the Orient.   Madeleine alone
was crowned with gold.

After a time Zenayi returned and beckoned the spectator of
this novel scene away.   The curtain fell and the dream-like
loveliness vanished.   As they resumed their own costumes and
passed out from the palace into the open country again, the
Ghebre said :

"Will you wed now the unveiled girl of the *anderoon*, she
who wore the badge of the Sun Lion upon her veil?"

Debaena was silent.

"The point of honor is perplexing you, Alfonso," said his
friend.

"Yes, I have *sworn* to love her," was the soldier's response.

"But *can* you love her, Alfonso?"

"I fear not. A revulsion of feeling has come."

"Are you bound by an oath to do that which is impossible ?" inquired the Ghebre.

Debaena smiled. Then he replied :

"No, but what shall I say to her ?"

"Tell her a revulsion of feeling has come," replied his friend.

"I fear I must do that, Zenayi. But who is the girl ?" The Ghebre placed his finger upon his lips. That sign was sufficient for the soldier. It informed him that the subject was not to be discussed, and that the girl must remain a mystery. In vain had Debaena, when her arms were about him in the garden at their last interview, sought to ascertain the details of her rank and history. She had replied to the effect that all inquiries as to her origin must be made directly to Zenayi. After the two had walked for a time in silence the soldier said :

"You alone appear to have the power of granting or refusing an interview with her. I will not see her again. To you I intrust the duty of saying to her that we must part forever."

"It is well," replied the Ghebre. "One of the three obstacles to the attainment and ownership of *the immortal beauty* has vanished, and sooner than I expected. There are but two impediments now."

"You are right, Zenayi. The obstacles are Madeleine and Irene."

"No woman can satisfy the heart, Alfonso," replied his friend. "That fearful, eternal craving after love which haunts the human heart, that agony of apprehension that old age may come with all its weaknesses and decay, and find the hungry heart more famished still, that lonely anguish which wakes the man from his sleep to tell him '*you will be forever alone,*' can never find its perfect solace on the earth. The beautiful creature that you wed and who seems for a time to be equal to all the demands of this heart-hunger will in time change. The two mortals who fancy that in their union is perfect peace and harmony, for a few years live in a sweet delirium of joy. Then arise discordant interests. The man discovers that the children who are born to him usurp a portion of that love which he believed to be utterly and absolutely his own. Less and less grow the attentions of his wife to him. The children steal more and more of her time and tenderness from him, and the better and purer and nobler the mother, the more does the man appreciate the truth that he is often, often alone. Then

the ambitions of the man strengthen with his years. To gain
his ends more and more of his time must be spent away from
her. He believes that all his labors, exertions and absences
from home are for the purpose of securing wealth or power that
his wife and children in their ever-increasing needs may be provided for. And thus two earnest hearts find themselves drawing farther and farther apart, and the heart hunger in them
cannot be satisfied as of yore by actual presence, because their
time for heart-communion is more and more limited. Once to
them constant presence seemed to be the perfect fruition and
only realization of love. Now that has become impossible.
The man sighs often 'I am alone.' The wife whispers to herself, 'How can he leave me so much alone.' Trust not the
illusions of married love, Alfonso. Love is only a *dream*
through which many must pass and to which there comes a
terrible awakening. Alas! the noblest hearts pass through
many such dreams and never learn philosophy. Therefore
would I have you early shake off this fearful illusion of love,
and seize the *immortal beauty* which may be yours. This is
the true height of human happiness, which you may gain by a
strong effort of the will. From the elevation I can lift you to,
you can survey the affairs of men with calmness and conscious mastery, and look upon the loves of women as trivial
matters, as the mere motes which glisten in the sunbeams."

As the Ghebre concluded, he looked earnestly upon the
face of his beautiful friend, and in his eyes Debaena saw again
that wondrous light, that consciousness and grasp of immensity
which had become the marvel and the awe of all Persia.
From that gaze the soldier seemed to take in magnetic ambition to his own soul. From those eyes, so fearfully and yet
exquisitely fashioned, he seemed to draw the inspiration of a
limitless desire, and yet they set him dreaming of his own earliest and vague recollections. The beautiful eyes dazzled him.
The possession of all worldly power, glory, riches, seemed to
reign there. The eyes seemed to say, "We have gained all
that the human heart can desire."

It was this consciousness that Zenayi had attained supernatural eminence that ever haunted Debaena's brain, and a
thirst to stand at an equal altitude was ever raging within the
soldier's heart. The temptation to abandon forever the sensual in love that he might gain this prize seemed at certain
moments of spiritual exaltation to utterly overpower him, and
at those times he believed the struggle with his own human

passions would be brief and the victory over them easy. And now with one beautiful illusion dissolved in an instant by the scene at the bath, secured for him by the Ghebre's power and influence, he wondered if he might not with equal facility be rid of all female illusions. But as he reflected he remembered that all his years had seemed to him to be wasted, and all his ambitions and successes tame if he could not have some human being to share his trophies, to be the light of his life and to satisfy the hunger of his heart. The craving to love and to be loved, to caress and to be caressed in turn, to have eyes brighten and flash joy at his coming, and a heart to grow sick and faint when he was absent, these had seemed to him to be indispensable to his happiness and peace. But now the demand was made upon him, " Renounce the love of woman forever. Thus only shall you be equal to the Ghebre."

"Oh! Zenayi, my friend," he exclaimed, "two powers are waging war in my heart. Love and ambition struggle for the mastery. I aspire to the highest, and yet my heart bids me beware lest in abandoning love I abandon that which yields the sweetest, most intense joy on earth."

"Too well I know the intensity of your struggle," replied the Ghebre. "Too well I know how sweet is the hope of a woman's love to a young heart. But in proportion to the pain of the self-denial is the splendor of the compensating gift. You have not even dreamed a dream like the effulgent scenes and powers which attend the possessor of this amazing gift. For it kings would yield up their thrones, conquerors break their swords, women abandon their children, and sages burn the libraries of the world. Do not despair of winning it, Alfonso. Bend every energy of your powerful will to crush the sensual in you. Those who trample upon the sensual are pure, and qualified for the receipt of this inestimable prize. But it is not and cannot be the reward of all who are qualified thus. A chosen few can share it. I have the power to offer it to you. It is within your reach now, but the time is short within which you can avail yourself of the offer. If you refuse it within the limited time, you lose your chance forever."

CHAPTER XXXV.

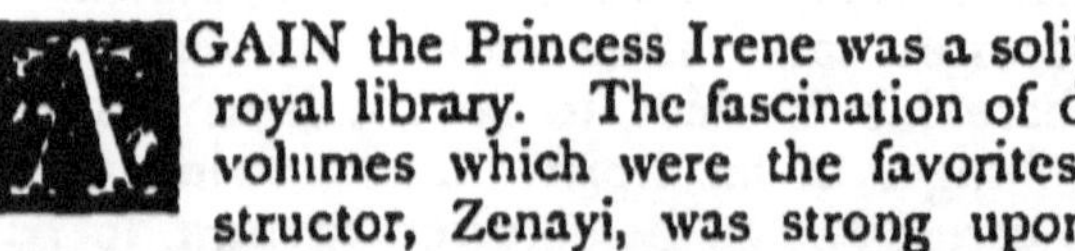AGAIN the Princess Irene was a solitary student in the
royal library. The fascination of diving into the rare
volumes which were the favorites of her former instructor, Zenayi, was strong upon her. The influence of that wonderful intellect had from her earliest recollections been potent in fashioning her literary tastes. Study had
become a second nature to her, and she realized the force of
the Ghebre's words : " *In anguish or in the overwhelming current of cares, fly for an hour to some book which engrosses the
intellect ; then will you rise refreshed for a new conflict with
fate.*"

The Ghebre had watched the dawning of the girl's intellect
with profound interest. With rare skill he had directed her
readings for years, and now in the full bloom of her young
womanhood he knew her to be the most scholarly woman in
the empire. Though he appreciated the diplomatic character
of her mind, knew that she would intrigue boldly for herself
and the few friends she acknowledged, and had used her to
further his own schemes at· the Persian court, still he loved
her, and was true as steel to her under all vicissitudes. Next
to his darling Debaena he valued her. He would forward any
scheme of Irene's concocting, save one. That one was an effort to gain possession of the great cavalry commander's heart.
Should she ever manifest a purpose to win Debaena, he resolved to thwart her. But no indication of such a purpose
had ever his penetrating eyes discovered. He was satisfied at
last that her regard for the great soldier was a noble, exalted
friendship, and when this conclusion was reached the Sphinx
was at ease, for he had determined to exalt Alfonso far above
any height to which her efforts could lift him. To attain this
ineffable altitude it was essential that Debaena be incumbered
with no love for mortal woman.

But one day the Sphinx was surprised by a letter from Irene,
requesting that he would immediately visit her for a consultation regarding Debaena's advancement, and that the soldier
should be a party to the conference. When Zenayi and the
commander reached the royal library they found the princess

as usual absorbed in study. On this occasion she was examining a rare and beautiful manuscript, written in the finest
Nastaalik character by the famous scribe, Muhammed Husein,
honored with the title Zerin Kalm, or "*The Pen of Gold.*"
Sixteen eminent painters had contributed to the embellishment
of this volume. The leaves of the manuscript book were of
soft, silken Kashmirian paper, and of modest shades of green,
blue, brown, and fawn colors, so that the eye was never offended by their glare, although richly powdered with gold. In
parts of Persia there is almost a continuous glare from the sun,
and the eyes are affected painfully from reading from white
paper.

The girl looked up from her study and greeted her friends,
who seated themselves on either side of her on the divan.

"You did not honor me with a visit, General Debaena, after
your purpose was carried out of discarding the fair one who
was so artfully put forward by Ayesha as to deceive even
Irene."

General Debaena answered in surprise, "So this artifice of
the veil was the work of the powerful Ayesha; and *you* were
deceived. This must be the first time in your life that a plot
was woven within the inner meshes of your plot and you failed
to detect it with your keen eyes.

"Yes; Ayesha deceived me, and your lips were so dis-
creetly sealed regarding the veiled beauty that I had no question as to her being Ayesha."

"And why should Ayesha send a substitute in her place?
Who is the mysterious girl, the heroine of the veil and the
broken star?"

"Hush!" interposed the Ghebre. "That name must not
be divulged now. Wait for the natural disclosures which time
will make. But you have summoned us, Irene. We await
your communication."

"It is in the interest of General Debaena that I have summoned you," she replied.

"Well," said the Ghebre.

"The favorite commander of Persia," replied the princess,
"must aspire to and must obtain the place of Mirza Sheffy."

"The attempt would be presumption and the failure would
be disastrous," replied Zenayi.

The eyes of the soldier glistened with pride and delight at
the boldness of Irene's proposition, and he listened eagerly to

12*

the discussion. The girl detected his pleasure and hope, and a smile played about her beautiful lips.

"There is no such word as presumption, Zenayi, for the fearless. The bold win that which they dare aspire to. I know the failure might be disastrous. But there shall be no failure."

"So said your royal brother, Irene, at the opening of the Russian war."

"Abbas Mirza is not Irene," she replied with dignity.

"No!" said the Ghebre, "I must do you justice. You *did* oppose the commencement of that war. But how would you dispossess so potent a dignitary as Mirza Sheffy? His ability is recognized throughout Persia. The precedents of the empire are antagonistic to your plans. He has the royal blood in his veins. No other stock can hope to win that high position."

"You have forgotten, Zenayi," replied the persistent princess. "The man may aspire to the position who is allied to the royal family. Such marriages *have* carried men to that post of honor and may carry men there again."

The eyes of Debaena were flashing now. He sprang to his feet and stood before the two in his eagerness. But he was silent. His eyes met the eyes of the princess in gratitude. The girl saw it and renewed the discussion.

"General Debaena is the favorite of the people. The Shah knows it. My father, moreover, cherishes a regard for him equal in intensity to that of the most loyal subject."

"But Ayesha will fight for Mirza Sheffy and ruin those who oppose her," said the Ghebre firmly.

"Not if her own daughter weds Debaena. I defy you, Zenayi, to refute me now."

The Ghebre started as if a thunderbolt had fallen at his feet. Turning to Debaena, who stood erect, he said sternly —

"Never wed the daughter of Ayesha, *never*, as you value the advice of Zenayi. What Irene proposes *is* feasible in the light with which she now invests her plan. To me she is incomprehensible now, but for you it is manifest as the day she cherishes a noble friendship. For your advancement she will trample down her prejudices and her animosities, and this manifestation of herself has made her *great* in my eyes. But do not wed the daughter of Ayesha. *Remember*, Alfonso, *remember*."

Again that deep, deep, mysterious voice pleading with the soldier in the interest of the *immortal beauty*. What was *the great secret* which seemed to beckon the ambitious chief on and still on ? What value rested in the secret which could render trivial the ambitions of the Persian court now so temptingly offered him at the hands of the wonderful Irene ? When first she suggested a marriage into the royal family, a thrill passed over his heart. He fancied that she would be the link to unite him to the potent monarch of Persia. But this was not her pleasure. Her acute intellect had planned for him an alliance with the daughter of Ayesha, "the power behind the throne." This would indeed make him the *prime minister* of the empire. For Ayesha would acquiesce in the fall of Mirza Sheffy. This result was as certain as fate. If Debaena should ask the hand of Irene for himself, he was confident that the noble Abbas Mirza, her brother, would lend his powerful influence to secure the marriage. This result *might* win him the place of Mirza Sheffy. But Irene had boldly struck for the *certainty*. Once married to the daughter of the powerful Ayesha, Debaena's advancement was as certain as an axiom.

A strange emotion passed over the commander's heart. He had fancied that the princess was inclined to regard him more tenderly than any other of his sex. But now the disinterested nature of her friendship was manifest. She was advancing his interests with the calm tenderness and zeal of a sister. Of the power of Ayesha he knew that Irene had ever been jealous. Trifles had told him this. Zenayi had told him this. But now in her zeal for him she was proposing an alliance with the daughter of her rival. This he acknowledged to be friendship of the purest type.

But the Ghebre was awaiting his decision. The mysterious eyes of the priest were upon him. The beautiful eyes of Irene were upon him. One offered him the highest rank under that of the Prince Royal of Persia ; the other offered him an unknown power, a vast, vague, undefined sovereignty which perhaps would give him a sceptre on the borders of the supernatural. Which should he choose, the love of woman and a certain empire, or the shadowy, phantom-like promises of the Ghebre ? The eyes of the girl were dazzling in their eagerness. The eyes of Zenayi were luminous in their wonderful depths of expression, and about the lips of the mysterious man that familiar smile was playing, that perplexing, persuasive smile of calm superiority. This seemed to exercise a mighty fascination over the commander. He gazed upon the calm, intellectual, superb face of his friend until all power of resisting the ambition recalled by that look seemed to melt away from him. He reached forth his arms to the white-robed priest and said with firmness:

"I am strongly tempted by the Princess Irene, but I cannot wed a woman I do not love. I will follow the advice of Zenayi."

The Ghebre folded his arms about the soldier and said to him tenderly: "Boy, you have chosen well. Your reward will be great."

Debaena was surprised by the calmness with which the princess heard the final decision so disastrous to her scheme. It was natural that the vanity of the woman should be offended. She had carefully planned the alliance and spread the temptation before the ambitious soldier, confident of success. The influence of the Ghebre was stronger than her own. She was utterly foiled. Still she manifested no dismay. She only smiled and said:

"It is not to be wondered at that the most astute intellect in Persia can hold forth inducements to an ambitious man greater than any a girl can offer. I was earnestly bent upon securing for General Debaena a position where he could display to advantage his great abilities, and where he could win new laurels, which the army could never yield him in times of peace. The motive of the girl cannot be misunderstood. It was the desire to recompense exalted merit."

"I am honored by your words and by your project so flattering to me, *Coadjutor*, and the memory of them will follow me to my grave. But I have learned that when Zenayi counsels me to avoid a particular line of action his counsel is dictated by the highest wisdom, and invariably results to my advantage. And the additional reason, ample in itself, that I should be wretched wedded to a woman I did not love, must have its full effect upon you who have stated to me your belief that when I did love that love would be utterly absorbing."

"Love and ambition, General Debaena, are rarely found together in this world. Fate generally decrees that the fruition of perfect love must exclude the successes of ambition. Else would this earth be Paradise and the realms of Allah have no charms for mortals. Allah grant that you may be one of the few who revel in perfect love and perfect realization of the dreams of ambition."

She looked upon the gifted soldier long and earnestly. Her eyes were full of intellectual beauty and her face wore the expression of a rich, warm, ardent nature susceptible to the sweetest and the grandest emotions. It was a source of delight to Debaena to possess the earnest regard of so beautiful and gifted a creature as "The Ornament of Persia," a woman whose life seemed to be spent in schemes for his advancement and glory. The exalted type of her loveliness and grace, the sweetness of her speech, and the richness of her intellectual culture were calculated to ensnare the heart of a man far less susceptible to the charms of her sex than the impetuous commander of horse who confronted her. The Russian war had taught him how Irene could plot and suffer for that which engaged her heart. There was an intensity of feeling in the girl, a depth of sentiment which some day must encircle a man like a wall of fire, eternal and constant. Was not the love of that gifted princess worthy the solicitation of an ambitious man? Would not the love of Irene fully and grandly satisfy a great want of his nature? As these questions awoke afresh within him they caused his dark eyes to regard her with more tenderness than he was aware of. An answering light seemed to awake in the eyes of Irene, and the Ghebre, watchful, admitted to himself that never had he encountered a couple so handsome and so apparently designed by nature for each other as his two pupils before him. He detected the magnetic fire kindling in the glances of their eyes, and hastened to part them before the possible mischief could be done. He knew that if this couple loved, the revulsion of feeling which had followed the love scene of the garden could not occur. The two before him were the perfect adaptation of nature. If once they loved their parting would arouse a tempest of agony. The *immortal beauty* might not be powerful enough to wrest the sceptre from Irene.

And so the Sphinx parted them at once, and hurried Debaena away with the words,

"Come; the day of the great trial is at hand. The hours are precious to us now, and we must prepare for the journey."

"And will you leave Teheran," inquired Irene, "for a long absence?"

"It will be the absence of weeks, Irene. But you are to meet us at our journey's end. Abbas Mirza and the Shah have given their assent to my meeting you at the foot of Ararat. I have proposed to them to instruct you in the geological formation of that mountain. You will be sent thither with an armed escort, and the American lady with the golden hair will accompany you."

"They have justly named you the Sphinx of Persia, Zenayi," replied the amazed Irene, "and when you speak the word I gladly follow the Sphinx."

"Abbas Mirza will give you the day and hour of your departure after a consultation with the stars. Until that journey is complete, guard yourself from every frivolity, and by inner contemplation prepare for a contingency which may realize for you the attainment of an object which you once told me was the brightest dream of your life."

"Impossible!" she exclaimed, "that I can be near the day of that effulgence. And may I, Irene, hope for this acme of delight?"

"No. It may be near to you and still elude your grasp. But I would have you ready for a contingency which may yield you the fulfillment of that sweet dream."

There was a mysterious sympathy between Zenayi and the lovely girl, a knowledge of some possible fruition, which puzzled the commander of the Persian horse. But he surmised that in some way it concerned himself. He had no time for words, however, as the Ghebre hurried him away. As he passed through the parted drapery at the end of the library, he looked back. Irene had not resumed her book, but was looking after him, and their eyes met once more. He kissed his hand to her before he vanished, and a blush stole to her cheek.

When the commander regained the seclusion of his own palace, he wandered into his quiet garden and seated himself beside his favorite fountain. In his hands were the two miniatures once more. Again he studied them, and dreamed of the originals who occupied now so much of his time and thoughts. Dark hair and golden hair, the Oriental and the Occidental, which should he choose? In the two had nature exhausted her treasury of gems. The types, so opposite, and yet so exquisite, bewildered him. One was not more beautiful than the other. One was not more graceful than the other. It was difficult to define the differences in their intellects. If one might be pronounced the stronger intellect, it was Irene. But the soldier corrected himself in the latter conclusion by recalling the fact that he had enjoyed comparatively little opportunity of seeing Madeleine's strength of character and mind tested. He had lived to a certain extent for years under the dazzling influence of Irene. Time and trials had proved her worth. But Madeleine had been a reminiscence, a girl, a youthful creature idealized by absence, and exercising over him fascination by the mere potency and halo of a boy's memory. Now like a pure, fresh creation she had fallen to him as if from Paradise. Could he love her with the full, developed powers and character of manhood upon him? Would she love with the intensity of which the Persian was capable? That thought, *intensity*, seemed to halo the head of Irene like a circle of scarlet fire; while about the pure, blonde brow of Madeleine was a soft, spiritual glamour which told of a soothing nature, a peaceful, calm, loving nature, which would eternally love, and by its serenity lull the man of her choice to happiness and peace. One would dazzle, cling to him, fire his soul to the loftiest ambitions, and arouse every intensity of his heart. The other would sit calmly beside him in loving sympathy, and with her fair hands part hallowed from unhallowed ambitions, and influence his soul to avoid all that might bar the light which fell upon it from Heaven. The soldier was in a dilemma. How should he solve the problem of beauty?

CHAPTER XXXVI.

N the little chapel of the Armenian monastery, on one of the slopes of Mount Ararat, the commander of the Persian cavalry was standing, engaged in studying the details of the sanctuary. He was alone, and silence reigned in the holy place. Curiosity had drawn him thither, and finding that the church was entirely deserted, he determined to examine the details of this repository of Christian symbols. The soldier had been baptized in his infancy in the Christian church to which his mother had belonged. So she had informed him, and the memory of her words had remained with him always as a link binding him to the Christian faith. There was but a vague idea in his mind as to the sacramental tie which united him with the church of his dead mother. But nevertheless through all the vicissitudes of life, and the oblivion which worldly pursuits entail, he remembered that his poor, struggling mother had been a Christian. Thus even when he became a Mohammedan for the purpose of securing a position in the Shah's body-guard, he noticed particularly that the Christ whom she had adored as God was held in high veneration as one of the great and true prophets of the Persian state religion. But to the girl, Madeleine, he owed more of his knowledge of the tenets of Christianity than to any other person. The labors and poverty of his mother had given her little opportunity for developing in her child the proper reverence for holy things. From his earliest childhood he had been taught to run here and there for his bread, finding employment wherever he could, and thus he had been withdrawn from his mother's direct influence, and had been seldom with her. He had vague recollections of a church where she had taken him occasionally in early childhood. But there was nothing distinct in his mind regarding dogmas and worship, until the girl, Madeleine, his early friend, endeavored to instill her own faith in his heart. With her teachings, imperfect as they were, he had fought the battle of life, and when the temptation came in Persia, he abandoned the church of his mother and of Madeleine with little remorse. Faith had really taken no strong hold upon his heart. He was too ambitious to allow his thoughts to dwell upon the affairs of the future life. And then the influence of the Ghebre had unconsciously wrought in his mind a reverence for the past, the past which was before Christ came. He saw in Zenayi's religion some influence which made him just to men and reverent to God, and this upon cursory view he deemed all that was essential in religion. If the religion of the ancient Magi inculcated this morality, what need could there have been for a later religion, or manifestation of God? The subject interested him, however, but little. There was in him a certain innate liberality which made him extend the hand of charity to all men who appeared to be true and just, whatever form of religious faith they espoused.

Once he had asked Zenayi his opinion of Christ, and received in response these words: "He was the purest man who ever lived, and His teachings, if followed, would turn the hearts of all men to Ormuzd."

But now the soldier stood alone in a Christian place of worship, and studied the decorations and peculiarities of an altar and sanctuary of that faith; it was all Greek to him — gold and silver, brass and wood, lights, colors, pictures — what did they all mean? He could comprehend the reverential awe which attended the Ghebre's movements when he prayed to the skies in their immensity of space, and towards the distant lights of the heavens, which suggested the vast and incomprehensible power of their Creator, who doubtless dwelt in the immensity of space beyond these eternal and luminous creations; but worship which was restricted by a roof of man's creation, and whose symbols were the tinsel of a day, was incomprehensible to him. The roof, as his thoughts would at that moment soar to the contemplation of God, seemed to bind in his soul to earth, and to suffocate him like the roof of a low cavern. He walked to the door of the chapel, and looked upward to the serene skies above the ice-clad peak of Ararat, and his soul seemed to break loose at the pure, free vision. "Aye!" muttered Debaena, "*there* is my God, when I shall choose to shake off the trammels of scheming ambition; there is the sanctuary to which I shall look to *realize* God."

"And what will you do for a sanctuary for the poor prisoners who languish in dungeons, General Debaena; shall they not worship as well as you?"

The voice was startling but sweet, and close behind him. She had entered the chapel from the opposite side, and crossing to his side of the church had overheard him talking to himself.

"Beautiful vision," exclaimed the soldier, as he turned and beheld her like an angel clothed in white; "I knew you would be here, but never dreamed you would come so soon."

"And I, Alfonso, never dreamed, since dreaming is the poetic term for thought, that I should find you in a Christian church meditating upon the unseen and the eternal."

"Yes, we all at times soar in contemplation to the supernatural realms; this is the evidence of our immortality. Do you know at the instant you startled me so I was diving into a sea of meditation, suggested by the great poem of Jelaluddin; this sublime poem on Divine Love, and the Sufi Philosophy, you must read to divest yourself of any narrow idea exclusive Christian readings may have given you that the fire of divine enthusiasm is confined to any one sect or country. All peoples are the beloved of God, and purity of thought and purpose live throughout the earth. We shall all be judged by a God of love, and shall find that we are indeed his *children.*"

"True, true, Alfonso," she replied; "but we must each follow conscientiously the light which is in us."

"I accept that test," he replied. "I have never yet followed conscience strictly, but, doubtless, some day I shall yield to it implicitly; but when that day arrives I know that my heart

and my religion will impel me to love and cherish all men who
live strictly up to the faith they profess."

"Then, Alfonso, you will love very few. But come with
me before this altar, which is not an altar of my church, and
lisien to the reading of those prayers, which long, long years ago,
when you were in trouble, seemed to soothe your wounded, outraged heart. Come with the girl Madeleine of other days, and
listen to the prayers she read you then. Come. You will
find them still as sweet, as beautiful, as soothing, as in that far-
off land they were then. Come. We are two children again."

With irresistible sweetness of tone and manner she drew
him through the deserted chapel, and they knelt once more
together in prayer; he, with uncovered head, and silent, listened to the sweet voice of his early friend, as before the altar
of a Christian church she poured forth in low tones the words
of the heart-touching prayers of the English church, and as he
listened to the simple but majestic words of the heart, calling
upon the mercy of the holy God and Father of all, memories,
aspirations, holy impulses of other days came crowding upon
him, and the tenderness of his heart was aroused from its
mighty depths, and he longed to be a partaker in the simple
and childlike trust Madeleine so evidently possessed in the truth
and sublimity of her faith; and his eyes were upon the girl as
she prayed, and the sweetness and purity of her soul were
manifest in her face. Into the chapel window glanced a pencil
of sun-beams, and looking for something sweet to caress they
fell upon her cheek and golden hair, and glorified her as she
prayed, and to the eyes of the soldier this seemed a celestial
testimonial to the purity and loveliness of the girl. There
seemed to him, at that moment, to be a protection for the beleaguered soul in the simple companionship of Madeleine; the
heaving of her breast, the melody of her words, the tenderness
of her supplication, and the magnetism of her presence,
worked upon his sense of the innocent and the beautiful, like
the sleep of a pure, lovely infant in perfect repose.

And when the prayers were finished, and for a few moments
she bowed her head in meditation and secret communion with
God, as in the days long gone, he felt a tremor creeping over
him, and his eye moistened, and a sweet, heavenly purpose of
living a spotless life stole over his heart, and he bowed his head
also in recognition of the divine inspiration which was upon
him. Then Madeleine arose, and with a smile led him away
from the chapel.   ..   .   .

The Armenian monks, aware of the distinguished persons who were honoring them with a visit, made every effort to render them comfortable during their sojourn on Mount Ararat. Zenayi, with that liberality of sentiment which made him so great a favorite throughout the empire, had often persuaded Abbas Mirza to donate money and supplies to the good monks, and they ever in return greeted him as a friend in the occasional solitary expeditions he made to the mountain. They now relinquished to him several apartments or cells for the use of his distinguished friends, while the court-yard was occupied by the cavalry who escorted the females. The two parties had met at the monastery, which was to be their headquarters during their exploration of the mountain. The Ghebre had his own private reasons for conducting Debaena, Irene, and Madeleine Delaplaine to this locality. The ostensible one was to afford them views of the surrounding country and to familiarize them with the geological formation of the mountain, in which the Persian princess was interested. She was still under the intellectual guidance of the Ghebre, and Abbas Mirza desired that she should master the science of Oriental geology under that eminent teacher. Thus day after day they all inhaled the pure air of the mountain, wandered over its evidences of ancient volcanic formation, and in the heat of the mid-day refreshed themselves from their ample supplies under the shade of the woods which encircled the Armenia monastery. Under the magic words and learning of Zenayi, every object in the neighborhood assumed new interest for the delighted and happy party.

One noon, as the explorers were picturesquely grouped in the shade of the woods, and near to the bank of the cool stream which flowed down from the eternal ice-cap of Ararat, Debaena found himself and Irene sufficiently remote from Zenayi and Madeleine to engage in private converse. Their backs were to their companions, and the princess had cautiously drawn her veil to one side, and was allowing the commander a full view of her countenance as they earnestly conversed.

"Are you aware," she asked, "of the ulterior purpose of the Ghebre in conducting us to Ararat?"

Her companion hesitated to reply, as he feared to betray more of the Ghebre's mysterious object than had been intrusted to the princess. He knew that it related to the revelation of the *third and last great secret* of the Sphinx. This was his only knowledge of the matter.

"Zenayi has promised," he said at length, " to reveal to me here something which I have long desired to know. It is a mystery. It is a secret to me. That is all I can say."

"And you have no knowledge of the nature of the secret ?" she asked, regarding the soldier earnestly with her exquisite eyes.

"I have no idea of the nature of the secret. I have told you all I can."

"I know what the Ghebre has in reserve for you, General Debaena. I alone of all the women of the earth know the great trial to which you will be subjected on this mountain.

"You ! Irene ! "

"Yes. The sister of Abbas Mirza has the unparalleled honor of knowing the Ghebre's inner heart. You will be tested severely. You have never even conceived the brilliant temptation which that mysterious man will spread before you."

"And do you know the terms upon which the great secret can become my own ? "

"I do," was the response.

This was a surprise, indeed, for the soldier. He saw the lovely being beside him look down to the earth, and an expression of intense sadness gather upon her features.

"Why are you sad, Irene? That face was made for sunshine, gladness, science, hope, all that cheers and rejoices the heart of man."

"To all humanity," she replied, "the day of anguish must come. None of us are exempt. Then why should not I experience at times the sudden check to the flow of my spirits ? Why should not I repine at the decrees of fate ? "

"Because, Irene, you are blessed with so many gifts of intellect and enjoyment beyond the reach of most of your sex. You have the blood of ancient kings and heroes coursing your veins. You are the idol of princes. Wealth and luxury are at your command. Your intellect has given you the proud appellation of ' *The Ornament of Persia.*' Fate has dealt kindly with you. Why should the Princess Irene be sad ? "

"All these gifts would I gladly relinquish for one gift. That gift, priceless to me, is the daily possession of humble women. I, the princess of a glorious line of ancestry, hunger for that which the poorest subject may and often does possess. I would fling to the winds, wealth, power, rank, to possess that, only that."

Debaena listened to the earnest reply of the proud, beautiful woman, and the tones of her voice reached to the depths of his heart. Intense suffering was in those accents. The coveted of all, the honored of princes, was in agony, and the truth had escaped her at last.

"Irene," he said, regarding her as she sat in speechless agony and with eyes half closed in the intensity of her pain, "there is but one thing on earth for which *I* would fling aside the gifts you have named."

"And what is that, General Debaena?" she asked softly, but without looking up.

"The entire heart of the woman I love," said the soldier earnestly. "Aye!" he continued, his voice rising into vehemence, "for that I would trample under foot principalities and powers, and all that men can ever possess. But into my brain has burned the truth that no woman ever gives all. Something is reserved of her heart. The entirety of her heart is never given to the man she loves."

"Seldom, General Debaena, seldom," was the response. "But you do not know yourself. The Ghebre will unveil to you a loveliness for which you will relinquish the entirety of any heart, the deepest and most unselfish love that could be conceived in a poet's reverie."

"The Ghebre can never tempt me to abandon an entire heart when I see it really and truly offered to me. I mean the whole of *that heart* which haunts my dreams. One woman I love, one who is enthroned queen over my life. But for a portion of her love I would sacrifice nothing. For the whole of her love I would sacrifice all."

"You do not know yourself, General Debaena. You have never been tempted as Zenayi will tempt you. When upon your dazzled sight breaks the vision of loveliness he will unveil, all that you have ever dreamed of a woman's heart will vanish, and you will fly into the arms of his temptation. You will yield all. For you are human, and the gift he offers will transcend all that you have ever dreamed of power, and wealth and glory."

"You amaze and startle me, Irene. But still I say to you, and say it upon the honor of a soldier of Persia, that should Zenayi by supernatural power open the gates of paradise and bid me enter, I would refuse if by that refusal I could gain the utter abandonment of that woman's soul to me."

"Mortal man," said Irene solemnly, and yet looking up to the beautiful face of the commander, which was radiant with the intense love of his heart, "you know not what you say. That noble prince of thought, that faithful friend who has bound the very strings of his heart about you, has in his intense affection destined you for a wonderful fate. From that glorious fate you will be powerless to escape. The novelty, the splendor, and the power of the acquisition will dazzle your imagination, cause your blood to run quickly in your veins, and your form to expand with pride at your eminence. The face of the woman you love will grow hazy in the distance and then vanish. You will think of her no more, but entering upon your glorious career you will move on in majesty along the path of your beautiful future."

She paused and eagerly watched the play of his expression. He was all fire now; his curiosity and his imagination were powerfully at work. He saw that Irene was indeed possessed of the secret, the great secret which had engrossed so much of his thoughts. But still the intensity of his mortal love for a woman was burning within him, and when at last he spoke it was in accents which would have made the heart he loved leap for joy.

"Irene, I love, and all the powers of the tempter can never make me abandon the sweet hope I cherish of one day winning *all her heart* to myself. For this consummation I daily wear the yoke of uncertainty, and for this consummation I will sacrifice all things in the gift of men."

Then they heard the voice of Zenayi calling them.

CHAPTER XXXVII.

HE mountain trembled, and a rumbling sound was heard under their feet. All started to the floor except the Ghebre, who remained in his chair, calm and unconcerned. The countenances of his companions bore marks of apprehension as the jarring of the mountain continued and the subterranean thunders increased in violence. Then all was still again. Zenayi and Irene exchanged glances. Then did the princess detect in the eyes of the Sphinx an intelligence which seemed to say to her, " The hour has come."

Debaena and Madeleine, recovering from the shock of the volcanic commotion, looked towards the unruffled face of Zenayi for an explanation of the mystery.

" There is no danger," he said, interpreting the look. " Ararat was once a volcanic mountain and flames issued from the peak where now is perpetual ice. But the internal fires of the earth at great intervals still influence the fissures in its lowest foundations. This has caused the commotion. It will not continue long."

The Armenian monks, as he concluded, came hurrying into the apartment, as if Zenayi alone was the intelligence who could dispel or confirm their fears. His calm expression reassured them, and they listened to his theory of the disturbance grouped eagerly about him.

The oldest member of the brotherhood was inclined to dispute the Ghebre's statements.

" I have lived upon Ararat," he said, " more than fifty years, and never before did I feel the mountain tremble, or hear subterranean noises."

" I said at *great* intervals there were manifestations of subterranean power," was the reply of Zenayi. " Fifty years is a trivial matter in the lifetime of the globe. But come," he added, addressing the members of his exploring party, " we must mount our steeds and be-off. We have much to inspect to-day."

The monks dispersed to their duties, and the explorers proceeded to the courtyard of the monastery, where their horses were saddled and awaiting them. They mounted and were off, a small escort of cavalry accompanying them. Proceeding down the mountain, which had become perfectly quiet again, they reached a belt of woods, where Zenayi directed the cavalry to halt and await the return of himself and his three companions. Leaving their horses in charge of the soldiers, the explorers proceeded on foot, following the Ghebre. The silent and mysterious priest led them away through a little path under the trees, and emerging at length upon an open part of Ararat exhibited to them a pass leading through broken and disordered masses of rocks. They entered this pass, and in cheerful converse made their way through its windings, with the brilliant sunlight above them and a little stream murmuring its way down the mountain beside their path. Madeleine clung close

to the side of their guide, who assisted her over the more difficult obstacles in the rocky pass. But Irene received the assistance of Debaena, who often found her soft, warm hand in his,
as he aided her over the masses of fallen rocks which blocked
the way. The two were engrossed in each other's society and
conversation and a magnetic sympathy warmed them. Irene
was veiled in the fashion of her country. There was an innate
harmony between these two impetuous natures, and the more
frequently they were brought together, the more vividly did
both recognize that accord. There was a peculiar tenderness
in the manner and voice of Debaena on this occasion which
did not escape the attention of his companion. The soldier
knew that he was soon to undergo an ordeal which might separate him forever from the love of any mortal woman. Should
the temptation about to be offered him by the Ghebre be sufficiently potent, he would from that day discontinue all intercourse with women which verged upon the sensual. From that
day forward not even could a woman's hand rest *tenderly* in his.
He must avoid them and restrain all ardor in their society, or
the gift of the Sphinx would be forfeited forever. Involuntarily
perhaps, or from the consciousness that woman's tenderness
was about to escape him for all time, he pressed the hand of
the beautiful princess when the impediments in their path
obliged him to take it, and at that gentle pressure a warmth
seemed to respond to him from the girl. The two grew more
and more silent as they proceeded. There seemed to be a delicious sense of congenial companionship in the two, and before
they were aware of it their pace slackened, and they fell far
behind the Ghebre and Madeleine. Closer and closer the two
loiterers seemed to draw to each other, more frequently did
Debaena extend his hand to aid his beautiful companion, and
presently at an impeding rock, which demanded unusual vigilance to surmount it, the soldier passed his arm around the
waist of the princess and lifted her from her feet, carrying her
entirely over the obstacle. The instant the powerful arm of
the commander encircled her, Irene felt the blood warming her
cheek. She was powerless in his manly grasp, but she was not
offended. There seemed to be a refuge for her weakness in his
strength. But she trembled and was faint with pleasure, and
when the soldier placed her on her feet on the other side of the
rock she looked up into his face and said timidly, " I thank
you." He caught the glance of her bright eyes through the
openings in her veil. Their expression fascinated him. He

did not relinquish the clasp of his arm about her waist, but held her firmly pressed against him for an instant. Then he said impetuously:

"Forgive me; forgive me, but you are too lovely for this earth."

She struggled then to emancipate herself, but she was held by arms of iron. He spoke again, his impulse obliterating every barrier of reserve.

"Do not struggle away from me. Irene, I love you."

At those words her resistance grew feeble, and she mur. mured, "Oh, no! not me."

"Yes, you, Irene — beautiful, peerless angel of the East, I love you, and the love which now I offer you is offered with all the energy of my being. Love me, love, me, love me; *dear* Irene, love me."

At those words of ineffable tenderness, the Princess Irene remained passive in his arms, and silent.

"Love me, dear Irene, love me," pleaded the soldier again. She leaned her head upon his breast. That token was enough. He raised her veil tenderly, exposed to the sunlight the loveliest face in Persia, and pressed a fervent kiss upon the lips of the peerless woman who adored him.

Zenayi had turned a corner in the pass with his immediate companion, and did not witness this sudden protest against his grand scheme for the day. But his voice was heard calling to the loiterers. The two hastened on to rejoin him, and the princess said, as they passed along:

"You will be tempted beyond the power of resistance to-day, and Irene will be forgotten."

"You do not know me, Irene," he said, tenderly. "Already has the curiosity to learn the Ghebre's secret passed away. It were better for me to tell him at once that I renounce all claim to his mysterious gift."

"No, no, General Debaena," she exclaimed. "Face the fearful responsibility of a decision, and then decide with the . calm, majestic front of reason. It is just that you should know the splendor which is offered to you, for the opportunity seldom comes to man."

"And what splendor can equal the splendor of my Irene? What treasure can tempt like the heart of my princess, my heroine, my life?"

"Hush!" she said. "You know not the peerless beauty that is just before you. You are estimating Irene by false standards of excellence. Wait, in the name of Allah, wait. You will be tempted as you never were tempted before. I could relinquish the fresh, noble, ardent love given me by my hero, Debaena, to see him clothed with the majesty of Zenayi's gift. For why should a woman stand in the way of my hero's advancement? Forget me, Debaena, and accept the nobler gift of the Ghébre."

"*Never*," was the ardent response. "You once told me that I would forsake all wealth and power for the woman I loved. So would I. And now that the matchless loveliness of my Irene and her surpassing breadth of intellect have become my treasures, the splendors of empire, wealth and glory are coming like falling stars to the dust beneath her feet. In the effulgence of her eyes is my soul entranced and happy. In the depths of her love is my heart sweetly sleeping, its long looked for dream, and upon her lips shall I drink forever the nectar of joy and unutterable peace. Oh, Irene, my precious Irene, you are the fullness of a lover's dream. Close to your dear heart press me. Fold your arms about me, who have so long panted for the fruition of a great woman's love."

"Come, come," called the voice of the Ghebre again. "The hour is at hand. Hasten to the sight which is about to be yours, and which will soon pass away forever."

The two immediately hurried on and rejoined their companions. Before them was the rock elevated upon smaller ones to which Zenayi had once called Debaena's attention, and bade him remember. Before it stood Madeleine and the priest, the latter with folded arms. As the lovers came up, the Ghebre said:

"Under the influence of the subterranean fires, now at work in the base of the mountain, the earth will open in a great fissure just before us. After a time the fissure will close up again. This phenomenon, the history of past ages tells us, occurs but once in every thousand years. It opened one thousand years ago to-day. It will close to-day, and will not re-open until another thousand years are fulfilled. While it is open we shall descend into it, and behold a mystery which the power of Ormuzd has created. Observe now closely, for I hear the subterranean noises which indicate the opening of the earth."

A trembling of the mountain ensued. Then came a heavy booming sound from the earth, and a few paces in front of the party a threadlike fissure in the rock, scarcely noticeable before, slowly widened, spread, yawned until it exposed a great cavern in the earth, through which a red light seemed to be shed from a great depth."

" Come on without fear," said Zenayi. " Natural steps in the rocks give us access to the subterranean marvel. Alfonso, support the Princess Irene in the descent."

The voice of the mysterious guide was commanding and re-assuring, and they followed him as he escorted the wondering Madeleine down the shelving rocks into the unknown. They were approaching the great cavern laterally, and the light was first a dim red, but when they had descended about two hun-dred feet, they entered a high arched cave, through which the bright, red light from the volcanic fires which once had as-cended to the peak of Ararat was playing fitfully but brilliantly. The floor of the cavern was covered with white pebbles, upon which the party walked until they reached a grotto large enough to contain a hundred persons with ease. To the amazement of the explorers, this grotto was covered within, floor, sides and roof, with masses of tiny crystals which bril-liantly sparkled in the distant firelight. But the greatest mar-vel of the place was the object in the centre of the floor of the grotto, and all eyes were instantly fixed upon it. It was a natural basin of crystal filled with sparkling water, deep enough to submerge the human figure to the waist. The pellucid fluid was bubbling up on every inch of its surface, and as it rose and swelled and murmured, supplied from some hidden source, a sound of gentle music in the air accompanied its melody.

All voices were hushed in the awe of the supernatural, and all eyes were turned upon the Ghebre, who was kneeling reverently upon the brink of the fountain and praying to Ormuzd. Brighter and more merrily played the up-gushing water, and sweeter and more gently whispered the unknown music in the air. Gentle suggestions of the pure and holy seemed to come from that divine melody, until all hearts were elevated to contemplation of the spiritual and the hea-venly.

At length the Ghebre arose to his feet and looked upon the beautiful faces of his companions, radiant with the red light which was cast upon them.

" In the tenderness of my love for you, Alfonso," he said, " I have brought you to this mystery. You know the terms upon which you can enjoy the last great secret of your friend. I have offered you this in gratitude for your saving my life at

Echmiadzin. By violence the Ghebre may die. By the wasting of disease and the decay of the vital powers I can *never* die. *I am immortal.* Bathe in that fountain and you can never die. Take with you into that priceless bath these beautiful friends of yours, and they can never die, but will ever flourish in unchanging beauty, for this is the *Fountain of Perpetual Youth.* I bathed in these waters at my mature age; so shall I always remain as when I made that exquisite plunge into immortality. Enter this fountain now in the splendor of your young manhood, and you shall always be the same as now. Wrinkles, decay, old age can never put their painful marks upon you or upon these lovely women, when they shall make the eternal renunciation of mortal love, and bathe in these celestial waters, offered once in every thousand years to mortals by the inscrutable decree of the pure Ormuzd. But at the first yielding to the sensual love of. mortals the priceless gift passes from your possession, and you become subject to decay and death. Look into the eyes of Zenayi and recognize the man who has outlived dynasties and empires, and upon whose face and form *thousands of years* have fanned their wings, and could not change him. See you not the plenitude of power, the profundity of learning, and the knowledge of the human heart which immortality upon the earth shall give? Hunger and thirst can never slay you; only a death of violence can cheat the bather of his immortality. Ponder this mystery, and then plunge into the fountain, Alfonso, Madeleine, Irene, and forever free yourselves from the sensual, and you shall, like Zenayi, live forever. Soon the hour will come when we must fly from this place, and the fountain be concealed for another circuit of a thousand years. Oh! was so inestimable a gift ever offered to three mortals in the bloom and freshness of their life and beauty?"

Into the faces of each other looked the three companions of the Ghebre, turning their eyes to one and then to another, as if to read the hidden secrets of each other's thoughts. The immensity of the proffered gift thrilled through the intellectual appreciation of them all. What they should gain all dimly saw. What they should lose by the renunciation of mortal love all pondered deeply. They looked upon the fountain merrily playing in its liquid light, and at their hesitancy the aërial music seemed to murmur a sweeter, more tempting melody. The fullness of joy was in the pulsations of harmony traversing the air, and the pure waters of the immortal foun-

tain seemed to leap up in eager invitation. Debaena pressed
his hands to his temples in the agony of his indecision, and the
eyes of the two beautiful women studied the expressions of his
face as he turned to them in the intense thought of his inquiring eagle eyes. How could he make a decision now, when
the magnitude and the surpassing brilliancy of the issues at
stake overpowered him, dazzled him, bewildered him? All
power but no love. This was the edict of the beautiful fountain. Eternal youth but no tenderness, no, not to the end of
countless ages.

The Ghebre spoke again, as with his calm smile of superiority he surveyed the faces of them all.

"One woman bathed in these immortal waters ages ago.
As she was in youth and beauty so did she remain, every feature, every limb as it was when she entered the fountain. In
learning and in culture she became a wonderful power. But
the hour of temptation came to her. The experience and the
wisdom of ages was wiped out when she saw the face of a man
of extraordinary beauty. For the kisses of his lips she forfeited
immortality in an instant. She can never regain the immortal
gift; she will decay and die. And the man for whom she sacrificed all has turned his back upon her, because he watched
her in her bath in a royal *anderoon*, and saw that the perfections of her form did not equal the beauties of her face."

Debaena started and looked in amazement towards the
Ghebre.

"And did she wear upon her veil the badge of the Order of
the Sun Lion?" he inquired.

"The same, the same," was the response. "You have
solved the mystery, and for that man's kisses she sacrificed
perpetual youth."

At these words the beautiful face of Madeleine turned from
Debaena to the fountain. She approached nearer and still
nearer to the pellucid waters, and gazed earnestly upon their
riotous play as they danced in the red firelight. For a moment she appeared to hesitate in uncertainty. But as she
clasped her fair hands over the brink, and studied the tempting fountain, the mysterious music swelled louder and sweeter
upon the ear, and the notes were those of temptation calling
for the sacrifice of love and the acceptance of immortality and
perpetual youth. She rapidly flung aside the covering which
fashion had placed upon her golden hair, shook out the heavy
masses of her silken locks, and with a quick, eager movement,

stepped from the brink into the water, sank to the waist, and then, with a cry of exultation, plunged her arms into the encircling flood, and poured the immortal waters upon her head.

CHAPTER XXXVIII.

AS Madeleine revelled in her bath, which forever sealed upon her the freshness of perpetual youth, the Princess Irene with eager eyes gazed upon her. The drops of water falling from the golden hair and from the uplifted fingers of her hands flashed like rubies in the red light of the volcanic fire. A radiance unearthly was upon her face as she smilingly looked towards her companions, and the sweet notes of the supernatural music seemed to call louder for the remaining two to secure forever the freshness and beauty of their youth. Nearer and nearer to the fountain pressed the figure of the Persian princess, and more alluringly upon the air trembled the melody of the tempting harmony. Would she too, the Ornament of Persia, yield to the greatest temptation ever offered to woman? Eternal beauty, eternal power to rule and fascinate the hearts of men, ever-increasing learning, new resources of power through all the ages, these were the rewards of the immortal bather. Would the scheming intellect of Irene fail to grasp the very source of power? She stood trembling upon the brink of the fountain. She flung aside her veil, and the surpassing loveliness of her features seemed to gather a more heavenly lustre from the light which emanated from the fountain itself.

The magnificent eyes of Debaena were upon her. The mysterious eyes of the Sphinx regarded her expected decision with undisguised interest. Why did she hesitate to plunge into the immortal waters? Madeleine was calling to her. The mysterious music of the supernatural was calling to her. Power, the eternal future, the glories of ages to come, all were calling to her. Why did she pause and shiver upon the brink of so glorious a destiny? At last she turned and gazed upon the face of the great soldier of Persia. His eyes met her inquiring look, but 'he spoke not, moved not, gave no indication of what was passing within his soul. Then she looked away upward to the roof of the grotto as if she implored the guidance of Allah. At last she turned abruptly from the fountain, and kneeling at the feet of Debaena said in tones of thrilling sweetness :

"My lord, my prince, my hero Debaena, *I sacrifice eternal youth and beauty for you.*"

The eyes of the commander flashed brilliantly at these words, but he turned to look at the eyes of the Ghebre.

"Stand back, Irene," hoarsely called out the voice of Zenayi ; "stand back until I summon to the aid of the *immortal beauty* the forces of reason."

The lovely girl arose to her feet, retired a few paces, and there stood silently and with clasped hands awaiting the result. Even the immortal Madeleine paused in her bath to listen, so unexpected had been the decision of the Princess Irene. Then the immortal Ghebre addressed himself to the idol of his heart :

"Alfonso, when the inhabitants of Io buried with magnificence the corpse of Homer, I was a witness of the superb spectacle. I stood upon the Acropolis of ancient Athens when the Parthenon and the Erechtheum were in the plenitude of their glory. I was the companion and instructor of the youthful Cyrus, and in the zenith of his glory he loved Zenayi. I have been face to face with Alexander the Great. I witnessed his early battle of Chæronea and his conquest of the sacred Theban band. I saw him die with the fever of the Assyrian marshes ; and all my efforts to save him proved of no avail. I stood by the cross of the great prophet, Christ, when the false and the cowardly forsook him and fled. Aye, before all these and their epochs I lived. When the Ararat, within whose cavern we now stand, was crested with verdure to the very summit and while the timbers of the Ark still mouldered at the peak, I was familiar with the secret places of the mountain and knew the history of the postdiluvian races of men. By the cradles of historic kings and conquerors I have given counsel, and my fame as scholar, councillor and sage has been in many climes. By one name here, by one name there, I have been reverenced or feared. The great have valued my counsel, the weak have returned again and again to the Sphinx whom they have driven forth and undervalued. When Persia extended from the Indus to the Mediterranean, and from the Euxine and Caspian to the Persian Gulf and Indian Ocean, I was an inhabitant of the great empire and my name was in the mouths of the learned and the great. I have seen the mighty in their glory, and witnessed the proud shivering in the glance of death. The pale conqueror of men has gathered the lofty and the beautiful of all climes to his mouldering clasp, and I survive them all. Dynasties and races pass me by on their march to *death*, and I smile calmly upon his skeleton form and all-conquering sickle. For by the hand of time and the wasting of disease I can never die. I have looked upon the peerless charms of Statira, and Semiramis from her battle-horse has flung to me a kiss. Into the libraries of all lands I have walked for study and to them given some of the rarest volumes rescued from the destroying fires of thoughtless conquerors. I have seen libraries in all ages given to the devouring flames and witnessed the tears and lamentations of the learned. Palaces and temples have been my refuge, or in the caverns of the earth I have hidden from violence. I have been courted and caressed in one age, hunted and persecuted in the next. I have seen the development of every human passion in prince and subject, and neither knew the truth that I was the eye of the Past, and the eye of the Future. In all the schools of philosophy I have been a student, and the knowledge of Thebes, Memphis and Heliopolis has been taught to me by their priests in all ages. What I have been in the past you may be in the future, the sage of sages and the adviser of countless kings. The hidden treasures of empires will be known to you and the secret motives of human hearts. Experience, experience, that mighty tutor of the great, will show to you the reins of empire by which you may drive all men. Listen to the supernatural music which summons you to power and to the immortal possession of all your youth and beauty. Listen while yet the celestial strains allure you to the priceless gift. The woman of to-day will be the mouldering dust of the morrow. I have witnessed countless throngs of the beautiful go down to death. Fair as Madeleine, spirited and beautiful as Irene, they have mouldered and their faces have fallen in and worms have eaten them. But the immortal beauty, the perpetual youth can be your own, and unruffled you can witness the flight of ages. Hasten to the fountain where Madeleine is saved, and through countless epochs you shall contemplate her as a remote star, ever growing in learning, power and witchery. Shake off the sensual, abandon love, and enter forever the immortal life. Hasten, for the hour of your trial is short. The mountain will close for a thousand years and when again it opens you will be forgotten dust."

The Ghebre with his glorious eyes of immortality contemplated the soldier. Then with his white-robed figure erect and majestic he turned and pointed to the fountain. The music of an unknown realm swelled forth enchantingly upon the ear. It seemed to embody in its notes the suggestion and the realization of the wonderful gift. Endless power, endless life, endless youth and beauty were in the bath where Madeleine revelled, and the commander approached the brink with his ambitious soul on fire. The consciousness of coming power so near at hand, the effulgence of the immortal bath shining upon his hero-face, and the inflaming words of his long-tried friend seemed to draw him onward, nearer and nearer to the fountain. And the alluring music in the air urging him to the step which would secure his matchless destiny transcended all power of resistance, until he turned and looked upon the trembling figure of the lovely woman who had sacrificed all for him. There she stood, the queen of the Orient, with her woman's soul in her eyes regarding him. The intensity of her thought blazed in her beautiful eyes, her hands were clasped, her attitude that of loving helplessness and eternal trust.

Debaena turned from her to Madeleine and the fountain, contemplated the two for a moment, and then with an air of proud disdain that he had been for an instant tempted from the great within him, stepped back a pace and *folded the proud and beautiful Irene in the arms of his love forever.*

The Ghebre fell senseless upon the floor of the grotto and the celestial music ceased.

For an hour the trio made every exertion to restore Zenayi to consciousness. Madeleine, emerging from the fountain, found to her amazement that instantly the clothing upon her dried, and not the slightest indication of moisture remained upon her heavy mass of hair. She scooped up with her hands the immortal water and poured it on the Ghebre's head. She bathed his forehead and hands, while Irene sustained his head upon her lap. But every effort was unavailing to restore their venerable friend. At last they were startled by a recurrence of the heavy rumbling in the mountain which had preceded the opening of the fissure. Some instinct warned them that the closing up of the mountain was at hand. In their terror they raised the Ghebre in their arms, and by their united strength carried him slowly up the natural steps in the rock by which they had gained access to the cavern. As they toiled away upward with their burden, they felt the mountain tremble, and heard repeated detonations of the subterranean thunder. Sudden and brilliant lights flashed up from the red fires, deep in the earth, as if from explosive gases. Their alarm increased at every step. They might be imprisoned forever in the earth by the sudden closing up of the fissure which, Zenayi had notified them, must close sometime during that day. Their burden hung like lead upon their arms. But they would not abandon him and seek safety in a precipitate flight. They heroically clung to their friend, and slowly bore him upward. At last, to their joy, they reached the summit, lifted the body of Zenayi through the fissure, and, panting with fatigue, carried him far away from danger and laid him beneath the shade of a cluster of bushes. Scarcely had they been relieved of their load when they heard the detonations in the earth louder than before. Again the mountain trembled, and immediately the fissure in the rocks closed up, and the fountain of perpetual youth was lost for another thousand years.

At last, to their great relief, the Ghebre opened his eyes, and in another moment spoke to them.

"My distress at Alfonso's refusal of immortality," he said, after he had learned of their escape from perpetual imprisonment in the cavern, "overpowered me and I fell. My sweetest hope in in life was that my great soldier might share with me the priceless gift. But Ormuzd has decreed otherwise. Live then, Alfonso, a pure life during the years that remain to you ; and at your death the eternal Ruler will seat you in Paradise. May the great and astounding love you have both manifested for each other render you happy and peaceful to the end. Had the cavern closed upon you and Irene, death would in time have come to you both. But Madeleine and Zenayi would have lived in that fearful prison for a thousand years, until the fissure once more opened to us the light of day. Go now, Alfonso, for our escort, and bid them bring here a litter for me. I must be carried to the monastery. My natural strength will soon return to me."   .   .   .   .

When Debaena was once more at the capital of the Persian empire, he solicited from the Shah, through the medium of Abbas Mirza, the hand of the Princess Irene. The royal assent was readily obtained for so desirable a match, and the lovers who had sacrificed the immortal life were united in marriage. So beautiful was the pair as they knelt before the Shah to receive his blessing, that a murmur of delight ran through the crowd of princes and nobles who thronged the court. Madeleine was there in her immortal loveliness, and the white-robed Ghebre stood beside her, gazing with his mysterious eyes upon the scene.

.   .   .   .

Years have rolled away since the hero of the Russian war folded in his arms the peerless princess as his wife. Beautiful sons and daughters have blessed the union of this happy pair and to-day occupy places of honor and power in the Persian empire. The marks of age have traced themselves upon the brow of Debaena and his loving wife. Their hair has put on the silver hue, and in a few years they will go down to death. But Madeleine, the golden-haired, is still a fresh, exquisite, blooming girl, as lovely as when she paused upon the fountain's brink and studied the tempting waters of immortality. Not a line has deepened in her fair face ; not a thread of silver has stolen into her silky mass of hair, and her eyes still gleam with all the lustre and beauty of her youth. Her kindred have all passed to the tomb, but she will never die. All the luxuries of wealth are in her grasp. The knowledge of the Ghebre has opened to her the buried treasures of many ancient empires ; and with that mysterious unchanging guide she has traversed many lands and studied deeply the lore of ages. On, and still on into the future, shall tread her beautiful feet. Kingdoms shall pass away, and she remain ever beautiful, ever young. The mysteries of science and the lore of all lands shall in time be within her intellectual grasp. Her eyes have begun to take on that mysterious and profound look of the Ghebre. Year by year shall it deepen and startle men, that luminous, fascinating look of immortality.

The girl who forfeited immortality for the sake of Debaena's kisses, and who was sent by Ayesha as her substitute beneath the veil to entrap and hold the heart of the young commander, has long since mouldered into dust. But Madeleine, the sweet, pure type of innocence and loveliness, will live on and on, until the end of time shall unite her to the holy God she loves. In the streets of many cities of the earth the passer-by is often startled by a vision of female loveliness which haunts his memory ever after. It is that of a mysterious girl of peerless beauty, and with golden hair, whose eyes are radiant with a mysterious power, and whom no one ever knows. She passes in her matchless loveliness, clothed in mystery; and when she has gone the memory of her lingers and oft returns again like the ideal images seen in dreams.

THE END.